SAVAGES

THE SAINT-ÉTIENNE QUARTET, PART 2:

THE SPECTRE

SABRI LOUATAH

corsair

CORSAIR

First published in France as *Les Sauvages, Tome 2* by Flammarion/Versilio in 2011
First published in Great Britain in 2018 by Corsair

1 3 5 7 9 10 8 6 4 2

Typeset in Janson MT Standard by SX Composing DTP, Rayleigh Essex
Printed and bound in Great Britain by CPI Group (UK) Ltd, Croydon, CR0 4YY

A CIP catalogue record for this book is available from the British Library.

ISBN: 978-1-4721-5324-1

Papers used by Corsair are from well-managed forests
and other responsible sources.

Corsair
An imprint of
Little, Brown Book Group
Carmelite House
50 Victoria Embankment
London EC4Y 0DZ

An Hachette UK Company
www.hachette.co.uk

www.littlebrown.co.uk

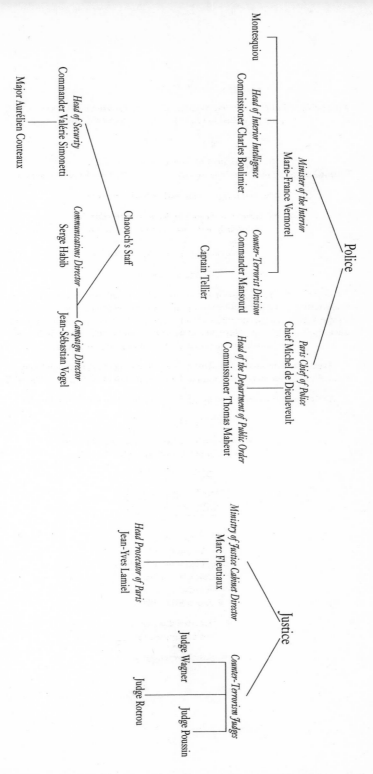

Police

Montesquiou

Minister of the Interior
Marie-France Vermorel

Head of Interior Intelligence
Commissioner Charles Boulimier

Major Aurélien Couteaux

Head of Security
Commander Valérie Simonetti

Counter-Terrorist Division
Commander Mansourd

Captain Tellier

Chaouch's Staff

Communications Director
Serge Habib

Campaign Director
Jean-Sébastien Vogel

Paris Chief of Police
Chief Michel de Dieuleveult

Head of the Department of Public Order
Commissioner Thomas Maheut

Justice

Ministry of Justice Cabinet Director
Marc Fleutiaux

Head Prosecutor of Paris
Jean-Yves Lamiel

Counter-Terrorism Judges

Judge Wagner

Judge Rotrou

Judge Poussin

THE SPECTRE

SUNDAY

1

MURDERERS

1.

At the very moment when our secret services' satellites registered the first worrying crowd movements on the outskirts of Paris, at the very moment when, throughout the country, stadiums, bars and squares with giant screens seemed to implode under the simultaneous surge of shock, disbelief and anger, Henri Wagner, investigating judge in the Paris prosecutor's counterterrorism division, was peacefully admiring the stone saints that looked out over St Peter's Square in the Vatican.

He had joined his wife the day before and planned to leave the next day. Paola wanted to visit the Sistine Chapel, where they had met twenty years earlier, but half an hour after buying tickets the judge had abruptly left, unable to concentrate, his mind occupied by work anxieties.

Madame Wagner was a reasonably famous pianist, known to music fans by her maiden name, Paola Ferris. At this particular moment, she walked over to her husband, who stood motionless, leaning like a young man against one of the crowd-control barriers, though strangely there were no lines of waiting tourists on this beautiful spring Sunday.

'What on earth has got into you?'

The judge shrugged and seemed to hesitate before speaking. Beneath his white hair and bushy black eyebrows, beyond the lines that marked his face, there was something irrepressibly youthful about his appearance: his slightly gangly frame, his prominent Adam's apple, and his casual clothing, accentuated by the two undone buttons of his polo shirt. He put his hands on his hips and looked up at the sky.

One of the judge's two bodyguards moved away to take a phone call. The second one eventually looked in the same direction as the judge. Part of the VIP Protection Service, which regularly rotated the bodyguards of threatened judges, the two new officers were identical even in their choice of week-end outfit: leather jackets, trainers and dark sunglasses. Judge Wagner felt sure this was not planned. At lunch, he had called it 'professional camouflage' – a witty remark that neither of his shaven-headed apes had dignified with a smile.

'Strange, don't you think?'

The judge was speaking to his wife, who heard her mobile vibrate for the third time in a row inside her leather handbag. She asked what was strange but didn't wait for a reply before pressing the green button on her phone. Hands behind his back, Judge Wagner took a few steps towards the foot of the stairs that led to the hanging gallery. The statues were sharply silhouetted against a bright spring sky, dappled with small, fast-moving clouds. The wind chasing them was bitingly cold, so Judge Wagner popped the collar of his jacket as he contemplated an optical illusion that delighted him, even as it left him unnerved and dizzy. It seemed to him that it was not the clouds making their way across the sky, but lofty saints suddenly awakened from their eternal sleep, just as it sometimes appears, from a stationary train, as if the train next to yours, moving imperceptibly, is in fact the one standing still while your own has begun to move.

'Paola, look . . .'

But when he turned towards his wife, her face had drained of all colour. Her hand was half-covering her gaping mouth and her large, clear eyes were already welling with tears of horror.

The security officer, who was also on the phone, grabbed Judge Wagner by the elbow and pulled him to the edge of the square as he handed him the phone. As the head of the counter-terrorism division explained the situation to him, his wife called Aurélie back in Paris to make sure she was okay. Her daughter's voice was a bit sleepy. An aunt would come and take care of her until they returned. Surprisingly, Aurélie didn't argue.

In the car back to the hotel, Paola took her husband's hand, which, unlike her own, wasn't trembling. His eyes, too, remained steady and solemn as the umpteenth caller shared tragic new details.

When he hung up, she looked lovingly at his steady, serious face, his white hair.

'The future is now,' she murmured.

Her husband put his hand on hers.

'I always thought his campaign slogan was . . .'

She couldn't find the right adjective and fell silent.

'Prophetic?' the judge suggested, without taking his eyes from the screen of his BlackBerry.

'Um . . . No, that's not what I meant . . . But, for God's sake,' she said, suddenly sounding angry, 'this doesn't even seem to bother you! A presidential candidate's been shot!'

'Paola—'

'It's so horrible! They shot him. My God! I just... I don't understand. With all this going on, how can you keep such a... Herculean calm?'

Judge Wagner smiled inscrutably. He cleared his throat, seemed to think of ten other things to say, and then answered his wife as their rented estate car sped along the banks of the Tiber at breakneck speed.

'Darling, unless Roman mythology has been mistaken all these years, I'm pretty sure Hercules was anything but calm...'

2.

First to arrive at the Grogny University Hospital's emergency room was a phalanx of men wearing earpieces, followed a minute later by two waves of uniformed motorcycle units. The shouts of the first unit were soon joined by the cacophony of whistles from the second, carrying out their orders to evacuate the ground floor. A nurse complained as she wheeled a patient from a room, but the department head ordered her to obey without another word.

After the storm came the calm, a more terrifying calm, barely disturbed by the beeping of the machines. No one on the hospital staff dared even swallow. It felt as if the slightest sound might make these stocky, tense, adrenaline-fuelled men explode.

A puny house officer dropped his stethoscope on the tiles. A security officer, who was violently chewing gum, shot him a murderous look. Clearly gifted with superhuman powers, he was the first to hear the procession arrive. A split second before everyone else, he rushed towards the door, which opened automatically.

The stretcher was carried quickly past nurses, all of whom were left stunned as they saw with their own eyes what they had only suspected: the identity of the patient for whom the unit had been transformed into a high-security zone.

A female house officer was charged with looking after the candidate's wife, checking her blood pressure and bringing her water.

Esther Chaouch allowed herself to be led into a small room, where the young trainee doctor could not hold back a sob. She was joined by an experienced A&E clinician, who immediately checked the patient's pupils.

'Madame Chaouch, I can assure you your husband is in good hands. Professor Lu—'

'Where have you taken him? What are you going to—'

'Please remain calm, Madame. Your husband is in good hands.'

Esther Chaouch got up and took advantage of the doctor's momentary lapse in attention to leave the room and cross the corridor, where none of the bodyguards had the heart to stop her. She stood, alone, at the red-silled window through which the blood-covered face of her husband was visible, starkly lit by fluorescent lights. While the bullet had passed through his left cheek, it was the flesh on the right side of his face that had exploded outward, creating an unbearable sight.

Esther Chaouch fainted. When she came to, she was surrounded by bodyguards and Jean-Sébastien Vogel, her husband's campaign director, who had taken off his tie and was looking at her, less with compassion than with a sort of anxious, shellshocked curiosity.

She spent fifteen minutes on the phone with her daughter, Jasmine, who had chosen, a few hours earlier, to go home to her apartment on the Canal Saint-Martin, which Vogel confirmed was one of the safest places in the capital. After half an hour, the head of the unit came in and helped her sit up on the bed. He explained the situation to her in a voice so gentle she thought for a moment that she had been cocooned in morphine or some kind of invisible cotton wool designed to protect her from the world's violence.

'Madame Chaouch, I'm Dr Lucas. We've just spent half an hour . . .'

He halted mid-sentence as something caught in his throat. He lifted a finger and turned around for a moment to cough. The doctor's tone, the timbre of his voice . . . Esther Chaouch put her head in her hands. She felt sure it was all over, that he was about to inform her that her husband was dead. She even had enough time to put herself in the shoes of this doctor who was tasked with explaining why they hadn't been able to do anything, this grizzled doctor who must have notified hundreds of families about hundreds of deaths, and who must have used the same horrific and supposedly earnest euphemisms each time: 'has passed away', 'didn't make it', perhaps even the despicable *'has left us'* . . .

But she was wrong.

'Please excuse me. So, where were we? The scan shows the bullet did not touch his brain. The bullet essentially went straight through both cheeks. It's a stroke of luck, but it's very likely that the shock resulted in a ruptured aneurysm. We have spent half an hour stabilizing his blood pressure so that we can safely transport him to a specialized hospital. The neurosurgeons and neuroradiologists at Val-de-Grâce have been alerted—'

'Will he live?'

'Madame, his condition is . . . extremely serious. I won't lie to you, the operation is very difficult. But I can assure you that the procedure will be carried out by some of the best surgeons in the country. You can count on that.'

Esther Chaouch stifled a sob. Yet again it was the doctor's gentle, professional tone that had pierced her natural reserve.

'How are you taking him there?' she asked brusquely, standing up to go with them.

'By helicopter. It's a ten minute trip. You can follow by car. I think the convoy is ready to leave. Your daughter,' added Dr Lucas, after a glance at Vogel, 'is being driven to Val-de-Grâce right now.'

In turn, Esther looked at Vogel.

'Jean-Sébastien, was it a terrorist attack?'

'Yes, of course, but it's too early to—'

'But why did no one tell us he was *really* at risk? Where was . . . Valérie Simonetti? She didn't know? But you knew, right?'

'Esther, there'll be an investigation. The people who are responsible—'

'And now, is he safe? *Tell me*: is he safe?'

'Esther,' Vogel replied, looking at the floor, 'the chief of police in Paris called to say he'd sent six riot control squadrons to cordon off the area around Val-de-Grâce.'

Esther Chaouch raised her hands and shook her head from side to side in rage.

'The chief of police? Dieuleveult? He hates Idder, for God's sake—'

'Esther, that's enough,' said Vogel sharply.

The man first in line to become Chaouch's prime minister

took Esther's hands, which were flushed with anxiety, in his own.

'That's not how it works. This isn't politics any more. France has just been attacked, don't you see? France.'

A few seconds later, an air ambulance took off from the roof of the Grogny University Hospital and headed towards the sun, flying over the suburbs, the highway, the eastern neighbourhoods of Paris and the Seine, before landing in the courtyard of the Val-de-Grâce military hospital, where half a dozen people in white and blue scrubs stood around a stretcher, preparing to receive their most important patient of the year.

3.

'Horses of fire.'

They were Rabia's first words as she emerged painfully from a sleep she thought had lasted a whole day. When her eyelids could open almost normally, she added that these fiery horses were in the sky, and that she had seen them move with a mute but portentous roar. Fouad checked her pulse and put the back of his hand to her sweating forehead.

He had finally managed to break down Rabia's door after throwing himself against it several dozen times, which would probably mean pain and bruises the following day. He'd been surprised to see shards of glass on the tiled floor, but then had finally found his aunt asleep on her bed, without sheets covering her.

As she raised a hand to bring to life the horse race from her dream, Fouad saw her expression change. The otherworldly haze had dispersed. She remembered.

'Where's Krim? Where's my son?'

She grabbed Fouad's wrist and leapt out of bed.

'Auntie, what happened?' Fouad shouted. 'Tell me!'

Rabia lost her balance and fell back on the bed. She stammered a few words that Fouad found hard to make out: Omar, telephone, Paris.

'Omar?' asked Fouad.

'Like Omar Sharif,' said Rabia deliriously. 'We met on Meetic, and afterwards . . . I . . . after . . .'

'I'm going to get you some water.'

'And Luna? Where's my daughter?'

While Fouad filled a bottle so he wouldn't have to make multiple trips to the kitchen, he grabbed the phone in his left hand and was horrified to see that he had more than thirty missed calls – he had switched it from vibrate to silent, and the red light had been blinking for fifteen minutes without him realizing it. He squeezed the plastic-covered keypad until his knuckles turned white.

He let the water run and looked at the broken door. At that very moment, Fouad knew that he knew, but he didn't yet know what. Because, instead of calling back the last number displayed on his phone, instead of answering Rabia's phone, which had been ringing incessantly since he had entered the flat, he opened the living room's glazed doors and switched on the TV. All the network shows had been interrupted and replaced with special breaking news bulletins. He clicked over to LCI News. He was used to the red 'Emergency' notice scrolling at the bottom of twenty-four-hour news channels' screens. A law had been passed, a missing girl had been found dead, a damning statement had been made at a political convention . . . But this time, the Socialist Party's presidential candidate had been the victim of a terrorist attack. That much, Fouad knew. But there was something else.

He turned up the volume.

There hadn't been time to give the expert commentators the usual makeover. Their noses were shiny and sweat had glued entire locks of hair to their creased foreheads. To Fouad, those feverish voices, required to make their point in less than twenty seconds for fear of being cut off, had never sounded so strident. He had appeared on a few shows himself; he was due to appear on many more soon, to promote a big-budget comedy film due out that summer, in which he played the most prominent supporting role.

'Fouad?'

Rabia's figure looked distorted through the convex panes of the glass door. Fouad didn't have the chance to turn the sound down. He ran over to his aunt to keep her from coming in. The voice of the lead news anchor was finishing a recap of the breaking news story of the century.

'At present, the identity of the gunman is not known. In the video of the attack, which we have chosen not to air, the suspect appears to be a young man, perhaps even a teenager, of Asian or perhaps North African origin. We'll be back soon with an update . . .'

Fouad wasn't able to hold Rabia back for long. She seized the remote from her stunned nephew, who finally knew what he had sensed from the beginning. And yet he still didn't believe it. It took Rabia's furious clicking, a dozen times or more, for it to sink in. She kept on until, instead of the greedy, obscene faces of the journalists and commentators, the screen showed the frozen, enlarged image of the young gunman, his flat cheekbones, his wide eyes filled with terror and, visibly despite the pixellation, with tears.

'Krim . . .'

4.

It was 5.30 in the afternoon when Krim was released by the doctor and declared fit for police custody. It had taken two hours to calm his spectacular panic attack in the police van, as tense voices argued over where to take him: 'to the 36' or 'to Levallois'. Krim had followed these esoteric disputes until he couldn't breathe any more. Levallois-Perret housed the brand new headquarters of the Central Directorate of Interior Intelligence (CDII), the result of a merger between the RG intelligence service and DST domestic intelligence agency – the French equivalent of the FBI. It included, among others, the counterterrorism division. When he heard that he was to be interrogated Krim had vomited onto a pair of combat boots that had automatically taken their revenge with a swift kick to his upper lip.

The blow made no visible difference: his face was already swollen from the kicks and punches he had received from a crowd that, without the intervention of the bodyguards, would probably have lynched him. Nevertheless, apart from the medication to prevent him from hyperventilating, they had had to give him a few quick stitches around the mouth. While his young patient, knocked out by the tranquillizers, slept under strict surveillance, the doctor complained about the behaviour of the policemen.

'Did you really need to be so rough?' he asked in a tone that was all the more reproachful since he was obviously not going to report anything.

Krim opened his eyes while they were moving, transported at a speed he had thought possible only in video games. Strangely, it seemed to him that he was sinking rather than taking flight, sinking into the weight of time where he would explode in a million little air bubbles.

People asked him questions, and he heard himself attempt to reply.

Again he fell asleep, opening his eyes just as a futuristic structure emerged in the distance: twin buildings made entirely of glass, sparkling in the sweltering sun. The motorcade sped into a multi-storey car park. Krim let himself be lulled by the screeching of the tyres.

When he woke up, he was no longer surrounded by policemen screaming at him to spell his last name, but in a strangely calm basement room, where hot, dusty rays of sunlight spilled through two long, barred windows onto sleeping computers. Looking up, Krim occasionally saw booted feet stop on the ground-floor courtyard. The lowered barrel of an assault rifle suddenly appeared. It was followed by grey trousers above black loafers. The courtyard's furious activity contrasted sharply with the crushing silence that reigned on his side of the double-glazed windows.

Having fully regained consciousness, Krim realized he was handcuffed to the arm of his chair. This wasn't the first time he'd felt the restraint of metal bracelets, but never in the course of his previous misadventures had the police fastened the cuffs so tightly. The slightest wrist movement ground together bracelet and bone, sinking metal into flesh, which consequently reignited pain all over his face and torso.

At last, two men entered. They were both the same height and wore the same suit and no tie. The meaner-looking one wore an undershirt visible beneath his white button-up, and had deep-set eyes and a half-open mouth. He remained standing beside the open door, behind Krim, leaving his sharp-eyed colleague to sit on the edge of the desk.

14

'So, Abdelkrim. I'm Captain Tellier.'

He was a restless, clumsy man, as if burdened by his own size. His blonde, greasy hair was tied in a ponytail, and it looked like this was the first time he had ever worn his suit jacket. Krim didn't notice right away that he had a harelip but once he'd spotted it, it was all he could see: the upper lip split in the middle, the raw flesh that explained everything: those sharp eyes, the uneasy posture, the vengeful voice.

'How are you, Abdelkrim?'

Krim wanted to say something about his handcuffs being too tight, but he was afraid he wouldn't have the chance to make another request for a long time. He cleared his throat to try to explain as quickly as possible that his mother must be looked after, but, as she came into his mind, he had a swirling memory that she had been imprisoned by Mouloud Benbaraka, that she was still in danger, that Nazir . . . He didn't have time to get anything out; Captain Tellier hadn't asked Krim a question to get a reply, just to make him listen to the sound of his voice.

'We're not going to do this all night. You shot at a presidential candidate. You're going to tell us why you did it, who gave you the weapon, and why the gun says "SRAF". You're going to tell us everything. But you're going to start by telling us where to find your mobile phone.'

'My mobile phone?'

'Yeah, your mobile phone. You really expect us to believe you don't have one? So where is it? It wasn't on you, or near the town hall. So . . . where is your mobile phone?'

Krim didn't answer. He would have liked to say he had thrown it off a bridge, but he didn't know if he had dreamed that or if it had really happened. Captain Tellier could see that the boy was completely out of it. When he uttered 'mobile phone' again, it had the same effect on Krim as a word in a foreign language.

'All right, let's back up,' the captain went on. 'You don't know what a mobile phone is, but you still remember what a phone number is, right?'

Krim muttered, to hear the sound of his own voice and because absolute silence made his head spin faster.

'Well then, you're going to write down the names and phone numbers of all your family and friends. Understand? Can you do that for us?'

Krim reacted suddenly.

'But they don't have anything to do with . . .'

A policeman entered the room and handed the captain a document. It was Krim's file from the Criminal Office Processing System, which contained the list of offences on his police record. The captain's lower lip twitched as he read.

'Theft, assault of a police officer, possession, dealing, damage to property . . . Well, I can see you're a regular customer. You'll have to tell us how you got from dealing weed to political assassination, but for now I just want you to make the list I asked for, okay? Come on, your whole contacts list, plus your family.'

'Can I make a phone call first?'

The captain looked at his colleague for the first time with a comically distressed pout, so exaggerated that it seemed clear that if he hadn't been a captain in the counterterrorism police, he might have haunted indie-rock festivals grasping a can of Heineken, a rolled cigarette hanging from his lips, his hair tied in the same faded blonde ponytail, like one of those sad middle-aged people who strive desperately to preserve the trappings of being a hip, open-minded teenager as the decades pass.

Nonetheless, however much Captain Tellier's voice might have tried to sound approachable, to make you forget his deformity, it was only intermittently sympathetic. He ignored Krim's question and continued.

'Write down everything you can: brothers, sisters, cousins, uncles, dad, mum . . .'

'But what are you going to do to them?' Krim said, sounding worried.

The captain stood up. His exasperation showed through the deep breaths he took, the mechanical way he softened his voice.

'We need to question the people who know you. It's standard procedure.'

'I threw away the phone,' Krim declared. 'I threw it off a bridge, into the river.'

'You threw your phone into the Seine? What time? Why?'

'Because of the pictures . . . The pictures of . . . But it didn't fall into the water,' remembered Krim, without thinking about sorting through the information that was coming back to him, the way you remember the details of a dream in the late afternoon.

The captain tipped his head back and looked at the ceiling.

'And the watches? Why did you have two watches?'

'I . . . I forget . . .'

'Listen, pal, I don't think you realize what you've just done. But we'll have time to talk about it. Lots of time.'

Krim looked at the floor.

'You've already been in twenty-four-hour lock-up twice. You know how that works? Hours of questioning by people like me who yell at you. Except that we're not two-bit cops from Saint-Etienne – this is counterterrorism HQ. So let me explain: the prosecutor is going to charge you with the most serious charges in the entire Penal Code. And we're going to question you for forty-eight hours and then the prosecutor will extend custody another forty-eight hours, and so on until we reach a hundred and forty-eight hours. Try to imagine how you'll feel in a hundred and forty-eight hours. Are you good at maths? You Arabs are usually good at maths, aren't you? How many days is a hundred and forty-eight hours? I'll let you work it out.'

The captain made a lopsided grimace and passed a finger over his eyes, as if to wipe away invisible beads of sweat.

'Of course, we could get this over with in one night if you tell us everything. It's up to you – everything is up to you from here onwards.'

5.

Krim's muddled brain tried to work out how many forty-eight-hour stretches it was. He had rounded up from forty-eight to fifty to make it easier, and he ended up coming to the absurd figure of six days while his trembling hand wrote down his aunts' first names. He soon realized he couldn't remember any phone numbers, not even that of his own home.

The captain noticed the pen was motionless at the top of the second column. He slowly drew the paper from the desk. Krim was about to ask the captain to help him find his mother's number when he heard Nazir's voice in the hallway.

Paralysed, he kept his hand around his wrist and began to breathe more quickly, until he felt his pulse begin to race in the bulging vein of his forearm, swollen and bruised by the handcuffs.

'Come on, now,' the captain asked. 'What, did you see a ghost?'

Krim turned his head and saw a tall, dark figure outside, giving orders to policemen in the same authoritative tone as Nazir. But perhaps it wasn't him? This thought was confirmed when the figure turned around. It was a young man with unremarkable features and icy blue eyes, as fair as Nazir was dark, wearing a black suit, dark blue tie, supporting himself with a walking stick.

He approached the cell without taking his eyes off Krim. When he entered, the captain stood up and straightened his jacket respectfully.

'So this is the hitman?' the man said with the same sinister laugh as Nazir. 'My God, he's barely reached puberty . . .'

'Sir. We've just started the questioning.'

'Then, by all means, please continue,' he said softly, while continuing to glare at Krim. 'The minister would like to assure you that you have her trust. A word with you, please, Captain.'

The captain rushed after him. Krim was fascinated by the power this man must possess to command such complete silence in those around him. He hadn't even glanced their way, but the two officers, who must have been twenty years his senior, had jumped to attention like schoolboys at a disciplinary hearing.

Outside the office, the man asked the captain what Krim had revealed so far. Tellier told him about the mobile phone, the bridge, and other details that had come back to the 'kid': a sightseeing boat, the back of Notre-Dame . . .

'You can see how important you've become,' Captain Tellier commented once the blonde ghost had left, leaning on his cane. 'Even the Minister of the Interior's chief of staff is interested in you.'

Krim wasn't listening. He couldn't remember even the

smallest feature of the man's face. Everything had been sucked up by those unnaturally blue eyes, everything except a dimple that split his chin in two.

'Right, so where were we?'

'I know I have the right to a lawyer,' ventured Krim, recovering his wits.

'Come on. Just shut up,' replied the other policeman, whose husky voice Krim was hearing for the first time. 'You think I'm going to believe you know a lawyer?'

Krim went bright red. He had seen what legal aid lawyers were like from his previous visits to lock-up. Law students who peered distractedly at the client-of-the-day's file while writing text messages to their friends. On the other hand, he clearly remembered a *Special Correspondent* report on Maître Aribi, nicknamed 'The Arab's Advocate' by reporters trying to destroy his reputation. He was a hot-shot lawyer who spoke like a Frenchman and had won acquittals for dozens of people, all of them Arab.

'I want my lawyer to be Maître Aribi.'

It felt as if he had named a *Dragon Ball Z* character.

'Maître Aribi?' mocked the lieutenant. 'Which Bar?'

'What?'

Krim didn't understand, and the lieutenant didn't seem to want to help him. The captain helped him along.

'What city does he work out of, your Maître Aribi?'

'Oh – I dunno . . . Paris.'

The lieutenant took the cap from a felt-tip pen and wrote down the lawyer's name.

'We'll call him once you've started getting down to business.'

'Monsieur,' Krim said, suddenly in a panic. 'My mother

– you've got to do something. She's . . .'

'She's what?'

The lieutenant seemed so full of hate that Krim was at a loss.

'I want to speak to my mother. I've got to call her. She's—'

'No,' interrupted Captain Tellier, 'the prosecutor has expressly forbidden any phone calls. It could negatively affect the investigation.'

'But . . . they've got nothing to do with it! It's my family—'

'To you it's a family,' Tellier cut in again, 'to us it's a network. We're not going to let you warn the other members of your network. You can understand that, can't you?'

6.

At Saint-Etienne's North Hospital, Fouad made several trips between the room where old Aunt Zoulikha was being kept, after fainting the night before, and the emergency wing where blood samples taken from Rabia revealed a low dose of GHB, the infamous date-rape drug.

The A&E nurse was overwhelmed. She gave her patient tranquillizers; Rabia was suffering her fourth anxiety attack since hearing the news. Fouad asked to speak with the nurse in private. She had bags under her eyes and always seemed to be holding back an exasperated sigh.

'Are you going to examine her, to see if she's been . . . assaulted?'

'You mean sexually assaulted? Yes, yes, we're going to do that. Listen—'

'When?'

The nurse, who was in the process of changing the IV bag, stopped, stared and closed her eyes.

'Monsieur, as you can see, we're short-staffed, so please go

21

and keep your aunt company, have some coffee – do whatever you want – but let us do our jobs, okay?'

The nurse's condescending tone irritated Fouad so much that his jaw and neck stiffened like a bull about to charge.

After visiting Zoulikha, who was sleeping alone on the fourth floor, making sure that little Luna was safe and sound at her granny's, and spending each trip in the lift focused on the soupy hospital smell to avoid thinking about what had just happened, Fouad found himself in front of the sleeping Rabia and realized he wouldn't make it to the end of the day unless he found out where Jasmine was.

He got out his phone and checked the missed calls to see if his beloved's first name was there. It was not. As he was about to press the green button on his immortal Nokia, purchased seven years earlier, he realized he couldn't do it, that he couldn't just call her: his beloved was Chaouch's daughter; Chaouch was the man his young cousin had just shot at point-blank range.

He dreamed there was someone he could ask not only for advice but for a precise, detailed and, above all, indisputable order on how to proceed. But he was on his own. And, anyway, how were you supposed to proceed when the way forward had just disintegrated before your very eyes?

While pacing the hallway of the emergency wing, he caught sight of his Uncle Idir, who was anxiously questioning a peroxide-blonde nursing assistant standing in front of the admissions list. Uncle Idir had not shaved since the day before and, seeing his prickly cheek from this angle, Fouad thought that after the hour he had just been through, the previous day seemed more like a month ago. His brother Slim's wedding, venerable Uncle Ferhat's desecration. The passage of time began to overlap and spin like in a kaleidoscope, and Fouad, who hadn't slept in at least thirty-six hours, had to lean against a bare wall for a moment, so as not to lose his balance.

'Fouad, where's Rabia?'

Idir had tears in his eyes. The heat, added to the red-checked sweater he'd thought it a good idea to put on over his shirt, made his narrow face flush, giving it a disturbing colour. Fouad put a hand on his uncle's shoulder. It took all his remaining energy not to break down in tears.

'You see him on TV? You see Krim?'

Idir was in a state of shock. Fouad led him into Rabia's room and sat him down in the only empty chair.

'Do you want a glass of water? Uncle? Do you want a glass of water?'

Idir did not reply. He was looking at his sister-in-law stretched out on the bed and trying to control the terror that had taken hold of him the moment Krim's face appeared on every TV screen in France.

'Did you call the police to tell them?'

Fouad wanted to snap back: why me? Why am I supposed to have called the police?

He went to the bathroom with a plastic cup, braced himself on the edge of the toilet bowl and forced himself to throw up. When he got up, he splashed some water on his face and comforted himself with the illusion that things were better.

'I'm going to call them now,' he said to his old uncle when he returned. 'But we also have to call a lawyer. Krim's going to need one. And us too.'

'Us too?' Idir repeated, looking up at his nephew, his face

clouded by anxiety and incomprehension.

Fouad remembered imitating his uncle's thick Marseilles accent in the community centre – Rabia had laughed so hard she'd had to cross her legs to avoid pissing herself.

'All of us.' Fouad didn't even try to camouflage his emotions as he left the room.

7.

At the corner of the main residential street in Grogny's Rameau-Givré housing projects, the first vehicle to go up in flames was not a car but a scooter. And for twenty minutes, its owner had no idea. Yael Zitoun, who had come to spend this particular Election Sunday in her father's company, was in the bathroom at that moment, busy reading Avernus.fr on her MacBook. The site was her father's new bible, and its morning editorial, written by editor-in-chief Puteoli, called on voters to staunchly reject Chaouch:

> Fifteen hundred years of history just to end up here? Fifteen hundred years of blood, sweat and tears, fifteen hundred years of France, just to end up with a permissive, multiculti member of the European Parliament dressed up as the Nation's Saviour by cynical ad-men? Fifteen hundred years of patriotism to end up with this: a PR expert who bats his eyes at the ratings agencies and is more worried about showing his best side in photographs than in France's future?

Yael was about to come out of the bathroom to argue with her father for the second time that day, when the most familiar picture in her contacts list appeared on her iPhone's screen:

24

Fouad's.

'Yael! Can you hear me?'

'Fouad, oh my God, did you see? It's a kid! An eighteen-year-old kid!'

'Yael, I'm going to tell you something really serious.'

His voice was weak and full of pain. Nothing like the lion, the stentorian orator whose career she had managed since landing Fouad a role on *Man of the Match*.

Yael combed her fingers through her thick red hair while Fouad explained that the eighteen-year-old kid was his cousin Krim.

She was silent for a few seconds, her eyes wide open and yet completely blind to the computer screen balanced on her bare knees. Fouad, who couldn't see what she was doing, wondered if the connection had cut out.

'Yael?'

'Fouad, I . . . Oh my God, I don't know what to say.'

'You've got to help me . . .'

'Of course,' Yael replied, with no clue what he was going to ask for.

'I need a lawyer, Yael. The best one possible.'

Yael finally came to her senses. She put her iPhone on the pile of toilet paper rolls and put it on speaker so she could search for the name of a criminal lawyer her agency's director had used two years before.

'I'll find one, no worries. I know a lawyer, a young one. He's with a big firm . . .'

'I don't want to be a pain, but it's very, very urgent.'

'Yes, yes, I . . .'

But Yael didn't get the chance to finish. Her father was

hammering on the bathroom door.

'What the hell are you banging for?'

'Yael! Your scooter's on fire!'

'I'll call you back,' she told Fouad.

She came out of the bathroom and saw her father standing on a chair to get something from the top of the bookcase that covered almost the entire wall.

'Papa, what are you doing?'

Monsieur Zitoun didn't reply. Yael rushed to the window and saw, next to the rubbish bins, that her scooter was indeed in flames. When her father got down from the chair, he was holding his rifle from the Algerian war.

'What are you doing? You're crazy!'

'This is just going too far!' Monsieur Zitoun said angrily, almost exaggerating his *pied noir* accent. 'They made Madame Zelmatti leave. They made poor Serge Touati leave. You think they're going to make me leave too?'

Yael would have liked to take the gun from her father's hands but she was terrified of weapons. Anyway, the old man couldn't get the magazine open. Yael could see the anger leave his trembling hands and gather around his mouth. He was going to choke on his own words, his bitter complaints and threats. He was going to rant and rave to himself in private, as usual. Everything would be fine.

Yael called the police and, from the window of her father's house, watched the crimson rays of sunset painting the end of the street. Her scooter burned silently; the image seemed unreal and Yael hardly gave it any more thought.

Fouad's cousin had shot Chaouch.

The more she repeated this to herself, trying to give it

26

some meaning, the more the words took on a life of their own and appeared to her as abstract shapes, cut off from all reality, incapable of any sense.

She closed her eyes and reopened them on a silent, seemingly paralysed neighbourhood. In the distance, the Baldassare Galuppi Auditorium sat calmly dominating the landscape. Whenever she was here, there was a moment when, on fine evenings, the disc of the setting sun nestled into the perfect rectangle formed by the arch of this ultra-modern, very costly and – according to her father – completely useless building. It had been erected by Chaouch at the start of his first term as mayor of Grogny.

'My God,' Monsieur Zitoun grumbled, 'you know people are still voting?'

'People are still voting? How?'

Monsieur Zitoun gestured at his daughter to shut up so he could watch the news. The election coverage had started with a special newscast, four hours earlier than planned. A permanent inset showed an image of the square outside Grogny's town hall, now emptied of its crowds and dotted with sinister yellow police tape. In the studio, guest speakers took turns: the politicians' 'thoughts were with' Chaouch's family. The most recent update was that he was hovering between life and death but, without exact information about his condition, the election continued. It had been announced that the Ministry of the Interior, in charge of organizing the presidential election, would be holding a press conference in one hour.

While waiting for the police to arrive, Yael went out onto the balcony of the second floor to smoke a cigarette and call her lawyer friend. And it was then, as she tapped the filter of the

Marlboro Light against her thumbnail, hesitating to light it, that she made out the first, still distant, murmur of the riot.

Behind the last house on the street, the Rameau-Givré housing project's low-rise blocks of flats released a tide of hooded kids. Strange explosions reverberated all the way to the Zitouns' peaceful neighbourhood.

Yael gestured to her father to join her on the balcony; together they watched more than a dozen teenagers charge down their street brandishing Molotov cocktails that they threw at all the vehicles they could find as casually as they would have thrown fireworks, screaming what would be the slogan of the coming unrest:

'MURDERERS! MURDERERS!'

'Who are they calling murderers anyway?' asked Monsieur Zitoun.

His daughter replied, somewhat dreamily, 'The state, the government, I don't know – France, those who own the country. They want their president back.'

'Get back inside!'

Monsieur Zitoun quickly closed the shutters and in the gloom, barely lit by a defective halogen lamp, he now began to search seriously for bullets to load into his old rifle.

8.

Fat Momo had waited for Fouad and Krim's mother to leave before returning to the cellar and fetching the pistol that was wrapped in a piece of cloth. This accomplished, he hid the weapon in his tracksuit jacket. Never in the past months had it felt so heavy, not even the first time Krim had passed it to him so he could practise too. At first, Fat Momo had thought it weird, but then he had developed a taste for it, encouraged by Krim's cousin Nazir, thanks to whom they'd got hold of the weapon, as well as the money to set up what they called their 'little business'.

He caught the tram at Sadi-Carnot Square and had the bright idea of buying a ticket, validating it and sitting down just behind the driver, thinking to himself that the local police, summoned as back-up for the conductors, generally focused their attentions on the rear of the tram. The trip felt like it took an hour. Fat Momo had only one vague, fragmented thought in his mind, centred on his best friend, but it never turned into a coherent picture of the situation in which Krim, and by extension he himself, was caught.

When he finally reached Bellevue Square, on the city's south side, he was sweating like a pig. A guy from the neighbourhood recognized him and came over to say hi.

'You crazy fucker! A tracksuit jacket in *this* weather? What are you, a Turk?'

Turks had a reputation for dressing warmly in the summer and in t-shirts in the winter. Fat Momo was afraid the weapon might end up falling out if he hung around too long. He said goodbye to his tiresome neighbour and went home, checking to make sure the police weren't hiding in the hedges by the ground floor of his small residential building.

His elderly father was dozing in front of the TV. His snoring did not entirely drown out the overexcited voice of the female newscaster who was repeating the day's news for those who might be tuning in after a visit to outer space.

Sultan, his beloved Alsatian, noticed his young master's agitation and barked at him a few times.

Fat Momo whimpered as he stroked the dog's head. He ran

into his bedroom and stuffed some clothes into a gym bag. As he was closing the bag he wasn't sure whether to add the gun – it would be better to throw it away somewhere en route. But the idea of having to secretly carry it once he was outside seemed insurmountable. After trying to hide it in one of his trainers, he rolled it up in a towel and placed it at the bottom of the bag.

Then he stood still in the middle of his messy bedroom.

Slackjawed, Sultan looked at him to find out what he would do next. Fat Momo unzipped his jacket the rest of the way and noticed that his t-shirt was so soaked with sweat it had changed colour. He took off the jacket and t-shirt. Naked to the waist in front of his dog, he was wondering if the animal understood how ugly his rolls of fat were, when the ringing of the doorbell froze him to the spot.

If he didn't answer it right away, his father was going to wake up and he'd have to tell him everything. If he answered it right away and it was the police, he was fucked.

He struggled into another t-shirt – the first one he found: his Algerian football team shirt – then went over to the peephole in the front door. The neighbour had come to give them some of the tagine she had made that morning. His widowed father was so courteous that the neighbourhood women had become fond of him and always brought him a plate of couscous, pastries or even an extra helping of lamb. Fat Momo took the tagine from the woman and explained that he was in a hurry.

'What are you plotting, you little devil?'

'Nothing!' Fat Momo cried.

The neighbour, who had never heard Fat Momo use such a tone before, turned on her heel and left to avoid any further insult.

The hardest thing then was saying goodbye to Sultan.

Sensing that his father's uneven breathing presaged an imminent awakening, Fat Momo was forced to dry his tears and hurry out. He could still taste his dog's dependably fetid breath in his own mouth, however, and he held on to its memory as he walked through the hot streets again, and discovered that a firearm, whether hidden in your jacket or at the bottom of a gym bag, is still just as absurdly, monstrously heavy when, as was the case here, it was connected, however indirectly, with the assassination of a servant of the Republic.

2

THE MACHINE

1.

The square outside Grogny's town hall had been cordoned off so the forensic technicians could examine it in search of evidence. Behind the barriers guarded by the CRS riot police, shopkeepers, residents and passers-by were not yet ready to leave this place that, to their disbelief, was now a crime scene. Journalists continued to swarm, only to be unceremoniously pushed back by law enforcement. The mood deteriorated when a municipal adviser close to Chaouch shoved a cameraman, knocking over his boom operator.

Directly across from the town hall, immune to all this activity, a Chinese restaurant owner dressed in a vest was sweeping confetti from the doorstep of his establishment. With a deft twitch of his lips, he steadily rained clumps of ash from his cigarette onto the just-cleaned pavement, perhaps wondering when all these people who were hanging around would start to feel peckish.

On the front steps of the town hall, everyone was waiting for the prosecutor to arrive from Paris. When it came to terrorism, the Parisian courts had national jurisdiction, its judges enjoying a change of scenery, and its prosecutors systematically learning the facts of different cases, whether they'd originated under the Corsican sun or in the forests of Brittany.

But even before the arrival of the prosecutor, who would choose which law enforcement branch would lead the investigation, Valérie Simonetti, the head of Chaouch's bodyguard, was being questioned in an unmarked van at the far edge of the square. The 'Valkyrie', as she'd been nicknamed, was sitting ramrod straight on a bench normally reserved for people under arrest. Two counterterrorism officers had relieved her of her weapons and earpiece, and the commander replied to their questions in short, precise sentences. Her voice didn't quaver. Her face showed no sign of anxiety. Her hands rested on her knees. It was in the very austerity of her demeanour, her smooth cheeks a little more taut than usual, that one could guess at her devastation.

'So there was no procedural error,' one of the policemen mused aloud, as he filled out the form. 'According to you, the only aberration was Major Couteaux wanting a last-minute change of assignment ... But you refused to let him be the Kevlar, and you moved him to the second ring of defence?'

'That's right,' the commander replied.

'And you think Major Couteaux is responsible for missing the gunman in the crowd?'

'I don't accuse my men without proof,' Valérie retorted before locking eyes with her subordinate. 'If there's one person to blame for this, it's me.'

The officer turned the page of his notebook.

'Can you tell me about the threats the CDII passed on? When were you made aware of the existence of Nazir Nerrouche, the gunman's cousin?'

'Just two weeks ago. I was given access to the investigative team's file, and I met Boulimier several times.'

Boulimier, the chief of police, was close to Noyer, the soon-to-be former president, and had been director of the CDII since its creation in 2008.

'And there were never any conflicts between your team and the one monitoring Nazir Nerrouche?'

'Not to my knowledge. I was apprised of the new information, and I increased surveillance of Deputy Chaouch. I adapted. All my men had a photo of Nerrouche on them, but we gave priority to the Al-Qaeda lead. The other threats didn't seem that credible. Anyway, you know—'

The commander was interrupted by the arrival of two men wearing dark suits like the counterterrorism officers and, like them, if you had passed these men on the street, you would have thought salesmen, not supercops. But they weren't CDII civil servants: they were part of an elite police force and an unease spread through the van, a reaction they were used to. The woman they were here to question, however, did not raise an eyebrow, not even after they had announced her suspension for the duration of the investigation.

Without bothering to introduce himself, the first of the new arrivals declared, 'Internal Affairs investigation. We've just been told that the Paris prosecutor is on his way. Commander, I suggest you follow us to our offices. It'll be more comfortable for us to talk there.'

Valérie Simonetti stood up gracefully and confidently. She bent her head so her blonde hair did not touch the van's ceiling, then got out, towering over the two men from the police's police who stood beside her. As they led her towards their vehicle, she took one last look at the steps of the town hall. The memory of the gunshot caused her to inhale sharply. She put her hand on the back door of the car in which she would be taken away like a common criminal. So much rage had built up inside her since the gunshot that she almost tore off the door handle before the driver could unlock it.

2.

'You're young, but there's something you absolutely must understand, my dear *assistant*: in our old country, every department is in competition with another. And though they share the same goals and have the best interests of the nation similarly engraved above the entryway to their headquarters, each will always prefer to trip up the opposing department rather than work together in harmony. Oh yes. The Ministry of the Interior and the Police Department in Paris, the counterterrorism division and the CDII . . . Because, you know, for those who are tasked with navigating these high seas, the war among departments is a given almost as fundamental as the very existence of crime . . .'

Jean-Yves Lamiel, the powerful Paris prosecutor, often engaged in this sort of rambling. As their car reached Grogny, his victim this time was the young assistant prosecutor for counterterrorism. Lamiel had the most spectacular face in the Paris court system, like Daumier's caricature of a pear – except that in this case the pear was overfed and looked like a true GMO: enormous cheeks and jowls so swollen they looked like they were about to explode. In contrast, the upper part of his face seemed weirdly constricted, his forehead ridiculously shrunken and his eyes bulging from their undersized sockets.

To counteract this boorish appearance, his eloquence had become cunning and extravagant with, as its climax, *the lesson*: this passion for explanation was the great judge's particular hobby horse and took up so much of his days that, as the fourth Madame Lamiel could testify, it was only at night that . . . Well, he was never happier than when he found an unusual way of stating the obvious facts that practice, habit and the mechanical nature of everyday life had caused his young colleagues to lose sight of, exasperated as they were by his copious timewasting.

'Look, I'm going to draw something for you,' said Lamiel excitedly, sensing that his assistant was not giving him his undivided attention. 'These are things you know, of course. You know them, but only *abstractly*. Whereas – whereas! . . . When you have to make decisions, decisions like the one I'll make in a few hours, the important thing is not knowing something in theory or even acting in possession of all the facts. The important thing is to *see* . . .'

At the word 'see', his eyes became saucers. He took a paper napkin from his three-button jacket, an expensive fountain pen from his attaché case, and drew the following diagram:

'What does this remind you of, without a caption?'
The young assistant pretended to concentrate. He didn't dare

say it in front of his esteemed boss, but the only thing it really reminded him of was Pac-Man.

'I'll explain it to you. The head swallowing the smaller one is the CDII, the big fat CDII of dear Commissioner Boulimier. Well, imagine investigative teams with secret clearance, a whole undefined group of cops in the shadows with their ears to the ground . . . And the little ball there, all tense and tough, sharing its headquarters in Levallois, well, that's the ATSD, the Anti-Terrorist Sub-Directorate. I'm going to tell you what I think: the ATSD are the best counterterrorism cops in France, the elite. What's more, it's a branch of the judicial police. When we judges have to choose men to lead delicate investigations, we'd rather have the word "judicial" before police, don't you think? . . . Therefore, the choice is simple: Boulimier's CDII, which answers directly to the government, or the ATSD run by Mansourd, who, as we speak, is waiting for me in my office at the Palais de Justice – shadow men or supercops.'

'Yes, but—'

'You don't have to say it: the CDII had been watching Nazir Nerrouche for a few weeks. I myself authorized taps on four mobile phones and physical surveillance of a few suspicious characters . . . Then it would follow that I'd allow the investigative team that's already worked on this Nerrouche to continue its job, right? And yet I'm going to hand the investigation over to the competing department, the ATSD. Can you tell me why?'

'Because to the public the CDII seems too close to power? Because President Noyer and Boulimier are old friends?'

'Of course, but there's another reason. Can't you see it? I repeat: can't you *see* it?'

The car had stopped in front of the yellow tape that surrounded the square outside Grogny's town hall. The chauffeur waited for a sign from the prosecutor that he could turn off the engine, but the latter was shooting a hypocritical and tyrannical look at his poor deputy.

'It's Pac-Man!'

The assistant grimaced.

'Yeah – yes, I thought that's—'

'Look at the drawing! I too am the little ball swallowed up by the big head, the only high-ranking judge nominated without the approval of the president. What did they call me in my profile on the back page of *Libération*? "Prosecutor Lamiel, a small island of resistance to Noyerist cronyism". A small island of resistance, ha! They should have said: "Prosecutor Lamiel, an indigestible hairball stuck in the Pacnation's craw". Well, this is what we're going to announce, my dear *assistant*: that we are opening a judicial inquiry, with an appointed investigating judge, and that the inquiry will be headed by the ATSD. And when we announce this, there'll be muttering, conjecture. People will think: here at last is a public prosecutor's department that doesn't lie down and take orders, and so on. A prosecutor's department so independent that it's even willing to entrust the proceedings to an investigating judge . . . Keep the drawing,' he concluded, as he tore himself from the comfortable seat, breathing heavily with his tongue out. 'This drawing encapsulates the whole state. It might be of use in twenty years, when you're in my shoes . . .'

Lamiel saw a cavalcade of riot police vans go by, speeding towards the low-income neighbourhoods that were now in flames. As he buttoned the third button on his suit jacket, he added, 'That is, if the state still exists in twenty years . . .'

3.

At first, the trouble was confined to the Rameau-Givré housing projects in Grogny, but by 6 p.m. a hundred burned-out cars were found in the areas where crowds of voters had gathered: at the exit of Charléty Stadium, on Marseilles' Canebière main street, and in a few provincial town centres where spontaneous unrest was a common occurrence.

Another kind of fire was burning in the heart of the capital, just a few metres from the Elysée Palace. Minister of the Interior Marie-France Vermorel had summoned around thirty people to the ministry's basement: the high-tech inter-ministry crisis room consisted of a huge round table with microphones, telephones and private screens. She welcomed all the top brass from the French police, including Commissioner Boulimier.

One by one, each of these eminent officials was given a thorough dressing-down by Place Beauvau's own Iron Lady.

'Can anyone tell me how I look at this moment? Anyone? An assassination attempt on a presidential candidate ... What the hell is happening? Is this an American TV show? Did I miss an episode? Nobody is irreplaceable – get that into your pathetic, incompetent little heads!'

When it came to the turn of Commissioner Boulimier – whose elite units had not foreseen the machinations of the enigmatic Nazir Nerrouche – his studious colleagues, in a row against the wall, thought the gigantic luminous saucer hanging above the table might explode onto their very honourable bald pates.

The meeting was almost over when a Renault Vel Satis sped into the ministry's courtyard. The Republican Guardsman who opened its door saw the gilded handle of a walking stick emerge and recognized it as belonging to the minister's young protégé. At twenty-nine, Pierre-Jean Corbin de Montesquiou (called Monsieur de Montesquiou in hallowed halls and 'P-J' in private) was by far the youngest chief of staff in France. He had graduated second in his class from ENS, the elite National School of Administration, but, instead of taking one of the exclusive *grands corps* public-sector jobs, he had committed sacrilege by choosing to join the Prefectural Corps. Administration truly impassioned Montesquiou. Or, more accurately, the royal machinery of power held an inordinate fascination for him, particularly when its all-powerful gears were in motion. He had started at the ministry as a technical adviser, where he had learned in a very short time how to make himself indispensable. Strictly speaking, he wasn't chief of staff, the position held by an older and less brilliant man; he was deputy chief of staff, but Minister Vermorel, one of those in the president's innermost circle, spoke of him as her 'right-hand man', adding that he was the person most crucial to the ministry.

Not many people understood this, but Montesquiou did: his office was next to the minister's, he had a chauffeured car and the right to speak rudely and condescendingly to sixty year olds who had been important commissioners, fearless inspectors and men of action while he was still in his cradle.

Upon entering the antechamber of the crisis room, where the minister still hadn't finished haranguing the officials, he was handed a piece of paper that he read quickly, commenting, 'Things are going to change.'

Montesquiou gave no sign what these figures meant to him. The voter turnout numbers gave him pause, but not the election results. He put his walking stick on a pedestal table and used the adviser's back to scrawl the rough percentage of people that had just crowned the new President of the Republic on a little sheet of paper. He folded the sheet in half and entered the room. After the ministerial lambasting, a video conference brought together the commissioners on a large screen visible to all.

'Please stand up,' the minister ordered the chief of the riot police, 'so my chief of staff can take a seat.'

'Of course, Madame Minister.'

The riot police chief got up with a self-conscious smile, but the edges of his receding hairline reddened in anger and shame.

A tall, greying police commissioner described the measures being taken to close the airports and reinforce border controls. The lists of PVI (Points of Vital Importance) were being sent to all the prefectures; some MFUs (Mobile Force Units) were being sent out to high-risk areas like harbours, electricity power stations, railway junctions . . .

'The executive office is calling an emergency meeting,' the commissioner went on, 'of a restricted security and national defence council. In the meantime, we've taken it upon ourselves to raise the National Security Threat level to red for the first time since its implementation.'

Faces darkened. Throats went dry. Several glasses of water were drained in the silence following this announcement, which represented a leap into the unknown, even for these men accustomed to handling crises.

Having cleared his throat, the commissioner went on: 'VIP security has been tightened and the president has moved his campaign headquarters to the Elysée bunker . . .'

Rue du Faubourg Saint-Honoré (where the Elysée presidential palace is located at number 55) was indeed – Montesquiou's chauffeur could testify to this – blocked by four riot police units as well as reinforcements from the Republican Guard.

'Across France, law enforcement has been put on red alert. Their primary objective is to stop the riots from spreading beyond the Paris suburbs.'

Montesquiou waited until the commissioner had stopped speaking before passing the note to the minister.

She also showed no reaction. But, a few seconds later, she interrupted the next speaker, a prematurely bald adviser, who looked totally shocked.

'Okay, enough. The way things stand, we can't wait any longer for the press conference.'

The election results would soon be posted on Swiss and Belgian newspaper sites, which were not subject to the same draconian regulations as the French media.

'Yes, Madame Minister,' replied the chiefs as they stood simultaneously.

But the minister stood motionless for a moment, looking closely at Commissioner Boulimier. Noyer's wife had called her 'The Dragon' in leaked footage that had been the talk of the town during the holidays: the First Lady confessed in the video that Vermorel gave her the chills, and lamented that the Minister of the Interior was only person in the country with whom her unruly husband occasionally showed any humility . . .

The head of the CDII also ended up bowing before the minister. She folded in half the paper Montesquiou had given her and passed it to her neighbour on the left, who passed it on in turn. After everyone had seen it, 52.9 per cent was the only thing in the minds of the police chiefs, just as thoroughly as their minister's screams had been a few moments earlier, screams that still seemed to be echoing through the beautiful, luxurious corridors of that old mansion.

4.

Such a fit of anger was normally the president's prerogative. That Vermorel felt she could berate the chiefs of police and gendarmerie in such a way proved her special status at the epicentre of the country's political machine. Besides, being a born politician, she took a mischievous pleasure in castigating these loathsome police commissioners. However, one man had escaped this dressing-down: the powerful chief of the Paris police, Michel de Dieuleveult, whose authority in the police command rivalled the minister's, a man whom Montesquiou, demoted to pageboy for the occasion, accompanied into the minister's office. The Paris police headquarters faced Notre-Dame, right at the heart of the Ile de la Cité: it had nearly forty thousand men at its disposal, its own interior intelligence service and a world-famous stronghold at 36 quai des Orfèvres. It was a veritable state within the state.

Vermorel was meeting with him in private to pool what little information they had on Nazir Nerrouche. Dieuleveult, who dyed his hair black, was a rigid, suspicious man. He looked like a deacon who had been elevated overnight to cardinal. And so a certain calm amazement issued from his eyes, hidden behind thick horn-rimmed glasses whose lenses had long since lost their anti-glare coating. He hadn't yet reached an age where a large gut might have justified wearing his belt so high, just above the belly button: it was a sort of retrograde, almost unnoticeable vanity.

'Madame Minister,' said the chief of police, a hint of aggression behind the polite words, 'we don't know anything more than what's in the CDII file.'

The minister did not want to meet his eyes, which, in any case, were hidden by her own reflection. Even in the rare moments when they appeared, thanks to an uncontrolled movement of his head, they were flat, inexpressive ovals that betrayed no emotion, not even the contempt his eyebrows permanently displayed.

'Chief Dieuleveult,' she said solemnly, 'I assume that in these, shall we say, apocalyptic circumstances, we can count on the complete support of your teams?'

'Of course, Madame. The security of the capital is the security of France . . .'

The chief of police's words were clearly duplicitous, but the hostility between these two right-wing leaders was so old that no one thought to address it.

'So, we shall see,' concluded Vermorel, who wanted to have the last word on that.

Fittingly, they next discussed the measures he would take to ensure the capital's security.

'Excellent,' concluded the unflappable chief of police. 'Then all that remains is to wish you good luck. Or rather . . . to wish *us* good luck.'

Left alone with Montesquiou in her office, the minister let out a deep sigh and watched the red lights blinking on her phone.

Montesquiou was reading newspapers online from his phone. He had sunk unthinkingly into his chair and, for a brief moment, he looked like a grumpy teenager in the headmaster's office. Then something made him sit up straight.

'Good God, it's blowing up online. People are spouting all kinds of crap,' he said, looking up at Minister Vermorel who was staring at the corner of her marble desk. 'Listen to this: "The opposition tried everything to smear Chaouch – anonymous letters, dirty tricks, digging into his past looking for mistresses, questionable friendships, controversial statements, even embarrassing votes. To no avail. So they counted the number of times he had been to mosque, and for each occasion tried to find a radical imam or the cousin of some obscure Salafist preacher so they could skewer him for keeping bad company. Except that there weren't any. Nothing to hide, nothing to blackmail him with. Chaouch was hopelessly clean ... And then he's shot on the day of the elections. No need to be a conspiracy theorist to wonder—"'

'Pierre-Jean,' the minister cut in with a sigh.

'It's from a blog run by the host of a morning radio show, Madame. Already picked up on Twitter by three big shots from the other party. Government officials! Peddling this kind of bullshit! What happens if they continue making accusations like that?'

'All in good time. Right now, we've got bigger problems than the rants of these stupid bloggers.'

The minister cleared her throat. The tension of the last two hours had returned. Montesquiou saw she was doing lip exercises and, realizing who she had to call next, vacated the room. Alone, Vermorel opened a drawer and threw a paracetamol into the glass of water she had poured before the meeting. She watched the tablet fizz around the glass with a kind of resigned placidity that, to the tired minister, seemed almost noble. That evanescence was her law, her fate, her duty, the duty of the state's top civil servants and all those who had France's best interests at heart: you had to be willing to dissolve your sense of self in order to serve.

When the tablet was no more than a tiny disc bobbing on the

water's surface, Madame Vermorel downed the concoction in one go and dialled the president's number, trying to think of the best way to tell him that the police and judicial juggernaut was under way, but at the same time incessantly thinking about that stupid, fatal 52.9 per cent that would never disappear, not even if it were doused with sulphuric acid.

5.

The plane carrying the Wagners landed at Roissy just before 7 p.m. Alerted by his court clerk that the Val-de-Grâce Hospital press conference was imminent, Judge Wagner insisted his security detail find him a television before they reached Paris. Thierry, the agent Paola had nicknamed Aqua Velva, glanced around the terminal. He made out a crowd gathered behind the line for a fast-food restaurant.

A few dozen passengers were avidly watching a television – they would remain in transit for quite some time, given that all planes were now grounded. Sitting on their suitcases, people were sweating profusely. They began to hush each other as if they were at the movies the moment a podium appeared on the screen. A small, bespectacled assistant was struggling to adjust the height of the mic.

'I know of at least one person who must be happy,' Paola murmured.

Judge Wagner did not react. He stayed at the back of the crowd, flanked too closely by his bodyguards. Paola could not bear the silent expectation that gripped the small group of viewers. She looked long and hard at her husband to gauge his level of focus, and interpreted a slight twitch in his left cheek as a sign that she could speak to him.

'Seriously, Henri, it's going to be hard for me to speak to

Xavier Puteoli again after all this. I know you're old friends but this is too much. And then there's Tristan hanging around Aurélie . . . I'm sorry, but no . . .'

'So, he blew a fuse. I'd be the first to admit that. But to say he's happy about a terrorist attack . . .'

'He's exultant!'

'Now, come on. As for his son, what am I supposed to do? Charge him with flirting without the consent of her parents?'

'Shh, he's coming on.'

Just then, Val-de-Grâce's chief medical officer walked up to the microphone and cleared his voice while grimacing severely so he'd be told which camera to address. He held a sheet of paper in his motionless hands. His inscrutable face was that of a man accustomed to secrecy: both as a doctor and a military man. And it suddenly seemed to Judge Wagner – and probably also to the several million French citizens watching that face at this moment – completely incongruous that a man so obviously uncomfortable with public speaking should be on the verge of delivering the most eagerly anticipated news of the year.

The surprise was even more complete when he began to speak in an unabashedly south-western accent that made him sound like a butcher from Gascony.

'Good evening, I'm Professor Saint-Samat, Val-de-Grâce's chief medical officer. Upon Monsieur Chaouch's arrival at five minutes past four this afternoon, an angiography was carried out and confirmed the initial diagnosis of a ruptured cerebral aneurysm. The operation carried out by Dr Neyme and myself consisted of removing the vascular malformation. It went well: there were no complications, and we successfully stopped the haemorrhage. The hope is that the haemostasis will hold.

Fortunately, Monsieur Chaouch's haemodynamic state remained stable throughout the operation, but you must understand that, given the gravity of the situation, he has been ... uh ... kept in a medically induced coma.'

Professor Saint-Samat flipped the piece of paper unbelievably slowly.

'Deputy Chaouch will remain in intensive care on a ventilator, closely monitored with the usual medical supervision. Of course, the next few hours will be crucial.'

Camera flashes continually illuminated his long, unperturbed face. He stopped reading from his paper and added, looking for the first time at a different camera, 'To conclude, I would like to add that the medical team cannot make a conclusive short-term prognosis for Deputy Chaouch. Thank you.'

The entire terminal exploded with chattering, commenting and making conjectures. Judge Wagner and his wife were led to his car, which had been waiting at Departures for nearly a quarter of an hour.

'But what happens,' Paola asked, 'if he wins the election while he's in a coma?'

'He simply wins the election. I suppose if he doesn't come out of it very quickly, the Constitutional Council will cancel the results and reschedule for the following month ... after the parliamentary elections. In other words, it will be a complete mess. And if Noyer wins, my God, it won't change anything except that his rival is in a coma. Unless the Constitutional Council says otherwise. The Council has absolute authority in the matter.'

Paola couldn't decide if this was a good or a bad thing.

Once the car had left the airport, she asked in a disappointed voice, 'I suppose you're going straight to the Palais de Justice?'

The judge reached over to touch the nape of his wife's neck. She began to turn towards him, but rejected his gesture with a shake of her head as soon as she felt his touch.

Since the death threats from Corsican nationalists, Paola was upset about her husband's chosen profession – maddeningly demanding, absurdly time-consuming – in which the excitement of the investigation ended up seeming like its own reward. The attempted hit, which had culminated in the discovery of a homemade bomb under his car, had even changed her husband's face: his jaw jutted out more, his forehead shrank. Above all, his eyes hardened: it was gradually becoming rarer to see a fanciful gleam or wide smile light up his face. It seemed constantly shadowed now: rivalries at the heart of the counterterrorism centre, death threats and bad ratings, the feeling of being sidelined. During the past year, he had been assigned only five new cases . . .

Paola's mouth contorted into a humourless smile.

'Our first weekend alone in six months . . . Some weekend . . .'

6.

Two men were waiting for Judge Wagner at the Paris prosecutor's office: Prosecutor Lamiel, with whom Wagner played tennis on Tuesdays, was sitting on the edge of his desk, and standing in front of the window was Commander Mansourd, the legendary chief of the ATSD. The judge was forever in his debt because he had been the one, three years before, to discover the Corsican nationalists' bomb under the judge's car.

'Your Honour, you were the only one missing. Have you seen the turnout?'

'Yes, eighty-nine per cent, very high.'

'Unheard of, you mean!'

Lamiel had just appointed Wagner and Poussin, the two judges most averse to the methods of Judge Rotrou, who had been in power for twenty years and was the embodiment of the counterterrorism judge, in both public opinion and action. The prosecutor had nicknamed them 'Le Lorrain and Poussin', after the seventeenth-century painters, or simply 'The Artists', and selected them for the most important legal procedure of the year.

Politically, Lamiel was actually considered to be on the left, something that irritated the powers that be. One year before the election, during the game of musical chairs that began with the retirement of the presiding judge, the Supreme Council of Magistrates had rebelled, vetoing everyone put forward by President Noyer and the Elysée for the notoriously key position of head of the Paris public prosecutor's department. The president had finally been forced to appoint Lamiel, but, despite everything, had succeeded in placing one or two of his own people on the team, although in the view of those who understood such matters, it was a wasted effort: everyone knew that the real head of counterterrorism was Judge Rotrou, nicknamed 'the Ogre of Saint-Eloi', after the high-security top floor of the Palais de Justice, where the counterterrorism judges had their offices.

The campaign had deepened the divide between Noyer and the judges (a double murder by a repeat offender, yet another statement by the president about the laxness and irresponsibility of the judges), while Chaouch campaigned in favour of true independence for the prosecutor's department from the executive branch. By promising a 'Marshall Plan for Justice', to be implemented over ten years, he won the support of a majority of the judiciary who finally felt that the tide had started to turn. And so, at the helm of this institution and at last going against the currents of power was Jean-Yves Lamiel – who, glancing at his desk, darkened by the burgundy wall-hangings and oak panelling, solemnly handed a document to Wagner: it was the introductory information, the basis of the investigation from which he would take the main elements for his first press conference.

'All right, Henri, you won't be happy at what I'm about to tell you. No happier than the Minister of the Interior was . . .'

'The gunman was under surveillance?' Wagner asked in anticipation. 'The police knew all about him, is that it?'

'No, no, I just went to see him,' replied Lamiel, still sitting on his desk. 'He's eighteen, he's a petty criminal, and he's been convicted twice for minor offences, both times with a suspended sentence. No, the person under surveillance was the one who's probably the real brains behind the shooting.'

He unbuttoned his jacket, got up and walked around his desk.

'The CDII called me five weeks ago to alert me to the activities of the SRAF, a previously unknown group. Nobody knows what the letters stand for, only that it's a secret movement led by a certain Nazir Nerrouche, the cousin of Abdelkrim Bounaim-Nerrouche, this afternoon's gunman. I've opened a preliminary investigation for criminal conspiracy in connection with a terrorist undertaking and authorized wiretaps. The investigation hadn't made any headway until today, basically because this Nazir Nerrouche is extremely paranoid and doesn't trust anyone.'

'How could we not have got anything from the wiretaps?' asked Wagner incredulously.

'The group from the CDII thought they had located a

weapons cache and caught a supposed accomplice, a member of the SRAF. But it was a set-up.'

'The accomplice?'

'Everything! The weapons, the accomplice; we were listening to three of his mobile phones, and on the first two Nerrouche knew he was being listened to, and, well, there's no point in beating about the bush: he was completely manipulating the investigation.'

Wagner was flabbergasted. How could the CDII team have been such amateurs? He had often worked with the agents of the CDII, and had never questioned their competence.

'And the third phone?' asked the judge.

'Well, I haven't been given access to the transcripts yet. It's been really difficult to requisition them. Anyway, he must have destroyed his phones since the attack. He's very . . . wily.'

'How old is he? Is he an Islamist? Has he been linked to any known groups? Al-Qaeda?'

'Nothing,' the prosecutor replied. 'Nazir Nerrouche is twenty-nine. He's been to college, the Sorbonne – started off majoring in French literature, then switched to classical literature, then changed tack again and studied insurance law. He started up a couple of small businesses, one in Saint-Etienne, where his family is from, and a private security firm that went bankrupt. He got involved in local life; looked after the Muslim sections of the cemeteries, lobbied for the construction of that mosque everyone was talking about during the campaign. That's when the CDII got interested in him. The problem was that he didn't attend any suspicious mosques, and had no link with any known terrorist networks.'

'But then what? He put together a sleeper cell?'

'Worse than that. Our worst nightmare: a movement that is, how shall I say, radically autonomous. A sort of self-sufficient ghost that's undetectable on the usual radar. Good luck explaining that to the press . . .'

'And the gunman?'

'For now, he's not giving us much, but I don't think he's lying about not knowing where his cousin is. So I'm having a hundred thousand copies of a Wanted poster printed with Nazir Nerrouche's face on it. I think we have to issue a European arrest warrant . . .'

Judge Wagner shook his head.

'How could we have lost him?' he thundered. 'It's unbelievable that we couldn't arrest him before this. Was he being physically watched? What happened?'

'The CDII's umpteenth blunder,' Lamiel replied. 'Which, by the way, Commander Mansourd has his own thoughts about. Commander?'

The commander kept looking through the window. He was probably the only officer in France's judicial police with such a luxuriant beard: a real man's beard, black and curly like his Samsonesque mane of hair. He wore a long-sleeved black t-shirt that hugged his thick, muscular torso, which owed nothing to time spent in a gym, and instead seemed to belong to a different century.

His black jeans seemed to vanish in the shadows, and Wagner suddenly thought that, if you pointed a torch where his legs were, its beam could have revealed a horse's sturdy legs. But when the commander-centaur moved away from the backlit glare, Wagner saw that wasn't the case: Mansourd had human legs and a hand on his holster; he was stroking the butt of his side-arm with a gentleness that belied his size, like a giant stroking a kitten.

'He probably had four phones,' he replied, 'maybe more, and on the ones the CDII was tapping, he gave false information to numbers registered to fake names. They botched the investigation and our colleagues are only sharing information from the taps in bits and pieces.'

'Things are going to change,' declared Wagner. 'We're no longer hunting the presumed head of some weird little movement, he's now the man behind a political assassination attempt. I'm telling you, we're going to get every last one of the wiretap transcripts.'

'Okay,' continued Lamiel, turning towards Mansourd, 'this is your big chance to prove that you're better than your friends at the CDII. For tonight you'll work with the Saint-Etienne police. No need to go to Levallois for the interrogations; you can watch from here.'

'Absolutely no cameras!' interjected Wagner. 'I'm not going to let the press stick its nose into my investigation. I hope we're on the same wavelength, Commander?'

The commander puckered his lips in acknowledgement. He noticed the prosecutor looked upset: his arms remained folded, and his eyes were bulging without focusing on anything particular on his desk.

Before leaving the room, Mansourd stared long and hard at Nazir's face on the Wanted poster. As for Wagner, he was less fascinated by the picture than by the intensity of the ATSD bloodhound's eyes. Framed by the sculpted, bearded face, his eyes seemed to glow red.

He stated in a gruff voice, 'We'll catch him, your Honour. You have my word.'

'Keep me posted, Commander,' said Judge Wagner.

Commander Mansourd left the office.

The two men looked at the spot where the commander had been standing. He'd left them both with the same impression: that he was a force to be reckoned with. One that for now was focused to their advantage and might tomorrow benefit someone else, but was only concerned with one objective: the capture of Nazir Nerrouche.

7.

'Quite a character, that Mansourd,' said the prosecutor. Then, changing tone: 'Henri, I have to tell you something: Nazir Nerrouche is the brother of Fouad Nerrouche, the star of a television show on Channel 6. I'm guessing you don't follow the tabloids, but if you did, you'd know there are rumours of a relationship between this actor and Jasmine Chaouch.' Surprised, Judge Wagner raised his eyebrows. Lamiel continued, 'That's right, Chaouch's daughter.'

'Does Mansourd know?'

'He's the one who told me just before you arrived; one of his men checked with Chaouch's security detail.'

'And?'

'And, not much to report . . . The team obviously knew him, but that's it. No criminal record, no bar fights, not even a speeding ticket; on paper, by all accounts, he's a boy scout.'

'We'll see about that.'

'There's something else, Henri,' said Lamiel hesitantly. 'Let's cut to the chase: I'm not convinced it's a good idea to leave our friends in the press completely in the dark about the investigation.'

'Except that if we start to share information left, right and centre, the CDII's mistakes will be exposed and plastered all over every single news outlet. It'll spin out of control in no time if we agree to play along.'

'Henri, I have to give my first press conference tomorrow morning. Do you realize I'll have to give one every day until this is over?'

The judge wouldn't budge an inch on this point. A ray of sunlight slipped between the curtains and lit up his white hair. In contrast, his raised eyebrows had never seemed so dark.

'They're going to need someone to blame, Henri. I'm not saying we're going to give that to them, but we'll have to find some way to appease them. Plus, it's not just the media, the General Prosecutor is going to follow this very closely. I spent half the afternoon on the phone with the Ministry of Justice. Everyone's career is at stake in this affair. Everyone's.'

'Prosecutor Lamiel,' Wagner solemnly replied, 'I have been appointed to head the preliminary investigation of an attempt on the life of a deputy of the Republic and a presidential candidate, and I intend to chase down every lead. I'm also going to widen the scope of the wiretaps and take all necessary measures to uncover the truth. But I am telling you now: don't expect a round-up of the entire family just to put on a show for the media circus. That would be completely counter-productive. Just look at Rotrou's recent exploits. Seriously, those methods . . .'

'We're in agreement, Henri, of course. Those methods are unconscionable. Or, rather, they can be better described as inefficient. The tide has turned; we've cleaned up the mess. There won't be any bad blood between the prosecution and the investigation and, above all, this time there will be no disagreement among the police services. I won't say that we're the future of counterterrorism law, but . . . it seems to me that it's not an exaggeration to say that it's in our hands.'

The judge was waiting for another 'but'. His mouth still open, Lamiel stood up and joined his tennis partner by the window. The courtyard of the Palais de Justice was buzzing with an unusual amount of activity for a Sunday.

'But for the moment they're going to ask us for the impossible. They're going to ask *you* for the impossible, and, not only that, they'll want it done yesterday. I hope you're ready.'

8.

As soon as the Val-de-Grâce chief medical officer's press conference was over, Fouad was told by the nurse – the same nurse with whom he'd argued earlier – that Rabia had just undergone an examination for possible sexual assault.

'She was raped?' asked Fouad, horrified.

'Sir, please calm down,' replied the nurse.

'Answer me, for God's sake!'

The nurse stepped back and nervously threatened to call security if Fouad didn't lower his voice.

'All right, are we calm now? Okay. The tests were negative.'

'She hasn't been molested then?'

'The tests were negative,' the nurse repeated.

'Thank God,' sighed Fouad, closing his eyes.

He wanted to thank the nurse, as if he owed her for the good news. Instead, he said nothing and he ran off towards Rabia's room. But Rabia was already getting dressed behind the door. Fouad knocked twice softly but could not enter, obstructed by his frantic aunt, her head lowered like a ram about to charge.

'We have to go find Luna now. *Miskina*, the poor girl's all by herself. Do you know what they did with my phone?'

'Auntie, calm down,' ventured Fouad as he finally pushed open the door. 'Calm down!'

'No, no,' said Rabia angrily, 'it's not time to calm down. We have to . . .'

She stopped and looked around the room, as if no longer looking for her phone, but rather for the reasons why we humans spend our time perpetually searching for something.

Fouad thought she was going to burst into tears. He rested a hand on her shoulder, as carefully as if he were handling a vial of nitroglycerine.

His Uncle Idir, meanwhile, wanted to say hello to Zoulikha, who was upstairs, but the nurse on duty informed him that visiting hours were over and that, anyway, Madame Nerrouche was sleeping like a log.

Disappointed, he went back downstairs and found himself face to face with Dounia, whose ragged appearance struck him almost as much as the guilty look in her eyes.

'What are you doing here?' asked Dounia, drying tears she unconvincingly tried to pass off as a cold by sniffling very loudly.

'I came to see Zoulikha and . . . Rabia . . . but, what about you? No one could get hold of you . . . You were . . .'

Dounia saw Fouad and Rabia; she stepped back but knew she was trapped. Fouad hurried towards her.

'Mum, where the hell were you?' he yelled. 'I've been trying to get hold of you for four hours! Four hours!'

Dounia reddened; in her son's anger, she saw an unexpected

escape route from the corner she was in.

'First of all, calm down. Don't forget that you're speaking to your mother, okay? I'm not your mate, all right?'

Fouad sensed she was hiding something from him but did not want to cause a scene in front of Idir. Dounia untied her hair, and then put it up again in an even tighter bun, going over to Rabia who didn't ask her a single question about her disappearance, relieved finally to be able to pour out her despair.

Fouad decided to drive Idir home. The old man did not really want to be alone after all this upheaval; luckily his son Raouf was waiting for him, and with him, the prospect of an almost normal election night spent listening to Raouf's explanations of why his father's generation understood absolutely nothing while his own possessed, in addition to the vigour of youth, the wisdom of statistics and complicated theories.

Raouf was waiting for his father in the stairwell, bewildered, sick of refreshing the browser of his iPhone, the screen now a smudge of fingerprints.

'This is . . . crazy,' was all he could stammer, noticing too late that the adjective was ridiculous given the situation, but that there existed in his vocabulary no word that was strong enough.

Fouad couldn't remember if he'd seen Raouf since daybreak. Raouf kissed him on both cheeks, bringing his mouth close to his haggard cousin's ears.

'Fouad, I've got to tell you . . .' whispered Raouf hesitantly.

Fouad sensed that what was coming was not a discussion he could face at the moment.

'We'll talk later,' he replied in a low voice, before putting him into the car with Idir, where Dounia and Rabia were waiting.

The sun was setting behind the slag heaps from the old

Clapier mine. Fouad scraped the kerb as he parked the car and looked up at the deserted balcony where, just the evening before, he had smoked a Camel with Krim. Some children stopped kicking around a ball to watch these people pass, these people with their strangely familiar faces, their party clothes and their tragic but determined way of walking.

In the lift, Dounia avoided her son's inquisitive looks by stroking Rabia's hair. When they arrived at the fourth floor, Granny's door opened suddenly to reveal Luna, who couldn't hold it together any longer. Screaming, she collapsed into her mother's arms.

Granny ushered everyone in so as not to attract the neighbours' attention, and in the subsequent bottleneck, Rabia and Luna, holding each other tightly, passed by the compassionate, terrified faces of uncles and aunts who had come for the wedding, then Slim, and finally Kamelia who, at the end of the line, held her arms out to her aunt so she could weep with her.

Rabia reached Granny's living room, which she knew like the back of her hand, and where the previous day the whole family had watched the videotape of Krim playing classical music on Granddad's electric piano before going to the community centre for the wedding.

Between sobs, Rabia found the time to ask, 'Bouzid's not here?'

'He's working till nine,' Rachida replied curtly.

Further away, the youngest of the Nerrouche sisters was holding Rayanne under one arm, rocking him as if to put him to sleep, while continually eyeing Rabia and Luna in a decidedly disapproving way.

Emerging from the bathroom, little Miriam ran to her

favourite aunt. She put her arms around her waist and pressed her face against her body. After an epic struggle, Rayanne escaped his mother's restraining arms and also went to embrace Rabia.

The children adored Rabia. And Rabia remembered, like a lightning bolt across the night sky of misfortune that had befallen her, that she adored the children.

3

52.9 PER CENT

1.

Although he was wiped out, Fouad was the only one in the flat whose face was not wet with tears or ravaged, in one way or another, by the enormity of what had transpired. Of course Granny kept her proud and grave appearance, but she wasn't trying to provoke anyone and instead was constantly looking for some task to do so she wouldn't have to face the heavy sorrow in the others' eyes.

Fouad went out onto the balcony and noticed a pile of ash behind the big flowerpot. The last rays of the setting sun made the pink concrete railing glow; the heat had not yet abated and light flooded the flat until finally Granny drew the curtains to eliminate the glare on the TV screen. Fouad recognized the news anchor's voice and stuck his head through the open window. The whole family was standing around the screen.

'Ladies and gentlemen, it is eight o'clock, and during this unique crisis, this remarkable situation, unheard of in our country's history, we can now give you the results of the second round of the presidential election . . .'

A large image of Chaouch's face appeared on the left of the screen. The bar graph showed his votes reached 52.9 per cent while Noyer's remained stuck at 47.1 per cent.

'Idder Chaouch is elected president with 52.9 per cent of the vote,' announced David Pujadas in a ragged voice, worn out by fatigue and the seriousness of the situation. 'With an absolutely extraordinary turnout: 89.4 per cent of the electorate turned out to vote . . . And for the first time in its history, France has elected a president who is in a coma,' he added, lowering his eyes, as if intimidated by the red recording light on the camera and the tens of millions of people watching the broadcast.

There would therefore be no acceptance speech from the president-elect in his euphoric campaign HQ. In fact, there were neither clips of elated supporters nor scenes of disappointment from the losers' camp. Although joy and disappointment were certainly present, they were cruelly mitigated by the extra-ordinary circumstances attending the results.

President Noyer cautiously accepted his defeat and wished his rival a speedy recovery from his coma. He then explained that, in this period of transition, his government was completely operational and announced that while the country waited for the Constitutional Council's decisions, a 'certain number' of measures had been taken to ensure the safety of the French people, beginning with the grounding of all aircraft and the raising of counterterrorism measures to level red.

'I want to reassure my fellow countrymen,' he concluded, 'that there is no reason to worry. In the last few hours, I have been hearing that there is concern, but there is no lapse in executive

63

leadership. The members of the Constitutional Council are intelligent and sensible, and I am completely confident in their ability to make the necessary decisions. France is strong, our institutions solid, and I am certain that after this unprecedented and – I repeat – *unspeakable* attack on national security, national solidarity will prevail . . .'

The president's speech was not yet over when the far-right candidate, who came in fourth in the first round of elections, rushed out a press release in which she acknowledged his firm approach but worried about the possibility of 'civil war'. On the radio, people were talking about imposing martial law as a pre-emptive measure. Others wanted the National Assembly and the Senate to give President Noyer full emergency powers under Article 16 of the Constitution. Conversely, on channel TF1, the leader of Young Socialists for Chaouch lost his composure while speaking to some right-wing leader, and stated that he 'understood' the uprisings that were spreading throughout the country. The right-winger even goaded him into saying that he was in favour of them. For a few seconds after his blunder, the camera lingered on the long-haired activist, no longer flushed with anger but rather with the certainty that, in one soundbite, he'd killed his fledgling career. And indeed, the Socialist Party's leadership waited only two days before firing him, partly to set an example and partly to dissuade embittered radicals from tarnishing the party's image as one that did not care about national security.

But that evening, most of France reacted as the Nerrouche family had: huddled together in their living rooms, nodding with raised eyebrows and a little relieved of course, but most of them, above all, immensely anxious, with the gloomy feeling that instead of witnessing the triumph of a man landing on the moon on live TV, as promised, they were being told the sun had just been kidnapped in some ridiculous last-minute plot twist.

2.

Fouad slipped out again onto the balcony and looked at the two mountains outside Granny's, the two slag heaps slumbering in the orange-red stripe of sunset, remembering the day when, as a child, he'd chosen the one on the left, while Nazir had taken the one on the right, decreeing it the best.

Again, Fouad looked at his list of missed calls. Jasmine still hadn't contacted him. He summoned up his courage and dialled her number. It went straight to voicemail, and he began to play with different hypotheses: her father was in a coma, and she wasn't allowed to use her phone in his hospital room – or the line was simply busy – thousands of people must be trying to call with words of comfort. He would just have to try again. Which he did. Ten times in four minutes. He left messages. It seemed as if he were leaving them in a void, like letters in a dead person's mailbox – except that no one, no agency, was there to tell him they had not reached the addressee.

He started theorizing again. This time, he wasn't juggling harmless rubber balls, but rather flaming clubs of terrifying possibilities, possibilities that pierced his pride and the love he felt for Jasmine: someone had told her that Krim was his cousin, she couldn't speak to a relative of her father's murderer, even if that person were her boyfriend . . .

He gave up and took a deep breath, trying to find the courage to go back to the living room where people were getting restless again. But Slim beat him to it, slipping a slender leg, still encased in the same white trousers as the night before, through the window.

'Fouad?'

'Yes, yes, all right,' his big brother replied, without trying to soften the fierceness of his tone, 'I'll be there in two minutes, okay?'

'No, Fouad,' Slim insisted, opening the curtain with a sharp tug, 'Krim's on TV!'

The first thing Fouad saw after leaping into the living room wasn't Granny's plasma screen but rather the family crowded in front of it, none of whom had moved since his flight to the balcony, though one thing had changed: they had all covered their mouths in horror. Every sentence the newscaster uttered about the gunman's identity caused a fresh flow of tears down cheeks that burned with shame. Down Rabia's face, mascara-tinted tears ran all the way to the corners of her trembling lips.

Granny began to speak in Kabyle, too quickly for her youngest daughters to understand. But even her little granddaughter Miriam could guess from her intonation that these were lamentations and macabre incantations.

Rabia turned up the volume, almost all the way. No one dared ask her to turn it down a little.

'We are now joined by a new guest,' declared David Pujadas, with some new-found enthusiasm in his voice, 'who can perhaps shed some light on this attack on President...' – he corrected himself – '... on President-Elect Chaouch. Xavier Puteoli, you're the editor-in-chief of Avernus.fr. This very evening you're publishing the first section of an article by Marieke Vandervroom about the CDII. The incredible failures of a top-secret investigation, the infighting between departments in charge of interior intelligence ... This article has created controversy – I remind you that the CDII completely denied all of these allegations in a press release. But first, the question on everyone's lips: do you think that the young gunman – for the moment only known by his first name, Abdelkrim – do you think he was acting on orders from the underground group known only by the acronym we'll no doubt hear a lot in the coming days: the SRAF?'

Rayanne, sucking his thumb at the foot of the television, began to smack the screen repeatedly. Two aunts rushed to stop him, but it was too late: the TV wobbled, and then fell from the too-narrow piece of furniture it had been resting on.

While Slim tried to reinstate it and switch it back on, a hush fell over the room, haunted by Rabia's ceaseless tears.

When she noticed that her phone was vibrating, she dried her face.

'It's the neighbour, Madame Caputo. Why is she calling me?'

The TV was working again. But Slim couldn't get it to show anything except snow. After a few more attempted calls, Rabia finally got up and answered to find out what her neighbour wanted.

At that same moment, Fouad got a message from Yael, telling him she had found him a lawyer.

3.

He went out onto the balcony to call Yael, closing the curtain as soon as the sinister voices on the TV began to resonate through the living room again.

'I just saw the situation on TV, Fouad. It's absolutely horrible, it's absolutely ... my heart goes out to you.'

'Thanks, Yael. So you've found a lawyer?'

'I've even called him for you. My contact works for Maître Szafran's firm, a top lawyer, and thinks that Szafran is the best man for the job. He defended some wrongly accused defendants in a terrorism case last year.'

'Krim is not wrongly accused,' snapped Fouad.

'Right, of course . . . Listen: Szafran's a top dog. He's president of an association that campaigns for better conditions in French prisons, he's had countless people acquitted and my contact at the firm says he often works pro bono. Do you have a pen to write down his mobile number? Call him right away . . .'

From the balcony, he heard Rabia let out a scream, which people in the car park of the library next door probably heard too, as he saw some people look round.

'Wait, Yael. Text it to me. I'll call you back.'

But Fouad didn't dare return to the living room.

He heard snatches of a confused argument in which the word 'police' figured heavily. The strident voices made it sound like a synonym for disaster. Fouad barely had time to register that he was starting to think like a criminal. He climbed through the window, pushing the curtains out of his way and saw his Aunt Rachida ranting at the family while pointing to the innocent faces of her young children as if they were proof of Krim's guilt.

'How can you possibly think of paying for him?' she screamed. 'You think I'm going to let my children have anything to do with all this? No, no, *wallah*, it's out of the question that we pay for the stupidity of your fucked-up kid . . .'

Fouad wanted to ask what was happening, but Rabia didn't give him time to defend her. It was less what Rachida had said than the shape her mouth made, so contemptuous that Rabia felt like she'd been slapped in the face.

Flushed with humiliation, she attacked her little sister with a flood of incoherent insults. Granny took the children by the hand and sent them with Kamelia into her bedroom.

Pressed against Kamelia's large breasts, the children raised wide eyes towards her, full of resigned bemusement. They were used to their relatives arguing, and they were, of course, too young to understand what was unique about this new conflict from which everyone was awkwardly trying to protect them.

'It's nothing, sweethearts,' said Kamelia, enveloping them in an uncertain voice. 'Mama is angry right now, but it'll pass. Nothing to worry about, my darlings . . .'

On the other side of the door, Fouad's handsome figure no longer cast its spell. Granny stood between the two raging sisters, and Fouad suddenly seemed tiny, insignificant next to this dark presence with her grey hair and inexplicably menacing charisma.

She calmed everyone with Kabyle phrases that sounded like magic spells.

With one look, old Uncle Idir forbade his wife, Ouarda, from choosing sides between Rabia and Rachida. But Fouad could see that the older sisters were strongly leaning towards supporting the youngest sister and her innocent toddlers.

The hand squeezing his phone began to shake. He went out onto the balcony, leaning on the railing, and forced himself to breathe slowly, his eyes closed.

When he reopened them, he saw that most hospitable of landscapes: the Tarentaize library with the slag heaps in the background, and on the right, the pink and green concrete towers of the housing projects, piled one on top of the other like Lego houses punctuated by fake windows – fake, because how could one seriously live in that convoluted jungle gym? Then, finally, to the left, the square where the neighbourhood children played, at the foot of the Saint-Ennemond church, with its rustic, oddly familiar facade; he felt that he knew it intimately, even though he'd never actually set foot inside.

He looked up: after a hot, sunny day, the windless sky looked like a crystal-clear lake high up in the mountains, gently painted with varying shades of blue and the sharp crest of a poplar tree reflected in it.

Fouad listened closely to the distant murmur of the city. In order to tear his attention from the tragic cacophony in the living room, he had to concentrate on the traffic noise, which was as reassuring in a city as the lull of the ocean or a breath of wind in a meadow. But suddenly the roar of cars seemed to swell and expand; an unusual number of vehicles appeared to be arriving on Granny's street. Fouad leaned over to check and saw more than a dozen police cars come hurtling past the library. Their sirens were off but their flashing lights quickly destroyed the subtle harmony of the watercolour evening.

'Fouad! Fouad!'

Dounia had been pulling his sleeve for perhaps thirty seconds. He turned to his mother and saw his own stupor reflected in her expression.

'Fouad! The police went to Rabia's place. They're coming here next. The neighbour gave them the address!'

'No,' murmured Fouad, in a stranger's voice, 'they're already here.'

Dounia rushed to the railing and saw at least thirty men

crowd into the entrance of the building. Some wore body armour and were carrying heavy weapons and battering rams. Others just wore white bulletproof jackets, on the back of which was written 'JUDICIAL POLICE'.

They all had guns and threatening faces. Before returning to the frenzy in the flat, Dounia spotted one in particular who was aggressively chewing gum: he had a beard and belonged to the judicial police. He suddenly looked up at her, as if he had felt her eyes on him.

The armoured men were first to enter, coming into the crowded living room like a herd of rhinos. They destroyed a table and knocked the TV over again. The bearded policeman called for silence and then shouted, 'Rabia Bounaim-Nerrouche!'

Rabia nervously identified herself.

'I am Commander Mansourd, from the Anti-Terrorist Sub-Directorate of the Judicial Police. This is Commissioner Faure, of the Regional Department of the Saint-Etienne Judicial Police. From this moment on,' he looked at this watch, 'twenty minutes past nine, you are officially in police custody.'

Stunned by these big words and the administrative and law enforcement nightmare they promised, Rabia let herself be handcuffed as family members screamed 'No!' and 'What's happening?' Fouad gestured at them to be quiet and asked the commander, 'For what cause? What is she charged with?'

The portly Saint-Etienne commissioner snapped back, 'With being her son's mother.'

The commander quickly shot the commissioner a dirty look and gave his own answer.

'The same thing as all the adults in this room: criminal conspiracy in connection with a terrorist undertaking.'

In the chaos that followed, amazingly, Fouad managed to impart to his relatives that they had the right to remain silent, that they had no obligation to speak, and that anything they said while detained would eventually be used against them.

A policeman forced Fouad against the wall and handcuffed him to shut him up. At that moment, Luna burst into tears. She had been outraged at her mother being handcuffed, but she was utterly humiliated by seeing Fouad restrained.

The commander asked that the cuffs not be put on the elderly. Faced with this unreal spectacle, Rachida was the first to lose control.

'But we haven't done anything! It was her son! He's the one who killed the president! We have nothing to do with any of it!'

Ouarda joined in, but Idir vigorously reprimanded her, and in Kabyle ordered her and the others to shut up.

'*Sesseum!*'

The word shivered across Granny's flat.

Standing in front of Rayanne, Kamelia placed her hands over her racing heart. Soon the only sound was the children's whimpers. Until, on top of the ocean of little cries, and with the brutality of a booted foot, Granny's imperious voice commanded them in Kabyle to follow instructions but say nothing.

Commander Mansourd looked at the old lady, whose stooped back and bovine eyes gave nothing away.

4.

Rabia didn't hear her two sisters' comments or Granny's command: she had already been led out of the building with Luna and Fouad and over to a vehicle that had been idling throughout the arrests. Fouad was put in a separate car, which immediately sped off. Commander Mansourd helped Rabia into the back seat by gently guiding her head.

In turn, her sisters, some handcuffed, some not, soon emerged from the block of flats. All the building's windows were open, filled with the gaping faces of neighbours in pyjamas.

The car carrying Luna and Rabia sped through the city to their home. On Commander Mansourd's orders, ten ATSD officers searched the sad little flat at 16 rue de l'Eternité with great pomp, rummaging through chests of drawers and cupboards, ripping open beds, pillows and the couch, and, with a calm, controlled voracity, removing all the photo albums, the hard disks from both computers, notebooks, report cards, sheet music, as well as all official papers on which there was even the most innocuous mention of Abdelkrim, the name having become, so to speak, radioactive. They also emptied the cellar, went over its contents with a fine-tooth comb, and sealed it off until the forensics team arrived.

'Damn, it's like Ali Baba's cave in here!' commented one policeman. 'They're going to have to tell us how our boy could afford all these toys.'

When he got back to the third floor, Mansourd took off Rabia's handcuffs and let her cry in her daughter's arms.

'Commander!'

One of his lieutenants beckoned him into Rabia's bedroom, where he'd made an interesting discovery: he handed it to his superior with a half-smile that immediately vanished at Mansourd's reaction. It was a dog-eared copy of *Preferring the Dawn*, the book released to coincide with the launch of Chaouch's campaign, and on whose cover the president-elect had never looked so alive.

5.

Jasmine Chaouch was alone in her father's room at last. She rested her forehead on the bed so she wouldn't have to look at her father, who was wrapped in bandages with tubes coming out of his nose and throat. The beeps of the electroencephalogram gracelessly joined the noise of other machines, vying stupidly against the monotonous spitting and wheezing of the respirator.

Jasmine let go of her father's hand, stretched out her slim body and let her mind float away on a stream of consciousness that moved from the absurdity of the messages she and her mother had been receiving for hours from the high and mighty to the piece from *The Magic Flute* that her father always asked her to sing for him: that moment when Papageno's glockenspiel defeats Monostatos's henchmen – the music stronger than violence. Her father loved that scene; he laughed like a kid when the henchmen began to dance, charmed by the childlike music that Jasmine didn't even realize she'd begun to hum, the sound drowned out by the chiming of the machines.

'Das klinget so heerlich, das klinget so schön ... La la la, la la la la la la, la la la la la la. Nie hab' ich so etwas gehört und geseh'n, la la la ...'

Jasmine looked at her father's mummified face, vaguely hoping to see him wake up, to see his handsome, clear-eyed, open face emerge from all the bandages and come back to life speaking of Mozart, so she could argue with him about how his monomaniacal passion for the composer kept him from discovering other things like the Baroque school, or contemporary music ... Or for him to look up to the sky with a broad smile, the way he did during the most ferocious debates, as he repeated yet again his theory that the most beautiful example of democracy could be found in *The Magic Flute*: the equal regard, or better, the equal concern and equal enthusiasm for the aspirations of both Papageno, the common man, and those of the hero, Tamino.

He only spoke about it at private dinners, with those closest to him, and wouldn't let it go: he espoused the idea of an ultimate reconciliation, talking of his duty, if elected, to make Mozart and the spirit of his music a mandatory class taught by experts for two hours a week. He had more or less already done this in Grogny, with his free music schools and the sparkling new auditorium. To him, the music of the classical age was the apogée of European civilization: its greatest treasure and its greatest gift to mankind. When he spoke of Mozart's *allegros*, his eyes, brown flecked with green, shone. He forgot about the national debt, ratings agencies and youth unemployment. 'They're going to think I'm a freemason,' he would joke into the ear of his wife or of the chosen one whose arm he'd mischievously grabbed – before bursting into laughter, with his loud, clear laugh that hadn't changed a note since his teens.

To Jasmine, having a father like Chaouch meant accepting that he would always be the largest figure in her life. But she hadn't foreseen that by becoming, for a few months, the largest figure in the lives of millions, it was possible, even inevitable, that tragedy would strike.

And now he wasn't laughing and he couldn't speak.

Jasmine heard the door open. Her mother came in. Behind her, looming in the corridor, Habib and Vogel were talking softly into their respective phones. Vogel covered his with his hand, while Habib, Chaouch's communications director, scratched his cheek with the stump of his arm. A tall, thin figure appeared and caught Jasmine's eye: it was Montesquiou, the chief of staff of the Minister of the Interior. Jasmine saw him exit her field of vision like a snake, leaving only his walking stick planted at a provocative angle.

'Honey, the convoy's ready. Do you want another moment?'

Her mother had tried to soften her voice but her eyes still had some of the hardness from her previous conversation with 'the president's men'.

'What's that guy doing here?'

'That's Montesquiou, from Vermorel's staff...'

'I know who he is, but what the hell's he doing here?'

'He's here to tell us about the investigation. Honey, there's something I have to tell you.'

Jasmine stared at her mother, ready to erupt at whatever she said.

'The young man who shot your father... his name is Abdelkrim. Abdelkrim Bounaim-Nerrouche. He's Fouad's cousin.'

Jasmine inhaled sharply in shock and covered her open mouth with her hand.

'Jasmine, has Fouad called you since the attack?'

'No,' Jasmine protested, her ears getting warm, 'that's impossible... Fouad...'

'Wait, Jasmine.'

'I don't have my phone on me anyway. I forgot it when I left... in a rush... But...'

Madame Chaouch grasped her daughter's shoulders.

'We don't know anything for now. No one is accusing Fouad. No one. I just want to know... if you feel up to speaking with the policemen from the...'

Jasmine didn't hear the rest. She rubbed her ears. But the

more she rubbed them, the more she felt they were actually going to burst into flames.

Esther Chaouch turned to look at Habib, Vogel, Montesquiou and a fourth man who was discreetly following the exchange from a distance.

'Sweetie,' she went on. 'About Fouad ...'

Jasmine got up suddenly, shaken by a single sob. She sniffed hard, once, to regain her composure and left the room, taking great care not to even glance towards the vultures outside the room.

6.

Taken aback, Esther, who had remained in the hospital room, beckoned to Habib and Vogel.

'I'd like to speak to Major Couteaux. Do you think that's possible?'

'Yes, yes,' replied Habib. 'He was questioned and quickly returned to Jasmine's bodyguard. Do you want to speak to him now?'

'Yes, please. Is the chief of the CDII with you?'

'Boulimier? Yes. Should I bring him in?'

'No,' replied Madame Chaouch after looking at her husband's bed, 'let's speak in the corridor.'

The head of the CDII, who had been scolded by the Minister of the Interior a few hours earlier, presented his respects to Madame Chaouch, bowing down as far as his paunch would allow. Charles Boulimier had a wide, square, expressionless face. In lieu of a mouth, the lower part of his face was crossed by a simple stripe, perfectly perpendicular to a dimple on his chin, which itself was devoid of both volume and depth. He had the perfect face for counter-espionage, if not the perfect body. He had put on weight since assuming his position – politics, with its banquets and receptions. His portliness was also accentuated – and not, as he must have imagined, elegantly hidden – by his habit of doing up only the top button of his jacket.

'Commissioner Boulimier,' Esther Chaouch began. 'Thank you for coming so quickly.'

'It's my duty, Madame.'

'Okay, then let's get straight to the point: I refuse to let my daughter be questioned. With all that's happening to her, if she also has to . . .'

'Of course, Madame.'

'That's all. Do what you have to do, but I don't want to know a thing.'

'There are alternative methods, Madame,' Boulimier insinuated.

'You understand,' Madame Chaouch continued, narrowing her eyes, 'I don't want her to get mixed up in . . . Her safety, Monsieur, her safety is all that matters to me at this moment in time.'

'Madame, I will see to this personally . . .'

Serge Habib beckoned to Aurélien Couteaux. Esther patiently thanked him for his thoughts and prayers before quickly getting to the point.

'Major Couteaux, you know Monsieur Boulimier, from the CDII. I'd like you to do something for me.'

'Whatever you wish, Madame,' the young security officer replied diligently.

'Aurélien, I don't want him to call her. Do what you like, but I refuse to let my daughter be mixed up in all that. You'll get the details from Monsieur Boulimier.'

Couteaux nodded silently, without daring to look at the powerful chief of counter-espionage. There was silence.

'I trust you, Aurélien,' Esther said in a single breath, obviously emotional, before addressing Boulimier. 'I'm never wrong with people, Monsieur Commissioner. I insist that Aurélien be on the front line of this . . . operation.'

Boulimier smiled deferentially. As for Couteaux, he bowed down so far that he showed the quasi-First Lady, on his well-coiffured cranium, the point where his vigorous brown locks took root and spread out.

7.

After learning by phone that the arrest of the Nerrouche family had passed off without incident, Judge Wagner had a strange idea: he asked his driver to press on to Grogny instead of returning immediately to the Palais de Justice. Night had fallen a few hours previously, so the judge's security officers pulled faces and felt it necessary to remind him that the town was cordoned off by the CRS.

The judge just waved a hand and went back to his thoughts and case files – the two things were, by this point, pretty much the same.

He was torn from his concentration by the screaming sirens and the shadows of the riot police vans lined up over a distance of fifty metres. Because of this urban unrest, he was going to be asked for results that were impossible to obtain in so little time. And now that he observed the long-deserted avenue, the shuttered storefronts, the night buses parked silently, and the high tensions of the CRS as it prepared for battle, he began to feel one of those twinges that might well foreshadow an imminent heart attack for a man of his age.

Amid a crowd of riot police, he spotted a sergeant who came over to him. Wagner introduced himself. The riot officer stiffened in a sign of respect.

'Your Honour, how can we be of service?'

'I just wanted to know what's happening, to see with my own eyes ...'

After a few words exchanged with the sergeant, Wagner was convinced of the gravity of the situation and the probability that the much-feared unrest could not be prevented. He looked at the powerful neck of this officer, his gloved hands, his torso swelled to monstrous proportions by the bulletproof vest. His eyes gleamed with enthusiasm in the middle of his tense face, like those of a boy about to meet his enemy for a fight after school. But, while the sergeant explained to him the reasons for such a large-scale operation and the techniques of urban guerrilla warfare 'used to remarkable effect by these savages', Wagner thought only of his own veins, which he could almost feel shrinking as the man spoke.

'Are you all right, your Honour?'

The judge nodded but could no longer keep his hands behind his back and his forehead bent forward to pretend he was paying attention.

Some gunshots sounded at the end of the avenue. He could make out, beyond the night-blue shadows and the ballet of helmets and Flash-Balls, the flame of a Molotov cocktail about to be thrown in their direction.

'Monsieur,' the sergeant advised him, 'it would be better if you didn't stay here.'

His bodyguards also insisted that they return without delay. Wagner breathlessly acquiesced and dived into the car. He again called Commander Mansourd and asked him for information on the behaviour of Nazir Nerrouche's brother, the actor Fouad.

'He was arrested without a problem, your Honour.'

Mansourd felt there was nothing else to add. The judge did not beat about the bush.

'Commander, we can't take any chances with him. He is – or was – the boyfriend of Chaouch's daughter. What do you think?'

'I'll know more once I've questioned him.'

Wagner kept silent for a moment.

'It's pretty obvious what was going on, isn't it? He goes out with the daughter of the candidate that his brother is plotting to have assassinated . . .'

'What do you recommend, your Honour?'

'He's isolated from the rest of the family, right? Listen: I think the best thing would be not to extend their custody.'

'Your Honour?'

The commander could not understand what he was getting at.

'Listen, if we keep them like that, I know that'll please everyone, Prosecutor Lamiel most of all. But I see dozens of these criminal conspiracies every year. Question them, spend all night if you need to, but I think it would be better to let them leave and place them under surveillance. Especially Fouad Nerrouche.'

Mansourd did not know how to react. To him, the idea seemed utterly crazy.

'He's most probably linked to the plot,' continued Wagner, who was now speaking more to himself than to the commander, 'and it's going to be no picnic making him crack. But if we release him under close surveillance . . . All right, listen,' he said impatiently, 'start the interrogations, and we'll have a better idea afterwards.'

Mansourd grumbled, 'Yes, your Honour.'

'Ah, yes, one more thing: the kid's phone. Did you recover it?'

'I have two men on the case,' replied Mansourd. 'They've done the tour of the riverboat companies and the lost property offices, but they've found nothing for the moment.'

'You think he was lying?'

'I don't think so, your Honour. And then there are still the boats at the Pont-Neuf to check, and another company whose name escapes me. It'll take a few hours, believe me . . .'

'Okay, okay,' Wagner concluded, 'keep me posted.'

8.

'You see . . .'

Fares jumped.

'. . . the most difficult one to do is the S.'

Fares glanced up at the rear-view mirror to see Nazir, Nazir, who had said almost nothing since they had joined the motorway. His head, helmeted with black curly hair, was looking down at an object stuck between his knees, which he manipulated in the shadows and with such intensity that it was best not to disturb him. Anyway, they already had in view the Franco-Swiss border at Basel. Nazir put away the mysterious object and turned around: the day was now no more than a smear of blood-red and golden glimmers in the bottom corner of the Maybach's rear window.

'Well, now it's like in the movies. Hey, you listening to me?' He snapped his fingers. 'Remember, you're the chauffeur of an Algerian diplomat, a chauffeur who's got bigger things on his mind, okay? Look at me, and act like the guy who's got bigger things on his mind.'

Fares turned his shaven head but saw only the profile of Nazir, who was staring open-mouthed at the horizon daubed with headlights and confusion.

'That's not normal,' he babbled.

Instead of the usual two or three customs officers, Nazir saw a dozen border police as well as soldiers armed with assault rifles. The vehicle two cars in front of theirs was asked to park at the roadside so it could be thoroughly searched. But what worried Nazir was that the occupants were a blonde-haired family who could not have appeared more ordinary and less suspect.

'Why are they stopping all the cars?' Fares thought it right to ask to prove that his mind was alert. 'Something must have happened,' he added, remembering the vans of riot police around Paris.

Nazir swallowed and rummaged in the suitcase to find his tie. He ordered Fares to put on his own, then returned to the position he had taken a few moments before: tense, panting, sitting up straight, completely still between the headrests of the two front seats, which his immense bony claws gripped as if the leather was living flesh.

What's more, his mouth had a tic that Fares found enormously irritating: his tongue slowly came out of the space left by his half-open mouth and licked the flesh of his lower lip in one suave and menacing movement. Fares had the impression that he was going to jump at his throat and tear out his jugular. He did not dare turn around to check where Nazir's fangs were pointing, no more than he dared look at the rear-view mirror – out of fear, of course, of catching that impossibly dark face that passed too quickly from one mood to another, from mad brutality to the sort of ingratiating warmth that was perhaps even more terrifying.

The two cars in front had also been asked to park on the side of the road, and it was at last the turn of their Maybach to be subjected to the watchful attention of the customs officers. The youngest whispered something into the ear of his neighbour, who didn't seem to be listening, concentrated as he was on his walkie-talkie. Nazir held his breath. It was the youngest officer who finally approached Fares's window.

'Papers for the vehicle, please.'

Fares took the false papers from the glove compartment and must have given a suspicious or, more probably, aggressive look to the customs officer, who opened the document and then advanced to the back seat window. The windows were eighty per cent tinted, which was technically not permitted. Nazir saw the customs officer's ruddy alpine face peering between his hands as he tried to see who was in this diplomatic car.

Gathering his courage, he wrapped a black scarf around his neck and got out of the car with his BlackBerry pressed to his ear. Side by side, Nazir and the customs officer formed a comical contrast: the tall, vulture-like figure of Nazir, and the stocky shape of the red-haired customs officer. In the eyes of a passing Martian, they would no doubt have appeared to belong to two distinct species.

'Can I ask you what's going on, officer?'

There was no photo of him with the stubble he wore at that moment in the evening's darkness; but all the same, he looked – or, at least, he imagined he did – like the pictures they had no doubt used on his Wanted poster. He stared into the man's eyes, on the lookout for a glimmer of suspicion.

But there was nothing in the depths of the customs officer's eyes, which could very well have been a bull's.

'Monsieur, this is a routine check. Can you open the boot?'

Nazir did not want to open the boot. There was only his suitcase in there, but he feared a crowd of customs officers would gather around their car if he let this cretin proceed with his 'checks'.

'Officer, I'm going to explain to you my problem,' declared Nazir, adopting an accent that was not very far from that of his Uncle Idir. 'My problem is that I must be in Zurich in half an hour.'

'Monsieur,' insisted the officer who was not intimidated, 'I'm sorry to ask you this, but, given the circumstances, we have orders to search all cars. *All* cars.'

In the middle of this nerve-wracking exchange, Nazir could not stifle an inward smile of satisfaction. He had manufactured these 'circumstances' with his own hands.

'Listen to me very closely. Do you see this hand? In half an hour, this hand must shake that of the Algerian Ambassador to Switzerland, and I'm telling you, I do not think that Monsieur the Ambassador of Algeria to Switzerland would appreciate a member of his diplomatic corps being held at the border.'

The moustached colleague of the young customs officer had ended his conversation on the walkie-talkie. He looked up at the sky and put a hand on the shoulder of his partner while looking furtively at Nazir.

'Excuse me, Monsieur, but you can go. Our apologies.'

Nazir stared at the clean-shaven neck of the young officer and wanted to add something. He took his time returning to the back seat, moving slowly enough to enjoy the diatribe the moustached man was giving to his colleague, constantly repeating the word 'diplomatic' until he gave him a sharp tap on the forehead.

'Come on, come on,' Nazir finally said to his red-faced chauffeur, 'let's get moving.'

And it was with these words, and without the slightest look through the rear window, that Nazir said farewell to the land of his birth.

4

THE ZURICH MOVE

1.

Nazir noticed that Fares kept yawning more and more as they approached the lights of Zurich. The Swiss highway was bumpier than Nazir had expected. He suddenly imagined an exhausted Fares losing control of their vehicle, going so far as to anticipate the vibration of the swerve, and the strange sexuality of the glide through the air that you knew would end in death.

Unable to allow himself any contact with France, Nazir decided to put the three BlackBerrys in his bag. Looking up, he saw Fares in quarter profile and noticed that he no longer bothered to lift his palm to his mouth when he yawned, to convince himself that he was fighting fatigue.

'You know what an accident is, Fares?'

Fares was surprised by Nazir's comment, the first that was neither an order nor a disguised insult.

'An accident is when the world goes faster than your ability to perceive it. When the world goes faster than us. You understand what that means?'

'Yes, yes, Nazir, I'm paying attention, so don't wor—'

'No, that's not that I'm talking about. We're going to take a break, anyway. As soon as you see a service station, pull over. But I want you to understand what an accident is, not just a car accident.'

He had a voice like his hands: knotty and unpredictable.

'The world has started moving faster and faster, Fares. You understand what I'm saying?'

Fares saw the universally comforting sign for food appear up ahead. It was like a lifeline. If he managed to reach the turn-off quickly enough, he would not have to reply.

'What can you do, then, to stop the world going faster than us?'

'Um, me, I dunno . . . Hey, look, there's a service station . . .'

'I'm going to tell you, Fares. I'm going to tell you in the hope that it's going to make a dent in your little head: the only way to stop the world going faster than us is, of course, for us to go faster than it.'

And while the car approached the floating building – a restaurant adorned with an immense plastic steak – Nazir explained to his chauffeur, who had not asked a question, what had just happened in France, what had just happened in the country where they had been born and where they would probably not return for a good while.

But he did not say that it was he, Nazir Nerrouche, who had fashioned the course of events.

'Honestly, that's killed my appetite,' commented Fares, who was having trouble finishing his double portion of fries. 'I liked him a lot, Chaouch. But who shot him? Fucking hell, I just can't believe it.'

Fares dropped his cutlery, which clinked on the plate as he raised his voice.

'It's disgusting! Just when—'

'Just when what?' sneered Nazir.

'Well, just when we were going to have an Arab president.'

'An Arab president, what rubbish . . . I'm going to pay and we'll see each other back at the car. We're going to have an hour's nap and then we're going to start off again. We're already an hour late if my calculation's right.'

Fares did not dare reply. His brain expanded and contracted like a sponge as he tried to process all of this information. The poor guy was lost.

'You sleeping?' he asked Nazir, whose elbow he saw move on the front seat.

'Hey, stop asking questions and get some sleep.'

And, suddenly feeling that he had to pace himself, Nazir added, 'I'm lucky. I never sleep more than three hours a night.'

Lulled by this mystery, Fares fell into the arms of Morpheus.

When he woke up, the car had, of course, not moved. He stretched his arms and shoulders, but knocked against the roof whose silky covering almost made him want to rub against it. Nazir did not seem to pay any attention to him, so he opened the door and did a few exercises around the car.

He had completely forgotten what had horrified him in the restaurant, but everything came flooding back when he sat down behind the steering wheel and saw Nazir. He was wearing white gloves and, with his tongue sticking out, was busy engraving an inscription on the butt of a pistol with an

Opinel knife, its pommel and rivets gleaming in the glow of the car's overhead light.

'Is that real?' Fares asked stupidly.

In reply, Nazir asked him to look at the object in the rear-view mirror: a majestic series of letters, F, A, R and S, impeccably engraved on the light-coloured wood grip. Fares thought it was his first name, but, however much he looked at it, the E was missing.

'Ah!' he exclaimed. 'So that's what you were saying: the hardest thing to do is the S! But what does "Fars" mean? And why the gun?'

'It's for you,' replied Nazir, taking off his white gloves. 'Read it in the opposite direction. Look.'

Without the inversion of the reflection it was indeed the letters S, R, A, F. Fares was still none the wiser.

'It's a welcome gift. I'll explain to you on the road. I want you to remember an address, in fact. Get a piece of paper and write it down.'

Fares rummaged in the glove box and found a sort of notebook. But, as he suddenly remembered, he didn't need it.

'I never forget anything, Nazir, you know . . . like numbers and stuff.'

'Yes but let's not take any risks. Write it down. For God's sake, you're not illiterate, as far as I know.'

'Uh, no,' Fares chose to reply.

'Hermannsweg,' dictated Nazir, 'number 7. It's in Hamburg, in Germany. If ever things go wrong, that's the meeting point, okay?'

Fares looked at this bizarre address, his mouth agape.

'Come on! There's a surprise for us in Zurich, I don't want to keep it waiting . . .'

Fares put the 9mm pistol in the glove box and started the engine. In less than half an hour, the car arrived in the centre of Zurich. Nazir knew the place like the back of his hand, and asked Fares to follow a blue tram, then enter a maze of impeccably paved streets that led them to the foot of a four-storey building with a smooth pale blue facade. Fares had scarcely switched off the engine before a BMW parked on the opposite pavement flashed its lights at him. The heat had made the evening dirty and misty, and the headlights were like spots of oil on the horizon.

Nazir ordered Fares to flash the lights in response. A few moments later, a man got out of the BMW, crushed the butt of a cigarette between his fingers and crossed the street, buttoning up his shirt to hide his gold chain.

'But . . . it's Mouloud!' yapped Fares, all excited. 'What the hell's he doing here?'

Without looking at the driver, Mouloud Benbaraka opened the door and sat down in the front passenger seat. He stared at Nazir in the rear-view mirror.

'Fuck, I've never seen so many cops! There were roadblocks at every toll!'

'Did they give you a hard time at the border?' asked Nazir, moving to the centre of the back seat. 'You had fake papers, right? No one followed you?'

'No, no one. *Wallah*, this fake passport, I've never seen anything like it. How did you get it? I didn't even know you could fake a biometric passport. It's a gem, I'm telling you, a gem!'

Nazir did not reply. He was looking right and left, with long stares that seemed to exhaust every visible inch of the horizon.

'No one followed you?'

'No! What do you take me for?' said Benbaraka angrily. 'I was in the slammer while you were still playing with your teddy bear. I know exactly how those drug squad *hmal* tail people. So you just fucking trust me!'

2.

The name Mouloud Benbaraka was eventually uttered in Krim's cell. Captain Tellier wrote it down on the transcript as well as on a Post-it that he handed to his lieutenant so he could immediately do some checks. Tellier noticed that Krim could no longer sit up straight. He was staring at the illuminated indicator light on the webcam that was recording the interviews but, as soon as the captain began typing on the computer keyboard, the monotone clicking of the keys made him close his eyes and nod off.

The captain banged his fist on the table. Krim sat up.

'You realize your story's completely worthless? On one side you have Nazir, whom you say is manipulating you, and on the other you've got this Mouloud Benbaraka who's taking your mother hostage . . . In short, it's everyone's fault, except yours! And this guy who takes you into his car and shows you photos of your mother, why didn't he do the shooting? Why would Nazir have asked an eighteen-year-old kid to shoot Chaouch instead of paying a professional? It's complete bullshit! Bull-shit! Isn't it? *Isn't it?*'

'Dunno. I want to sleep. I have the right to—'

'You don't have any rights! You shoot politicians, representatives of the state, so why would the state continue to respect your rights? What was he like, this supposed accomplice who drove you to Grogny?'

'Come on, I want to sleep.'

'What was he like?'

'He had red hair,' said Krim.

'Ah well, then. Red hair. We're making progress . . .'

And the clicking of the keys started again. Krim spoke to remain awake.

'With a little red beard, a . . . I can't remember what it's called.'

'A goatee?'

Krim nodded, but it was too hard for him. Sitting on the stool, his head started to spin on his slumping shoulders.

'I hope for your sake that you haven't given us the runaround with this mobile phone. Have you?'

'What?'

'We haven't found your phone. You say you threw it off the bridge, that it fell onto a riverboat. So why haven't we found it?'

Krim was falling asleep again.

'You want me to say I believe you.'

Krim opened his eyes slightly.

'Yes, I believe you. Your cousin who gives you weapons, cash, your train ticket, it's like a game, then your cousin sends you texts, you have the impression someone's listening to you, is interested in you. No, I understand. After you arrive in Paris, your mother and Benbaraka . . . no, no, I understand everything, I swear. There's just one thing I don't understand, at all. And that is why you fired the gun.'

'But . . . Benbaraka was with my mother, I saw the photos. What could I do?'

'Alert the police! Do something! You must have understood what that fucking meant, to shoot a presidential candidate!'

'I . . . I had smoked some dope,' murmured Krim. 'I was exhausted . . . I . . . it was like in a video game, you know?'

The captain's mouth hung open. He nodded, muttered an insult and decided to interrupt Krim's torture: he led him back to the cell and called his boss to recount the version given to him by the 'kid', thinking how well that nickname suited him at this moment.

Mansourd was in the Saint-Etienne police station bathroom. With his flies still open, he stared at the stainless-steel urinal. Distractedly, he caressed the photo inlaid in the medallion he wore on a chain around his neck.

Benbaraka's name made him wince.

'Commander?'

'That means something to me – Benbaraka. I'll call you back. Wait, have you seen the surveillance videos from the town hall square?'

'Haven't received them yet, Commander.'

'Well, what are you waiting for? Do I have to fetch them for you?'

Mansourd hung up. Emerging from the bathroom, he noticed that the detectives there regarded him as a celebrity. It was not completely unjustified. There were hundreds of counterterrorism operations in France every year, but very few, if any, concerned real nutcases bent on blowing everything up. There was no question that Mansourd had chosen counterterrorism in order to fight them, and not to assist Judge Rotrou – 'the Ogre' – when he carried out his media-friendly raids on networks of revolutionaries in the Larzac, who were more lovers of charcuterie and illegal camping than fanatics planning attacks on national security.

Having trained with the Anti-Gang Unit, Mansourd had spent his entire career in interior security before taking command of the ATSD. He led its dozen investigative groups and theoretically reported to his commissioner, but, in reality, the latter signed papers and liaised with the Ministry of the Interior. Given the sensitive nature of the cases he had to 'expose', Mansourd dealt directly with the ministry's staff. His reputation justified this statutory anomaly: he had tracked down and put behind bars two public enemies number one, and had contributed to thwarting more terrorist attacks than anyone else. His stubbornness knew no bounds, and if his maverick style had considerably slowed down his career (he had not wanted to sit the commissioners' exam and had never courted any politician), it had earned him the total respect of his men, and apparently also that of these policemen he had never seen before.

Beneath their gaze, he crossed the crowded room, which was scattered with little desks where the Elders of the Nerrouche family snivelled, repeating that they had never had anything to do with Krim or Nazir. The two children had begun to play with the switchboard operator, and their squabbles and high-pitched voices created a surreal atmosphere in the police station. Mansourd had asked that only those closest to Nazir and Krim be questioned in the cells upstairs. Some men from the ATSD therefore took charge of Nazir's brother Fouad, his mother Dounia and Krim's mother Rabia. Slim, bizarrely, had been left with the 'innocents' of the family and questioned in the main room, perhaps because the policemen had taken him to be a minor.

Mansourd entered Commissioner Faure's office without knocking on the door.

'Mouloud Benbaraka. Does that sound familiar?'

'Ah yes, he's our local godfather. We've been trying to nab him for years.'

Excited, Mansourd shut the door.

'Who's looking after the investigation here? The drug squad?'

'Yes, I've got a team working all hours on him. At first, the drug squad in Lyon was after him, but—'

'Call the captain in charge of his case.'

The commissioner did not like being given orders in this way. Nevertheless, he obeyed and called the captain in question. Mansourd was impatiently tugging at his beard.

'Pass him to me!'

He took the phone and asked for a summary of the investigation in less than a minute. At the other end of the line, the captain did not seem very cooperative.

'Listen, counterterrorism or not, I'm not going to let you screw up several months of investigations just so—'

'Captain,' Mansourd interjected, 'I am acting on behalf of Judge Wagner, of the counterterrorism unit at the prosecutor's office in Paris. I'm not asking for your opinion. I don't give a damn about your investigation. I'm just asking you to answer this simple question: did you tail him this weekend, yes or no?'

'No. We lost him this morning. He was at a wedding yesterday evening and . . .'

'Okay, I'm going to ask you something. You're not obligated to answer, of course, but let me remind you that we're looking for the man who ordered the assassination of a presidential candidate. So: did you put a GPS transmitter under his car? Something to geolocate him?'

If it was not authorized by a judge, this practice was illegal; but it was widespread in long-term investigations. The captain from the drug squad hesitated for a long time, obviously in great discomfort.

'Anyway,' he finally mumbled, 'your judge will never authorize—'

'Bingo!' cried Mansourd. 'Leave the judge to me.'

And while the commissioner took charge of calling the drug squad and the technicians who had done the GPS tagging, Commander Mansourd ran to the cells to ask Fouad, Dounia and Rabia everything they knew about Mouloud Benbaraka.

3.

His shirt half-open on his hairy torso, the crime overlord of Saint-Etienne turned a cigarette between his fingers while waiting for his lighter to produce a flame.

'Nice fucking car.'

'All right,' declared Nazir once he had written his text, 'it's time for us to go to the bank.'

Mouloud Benbaraka turned around. He hoped Nazir did not literally intend to go to the bank.

'How come?' he asked, his eyes wide open.

'Well, I'm going to get your cash. And Fares's. You think I walk around with two hundred thousand euros in my suitcase?'

'No, no, no,' retorted Benbaraka, raising his voice. 'That wasn't part of the deal. What is all this bullshit? . . . And since when are banks open at midnight?'

'No,' replied Nazir. 'I'm not going into the bank. Just next to it. I have to meet someone there.'

'Who? What's all this about? I'm coming with you.'

'Mouloud, don't mess with me. I've got to be in Hamburg tomorrow morning at seven. I'll get your money, I'll come back here, and after that we go our separate ways. Each to his own and God be with us all.'

'So you think I'm going to let you go just like that?'

'I'll leave you my passport, if that reassures you! We can swap . . .'

He plunged a hand into the inside pocket of his black jacket and threw the passport onto Benbaraka's lap. The latter moved his head from right to left.

'I'll take the passport, but we'll follow you with . . . Fares.'

'And you give me yours,' Nazir insisted. 'Your passport. I don't want you to run off with mine either.'

Benbaraka studied Nazir's reflection in the rear-view mirror: Nazir had the same concentrated and ironic expression, an eyebrow raised, his tongue passing slowly over the regular curve of his lower lip. He handed him his false passport.

'In that case, I'll take my car,' he said. 'There you go. I'll follow you with my car.'

'And while you're at it, just open the windows, put on some Rai music and stick the Algerian flag on the hood. Come on, use your head a bit: if I'd wanted to screw you, I'd have given you a fake meeting place . . .'

But Benbaraka did not trust him: there was always a trap with Nazir. He took back his passport and went out into the sultry night.

The Maybach set off, closely followed by the BMW driven by Mouloud Benbaraka as he bit his nails. Four blocks down, the Maybach stopped at the foot of a glass building. An endless word in German ended with '–BANK' above an imposing revolving door. Next to the bank, half hidden by a row of bushes pruned into the shape of flames, a sign flashed. Mouloud got out of his car and sat in the Maybach's passenger seat.

'But what's that thing flashing? I don't understand what's

going on. You're trying to fuck with me, aren't you? I'm warning you, I—'

'But you've got my passport! What am I going to do? Take the money from the boot and set off on foot? And what about my suitcase? I've got everything here! Come on, it'll just take twenty minutes.'

Mouloud Benbaraka had a bad feeling about this but he had no choice. Besides, it reassured him to have Nazir's passport: he therefore watched him walk down the path that crossed the lawn to the revolving door. He was wearing his usual black pinstriped suit, brown moccasins and white shirt, over which hung a slim Paul Smith tie. His BlackBerry pressed against his ear, he turned left after the door to the bank and disappeared behind the trees. At the last moment, he sent a strangely cheerful look in the direction of the Maybach's tinted windows.

Benbaraka pressed the cigarette lighter.

'By the way,' Fares asked him, 'I just wanted to know, about my brother—'

Benbaraka interrupted Fares with an incandescent look that mixed anger and hate. This emotion grew so strong that he couldn't stop himself screaming.

'Did I tell you to speak to me? Did I? How can you speak to me like that? Who do you think you are, you fucking bum, to speak to me about your fucking brother who's disappeared? You think we're in an episode of *Missing Persons*? Huh? Do I look like Jacques Pradel? *Do I?*'

4.

Judge Wagner's car came to a halt outside his Paris home, next to the Parc des Buttes-Chaumont. In the faint light of the overhead bulb, he was consulting the transcripts of the phone taps on Nazir Nerrouche. His bodyguard looked at the light on upstairs and saw Madame's silhouette pass by the window.

'Your Honour?'

Wagner took off his glasses and in turn looked up at the lit window. It was the first night he had come home after midnight – the first of many to come. He turned off the light and passed a hand over his face, rubbing the space between his eyes and the back of his aching neck. His encrypted phone started to ring.

'Your Honour, it's Mansourd. It's fine: we got a tip-off about the place where we might find one of Nazir's main accomplices, Mouloud Benbaraka, the man we were talking about. He's in Zurich, but I think we'll have to act fast. Tonight, if possible.'

'Commander, it's impossible to get an international commission request before the morning. Could take even longer if it's in Switzerland.'

'Your Honour, it's urgent. Very urgent. It's really the golden opportunity to—'

'Where does this tip-off come from?'

Mansourd used all his aplomb to lie.

'The questioning of Nazir's mother.'

'You've got it written down? The judicial police noted it all down, right?'

Mansourd replied in the affirmative while gathering the group of men around him in the superintendent's office.

'Well, I'm going to see what I can do. We'll wake up the Minister of Justice. Maybe it's best to sign for a joint investigation team. Listen, I just hope this tip-off is reliable.'

Wagner suddenly wondered if the commander was telling him the whole truth.

'Wait, Commander. Benbaraka was under investigation by the drug squad, right? I hope I'm not going to discover that you got the tip-off from illegal geolocating...'

'Your Honour,' replied Mansourd, 'the priority is to catch Nazir. You yourself reminded me just a moment ago...'

Wagner sighed. He had to think of procedure, unlike Mansourd, and if, at the trial of Nazir (and his accomplices), an illegal GPS device appeared in the prosecution file, it would be manna from heaven for the defence lawyers.

'The ends justify the means,' Mansourd added to put pressure on the judge.

'No, Commander. That is not true. The ends never justify the means.'

'Your Honour? It would be best not to lose time...'

'Do what you have to do, Commander. But no intervention.'

He switched his light on again and asked the driver to take him back to the Palais de Justice while he called Prosecutor Lamiel.

5.

Mansourd was not completely lying when he mentioned Dounia as a source of information. When he had stormed into the room where she was being questioned, he had asked the lieutenant, who was half-heartedly typing up the transcript, to go smoke a cigarette. Dounia did not stop coughing. The innocent look on her face – and the incomprehensible respect she inspired in him – made him choose the gentle approach: look, I'm not writing anything down, I just want to know if Nazir has been to Zurich in the past; look, I've turned off the computer. And it is true that he hadn't taken any notes, and Dounia had not noticed that he insisted on this point. So she had told him the truth, because she had nothing to feel guilty about.

But, half an hour later, Commander Mansourd returned to the room where she had dozed off a little and turned the computer back on.

'Okay, Madame Nerrouche, you're going to have to repeat to me what you said a moment ago, so everything is on the record.'

And so Dounia, who was completely exhausted, and more worried about the state of her lungs than the strange technique of this policeman, repeated, 'Well, I know he went to Zurich twice last year.'

'By "he", you mean your son Nazir, right?'

'My son Nazir, yes,' she said, feeling the tears well up.

'Take your time,' Mansourd said calmly, his knees trembling frantically under the table.

'So, the second time, I think it was in March last year, he asked me to transfer money to an account. And . . . you know, he was the one who was always putting money in my account. I have a job, but he insisted. He gave me some pretty big sums of money. I didn't always check, but sometimes it was two thousand euros, three thousand euros. And so, when he asked me to send him five thousand euros, which he would pay back, I had no reason to say no, you understand? So that's what happened: I transferred the money to Zurich. I'm sorry, but that's all I can tell you. I don't know why he was over there. I don't know why he wanted me to send money to that account. That's all I know.'

Mansourd had typed Dounia's testimony while she spoke. It took him ten seconds to read it all over again. When he had finished, he looked for a moment at Dounia, her beautiful open face framed by her peaceful grey-white hair, her gentle and tragic eyes.

'You should see a doctor,' he said nervously and without daring to look at her. 'Your coughing . . . it's not normal.'

Dounia raised her eyebrows, to acknowledge the advice he had just given her. Mansourd left the room with the transcript. He faxed it to Wagner's office and walked around the police station, waiting for the phone call and the judge's decision. Without an international commission, there was nothing he could do. The judge was going to wake up the Justice Minister's staff who, given the urgency of the situation, were going to wake that of the Swiss Justice Minister. As soon as he had confirmation that the procedure had begun, he could make contact with the Swiss police so they could arrest Benbaraka as soon as possible. Dounia's questioning and a personal intuition told him that there was a strong chance that Nazir was also in Zurich. But when his phone finally rang, the judge's news was not good.

'Mansourd, I've received the transcript. Listen, I've spoken about it with Prosecutor Lamiel, but the evidence is too weak.'

'What the—'

'Mansourd, listen to me. Lamiel and I have thought of an alternative solution: you put together a small team of three or four cars and do a surveillance mission. All unofficial, of course. You follow Benbaraka's car, but bear in mind that you are on foreign territory and cannot intervene.'

'Your Honour, with all due respect, the time it takes to set up . . .' He sighed. 'Listen, very well then. Okay. I'll send a team from Levallois. They'll get there before dawn. Thanks, your Honour. I'll keep you posted.'

The Saint-Etienne commissioner walked over to Mansourd,

looking grim. The commander listened to his grievances.

'Listen, all the neighbourhoods are in flames. I've got reinforcements arriving. I'm going to require you to leave my offices now.'

'Anyway, we've finished with the family. Just leave me three cells and that's all. All right?' he asked bad-temperedly. 'Is that okay with you?'

A riot van entered the police station car park, sirens screaming. Mansourd and the superintendent peered through the blinds: about twenty kids were under arrest. Some YVs. Code for Young and Violent. And they were, incidentally, all NAs: North Africans.

Mansourd explained to the family that they were free to go. Idir's face was soaked in sweat. He nodded to Bouzid and Mathieu, Rachida's husband, who had turned up spontaneously after receiving phone calls from Granny and his wife.

'What about Rabia?' asked Bouzid. 'And Dounia? Are you going to keep them all night?'

'We'll keep you informed, Monsieur. So, go back home, and if you remember anything, our door is open.'

It was literally open, in fact. A group of handcuffed petty thugs went through it before starting to scream and chant: 'Murderers! Murderers!'

The riot police smacked them on the head to calm them down. They were taken into the drunk tank before the terrified eyes of little Rayanne. As they passed Slim, one of them grimaced with disgust and stared into the young groom's eyes before disappearing down a corridor.

Rayanne was running around like crazy looking for his father. On seeing him pass, a riot policeman took him in his arms and gave him a wide smile.

'Well, young man, where are you going like that?'

Rayanne looked at the helmeted face of the policeman and his enormous fingers: the black gloves made them look like King Kong's. He sobbed gently, forcing the officer, who was out of breath from the athletic arrests he had just had to make, to put him down on the floor. As soon as his feet had touched the ground, Rayanne frantically ran off again in search of his father.

'That's how it starts,' murmured the riot policeman to his colleague. 'All cute and shy, and ten years later they're shooting at you. I swear . . .'

6.

The storefront Nazir stopped outside consisted of a window with white blinds and an excessively bright fluorescent sign flashing the words 'HAIR SALON'. The door did not have blinds, but pretty check curtains and a doorbell. When Nazir pressed it, he noticed that he had attracted the attention of three of the four occupants of the salon and realized that the other one must be his man, Waldstein.

Standing in front of the till, where he seemed to be looking at receipts, Waldstein was wearing the same immaculate outfit as his young colleague, who was busy daubing his shaving brush on the beard of a customer who stared at Nazir in the slightly sepia-tinted mirror. Slouched on a seat at the hair washing station, a teenage girl was flicking through magazines backwards, starting from the last page, not reading a thing, her mouth hanging open due to her braces. The look she shot the new arrival was somewhere between intense curiosity and bovine indifference.

'*Guten Abend,*' Nazir said to all present, while staring at the young girl.

A sudden blush appeared under the beautiful ovals of her eyes. The customer (her father?) greeted Nazir with a voice hoarse from the long silence that must have preceded this late and obviously unexpected visit.

The white uniforms of the two barbers made them look like laboratory assistants conscripted into an illegal experiment. It was the one attending to the customer who moved his head inquisitively.

Nazir spoke the first half of the code phrase, in a single breath: '*Ich mochte mir das Haar schneidenlassen . . .*'

He observed the reaction of the old man behind the till: he remained completely still, concentrating on his ledger. Nazir added, '. . . *Den Bart uberhaupt nicht.* But don't touch the beard.'

The man he was here to meet was probably the old one, but he was still not reacting. The young man gestured for him to sit down on a raised chair, next to that of the customer he had just started to shave. But Nazir did not want to take off his jacket. He absolutely did not want to take off his jacket. Taken by surprise, the young man tried to catch the attention of his boss. The latter closed his eyes and disappeared into the back of the salon, where he turned on a tap, waited for the hot water, then energetically washed his hands.

When he came back, Nazir had been covered from the neck down with a white sheet that swallowed up the armrests of the chair and went down as far as its footrest. Nazir saw him open a drawer in the marble counter and choose at random a pair of scissors and an old-fashioned razor whose metal blade gleamed brightly. Nazir had not foreseen that they would have company and have to act out this farce. Instead of a haircut, Nazir just asked for him to tidy up his neck and around the ears.

Herr Waldstein was not really called Herr Waldstein, and seemed to hide in every fold of his beardless, square-jawed face the memory of all the false names that his life as a secret agent had required him to use. A robust sixty year old, he had a wart at the corner of his left eye, which pulled down his leonine eyelid and directed all the movements of his face towards the other side. He had a strange, soft nose, almost as thick at the level of the nostrils as at the bridge but without the strength of a boxer's. It was impossible to mentally reconstruct his features once you looked away.

He put the razor down in front of Nazir, as if to intimidate him. With the scissors, he began to thin out his client's black hair. Nazir showed no sign of anxiety, but time was passing. He had said twenty minutes to Benbaraka: ten minutes had soon passed as he waited to be alone with Waldstein to settle their accounts. Nazir told himself to be patient, avoided looking at the girl in the mirror, and tried hard to remain alert in case Waldstein seized the razor to cut his throat in the middle of the salon.

The idea began to terrify him: would he have the time to free his arms to defend himself? The client beside him was presented with a hand-mirror to judge the quality of his shave. He studied his chin – from every angle. Waldstein had stopped thinning his hair. He took the razor and placed it a few millimetres from Nazir's neck. Nazir shivered.

'*Was machen Sie den? Nur den Haarschnitt, hab'ich gesagt!*'

Waldstein offered him a triumphant smile in the mirror. The other client got up to fetch his jacket and pay, followed by the girl. Once he had disappeared, Waldstein told his young colleague to leave. He looked like he was in a hurry anyway. As soon as the door closed, Nazir bounded out of the chair and said in French, 'What's all this about? We were fucking supposed to be alone. What's all this with clients at midnight?'

'We don't control everything in life, young man,' Waldstein retorted calmly, without an accent. 'We do late-night openings here, never usually this late, but . . . let's say it was a client we could not refuse.'

He took off his overalls before Nazir's furious eyes and led him into the back of the store. An enormous safe was hidden behind a wardrobe. He unlocked the door and took out the first metal box. He placed it on the table in the middle of the room and opened it before going to fetch the second one. In the first box, there was an incredible number of five-hundred-euro notes.

'Don't fuck with me. Hurry up,' declared Nazir while Waldstein carried over the second box.

Waldstein exhaled as he placed it on the table.

The other box contained half as many bills as the first one. There was also a metal suitcase to put them in, as well as a handgun and a passport that Nazir opened greedily.

'Nathaniel Assouline,' he read in a low voice. 'Born 25 September 1983, in Paris. Well, I'll need another week to grow a beard as thick as that . . .'

Waldstein helped Nazir to pack his 'personal effects' into the metal case. Nazir took out his phone.

'Only one more pawn to move, and I'll have checkmate.'

Waldstein smiled mechanically.

'I hope that, when they write my story, they'll have a chapter called "The Zurich Move". You play chess?'

Waldstein shook his head and finally spoke.

'You do not realize all the risks I take . . .'

'You're paid,' Nazir retorted. 'Lavishly.'

'If you think I do all this for the money . . . What's with the phone?'

Nazir did not reply. He dialled the number of the nearest police station.

In a rather convincing German accent (he rolled his Rs like a Bavarian), he informed the police that an armed robbery was about to be committed in front of the bank next door.

Waldstein took him through the back door to a private car park where two cars were waiting. Theirs was an enormous black BMW. Waldstein got into the driver's seat and Nazir sat beside him. The dashboard was of fine wood and the seats covered with luxurious beige leather. The car drove for a minute along a long, open-skied alley that came out on the other side of the block, two hundred metres from the bank's entrance.

7.

When the judge finally returned from the Palais de Justice, Mansourd received the order to personally carry out the interrogation of those he called 'the close family'. Luna had left with Granny without a tear: fatigue had overcome her unhappiness. Rabia's first words when she saw the commander enter the room were about her daughter: when would she be able to see her?

'Soon, soon. Please calm down.'

And her son?

The commander's only reply was a movement of the eyebrows.

He sat down in an office chair on wheels and began to read the transcript printed by the lieutenant who had dealt with the first interrogation.

'Monsieur, I'm sleepy. I've told your colleague all I know . . . That horrible man who attacked me, he held me prisoner, he drugged me and . . . I've had enough. Now I just want to see my son. At least tell me he's okay!'

The commander dropped the papers on the table.

'Madame, you declare that you knew nothing about the relationship between Abdelkrim and Nazir? You didn't know that they had been calling each other every day for months? You didn't know that Nazir regularly gave him money?'

'No, I thought that . . . I didn't know!'

'But then how do you explain the video game consoles in the cellar? The new clothes? All that treasure?'

'But I never went down to the cellar!'

'Never?'

'I swear on my children's lives, I never set foot in the cellar! There's normally nothing in the cellar! I swear to you I don't know what the hell he was doing there with Fat Momo. Anyway, I'm afraid of mice!' she added in a disarming explosion of sincerity.

The commander wrote down two words on the corner of a sheet of paper.

'Who's "Fat Momo"?'

Rabia bit her lip.

'He's a friend of Krim's. But he has nothing to do with—'

'His full name, please.'

'But you're not going to—'

The commander just sighed wearily.

'Mohammed, Mohammed Belaidi. But I swear to you, there's no one nicer than Fat Momo—'

'I'm also sure there's no one nicer than Abdelkrim. Address?'

'Oh, he lives above the Bellevue, in the rue des Forges . . . number 24.'

Mansourd changed his angle of attack.

'What do you know about the SRAF?'

'The what?'

Rabia passed a hand through her curly hair and pulled it down over her eyes, to stop herself from seeing the décor of this nightmare.

'The SRAF? You've never heard of the SRAF?'

'The *sraf*?' she repeated, pronouncing the word with a Kabyle accent.

The commander seemed interested.

'*Sraf*, in Kabyle, means nerves. *Zarma* means to be angry. To have *sraf* is to be irritated.'

He was about to ask more regarding this surprising piece of information when his phone rang. He left the cell and heard the excited voice of Judge Wagner.

'Commander, Mouloud Benbaraka has been arrested by the Swiss police, in front of a bank in Zurich. Thanks to an anonymous phone call. He was waiting in the car with an accomplice, a certain Fares. The police found a Parabellum nine millimetre in the glove compartment. The same as the kid's. And wait for this: on the grip was carved the acronym SRAF. That rang a bell with one of the Swiss policemen who, fortunately for us, had been watching the news.'

'And no trace of Nazir?'

'Ah yes, that's the really good news. Benbaraka won't give anything away, but the accomplice, this Monsieur Fares, who's apparently one of his henchmen, eventually confessed that Nazir was going to Hamburg. That he had to be there by seven in the morning. According to the police, he'll soon crack and say more about it. I'll take care of that now. You keep grilling the family. And about the phone taps: do you think the technicians have finished?'

'Yes, for the kid's mother's flat. There's still the other one, Nazir's mother's. I really think we should extend their custody until tomorrow evening at the minimum—'

'We've already talked about this, Commander. Excuse me, but I have to go.'

Mansourd hung up and hesitated before returning to Rabia. He did not share Wagner's enthusiasm about the Hamburg lead: it all seemed too easy to him.

He began to think of what Rabia had said about the SRAF. All the analysts had looked for an acronym when it would have been enough to question a member of Nazir's family to get the information. The CDII investigation had perhaps been even more botched than he had previously thought.

Some screams came from the drunk tank. The superindendent had taken off his jacket and came to inform Mansourd that two more riot vans were bringing in detainees.

'It's a while since we've seen this here,' he spluttered. 'The last time, it was what? The riots of 2005? You think the same thing's going to happen?'

Mansourd did not reply. Mopping his brow, the superintendent went on, 'All those idiots who think Noyer killed Chaouch! I can't wait to see the reaction of these savages when they discover that it's one of their own who did it . . . That'll shut up all their talk about a plot.'

In the meantime, insults aimed at Noyer rang out across the police station, and in many other police stations all over France.

Mansourd went to see those kids who were banging against the windows of the cell. The following day, they would all appear in court. Another night like this would not be needed to justify the 'exemplary' nature of the sentences.

'The *sraf*,' murmured Mansourd, as if to himself, when he saw the furious, swarthy faces of those teenagers under mass arrest.

The superintendent, who had followed the commander, asked him to repeat what he'd said.

Mansourd turned to him and replied to the question he had been asked two minutes before.

'It's not going to be like 2005. It's going to be worse. And you know why? Because this time, it's not one of their own who's been sacrificed through a police blunder, real or alleged. No, it's the guy who'd promised them it would never happen again, and they believed him. Their president has been killed, Commissioner. For the first time, they'd played the game: you know the turnout figures as well as I do. They'd registered to vote in their tens of thousands and now, their dream is shattered. No, believe me: it's going to be worse than 2005.'

One of the petty thugs, particularly agitated, kicked the door. The targets of his ire were the two policemen watching the kids as if they were animals at the zoo. Realizing that this would have no effect, the thug gathered all his saliva and shot his finest ever gob of spit at the window, provoking the roars of his colleagues and obliging the guardians of the peace to enter the cage and pacify them with truncheon blows.

8.

The air-conditioning wasn't functioning in the office where Fouad was being questioned. A deputy sergeant had dug out an old fan but hadn't managed to get it working. They had opened the first-floor window, which presented no risk as it was covered with a screen, overlooking the top of a pine tree standing motionless in the hot and windless night. The sound of a cricket disturbed the room's silence. And the room was very silent: Fouad refused to reply to the investigators' questions. He had held out for several hours: he knew his rights and wanted to speak to a lawyer before expressing himself.

Commander Mansourd pushed open the door and beckoned to his lieutenant. Fouad listened to the metronomic chirping of the cricket, thinking contemptuously of the third-rate poet who had first described this bland, repetitive noise as a song.

'Still nothing?' asked Mansourd.

'No. He wants to see a lawyer before talking. Bastard's tougher than we thought.'

Mansourd entered the room and asked the other policeman to leave. When he was alone with Fouad, he sat down behind the computer and went online.

'So, it seems that you're an actor? Some of my colleagues say they saw you in a TV series. So they weren't kidding? Let's see what our friend Wikipedia has to say ... *Man of the Match*, "Revelation of the series, Fouad Nerrouche..." and so on and so forth ... Well, we're not going to read all that, and anyway it's not our problem, television. No, our problem, I almost said our *equation*, is this.' He stopped and stretched out an index finger to start counting. 'So, the man of the match goes out with the president's daughter. The brother of the man of the match hatches a plot to assassinate the president. Are you following me so far?'

Fouad wanted to reply that they did not know each other: there was no reason for him to be spoken to in such a familiar way. He did nothing of the sort, but he couldn't help feeling intrigued by this bearded supercop in his black t-shirt. The hypothesis that he could be linked to the plot because he went out with Jasmine had never crossed his mind. It suddenly seemed to him terrifyingly plausible, if you took these people's point of view.

'Listen,' continued Mansourd, clenching his fist, 'let's not fuck around here: counterterrorism legislation means I could send you and all your family in front of a judge in a few hours' time. I just need to ask him to write a summons and, hey presto, at eight in the morning, I'll put everyone in a car to the Palais de Justice in Paris. And then, you know what's going to happen?'

Fouad now had to look down so as not to reply.

'The judge will charge you all with criminal association in relation with a terrorist enterprise. He'll ask for you to be remanded in custody and, as it involves terrorism, that can last for up to three years. Three years at the maximum-security wing in Fleury-Mérogis, among all the vermin. Your lawyers will be up in arms, so a judge will refuse custody for, let's say, the majority of the family. But those closest to Nazir and Krim – let's say you, your brother, your mother and your Aunt Rabia – you lot won't get out of this.'

Fouad, who had at first tried to blank out the sound of the cricket, was now trying to hear only that sound.

'So, how do these three years of custody work? Well, every four months, just before the committal order expires, the judge will summon you to his office to question you again. You will say you know nothing, that you've done nothing wrong, and the judge will send you before the sentencing judge to have your custody extended. But the worst thing is not even the fact that you'll all be in prison. The worst thing is not even that the mobilization of the support committee set up by your lawyer will run out of steam and that the media will want the people responsible for the death of their dear President Chaouch to rot in prison for the rest of their lives. No, the worst thing is not all that. The worst thing is little Luna.

'Ah yes, you can look at me like that, but little Luna, as soon as her mother is notified that she is being charged, will be handed over to social services and placed in foster care. I know what you're going to say to me, that your grandmother could very easily look after her, which is perhaps the case, but frankly, and without meaning to offend you, I didn't get the impression that the innocent members of your family were very hot about picking up the pieces. In fact, I rather had the impression that they had it in for you. So, there's another solution: if you refuse to talk, we'll delay the judicial hearing and extend your custody. Forty-eight hours, ninety-six hours. Until you've told us what we need to know.'

'But I know nothing!' Fouad finally blurted.

'No one ever knows absolutely nothing. Didn't you have some suspicions? Some doubts? I can't believe that all your family lived through all these months without wondering for a single moment what the hell Krim and Nazir were up to . . . And you, with the Chaouch girl, for fuck's sake, it sticks out a mile!'

'You don't know what you're talking about . . . I . . .'

'Yes?'

Fouad realized that, whatever he said, it would be too much: he was going to incriminate his entire family by putting the blame on Nazir. Because Nazir was part of that family, as sure as that stupid cricket was part of the night.

'I refuse to speak before seeing a lawyer.'

'Very well.'

The commander stretched and clenched his fists.

'Criminal association in relation with a terrorist enterprise was punishable by ten years in prison until a few years ago. The last reform of interior security laws raised the punishment to twenty years. You'll never do twenty years in prison, of course. You'll do four or five despite the aggravating circumstances; I mean participating in the murder of the first Arab president of our beautiful country. With a good lawyer, you'll do one or two. With a very good lawyer, zero. Except that, while waiting for trial in a special court, you'll already have spent three years in custody. The state will pay damages. It will be a huge scandal. Front-page news. And then the following day, there'll be those shocking remarks spoken by a re-elected Noyer, or the video of a chimpanzee in a bow tie capable of playing the first notes of *La Marseillaise* on a flute, and yesterday's huge scandal – the scandal of your life – will vanish without a trace.

'So stop fucking around, Monsieur Actor. This isn't your latest role, you know: the king of silence. All right, you're managing at the moment, you can keep it shut for two, three hours. We'll see how you feel in seventy hours' time. And yes, for acts of terrorism, we can keep you for three days *before* you see your lawyer. That said, bravo, you're staying silent, you're playing the hard man, fantastic, they should give you an Oscar. Except this is not a casting call. This is reality. And the reality is that if you continue your play-acting, in ten days your cousin will be fostered out and your little brother Slimane will be in the slammer. And he looks to me a bit . . . let's say, puny, your bro, if you know what I mean . . .'

The commander fell silent and stared at Fouad, so intensely that his silence continued to promise him hell on earth.

Fouad was concentrating just as intensely. He moved his jaw from right to left, but his lips remained closed and his teeth clenched. There suddenly passed across his face a long shiver wherein his whole dilemma seemed to concentrate and express itself. At its strongest point, his nostrils retracted. And once the torment had passed, he closed his eyes, sat up in his chair and said in a loud and intelligible voice, 'I refuse to speak before I see a lawyer.'

MONDAY

5

CUPID'S BOW

1.

Chaouch's great victory had, of course, been pushed into the background, in the French and the international press, by the tragedy that had descended upon the president-elect. It was compared to an earthquake measuring 10 on the Richter scale. Some even spoke of a 9/11 *à la française*. On the front pages, images of the attack competed with the latest figures from the Paris stock exchange, which had collapsed quite spectacularly. *Libération* replaced its front cover with an immense black page. Editorials around the world summoned the spectre of the 'Headless Republic'.

In France, it was the accounting of the 'first night of violence' that was bitterly crowned the media's favourite, the number one item on the major morning radio news shows. There were immediate and unscrupulous comparisons to the autumn 2005 riots. In fact, the count for that single night stood at: 2,150 cars burned, about thirty public facilities targeted, the offices of two youth clubs in the Paris suburbs vandalized, and, most seriously, a nursery school burned down to the north of Grogny. A few French flags had been torched for the cameras and police vehicles attacked: on some of them could be seen the impact of high-calibre bullets. The magistrates' courts, set up to dispense summary justice, were going to be packed all day.

The editorial writers noted that it had taken several days, in fact more than a week, to reach that level of violence during the chaos of 2005. Just as they might have commented on the audience figures for a probable new blockbuster by comparing them with those for *Avatar* or *Titanic*, our experts on public opinion prophesied unrest of an intensity that the country hadn't seen since episodes of civil war that, like the Paris Commune, had taken place too long ago to be relevant. What's more, the violence touched only the poor neighbourhoods in the Paris suburbs and a few provincial cities. The most important question was whether the President of the Republic, whose mandate was soon due to expire, was going to ask his government to proclaim a state of emergency in those areas.

The Ministry of the Interior indicated that the situation was completely under control and did not require special measures, and so instantly asked the media not to pour petrol on the flames. There were some political commentators who, in the morning debates, expressed outrage at the fact that the prime minister had not been in the front line since the 'events' of the previous day. President Noyer's mandate did not end until 17 May, in ten days' time; in the meantime, the government was responsible for managing current affairs. But panic had been sown in the ranks of the majority, and before Monday morning it had never seemed so obvious that the real head of the government was

Marie-France Vermorel, Minister of the Interior, the Overseas Territories, the Regions and Immigration.

After five years of Noyerism, the woman who had masterminded his victory had turned out to be the candidate's most effective soldier once he was elected to the highest office. He had her to thank for the 'nationalization' of his message and winning over votes on the far right, and, at the very moment when everyone was deserting him, she alone remained faithful to the former head of state.

2.

Contrary to appearances, it was still a sense of service that pushed her to make the media rounds on the day after the attack. She spent the morning going around radio and TV stations, and seemed to be the least punch-drunk personality in this terminally ill government. No, the nickname of 'Prime Minister Number Two' had never been more deserved, thought Montesquiou, standing still in the shadows offstage, his hand tightly gripping the handle of his cane.

France 2 had made exceptional arrangements, using the election night set to do a special edition. Vermorel played down the night's riots in front of a panel of specialists who dared not interrupt her. The female presenter was, however, finally forced to interject after being called to order through her earpiece.

'Minister, I am sorry to cut in, but we are now going live to the Palais de Justice, where the press conference of State Prosecutor Lamiel has just begun . . .'

Vermorel sat up, obviously offended. When she looked at you, you heard the sound of bullets. Maybe this impression of having a gun trained on you by the first policewoman of France even passed through the TV screen; in which case, the France of Vermorel was as frightening as a firing squad that lined up sixty-five million suspects . . .

She tightened the knot on the orange scarf around her neck, thinking angrily that she had not had the time to finish her sentence, and lifted her chin towards the large screen of the livestream, hoping that she would not be asked to comment on the prosecutor's statement about her relationship with the Minister of Justice – an old Chirac supporter who had betrayed the government between the two rounds of the election by declaring himself 'seduced' by the justice proposals of Chaouch.

Prosecutor Lamiel was standing in front of a sophisticated overhead projector. His genetically modified pear of a head diligently nodded as the technician gave him instructions that would make the computer work. As far back as any of the correspondents could remember, the Palace meeting room had never been so crowded. Lamiel had to pause several times because of the racket made by the pack of photographers and cameramen who were stepping on each other and pushing over chairs. He announced that, once he had finished being questioned, 'the gunman' would be accused of the following: the attempted assassination of a person in public authority (ah yes, Chaouch is not dead, he seemed to point out by raising his eyebrows), to which were added the aggravating factor of terrorism and the offence of criminal association in relation to a terrorist enterprise.

The climax of the press conference was, of course, the projection on the screen of the Wanted poster of Nazir Nerrouche: twenty-nine years of age, French nationality, one metre eighty-five, black eyes, very strongly suspected of being the person behind the plot against the candidate Chaouch, armed and dangerous, and for whom a European arrest warrant had been issued.

And while France and the entire world discovered Nazir's eyes for the first time on that close-up of his passport photo – his immense mad eyes, almost devoid of white, and his long, clean-shaven and sharp-featured face – while France and the entire world was astonished that Public Enemy Number One was this presentable young man, neither bearded nor even particularly stereotypical, Nazir was moving full speed ahead, driven by his accomplice, on an almost deserted highway whose bright yellow line markings and German signage were seriously beginning to weigh on his morale.

Waldstein wanted to turn off the radio now that the press conference had finished. Nazir turned it off himself and looked anxiously at the wing mirror, wondering if the slate-grey sedan that had been following them for the last ten kilometres was in fact the one he thought he had noticed on leaving Zurich.

'I wonder what photo of me they've chosen,' he said, in order to think about something else.

Waldstein did not reply. He began to yawn. Nazir saw a second head appear in the sedan, in the back seat.

'Take the next exit,' he ordered Waldstein.

'What! Are you crazy? We'd to have to do a U-turn. That'd cost us at least an hour . . . You've already forced me to do it before and now look at the time!'

Nazir insisted with some staccato taps on the dashboard.

'Come on, I'm not kidding! At the last moment, okay?'

Waldstein obeyed and turned off at the last moment. Nazir asked him to slow down and saw that the slate-grey sedan was no longer following them.

3.

Back from the TV panel where she had, in the end, not been asked to respond to the prosecutor's press conference, Vermorel welcomed into her office a small grey man with a face marked by two long wrinkles as deep as scars.

This little gentleman in a threadbare suit worked at the CDII and had a clandestine function: he led the defunct media department of the defunct interior intelligence service. His role was not exactly to watch the press but to feed true rumours and false scoops to the journalists who had – or did not have – his favour. No press service of any other ministry could rival the knowledge and networks of this intelligence mastermind who always remained anonymous. He had small, shameful, ink-stained hands, onto which Montesquiou fixed his contemptuous hawk-like gaze as he sat in the other chair facing the minister's sumptuous gold and mahogany desk.

The conversation was brief and the issues quickly defined: in exchange for an exclusive scoop, the editor of a favoured media outlet had to agree not to publish for a few more weeks the next stage of an inquiry that discredited what was, at this moment, the most sensitive branch of the Republic's law enforcement.

This branch was the Central Directorate for Interior Intelligence.

The editor of the newspaper was Xavier Puteoli.

As for the scoop, Puteoli learned what it was about fifteen minutes later by phone, from the very mouth of the little gentleman who worked for the defunct intelligence agency, who was calling from a phone booth a stone's throw from the ministry.

'We'll give you the stolen video of the arrests.'

Puteoli, who had initially refused any compromise on principle, went silent for a long time, seeming less to weigh the pros and cons than to privately rejoice at what being the first to broadcast this video would mean for Avernus.fr.

The prosecutor's press conference had in fact given no other detail on the gunman than his name, which was already known. The major TV channels had mobilized their best investigators and found the full name and address of 'Abdelkrim'. The images of 16 rue de l'Eternité were therefore being broadcast in a continuous loop but nothing was happening for the moment. When interviewed, the people of the neighbourhood wore the universal sheepish and incredulous faces of the neighbours of people whom tragedy has struck overnight: they described Krim as a shy boy, who had done a couple of silly things but who often helped out. And the Nerrouche family had of course become that inevitable chimera, as fictional as unicorns and astrology: a 'normal family'.

Besides, the newsrooms were already buzzing with the rumour that the gunman was the cousin of Fouad Nerrouche, the *man of the match*, but no one yet had broken the news. For the video of the arrests in which Fouad did not appear, it was a question of hours, perhaps minutes: some neighbours were eventually going to call the newspapers, some videos taken on mobile phones were going to be sold for a fortune, but, in the meantime, the TV channels did not have any other images to sink their teeth into except those of an empty block of flats and the other, more spectacular ones taken at the time of the attack and which Puteoli, at that very moment, was playing on loop in his office.

There were seven different versions of it: those of the TV channels who were covering the candidate leaving the polling station, and those taken with phones that showed, more than anything else, the panic and chaotic crowd movements after the shot was fired. On not one of these versions, however, did you see the candidate head on. If you pressed pause at the right moment on France 24's images, you could make out a bright red spurt on the left of the screen, but the camera shot seemed to have been arranged so that the only thing to appear distinctly was Krim's torso as he raised the weapon and fired. The absence of an image of the illustrious victim's splattered face perversely ensured the video's success, just like those videos of people jumping out of windows on 9/11, as horrifying as they were, could be viewed and viewed again – which would not have been the case had they ended with the flesh that had splattered onto the ground, all dismembered and unbearable to see.

Puteoli looked at his inbox.

'It's a deal,' he replied in a voice that betrayed irrepressible excitement at his triumph.

4.

Xavier Puteoli was a short, clumsy man, who wore a waistcoat, jacket and bow tie. He had shiny cheeks, pulled between a pair of menacing and obsequious eyes and the smile of an eternal business school student – even though he had never been one. He was one of those men who say '*enchanté*' in a suave and earnest tone of voice as they shake your hand, before having spoken to you and occasionally without even having really seen you. He smiled all the time, but never with his eyes: his overly affable appearance anaesthetized you while he, ever vigilant, anxiously looked you up and down with a sort of inexplicable rancour that made him look elsewhere if your eyes caught his.

Born in 1950 in Mostaganem, Algeria and arriving in France two years later, he had been in his last year of high school at the time of the events of May '68, in which he had taken part without managing to become leader of even the smallest committee. A rich bourgeois Maoist had called him 'sexually frustrated' during a meeting, and from then on he had an undying hatred of the French far left and its haughty leading figures. He had become a political journalist at *Le Point*, where he had conscientiously climbed the ranks at the price of a thousand betrayals and micro-degradations that explained why his eyes always looked so shifty. Having failed to become editor of that magazine, he had founded a 'free' internet news site that managed to attract all those – 'from the right as well as from the left' – who were sick and tired of the 'albatross of political correctness'.

Avernus.fr represented the peak of his career and his finest achievement. Its Latin motto was taken from Virgil: *facilis descensus Avernie*, which could be translated as 'the descent to Hell is easy'. To protect himself against this, he had married a rich girl from Normandy, who was aristocratic, blonde, Catholic, shy and reserved, and who had duly given him five blonde children, the youngest of whom, Tristan, was trying to get hold of him at that very moment.

He did not take the call because, through his office blinds, he saw the energetic figure of the female journalist who had investigated the CDII and Commissioner Boulimier rush into the open space. He turned off his computer screen and prepared to receive Marieke Vandervroom. She had no time for the small talk of other journalists and did not bother knocking on the boss's door: she came in like a fury, nostrils flared, wearing her ever-present leather jacket, threw her bag and her motorcycle helmet on the chair and brandished her phone, shaking it with extraordinary vehemence.

'Is this a joke?' she asked in her beautifully husky and rasping voice. 'Five months of investigation and you suspend publication just like that, overnight? And you tell me this by text? *By text?*'

At thirty-five, Marieke did not work for the editorial team of Avernus.fr. She had long ago decided that there was salvation in investigative journalism only as a freelancer. She therefore proposed her investigations to various newspapers, who paid her expenses and profited from her talents as a snooper without having to put up with her obnoxious personality.

'It's more complicated than that,' said Puteoli smugly, trying to calm things down.

'It's not more complicated than that!' screamed Marieke. 'I'm working on the most serious investigation team in counter-terrorism and the day before the article's supposed to come out there's an attack on a presidential candidate! And as if by chance . . .'

She didn't finish her sentence.

At the start, it had been about describing the opaque inner workings of Noyer's FBI, but then Marieke had stumbled upon the trail of a special operations group that existed nowhere in the official statutes, which was directly answerable to Boulimier and which had, therefore, dealt with the surveillance of Nazir Nerrouche.

'Marieke, let's calm down. Come on, have a seat.'

But Marieke refused to sit down. She furiously thrust out her chest. Her wide, oceanic face suddenly took on the colour of the bricks of her native Flanders. Puteoli turned his computer back on and pretended to read an email to avoid the lightning bolts sent from Marieke's angry eyes.

'I'm sorry,' he went on, appearing to finish reading the message. 'You see, Marieke, it's just a small delay, so there's no need to get yourself into such a state.'

'There's nothing in the first article! Nothing on Boulimier, nothing on the phone taps on Nazir Nerrouche!'

'There's enough to land us in court.'

'There's zilch! It's just an introduction to the shadiness of the operation, a basic organizational chart, *a fucking Wikipedia page*! We can't just stop there. It's completely absurd!'

'But I never said I wasn't going to publish the rest. You're going off the rails. I'm just asking you for a week. I mean, it's not the end of the world, one week. And if you don't mind me saying so, a Wikipedia page does not risk sending you to prison, the last I heard. While betraying state secrets by revealing the organization of the CDII in the very first article, on the other hand . . .'

Marieke swung around and stared at the occupants of the open space office, who automatically looked away. A fit of rage made her pull down the blinds and turn towards Puteoli while seizing her helmet and the strap of her backpack.

'Three days!' she declared, closing her eyes to stop herself from exploding again. 'If on Thursday you don't publish the sequel, I'm going to look elsewhere, or I'll post everything on the internet . . .'

'Come on, sit down and stop making such a fuss. You understand my reasons, no? I don't have the resources of *The Washington Post* or *Le Monde* here . . . I have to be sure that—'

'No, I don't want to know,' Marieke butted in. 'Besides, you'll never tell me the truth. So just promise me you'll publish the sequel in three days' time and we can leave it at that.'

'I promise,' lied Puteoli, getting up to lead his journalist to the door. 'But not in three days. Five. I'll post it on Saturday, okay?'

But Marieke was already out the door, imposing the sounds of her bag, boots and trademark jacket on a room that was intimidated at least as much by her tone as by the violent stomping of her heels.

5.

France woke up to the word 'Murderer' tagged on hundreds of walls. The blogosphere exploded with rumours about a plot hatched at the highest levels. Journalists ran amok. But Krim, who had finally been given the right to a few hours' rest, had only one goal in mind: to remember, before sinking into unconsciousness, the peculiar timbre of his mother's voice.

After a few hours' sleep, he had discovered that there were in fact two teams of interrogators, one at night and one during the day, and that the night team, led by Captain Tellier, had to be the nice guys, given the way in which the nameless lieutenants had woken him at six in the morning. They had forbidden him from sitting down or going to the toilet, and did not believe a word Krim said, unlike their nocturnal colleagues who kindly asked him for more details. The most brutal lieutenant from the day team looked like a raccoon and talked like a rugby coach; his deep voice ricocheted around the walls instead of passing through them. He had a foolish way about him that wasn't so much smug as controlling, and he was always on the verge of lashing out.

'Stop talking bullshit, you little turd!' The Rugby Player had put the chair against the wall. Krim now had to remain standing and, when he really could not continue, he was given a stool. But a stool was the worst because he couldn't take his mind off the fact that all he wanted was to lean back against the non-existent backrest.

It was between the Rugby Player's silences that Krim had sung to himself several times his mother's *lè lè lè lè*, those four oriental notes she came out with while touching the back of her hand to her forehead, her other hand on her hip and her large eyes dilated with an air of perplexity, stupefaction and indignation that was just for show. The phoniness now reassured him instead of irritating him. And it was against the shouts of the Rugby Player and his colleague banging his fists on the table, a guy with glasses and walking boots, that Krim now tried to retrieve the specific colour of her voice, its singular ring, which came back to him only in tiny mental sparks that never caught fire, like so many damp squibs.

In search of his mother, Krim's fingers moved in the rectangle of white light that fell on the desk in the room. He remembered those late nights spent listening to classical music. His mother would occasionally catch him at it, and he would pretend to be asleep or listening to hip-hop while gravely nodding his head, lips and eyes closed.

'You're going to rot in a hole till the end of your days. You've got nothing to lose, so tell us the truth!'

But the truth was that he had nothing to confess to them. He loved his mother; he hadn't told her that once since he grew taller than her, but it was true, all the same: he loved her. That was the only truth that came to mind.

A few metres from the cells, Captain Tellier learned by phone that Krim's mobile had not been found at the last riverboat company. There had, however, been a curious scene that the lieutenant in charge of this small mission recounted at length to the captain: when they had arrived at the office of the Pont-Neuf Pleasure Boats, the young woman behind the desk had made a few calls and began to tell them that no phone had been reported found.

'But then,' continued the lieutenant, 'a manager arrived and asked to speak to us in private. We went into his office and he told us that an American woman had come by on Sunday afternoon to pick up a mobile phone, one that had fallen from a bridge behind Notre-Dame.'

'Did you at least ask at what time?'

'No, no, boss, but wait: he told me she had brought the mobile to the jetty at the foot of the Eiffel Tower, where we were standing, and that a young woman had come to claim it.'

'What?' Tellier almost shouted.

'One of ours, apparently. She had police insignia, according to the manager. I asked him if he knew what department she belonged to, but he said that the police logo had been enough for him.'

Stunned, the captain paused for a moment before asking the obvious question.

'And what did she look like, this mysterious policewoman?'

'Oh yeah,' replied the lieutenant, who had not been at the ATSD for long, 'the manager told me that she was strange, with very blonde hair and . . . wait, what else did he say? Oh, she wore riding boots.'

'Riding boots? What the hell is all this crap . . .'

Tellier went into Krim's cell and asked the Rugby Player and the Rambler to take a break. Surprised, they obeyed.

'What do you know about the equestrian?' asked Tellier without thinking.

'The what?' asked Krim.

'A friend of Nazir's, a horsewoman ... What do you know about her?'

Krim gave an undoubtedly sincere look of incomprehension. Tellier closed his eyes and cleared his head. When he opened them again, they seemed gentler, almost friendly.

'Listen, my friend,' he continued in a voice that was almost sorry to break the silence, 'I'm not blaming you for this, but your version of events is not very easy to believe.'

This sudden courtesy made tears well in Krim's eyes. He frowned as hard as he could to stifle them.

'Put yourself in my place, Krim! That phone ... you threw it onto a riverboat and it can't be found ...'

He continued his list of events, without much conviction.

'Think, for fuck's sake. You're down there in Saint-Etienne, your cousin buys you a weapon, you practise shooting for weeks and, on the day of the election, he gives you a train ticket so you can go up to Paris, and at no moment do you think it's to assassinate Chaouch? I don't want to be nasty, but look, next door those guys are saying: either he's the best actor in the world or this kid is a total idiot!'

The idea that he could be a total idiot chased the emotion from Krim's heart. Cut to the quick, he shrugged and sighed, letting out a nonchalant 'pfft'.

'Why don't tell me the truth? That you were all in on it. Your whole family. Your cousins, your aunts, your mother ... How could they have seen nothing? And how would they have let you leave, just like that? Why on earth did you come to Paris? You know, right?'

Krim denied this with a tired but not yet resigned movement of the head. He believed he could convince them. Certainly not now, but once he had recovered some of his strength. For the moment, he couldn't go ten seconds without feeling the pain again, one way or another. His hands, his knees, his hip, his mouth, his head. His body was now just a conductor for pain, an anonymous pain that had seeped beneath his skin and was now taking up all the space inside him, tearing everything to pieces without warning.

'I told you, the red-haired guy—'

'And you haven't even given us his name ... And what did you do before going to see him? There's a gap in your story.'

Before going there, Krim had seen Aurélie, but he would never speak to them about that. He still did not remember his mother's voice but he suddenly remembered, with a precision that burned his lungs, Aurélie's mouth, the way it formed that little triangle above her upper lip, like the bow of a ship, and which he would have given anything to touch with his finger or his tongue.

In a moment of irrepressible exaltation, Krim dared to ask the captain, who appeared to be in a good mood and, unlike his barbaric colleagues, well disposed towards him, 'What do you call that part of the lip, there?'

The investigator was flabbergasted and, arms crossed, looked towards his lieutenant, who smiled and rolled his eyes.

'This little bastard is screwing with me, isn't he! Can you fucking believe that? He's screwing with me!'

Tellier lifted his head and passed a finger over his harelip. Before the Rugby Player and the Rambler came back into the interrogation room, however, he did at least reply, 'Cupid's bow.'

6.

It was certainly not her cupid's bow that Tristan Puteoli found interesting about Aurélie. He did not like her swimmer's shoulders and arms either: even if it was just an optical illusion, they reduced the size of her tits. Besides, she wanted nothing to do with him since the attack. She barely even deigned to look at him.

Tristan came to wait for her at the exit of the Joséphine Baker swimming pool late morning. He had brought a second helmet to take her home on his scooter but Aurélie, on seeing him, took off in the opposite direction and refused to speak to him – until Tristan, whose eyes glowed with cruelty, found a way to catch her attention and stop her beautiful wet head from moving away any further.

'You know I won't be able to stop them talking for very long? You realize that? We're accomplices if we say nothing, and my father's going to kill me . . .'

Aurélie, who had nevertheless kept on walking, now came to a sudden halt. Her eyes, reddened by the chlorine, stared at the surrealist block of the swimming pool suspended above the Seine, so close to the surface that it seemed to float there.

'For fuck's sake, don't do that, Tristan. Give me a little time.'

'And what are you giving me in exchange?'

Aurélie did not reply, but shot the teenager a withering look.

'Listen, Aurélie, this bullshit can't go on. Anyway, what difference does it make? Whether we say it now or next week, it's the same thing: we spent the afternoon with the guy who killed Chaouch, just before he did it! You can't hide that, it's just stupid! Worse than that: it's suicidal!'

'First of all, Chaouch isn't dead,' said Aurélie angrily, 'and secondly, yes, a bit of time would change everything, 'cause maybe I'll be able to speak to my father. Because, look, if they find out that he's the one investigating Krim, and Krim is linked to me—'

'Pfft. Linked to you, my arse.'

'If they hear that,' Aurélie went on, closing her eyes to stop herself from slapping him, 'they're surely going to say that my father isn't objective, and that—'

'And what? You're dreaming. What do you think will happen? You think you'll do a deal with your father so he discreetly gets Krim out of the slammer? Is that what you want? Fuck, are you high, or what? Anyway, I don't understand what you see in that little sand nigger . . . So it's thugs you find attractive, is it? Dream of being gang-raped by some ragheads, do you?'

Aurélie took the helmet from Tristan's hands. He was scared she would smash his face with it. But she just put it on her own head.

'You know why I'll never go out with you, Tristan?'

'Because you love me.'

'Because you're a *douchebag*. The word was invented just for you, you arsehole.'

'What makes you think I want to go out with you? I just want to . . .'

The rich boy from Neuilly burst out laughing and drove Aurélie, at her request, to the Ile de la Cité, outside the gates of the Palais de Justice, its gilded turrets sparkling in the bright spring sunlight.

'Now fuck off,' said Aurélie, handing back his helmet. 'And if you ever want to have the slightest chance of being able to tell everyone that you got me into bed, you'd better tell your cretinous friends to shut their mouths. Okay?'

Tristan smiled and replied, 'Deal.'

Then he pushed his scooter off towards Saint-Michel, zigzagging with excitement at the thought of being able to screw Aurélie in the near future.

Aurélie messed up her already dishevelled hair a little bit more before speaking to the policemen guarding the visitors' entrance. Smiling coquettishly, she succeeded in persuading the cop to lead her to the top floor of the Palace, just outside the Saint-Eloi gallery, where no one could enter without fingerprint recognition. Aurélie waited on a dilapidated bench for her father to leave his office. He had not slept at home the previous night: around one in the morning, Aurélie had heard her mother playing a few notes with the soft pedal on the grand piano in the living room, before violently striking a chord whose despair had thrummed through the walls and reached her bedroom at the other end of the apartment.

Her father the judge opened the door. He was in shirtsleeves, hands behind his back, his armpits circled with sweat. Leaning forwards, he asked, 'To what do I owe this impromptu visit? Nothing serious, I hope?'

Aurélie stood up. She had only a few seconds to gauge her father's mood and her chances of being able to make him pity her. Unfortunately, a pregnant woman opened the door, and without giving Aurélie the slightest look, tapped on the judge's elbow to ask him to hurry up.

'Papa, it's . . .'

But his head was embroiled in work worries. Aurélie could tell this from the fact that he did not ask her to finish her sentence.

'Never mind, forget it. We can talk about it tonight. What time are you coming home?'

'Late, but I'll come and see you if you're in bed,' added Judge Wagner, kissing his daughter's forehead.

'Did you come home last night?'

'No. I had a nap in my office.'

'Okay. I'll let you get back to work . . .'

But what Aurélie did not see, as she bounded down the stairs, was that her father stayed for a good thirty seconds in the doorway that led to the Saint-Eloi gallery – seized by the strangest of intuitions, so strange that he did not even dare express it in the secrecy of his own mind.

7.

The pregnant woman who had almost pulled Wagner by the sleeve was Alice, his court clerk. The judge could not do without her. Her olive-green and ever-smiling eyes provided him with an unexpected counterpoint to the violent drabness of his case files. At thirty-nine, Alice was expecting her second child, with a man whom Wagner had never met and about whom the two of them never spoke. When Paola was on the warpath, the judge found himself envying this unknown husband.

Alice was not conventionally pretty. She had a narrow body and thin arms, and she remained that way despite the pregnancy. She was, in all honesty, more energetic than elegant, and sometimes outright clumsy. But it was an ingenuous, childlike, *irresistible* clumsiness. A product of the 1968 uprisings, the judge's atheism did, however, make him suspect that there was something a little shady, or at least Catholic, about his court clerk's cheerfulness – that it was some kind of *exultation*, morally premeditated and the result of ideological coaching. In order to approve of them unreservedly, he preferred that the joyful outbursts of those closest to him be spontaneous and completely free.

Of course, Alice and he were not 'close', and joy was not exactly the daily bread of the Saint-Eloi gallery. Our judge was given a striking illustration of this when he returned to the ferment in his counterterrorism unit: young Judge Poussin, who had been appointed with him, was just coming back from the ATSD headquarters in Levallois, where Mouloud Benbaraka and Fares Ait Bechir had been transferred and interrogated.

'B-B-Benbaraka won't crack,' Poussin stammered, 'but this Monsieur F-F-Fares has told us everything. He drove Nazir from Paris to Zurich in a c-c-car with f-f-fake diplomatic l-l-licence plates; that was why they had no problem crossing the border. Once in Zurich, Nazir, "g-g-goes to the bank",' he said with air quotes, 't-t-to p-p-pay Benbaraka. But the Swiss police grab them, find an empty suitcase and a P-P-Parabellum nine millimetre engraved with the letters SRAF in the glove box. But the most important thing is that he f-f-finally told us this: Nazir had arranged to meet him, if things t-t-turned bad, in Hamburg. Yet again, B-B-Benbaraka will confirm nothing. We've got the address, and I've already alerted the Justice Ministry liaison officers so they can put us in t-t-touch with the Germans. Just as well a European arrest warrant was issued . . .'

With his painful shyness, you could not believe for an instant that Guillaume Poussin was an investigating judge; and when he began to speak, you could not understand how his rise had been so meteoric, propelling him, at the age of just thirty-eight, into the highly coveted pool of counterterrorism judges. He was the only judge in this part of the Palace to still have all his hair and, what's more, it was black and shiny. He was thin, had a big nose and a pronounced taste for turtleneck sweaters and jackets with elbow patches.

'I think they're going to send Mansourd,' Wagner replied. 'We have to ask the Germans to put their counterterrorism services on the case, not just the police. We can't afford to miss the hideout. What's at the address? A house, a hotel, or what?'

'It's a museum,' replied Poussin before adding notes off the top of his head: 'At 7 Hermannsweg, there's just a m-m-museum, with no flats above.'

'A museum?'

'Yes, a sort of d-d-doll museum. That said, it's in a slightly out-of-the-way area, with a big Turkish p-p-population.'

Perplexed, the judge dropped into an armchair and took his head in his hands. The hope of arresting Nazir the day after the attack invaded all his thoughts; it was dangerous not to resist these promises of glory, but fatigue was beginning to mess with his mind.

'Guillaume, could you go to Saint-Etienne to oversee the arrest of the kid they call Fat Momo and the search of that private security agency run by Nazir Nerrouche? And also to make sure that the Saint-Etienne police don't botch the investigation of the area?'

'V-v-very well. I'll leave this evening.'

'You also have to deal with the complaint lodged by Fouad Nerrouche, the brother, on Saturday night. His great-uncle was assaulted. There were obscenities written on his head' – he looked at the document faxed by the superintendent in Saint-Etienne – 'and a swastika. First of all, prevent the family from meting out justice themselves. Threaten them if you have to. And, above all, try to discover what connection that might have with our case.'

'Has the court in Saint-Etienne received the complaint?'

'Yes. The deputy public prosecutor has opened a preliminary investigation, but I've asked Lamiel to make you an auxiliary. I know it's a lot to deal with, but . . .'

But he did not have a choice. Commander Mansourd had been appointed coordinator of all police services for the hunt for Nazir, and Wagner was coordinating the coordinator and all the parallel investigations.

'Alice?'

The judge was going to ask her to draft two warrants: a bench warrant entrusting the police with the task of bringing the 'close family' to his office, and a simple court summons. He did not yet know which of the two options was preferable.

But Alice did not reply. Her eyes were glued to the computer screen.

'Your Honour,' she said in a limp voice. 'You have to see this.'

Wagner, Poussin and the latter's court clerk went over to Alice's computer. She pushed back the screen: the Avernus website was showing footage of the ATSD's arrest of the Nerrouche family.

There was no violence: everyone stood there calmly, but no jackets covered their faces (and for a good reason: Wagner had refused to alert the press). Even the children's faces were clearly visible, as the web team at Avernus.fr, though gifted enough to put the name of their site in big letters at the bottom of the video, had not thought – or, more likely, had deliberately not bothered – to blur them. The tactless owner of the smartphone enthusiastically zoomed in on all the faces in the room, including the uncovered heads of the ATSD investigators.

The judge was livid.

He switched on the small television hidden in the safe cupboard where the files were stacked. Maître Khalid Aribi, 'lawyer at the Paris Bar', was giving an interview on LCI, in which he said he had been appointed by the young Abdelkrim 'and his family', and was protesting the inhumane treatment by the counterterrorism 'cops' of women, the elderly and children . . . 'Children!' he insisted, furrowing his long brow and opening wide his large, dark eyes.

'I denounce a media campaign that is just beginning, a lynching unworthy of the justice system of the birthplace of the Rights of Man! I don't know who the judge is who sent thugs in jackboots to round up women and children at almost ten in the evening. Oh yes! They absolutely did! Don't be mistaken: we're talking about a roundup here! I hope he sleeps well at night, that judge, because if I were in his shoes, I'd need a lorryload of sleeping pills . . .'

The judge did not open his lips. With his shirt open nearly to the belly button, Maître Aribi let himself be filmed at length and fiercely moved from one provocative remark to another. Even through the screen, you could smell his five-hundred-euro aftershave.

'Turn that off,' was the judge's only comment.

8.

He was still angry a few moments later while listening to Captain Tellier's phone report on the interrogation of Krim. At the slightest hesitation in the captain's voice, he betrayed his impatience by inhaling a bit too sharply.

'So there you are: Krim and his mother's versions match on Benbaraka... But, your Honour, there's something else. A correspondent from *France Bleu* has been found in his home gagged and handcuffed to a radiator. He says that yesterday morning someone stole his press card and radio equipment.'

'Did he give a description of his assailants?'

'Assailant singular, your Honour. There was only one man. Red-haired. Corresponds to the description the kid gave us of the guy who helped him make his way through the crowd.'

'Okay, very good, Captain. Have they taken fingerprints?'

'We'll have them by tomorrow evening, but we should have the video-surveillance tapes of Grogny town hall square by tomorrow morning. Prosecutor Lamiel thinks we should make a composite photo and send it to the press.'

'Hmm,' Wagner hesitated. 'Listen, we'll sort out the composite. We'll send out a Wanted poster with Lamiel. I'm going to call him.'

The captain sounded surprised by the initiative.

'Uh... no. We've got three investigation teams on the case. The commander will tell you we can manage on our own.'

The judge nodded, unseen by Captain Tellier, and hung up. He was about to call Mansourd when he heard a familiar voice in the corridor of the gallery. He turned to Alice, who raised her eyebrows.

Judge Rotrou was back. From Pakistan, where he had reluctantly gone to reopen an old investigation, after repeated demands by the victims' families. Alice's raised eyebrows signalled that Rotrou must be upset at having missed all this excitement, and especially at having not been there in time to prevent Wagner being appointed.

He knocked on the door and did not look at Alice.

'Your Honour,' he began breathlessly. 'Congratulations!'

He was a massive, obese man who wore braces and sweated profusely. He was forever mopping his enormous and completely bald head, and he was recognized – and parodied – by the peculiar fact that his mouth was always open, in summer as in winter, a mouth with bulging lips, which were very red and turned into a permanent rictus of disgust.

Wagner stood up to greet the Ogre. While holding out one large, fat, clammy hand, Rotrou seized his colleague's shoulder with the other. His mouth approached Wagner's right ear, and, taking advantage of the fact that Alice could not hear him, whispered in an excessively polite voice, 'You're not going to succeed, your Honour. Withdraw from this case immediately and give it to me before you make a complete fool of yourself. You know full well you're not up to it, *your Honour...*'

Wagner freed his hand from Rotrou's paw.

'Thanks for your encouraging words,' he said aloud, 'but, without meaning to kick you out, we're rather busy, my clerk and I. Thanks and ...' – he could not resist the opportunity – 'please rest assured: the investigation is making very rapid progress.'

Alice was used to seeing explosions of animosity in these chambers, but the ones involving these two judges appeared to be wrapped in poisoned gauze. The dirty bombs they launched at each other were radioactive and much unhealthier than the tantrums of Corsican militants who, on learning that they were going to go to court, would call Wagner a 'dirty foreigner' before promising to blow him up, slit his throat, and other such activities. Wagner did not seem affected in the slightest by these exchanges. No more than he seemed to be after the one that had just taken place in front of his clerk.

He even went back to work with renewed gusto, as if the jealous hatred of the Ogre had revived him – as if, instead of hearing that he wished him to fail, he had just downed two cups of strong coffee.

He called Mansourd.

'Commander, how much longer until we get the video-surveillance tapes from the bank?'

The hairdressing salon that Nazir Nerrouche had probably entered shared a private car park under video surveillance with the Swiss bank outside which Mouloud Benbaraka and Fares Ait Bechir had been arrested.

'Quite honestly, I'm afraid it's going to be difficult,' replied the commander. 'Even in Switzerland, the banks drag their feet . . . We'd have to ask twice and start with the outside cameras, all around the bank. Whatever happens, we won't have the tapes for two, three days, maybe more.'

'I'll deal with this right now,' replied Wagner, scratching some notes on a file. 'You can release the ones we have in custody. I'll send the summons immediately.'

Mansourd could not hide his surprise.

'Your Honour? I thought we'd agreed about—'

'No, I've made my decision. All the close family members are being tapped. We've stuffed Nazir's mother's home with microphones . . . No, we'll learn much more by watching them this way, I assure you.'

The commander had begun to fiddle nervously with the medallion round his neck. One hypothesis burned in his brain:

the defence lawyer's tirade had scared the judge shitless, so he did not want to look like a monster.

'Your Honour,' he ventured, 'if it's because of this Maître Aribi . . .'

'I'm listening, Commander. Tell me what you're thinking.'

'I'm sorry, your Honour. It's your investigation. You do what you want.'

Wagner was no longer writing sentences but unreadable scribbles. He put down his pen.

'I'm going to tell you a story, Commander. There's something a high-ranking judge told me one day, at the very start of my career. I was an investigating judge in my native Lorraine. I was visited by a young mother who was a rape victim, suspected of suffocating her baby. She had not been able to have an abortion, so when the baby was born, she killed it. So . . . a child-killing mother. During the first cross-examination, she adopted a passive attitude, staring into space, giving me nothing. So, I charged her and sentenced her. She committed suicide on the second day of detention.'

'Your Honour—'

'Let me finish, Commander. I obviously felt very guilty. I felt that I had not questioned her properly. I went to see the presiding judge, who has since become a famous judge in Paris. He asked me to check that everything in the file was in order, that there was no court clerk signature missing, that I had been legally beyond reproach. I told him: "But that's not why I came to see you." He looked at me and said with a smile: "Oh, that? Get one thing into your head, young man: you cannot do this job without causing damage." You cannot do this job without causing damage.'

'Yes, your Honour, but—'

'Commander, I'm not going to remand an entire family into custody just because it keeps the media, the courts or the Pope happy. And if you think that lawyer's grotesque call to arms had anything to do with my decision, that's your problem. Have you received the summons?'

The commander looked over them.

'Yes, your Honour. I'm leaving right now to join the team in Hamburg.'

'You'll have the international commission within the hour. I'm counting on you to catch him for me, Commander. Wait,' he suddenly added. 'I almost forgot: do you have the mobile phone yet?'

'We've got a small problem. Someone has already claimed it, one of ours apparently, but I'll explain later. It's not as urgent as capturing this maniac.'

The judge agreed, hung up and felt Alice's admiring gaze upon him. He pretended not to notice and asked her to bring him a cup of coffee.

6

A SPECTRE IS HAUNTING
EUROPE

1.

On place Leon-Blum, in the 11th arrondissement, there was a bar frequented by the judicial police. Le Vidocq was divided in two: a veranda for civilians in front and a vast hall at the back of the establishment, where you could hear police captains pontificate on their exploits while devouring sirloin steaks. An unspoken rule forbade the brutes from the Anti-Crime Brigade and even sergeants from frequenting the place. At Le Vidocq you were among your own, careers were decided over a good Pouilly-Fuissé, and that Monday at noon, when the sculpted figure of Commander Valérie Simonetti appeared, a whole table of investigators made a show of standing up and leaving, happily skipping dessert in order to signal to the woman who had not been able to protect Chaouch that she had become *persona non grata*.

Valérie turned around to stare at them: the youngest one, unable to ignore her completely, gave her an apologetic frown to which the commander replied by fluttering her beautiful blue eyes. She had a meeting with Commissioner Thomas Maheut, one of the few cop friends she could be sure would not abandon her. He was neither in the hall nor on the veranda. She ordered a white port and sat at the bar.

She was wearing black trousers that clung to her powerful thighs, and a light jacket over a white t-shirt. Thomas arrived five minutes late. He had to stand slightly on tiptoes to kiss the Valkyrie's cheeks – he often claimed to have been the first to give her this nickname.

'You sure it's not a problem to be seen with me?'

Thomas froze in outrage.

'Has anyone said anything to you? If any one of those bastards says anything, I'll kill him.'

Without his uniform, Commissioner Maheut looked increasingly like the thugs he spent his life hunting. Granted, he wore polo shirts with no apparent brand, and gave himself a close shave twice a day, but, with time, his military tendencies had lost any of their reassuring qualities: with his hard eyes, jutting chin and heavy, mistrustful lower lip, he looked just like the sort of unsavoury character people avoid sitting next to on public transport. His nose was broken, his skin rough and his hair light and frizzy.

They were led to a table for two. As if by chance, the cops at the next table decided against coffee and went to pay the bill at the bar.

'Not one of those cunts can hold a candle to you. Christ, it makes me want to . . .'

Valérie liked Thomas a lot. He had been trying to sleep with her ever since they first met, and had been successful on three occasions – quasi-pugilistic one-night stands with the kind of woman he did not meet very often, especially in the cosy milieu he now frequented.

Thomas was the pride of his family, which was from what he still called, with a hint of bitterness, 'lower-class France'. He had become a policeman to avoid spending his life behind the conveyor belt of a factory: a brilliant law student and then the youngest superintendent in France, at thirty-five he was already responsible for the Directorate of Public Order and Traffic, thanks to the almost filial confidence placed in him by his mentor, Police Chief Dieuleveult. Desperate not to become one of those uptight arseholes around him, he exaggerated his working-class eloquence in public, said *shit* and *fuck* but was already becoming more sophisticated and could be heard to say *holy crap* more often than *holy shit*.

They did not waste any time: the conversation moved onto Chaouch before Valérie was even halfway through her port. For Thomas, there was not the shadow of a doubt. The attack was the work of a 'lone wolf'.

'You have to see these kids. They're crazy, I'm telling you. I mean, fuck, they're complete psychos! It had to happen one of these days.'

Valérie looked at her watch, whose face she always put on the underside of her wrist, against her pulse.

'I bet you there's going to be a whole load of shitheads saying on TV that it's society's fault and Christ knows what else. I mean, fuck, what more do they need? A scumbag shoots a politician on election day, and they still come out with that . . . that . . .'

The vast choice of insults with which he dreamed of bombarding these imaginary intellectuals overwhelmed him, and in the end, he just sighed. He gestured for the waiter to bring him something to drink.

'Don't give me that look,' he murmured, avoiding Valérie's eyes. She often behaved like a big sister to him. 'It's just a pick-me-up. With the way things are shaping up, you've got to pace yourself, right?'

Already calmed down by the first mouthful, the young commissioner went on, 'Look, seriously, the scumbag who fired the shot, who is he? Al-Qaeda? You're going to come out with big theories every time there's—'

'No, no,' Valérie interrupted softly, 'and, anyway, it's the counterterrorism squad that's investigating. Mansourd's ATSD. I hardly know more than you, just that quite a few heads are going to roll at the CDII. There's some dodgy stuff concerning Boulimier... Well, the kid couldn't have done all of it on his own, nor could his cousin. It's unbelievable that they were watched for so long and we didn't intervene in time... It's just... incredible.'

She took off her jacket, attracting a few looks with her muscular arms. A light blonde down covered them. At the slightest movement of her wrists, her athletic biceps swelled, prettily divided in two by a vein as blue as her skin was fair. Thomas raised his eyebrows and chased away memories of their last nocturnal combat, long before she was chosen by Chaouch to lead his security detail.

'Have you heard?' asked Thomas. 'They've already appointed a judge, to show that the investigation will be independent and all the rest. Guess who it is?'

'Henri Wagner?'

'The very same.'

'My oh my,' commented Valérie, looking again at her watch. 'I thought he was finished after that business with the Corsican threats . . . How'd he get the case of the century?'

'Ah well, that's politics,' the commissioner said. 'With the change of state prosecutor on the eve of the elections, everyone counted on Chaouch winning, and with the left in power . . . well, you can't imagine the Palace intrigues—'

His phone rang.

'Speaking of Palace intrigues . . .'

He got up to take the call on the veranda. Through the window, Valérie saw his face harden. When he returned, she asked him, 'Was that the big boss?'

'I've got to go. Shit. Sorry.'

Maheut insisted on paying the bill, but he couldn't wait for the waiter to come back with his credit card. So in the end he agreed to let Valérie pay and left the crowded room. Once on the veranda, some intuition made him turn around to look at Valérie, who was pretending indifference to all the dark looks being sent her way by everyone in the restaurant.

2.

Preceded by a police escort, a car with tinted windows double-parked beside Commissioner Maheut's car. The back seat window descended and a pale hand emerged from a charcoal-grey jacket sleeve, gesturing for the superintendent to get into the vehicle. Recognizing the car and the minimalist manner of the chief of police, Maheut obeyed and sat down on the seat. The chauffeur was asked to wait outside the vehicle and, without even glancing at his 'guest', Dieuleveult began to speak, flicking through a dossier filled with handwritten notes.

'I saw the Minister of the Interior last night. There's no point trying to conceal the truth from you: this is a very serious situation. When you think about it, the world's greatest civilization is sinking into violence worthy of an underdeveloped country. You'd think this was Algeria in the eighties. You remember President Boudiaf, Commissioner?'

This question required no response. Besides, the chief of police was still not looking at his interlocutor.

'If you want to know what I think, this is what happens when we invite everyone to the feast. Two generations later, here we are, repeating the mistakes of the past . . . Well, that's just my opinion. Our intelligence reports indicate that some gangs are planning to come and create havoc in Paris. I trust you to handle this. You're going to be on the front line over the next few days. I want reports every hour and increased security in the metro and at all the entrances to Paris.'

'Very well, Monsieur.'

'As for demonstrations, that's simple: there won't be any. No vigils, no solidarity marches, nothing. I want no crowd movements in Paris until order has been restored. I've already forbidden a concert in support of Chaouch. There will be no exceptions. I know there are people who would jump at the chance, who would use that to . . .'

Commissioner Maheut could feel that Dieuleveult was about to change subject. The chief of police was looking at a memo, knitting his brows so furiously that Maheut suspected he was just pretending to concentrate. Anyway, he abruptly closed the folder and finally turned towards Maheut with a look so neutral and blank that his entire face seemed featureless.

'Thomas, you are not unaware of the delicate situation in which we find ourselves vis-à-vis the Ministry of the Interior. The minister hates me. No, no, you have no idea how much she hates me. I cannot afford to put a foot wrong. No more, of course, than I could allow that from the men under my orders . . .'

Maheut was pursing his lips to hide his discomfort. The chief of police closed his eyes and made a strange grimace in which one of his nostrils got the better of the other. Maheut realized that it was an attempt to smile. And now that he thought of it, he had never seen his boss smile; he had not even thought that such a thing was possible for this ice-cold man.

'You are worth more than Public Order and Traffic, Commissioner. Spending nights in front of computer screens is okay at your age, but you have to think of the future . . .'

Here we go again, Maheut thought.

'I have big plans for you, Thomas. I have great hopes . . . One day, if things go well, you could be in my place. I am going to give you a mission that I could not give to anyone else. That said, you must promise me your unfailing support and your total discretion, and I mean *to-tal*.'

The commissioner did not know how to reply. His head had grown heavy and was hanging forwards. His neck, exposed by the lack of a tie, made him feel naked.

'In a war, you have two enemies: the opposing camp and, above all, your own side. The mission I am going to give you is directly related to this internal enemy . . . the so-called "enemy of the state", if you see what I mean.'

'Yes, Monsieur,' Thomas replied, sticking his trembling palms on the top of his knees.

'Such a mission is, of course, outside your usual prerogatives, and I am not going to provide you with the details right away. We will see each other again in the coming days, in line with events and movements at the Ministry of the Interior. Let's just say, to make your mouth water, that we are dealing with ... how do I put this ... Imagine a rotten edifice that is still standing only because it has abnormally solid foundations. Are you following me?'

'I ... I'm trying ...'

'So, imagine a rotten wood cabin on reinforced concrete stilts: your job will be to gnaw away at those stilts, if you like. Expose the rottenness. I am sure that you will excel in this exercise,' he concluded enigmatically, before giving a look that told Maheut to leave more effectively than the immaculate hand on his shoulder ever could have.

3.

Mansourd had already left when Fouad, Rabia and Dounia were released from custody. They were given back their phones and handed their summons, while it was explained to them that they would have a meeting tomorrow, Tuesday, at the chambers of Judge Wagner in the Saint-Eloi gallery of the Palais de Justice, Paris. The two sisters listened silently: they were in a state of advanced exhaustion; their gestures were mechanical and their eyes veiled with fatigue and sadness.

Fouad, on the other hand, was focused, tense, standing as straight as the I in Injustice.

When Rabia and Dounia were finally released, uncuffed

beneath the scorching sun of early afternoon, they fell into each other's arms and began to cry. They turned their phones back on, expecting to find dozens of messages left by the family. Instead, all the missed calls, without exception, came from unknown or hidden numbers. They listened to the first messages: they were journalists, from big TV channels, big newspapers and big radio stations, often from women with engaging and complicit voices, some of them with strong foreign accents . . .

Fouad did not wait a second to call Jasmine. But, after three more attempts and as many messages, it seemed obvious to him that she was unable to reply. She must be under surveillance. He had to find another way to communicate with her.

He dialled the number of Maître Szafran. A female voice replied and put him through. Fouad explained the situation: they were completely innocent, his brother Nazir was the only culprit, and the investigating judge had summoned them tomorrow at two in the afternoon. Maître Szafran listened to him attentively, a pencil in his hand, and replied that it seemed necessary to meet the next morning to prepare for the hearing with the judge. A hearing at which he himself would be present and which it was highly likely would not lead to charges, given the nature of the warrant Wagner had issued.

'Do you know the judge?' Fouad asked him.

'Yes, he's the only honest judge in that unit, as independent as you can be. Don't take this badly, but I'd even go so far as to say that you've had some luck in your misfortune . . .'

He had an intimidatingly deep, stentorian voice and perfect diction, helped by the old accent of the high intellectual bourgeoisie − majestic A's (proceduraaal, legaaality), clear consonants . . .

'That said, we should stay on our guard,' Szafran went on, 'and don't trust journalists, Monsieur Nerrouche. Do not reply to any request for an interview. Barricade yourself in a safe place until tomorrow. I'll give you one last piece of advice: take your car rather than the train when you go to the capitaaal.'

When Fouad hung up, he felt almost reassured; despite the prospect of meeting a judge, despite the impression that he had become a criminal overnight, the bass baritone of this lawyer had restored his faith.

But the thought of this good news that was not yet good news could not make him happy for long. When the carousel of conjectures and hopes stopped turning, there remained, frozen forever in the retina of millions of people, one stubborn, desperately stubborn little fact: his eighteen-year-old cousin had tried to assassinate the Socialist Party's candidate for the presidential elections, the man whom France had just elected with a comfortable majority – the man, above all, whom Fouad had one day considered, in front of witnesses no less, to be his future father-in-law.

He was filled with shame as he remembered that scene.

'I've just spoken to . . . the lawyer,' he said to his mother, who was caressing Rabia's grief-stricken head.

He had given up on saying 'our' lawyer, as if only criminals needed lawyers, and as if speaking about their lawyer constituted the first admission of guilt.

'And?'

'Mama, you didn't say anything to the investigators, did you? Did you sign anything?'

'Oh yes, a transcript.'

'And what did you tell them?'

'Oh nothing,' Dounia lied. 'What did you want me to tell them?'

'You realize that they can take something you said, and twist it to mean the opposite?'

'Of course, Fouad, I know. Listen, I'm in real trouble. Slim and Luna have left Granny's. Apparently, there was an argument when everyone went home last night, and they didn't want to stay.'

'What are you talking about? Where are they? Mama? Where are they?'

'They're at the house, it's okay. Slim had the keys.'

Fouad shook his head and took advantage of Rabia speaking on the phone to Luna to tell his mother, 'We'll go to Rabia's and fetch her things then take her to our place, okay?'

Dounia nodded and all three of them walked towards Rabia's neighbourhood. Hands in his pockets, Fouad repeated to himself the draft of what he was going to say to Jasmine when he finally got her on the phone. Lost in his thoughts, he didn't notice the looks from the passers-by who had recognized them. Yael sent him a text, asking if she could call him. He called her back immediately.

'We've just been released from detention, Yael, I haven't seen the TV yet. How—'

'Fouad, there's a problem,' Yael cut in, before continuing in a worried voice, 'I think it's best we see each other to talk about it . . .'

'I'm coming to Paris tomorrow morning. What's happening? I have to see Szafran and the judge in the afternoon. What's going on, Yael?'

'Listen, you've got other fish to fry. We'll talk about it in good time. Do you like Szafran? Does he seem okay? What does he think about all this?'

Fouad did not feel like talking. He kept his chat with Yael as brief as possible and hung up when the corner of rue de l'Eternité appeared in his field of vision. The street crossed one of the city's hills from one end to the other. Rabia's block of flats was situated just before the slope became really difficult to climb. Fouad suddenly saw a lorry mounted with a satellite dish turn the corner at full speed. He grabbed his mother.

An unusual crowd had gathered at the bottom of the hill. Onlookers were encroaching into traffic, and passing cars were greeted with honks and insults. Along fifty metres of a flat stretch, about thirty vans with satellite dishes hung around outside Rabia's building. They were all there: various French television channels (TF1, LCI, i-Tele, BFM-TV), major national radio stations, even foreign media. It looked like the caravan of the Tour de France. Journalists had colonized both pavements and part of the road; they were doing live broadcasts as their cameramen all repeated the same panning shot from the correspondent to Rabia's shuttered windows on the third storey. Some policemen stationed at the end of the block checked the residents' papers and kept out the journalists.

Faced with this spectacle, Fouad decided it would be better to fetch Rabia's things later. He had to tug on his aunt's hand to make her follow them: she just stood there, gaping at this dreamlike scene. It was a feeling that she had never had before: that of being locked out of her own home.

She suddenly felt like going to speak to those journalists, to tell them that Krim had nothing to do with any of this, that he had been manipulated; to tell them about the time in custody, all night having to reply to questions while the police completely ignored her replies; to shout at them that her son had been stolen from her, that she could not discreetly enter his bedroom that evening to turn off the classical music that he listened to when falling asleep, and plant a kiss of forgiveness on his forehead: forgiveness for the weed, the missed appointments at the employment bureau, the petty crimes and all the other things she did not yet know about, all of them, everything, because she was his mother and mothers were there to forgive their sons, just like she-wolves were there to protect their cubs, even at the cost of their own lives.

'Let them take me, instead of him,' she murmured tearfully. 'They're not going to send him to prison. I'm not going to let them send my son to prison . . . I swear on my life I'm not letting them steal my son . . .'

She was about to run towards the first TV van, about to scream out her she-wolf despair. And she would have, had Fouad's hand not tightened firmly around her trembling wrist.

'What have we done to God?' she asked her nephew in a voice worn down by sorrow. 'What have we done to deserve this?'

4.

'You're full of shit,' the Rugby Player decided after having tapped, with his large index finger, the 'Esc' key on his computer. 'Hey! You listening to me? I said you're full of shit and it's starting to get on my nerves. So let's start again: you arrive in Paris at about nine-thirty in the morning, you go to see Nazir, you don't dare go home, you leave and you walk around the streets, then you come back, Nazir's no longer there, instead there's a red-haired guy with a goatee, he gives you a weapon and tells you to fire at Chaouch, otherwise some guy at the other end of the country is going to murder your mother. I think we can agree that your story sounds like a fairy tale, but what the hell. What did you get up to before you returned to the redhead's apartment?'

'Dunno.'

'You'd better stop screwing with us, boy. What the hell did you get up to during all that time?'

The Rugby Player stood up, walked around the room and began hitting the door harder and harder. A voice on the other side asked him what was happening. The Rugby Player replied, 'It's okay, it's okay.'

Krim wanted to turn around on his stool to see what his torturer was cooking up, but he found himself on the floor before he could even move. With a violent kick, the Rugby Player had sent the stool flying against the wall. Krim got up and clenched his fist. The Rugby Player towered over him, planted his emotionless face in front of Krim's and said in a sinister voice, 'Go on! Hit me! You fucking little pansy, that's what I'm waiting for. Go on! Show you've got some balls! *Come on* – prove you're a man!'

Krim stepped back. A face emerged from the depths of his consciousness: that of his sister, poor Luna who was always defying him, always teasing him. He wondered what she was doing now. However much he tried to gather his thoughts, he could summon no credible backdrop for the immense sadness that must have filled her when she discovered that her big brother had assassinated the president. Especially as Luna found Chaouch irresistible. Whenever their mother shouted that he was on TV, Luna would leap out of bed and run over to the screen. Chaouch was the only external phenomenon capable of pulling her away from texting.

'I didn't know,' Krim ventured timidly, almost as if to himself, 'I didn't know I was going to shoot Chaouch. He'd told me I had to practise my aim. I thought . . . I dunno what I thought . . .'

The Rugby Player returned to the laptop, but wrote nothing. With a gesture of his chin, he told Krim to sit down and continue. Krim retrieved the stool and recounted that he had spent hours shooting at tin cans, taking great care not to mention Fat Momo. When he stopped speaking, the Rugby Player gave him an inscrutable look.

'Is that all?'

'I didn't know it was Chaouch,' repeated Krim, and then, thinking of Luna, he added, 'I liked him, Chaouch.'

The Rugby Player shook his head ironically and started again to press on the 'Esc' button on the top left-hand corner of his keyboard with the regularity of a pile driver, all the more so as it had no effect on the transcript of the interrogation.

5.

At Granny's, Rachida was pacing the room. She and her older sister Ouarda were screaming at each other, though what they said was essentially the same thing: that it was a shame on the Nerrouche family, that they would never recover from this shame, that the sky had fallen in and that this catastrophe had two names: Rabia and Dounia.

The first outbreaks of bitterness had made Slim and Luna flee. Slim wanted to stay and argue, but Luna had been intent on leaving, and the rational part of the family did not manage to stop them. This rational part had ended up sitting down on the couch and falling silent, unable to rival the dizzying flow of words from the two furious women, who followed each other from the kitchen to the living room and back again, looking for something to do (coffee, tea, dusting, tidying) and giving up as soon as a new broadside of indignant remarks burst forth from their lips.

The night in custody had awoken the maniacal element in Rachida's manic-depressive psychosis. A neutral observer, seeing her face that afternoon but paying no attention to the content of her words, would perhaps have noticed the intense jubilation she exhibited at letting her demon stretch its legs.

Busying herself at a chest of drawers, Granny seemed uninterested in the scene her two daughters were making; she raised her eyebrows from time to time, when their logorrhoea exceeded the acceptable volume given that there were children present.

After digging up some old lollipops and sending the children to play video games in her bedroom, she took her place on the edge of the couch and stared at the photograph of her tall, blonde son Moussa, the genetic anomaly of the family. The picture of him leaning against a jeep in the Algerian desert had never left the bottom corner of the monumental framed photo of Mecca that could be found in all the Muslim interiors of France: the famous black cube of Kaaba surrounded by an ocean of worshippers in white robes.

Granny was as calm and collected as if she had prepared all her life for that night in detention. But for the others, it had been a waking nightmare.

'*Some wedding*,' an old uncle summarized in Kabyle, trying in vain to extricate himself from the armchair.

Leaning against the bathroom door, Kamelia had stopped listening to Rachida's tirades, but while the words themselves were deflected by her inattention, she could not protect herself against the effect of their poison.

She saw her cousin Raouf, the son of Idir and Ouarda, whose damp eyes, when he raised his head, expressed an incomprehensible and shameful fear.

Kamelia was all the more amazed as the arrogant Raouf would normally have cut off one of his toes rather than admit his helplessness, his weakness, or even his ignorance on any subject. Outside his field of expertise – extending halal catering to the wider public – he seemed to know enough about almost any subject to hold a conversation in a respectable way. Whenever he was found lacking, or whenever someone else explained the facts to him, he acquiesced by closing his eyes and saying, 'Ah yes, yes, I knew that, yes, of course.' Kamelia had never hit it off with him. He was like the anti-Fouad, which the malicious gossipers of the family turned to their advantage by establishing between the two successes of the family a comparison that was as cruel as it was unquestionable: Raouf boasted a lot and did little, while Fouad did a lot and never talked about it. Fame played the role of justice of the peace and came down firmly on the side of the actor, letting one believe – wrongly, as Fouad repeatedly said – that it never made a mistake and always crowned the deserving.

'What's wrong, Raouf?'

The young entrepreneur lifted his eyes to the ceiling, as if to dry them. He stared at the naked lightbulb and declared in a low voice, 'I spoke with Nazir on Saturday. On the phone.'

He wanted to give Kamelia the time to understand what that meant, but the following sentence was burning the walls of his throat and found its own way out:

'It's too dangerous, I've got to get the hell out of here.'

'But why? What are you talking about? Did he tell you things—'

'Can't talk about it,' he said, looking at the cracks between the old kitchen furniture. 'Anyway, what's the point of staying here?'

'What's the point?' asked Kamelia angrily. 'Well, we're not leaving poor Rabia and Luna all on their own!'

This cry from the heart contradicted so candidly the general spirit reigning in Granny's flat that Raouf did not even feel obligated to reply to it.

'Yeah. Well, do what you want.'

Kamelia heard four phantom words behind those he had spoken, as distinctly as if he had written them in red lipstick on the tiles above the sink: save your own skin.

Indeed, her parents did not wait for coffee to be served to announce that they were leaving Saint-Etienne, as had been originally planned. Raouf had taken a week off, a fact he took care not to remind anyone of when he claimed that he had to return to London urgently.

The eyes of those stuck in Saint-Etienne then turned towards Kamelia, who began to sob, remembering Krim, stoned in the community centre, speaking about that girl he loved like a little kid, like the kid he was: an awkward guy on the surface, but the shy, gentle and even euphoric little cousin when they had played 'Name That Tune' in Granny's bedroom, and he had joyfully crushed the competition.

6.

As soon as he had seen Maître Aribi's intervention on TV, Fouad called Szafran to assure him that he had never appointed Aribi as counsel. Krim must have done it, thinking of the only lawyer whose name he was likely to know. Aribi was often on TV: his sensational declarations had, for years, made him a regular on talk shows, where his shameless cunning and spectacular sense of self-promotion were loudly applauded.

'I don't want to be defended by someone like him,' explained Fouad. 'Under no circumstances. And then, is it legal to proclaim yourself lawyer for people who haven't even asked you? I thought lawyers weren't permitted to chase after clients . . .'

'You're right. It's against the code of ethics and could lead to disciplinary proceedings. Listen, I'm going to call him. You go get some rest.'

Maître Szafran asked his intern to find the number of Khaled Aribi. The intern, Amina, had been making an odd face ever since she learned that Szafran and Associates were going to mobilize all their resources to defend the people who tried to assassinate Chaouch.

Fouad found his mother in the kitchen. She stubbed out a cigarette, coughing. When he went over to kiss her on the temple, she drew slightly away.

'Where's Rabia?' asked Fouad, his head in the fridge.

'Look, honey, I've cooked some *briks*, if you want one. Rabia? She's sleeping in my bed upstairs with Luna. The poor things . . .'

Slim appeared in the doorway, his arms laden with groceries. He quickly put down the bags to catch his phone, which was vibrating.

'Shit, I missed her. It's Kenza. Fuck, she's called me three times.'

Fouad recovered the Gold MasterCard he had given his little

brother to do the shopping, and helped him to put the groceries away in the fridge and the cupboards.

Looking worried, Dounia remained standing in front of the open window. This house, where she had lived for two years, had been miraculously assigned to her by the social housing office of the Loire, even though she had no young children and a steady job. With her nursing assistant's salary, she could easily have paid rent without help, but Nazir had thought differently: it was perfectly normal, he said, that the state provides a home for the widow of a man who had sacrificed his health maintaining its roads.

The house in question, with its walls of pink plaster, was part of a subdivision not devoid of luxury, perched on one of the city's seven hills, and had a pretty hedge-lined lawn where Dounia had organized a barbecue the previous summer. Apart from the fact that she was an exhausting half-hour's walk from Rabia's flat, it had only one real defect: the thin and dilapidated building that blocked the view of the hill of Monteyraud, the same hill topped by the apartment complex where Dounia had brought up her children.

According to her neighbours – a couple of nice music-loving retirees – the city council had promised to raze this eyesore of a building to the ground a year before Dounia's arrival. In the meantime, it stood there like a provocation, even if on some mornings, when the sky was clear, you could see the rays of the rising sun pierce the broken windows of the lower floors and gently illuminate the lawn and walls.

As he was starting to eat lunch, Fouad received a phone call from Madame Caputo. Rabia's neighbour told him that two journalists had come to ask her questions at around ten that morning. Fouad put his hand to his neck.

'Did you speak to them, Madame Caputo?'

'No, no, my boy, don't worry: I'm not one to talk about people. But I wouldn't say the same about everyone on the block . . .'

Fouad had scarcely hung up when he saw Slim come back into the kitchen, his face deathly pale.

'I've just spoken to Kenza,' he announced, not daring to look up.

Fouad turned to his mother. And then to Slim.

'So? What's wrong?'

'Pfft . . . Well, that old cow never liked me.'

'Who, Slim?' asked Dounia. 'Who are you talking about?'

'Her mother! Kenza's mother! She wants to kick her out of the house if she doesn't divorce me. She said it's shameful, that our family is shameful, that the wedding was a catastrophe, and so on and so forth . . .'

The silence that followed made the young man's cheeks go bright red. He would probably have burst into tears if Fouad had not asked: 'And Kenza, what does she think?'

'She says we have to get our own flat. But we've got no money. It's . . . oh God, it's a real nightmare. But I'm going to figure it out, I swear.'

'Tell her to come here if it gets that bad,' Dounia whispered, taking one of the last cigarettes from her packet of thirty. 'Anyway, I always said this house was too big for Slim and me.'

'But where will she sleep?' asked Slim, suddenly alert.

'Listen, my love, she'll sleep with you, in your bedroom. Where else would she sleep? I'll sleep with Rab and Luna, and tonight we can put Fouad on the ground floor in the living room, if that doesn't bother him . . . Fouad? What do you think?'

'I'm happy to sleep on the couch.'

The deal was struck in this strange and suspended atmosphere, as if everything was easy, as if none of it mattered.

Slim noticed nothing; he ran and kissed his mother on the cheek, pulled out his phone and, unable to hide his enthusiasm, called his new wife, Kenza.

7.

Waldstein had ended up disobeying Nazir. After four U-turns on endless sections of highway to shake the 'pursuers' off the scent, he had stopped on an *Autobahnraststätte* and refused to set off again.

'You understand I have to be careful, Herr Waldstein?'

Nazir's voice had become unbearable.

'Listen, my job is to drive you. I'm your taxi, okay? I'm not here to go around in circles.'

'Yes, but think: we would both be in a difficult position if we were followed. The people on my trail are very powerful. They've probably already obtained the tapes of the video-surveillance cameras outside the bank's car park and, if they've got them, I don't see why they wouldn't also have the ones for the streets leading to the motorway. So they'll know which direction we've taken. That's why I asked you . . .'

Herr Waldstein drove off again.

Half an hour later, some warehouses appeared on the edge of the road: they were approaching the main city. After glancing mechanically into the wing mirror, Nazir stared at his driver until a drop of perspiration quivered on his temple.

'If you don't like dirty work, why did you accept this?'

'What dirty work? I'm driving you, that's all!'

'Ah, so why would you want it to be about anything else?'

Waldstein did not understand. Or he understood only too well.

Nazir raised his voice.

'I'm going to tell you what I think, Herr Waldstein. I think that since Zurich and despite the labyrinthine route I've forced you to take, we've been followed by three cars and two motorcycles. We've shaken off the lot of them, and now you're waiting for just one thing: to take your phone to the first toilet you can find to inform our pursuers of the place you've driven me to. Which, of course, will not happen . . .'

Waldstein did not react. The car left the motorway and entered the city. He suddenly put on his best smile.

'I could have slit your throat back then, if that had been my aim. I had you at my mercy. I had my razor and your throat was exposed . . .'

'You could have, yes.'

'I don't envy you. I don't know how much longer you'll manage to stay on the run, probably a good bit of time given the money you've got in that suitcase. But I bet you'll be the architect of your own downfall, imagining ghosts everywhere . . .'

Nazir thought for a moment and replied in a steady, almost detached voice, 'I am the ghost. You know Marx's phrase: a spectre is haunting Europe . . .'

'What spectre?' Herr Waldstein reacted swiftly. 'The spectre of terrorism? Of political assassination?'

Nazir said nothing. He had recognized the street where he had to go.

'Drive around the area before stopping,' he ordered his chauffeur.

'Why?'

'To be sure no one's watching us, for fuck's sake.'

After looping around twice, Nazir opened the glove box and searched it with both hands. He turned to Waldstein and asked him for his phone.

'Are you crazy? Why?'

The negotiation lasted less than a minute, and Nazir got out of the vehicle after stuffing his pistol in a jacket pocket.

8.

About fifteen German police cars were hiding in the Hermannsweg area. Commander Mansourd had taken his place in the spy van closest to the museum entrance. It was not exactly a doll museum, but a museum devoted to puppetry. An effigy of Pinocchio moved in the front window. The building had three floors, only the highest of which was not painted in the bright colours of the rest of the establishment.

Hiding in the back of the car, Mansourd watched the end of the street through binoculars. He suddenly gestured to his German counterpart, who muttered a few words into his walkie-talkie. A car that had twice gone around the block stopped a few metres from the museum entrance. A man got out of the passenger seat: tall and dark-haired, he was wearing a black suit and looked preoccupied. He was constantly looking behind him and lifting his hand to his cheeks, as if to stop his jaws trembling.

He stopped in front of the museum entrance and looked up at Pinocchio. He put a hand in his inside pocket. Mansourd put down his binoculars: anyway, he could only see him from the back. When the barrel of a gun appeared in the man's hand, the commander put on his bulletproof vest and asked his colleague to launch the operation.

'*Es ist unser Mann,*' he said in broken German.

The fifteen cars secretly surrounding the area started up and disgorged a flood of hooded, armed men around the suspect. The latter dropped his weapon and immediately put his hands up. Mansourd, who trained his gun on him, was the first to realize it was not Nazir. According to his papers, it was a young man of Turkish origin, whose plans were perhaps not honest but had nothing to do with the plot against Chaouch.

Mansourd threw his binoculars to the ground and looked up at Hamburg's grey and misty sky. He called Judge Wagner.

At the same moment, Nazir was leaving Bern, where he had just bought a new BlackBerry. As the car set off again on the road going east, he told Waldstein, 'They're going to look for me in Hamburg and I'll be in the Swiss Alps. And when they hunt for me in the Swiss Alps, you know where I'll be? Somewhere else! They can't pin me down. Do you understand now?'

And without waiting for the reaction of his exasperated chauffeur, he added, 'Yes, I told you, Herr Waldstein: a spectre is haunting Europe . . . and that spectre is me!'

7

THE HAIR STRAIGHTENER

1.

In the middle of the afternoon, Prosecutor Lamiel summoned all his deputies to study the files and make a list of priorities.

The issue of the imminent court summons took up most of the meeting: was it right to put on trial fourteen-year-old kids caught red-handed burning cars but who declared, when in custody, that they did it to express their disgust at the attack on the president-elect? The courts had to apply the penal policy of the government and Lamiel offered a phrase that left no ambiguity regarding the strict hierarchy of the institution of which he was one of the most eminent members.

'In this period of crisis, the courts are expected to play the game.'

At the end of the meeting, he spoke with his deputy prosecutor in charge of counterterrorism. The latter was not happy with the boss's level of involvement but he had no choice in the matter, nor the effrontery to show his displeasure.

A few moments later, Lamiel was pensively walking up and down the corridors of the Palais de Justice with his rolling gait, hands behind his back. His big head, inflated by hormones, nodded mechanically in reply to the greetings of judges and court clerks who crossed his path.

At the foot of the final staircase, the one leading to the Saint-Eloi gallery, he took a deep breath.

'Your Honour,' he said to Wagner two minutes later, opening the door to his chambers. 'I hope I'm not disturbing you.'

He turned to Alice, the court clerk, and signalled to Wagner that he would like to speak with him alone. On seeing Alice's belly, he gave an approving nod and almost asked for news of her pregnancy. But his anxiety won out over his politeness. Alice threw a light jacket over her shoulders and made for the door, escorted by the nervous smile of the head of the Paris courts.

'Henri, I'm here to convey to you the concern in high places regarding the Nerrouche family, and the fact that you have released them so quickly . . . In particular the brother of Nazir Nerrouche, this young actor who was involved with Jasmine Chaouch.'

Lamiel kept his hands behind his back; with his right arm, he pointed to one of the chairs facing the judge's desk.

'May I, Henri?'

'Listen, these concerns in high places distress me, but I needn't remind you that I am independent. Statutorily independent.'

'Of course not,' retorted the prosecutor. 'And if Nazir Nerrouche had been arrested by now, that would have put us in a position of strength. I'm simply afraid that you don't completely appreciate the gravity of the situation . . .'

Wagner closed his eyes and shook his head.

'What do you want, Jean-Yves? For me to describe in detail the make-up of the team watching Fouad Nerrouche? There are at least three covert vehicles mobilized, probably fifteen police officers in total watching his every move, reading all his texts and emails. If he goes out, he's followed: wherever he goes we know what he's doing. If he scratches his ear, you'll have at least three members of the ATSD give you a report specifying whether he used his index or his little finger . . .'

The prosecutor swallowed a burp and nodded gravely.

'Ah well, so be it! I hope you know what you're doing . . . And as for tomorrow at noon? I suppose we'll have to cancel our tennis match, but I'd like to invite you to lunch.'

Wagner wanted to decline the offer: tomorrow at noon he had to be ready for the hearings of the close family. But the prosecutor's large eyes pre-emptively insisted. Wagner sensed that they would not be having lunch alone.

'All right,' he conceded. 'Tomorrow at noon.'

'And what about the Turk in Hamburg? Any news?'

'Nothing, I fear. Commander Mansourd insists it was no coincidence, but his interrogation is not very conclusive for the moment . . .'

2.

And Mansourd was right to insist. As Nazir could not help boasting to his chauffeur, it had taken him just two phone calls to send that poor decoy to the abattoir.

'That's why I changed phones,' Nazir explained. 'By the time they discover the number that led the Turk to the museum, it'll be too late. I could have just changed the SIM card, but I couldn't resist their new model. Take a look at that,' he said with a look of admiration.

The car had been snaking for an hour along a valley whose borders were dotted with larches and rare berries. Summits sprinkled with eternal snow could be seen through the tinted windows. Nazir gave a series of increasingly bizarre directions to his driver while continuing to frantically scrutinize the wing mirror. Waldstein sped into a thick forest, so thick that he had to switch on the headlights to negotiate the tight bends. During a clearing in the pines, he noticed that Nazir was writing a long text message.

Waldstein was relieved when they finally emerged from this nerve-shredding road into a clear and almost open landscape, where the multicoloured pattern of the foliage burst with life, humanity. Indeed, it did not take them long to reach a ski resort where Nazir suggested they take a break.

'I suppose your stomach must be rumbling.'

Waldstein parked in the deserted car park outside an inn. Nazir did not take his eyes off him. On leaving the heated car, he was surprised by how cold it was. He asked Waldstein to open the boot and take out the metallic case.

'Frankly, don't you think you're overdoing it here?'

Nazir's only reply was a brief snigger. He lifted his jacket collar to protect his neck and marched triumphantly over to the parapet of the panoramic viewpoint. Chalets stretched out at his feet like so many abstract miniatures, surreal in the rawness of the fading daylight. There had been a brief storm an hour before: the wood panelling of the little houses shone brightly, as did the pearls of rainwater decorating the pine branches.

On the resort's blue-green hillsides, the cable cars seemed

to have only just stopped. Their stillness troubled Nazir, who turned and walked back towards the inn. Waldstein went immediately to the toilets, where he grumbled at being unable to urinate for so long. When he came out, he did not see Nazir at the entrance. He looked around to check that the car was still there and walked around the ground floor. The oak tables were lined up beneath a maze of suspended beams, quirky baskets and trinkets in the shape of snowflakes and little hearts. Waldstein was beginning to hyperventilate: Nazir was nowhere to be found.

He slumped into a chair in front of the entrance. His gaze swept the cupboards whose glass doors were covered with delicate lace curtains through which gleamed, as if in the dream of a small, greedy child, a treasure trove of jam, honey and all sorts of biscuits. The manager appeared. Waldstein asked him if he had, by any chance, seen a man, this tall, unshaven.

'Ah yes, sir,' replied the innkeeper. 'He drove off with a lady.'

Waldstein rushed over to his empty car. He quickly searched his pockets and noticed that he did not have his phone on him. He knew very well he would not find it there, but still ran over to the toilets. Back with the innkeeper, he asked what car Nazir had taken. The innkeeper pinched the top of his enormous nose and closed his eyes to think. He replied that it was a black 4×4.

'What make?'

'Ah, there I can't help you.'

Waldstein ran out in the direction of the car park, but he heard the innkeeper shout to him from the steps of his ridiculous establishment: 'But sir, what about the rib steak? I hope we haven't cooked it for nothing. He said you liked it very rare!'

3.

A place had been set for Bouzid on Dounia's kitchen table but after half an hour's wait and a dozen calls from Fouad to his uncle, Luna decided she was too hungry and everyone began to eat. Except Rabia, who, scarcely awake, picked at a few lentils and left the table on the pretext that she wanted to rest some more. A few moments later, she came back into the kitchen and asked Dounia if she could straighten her hair.

The question made everyone turn around, including Slim, who was the first to react.

'But Auntie, your hair's very nice like that!'

Rabia was staring into space, an anonymous zone around the foot of the table. She creased her chin and forced a smile.

'Yeah, but I want a little change.'

Her smile turned into a grimace, and Dounia agreed to straighten her hair after she had eaten. She hesitated for a moment over coffee, and Fouad understood that she was trying not to take out a cigarette, for she had smoked one just before coming to the table. Slim took a call from Kenza on his phone and explained to Fouad, a few moments later, that the situation with her mother had improved a little, but that she was very touched by the proposal he had made.

'That Mama made,' Fouad pointed out.

Slim claimed that it was a slip of the tongue and ensconced himself in the best armchair in the living room to watch the news. Beside him, Dounia and Rabia had got into position: Dounia on the couch, her legs apart to be able to work comfortably on Rabia's hair, who was sitting on the carpet at her feet.

The contact of the hair straightener with his aunt's scalp gave

Fouad an unpleasant impression of disaster, but, yet again, it was Luna who intervened.

'Mama, you're making a big mistake,' she said, biting into a red apple. 'All the French women envy your beautiful, curly hair and now you want to spoil it all? This is ridiculous.'

But Rabia's resolve was unshakeable.

Fouad went out to phone Jasmine. She did not reply. He was wondering what shape his walk through the city would take when he received a call from Uncle Bouzid. His uncle spoke in a very low voice, and sounded ill. He wanted to see Fouad all alone, preferably in a public place. Intrigued by these mysteries, Fouad suggested they meet in a bar in the centre. His uncle turned up a good quarter of an hour late and with his left cheek swollen.

'What's happened to you?' asked Fouad. 'Did the cops do that?'

'No, no,' retorted Bouzid in a rush of sincerity, before realizing he had just missed the ideal excuse.

'Who was it then?' Fouad insisted.

'No, it's nothing. Sorry I'm late,' dodged Bouzid, looking left to right as if already impatient that no bartender was coming over to serve him. 'It's harder and harder to park in this fucking city.'

'Uncle—'

'No,' said Bouzid angrily, 'it was just now, there, in the bus. You know there have been riots in Montreynaud? I'm going through there, on the bus, at noon exactly, at the end of my shift, and what do I see? Three kids trying to open a car with a crowbar! Some kids, twelve, thirteen years old, smashing everything. I stop the bus, I open the window and I ask them what they're doing. They tell me to go away. Well, you know me, I don't like being pushed around ... I get out of the bus, *zarma*, to frighten them.'

'And then?' asked Fouad, who could easily guess what had happened next.

'They jumped me! I swear to you, I don't know what's happening with this generation. We weren't like that. *Wallah*, we weren't like that. We did some silly things, I'm telling you, but ... I swear to God, these kids ... It's like they're possessed, *wallah*, they're right little *shetan*.'

Bouzid passed a hand over his bald pate and asked for news of Rabia. Fouad was beginning to explain to him that she had moved in with his mother, that things were not easy but that she was being supported, when Bouzid interrupted.

'Hang on a sec ...' His hand trembled with the effort of remembering his nephew's first name. '... Fouad, don't you want to move to the bar instead?'

Fouad took his grenadine and sat down at the bar next to his uncle, who placed his elbows on the counter and ordered a beer.

'Hey boss! Boss!' he shouted to the owner, snapping his fingers. 'And some peanuts as well,' before adding to Fouad in the same aggressive tone, 'For fuck's sake, the price of drinks in bars these days. And, what's more, you have to ask for peanuts, I swear to God ...'

Fouad observed his uncle, who had a whole ritual for eating peanuts: he took a small pile, shook them for a long time in his half-open fist, before swallowing them in one go by tipping his head back.

'What were we saying? Oh yeah, Rabia ... Pfft, I swear to you ... Well, I've always said, if you're too lax with the kids, they'll walk all over you. Krim, he no longer had a father, there are kids like that, you can't have a discussion with them, you just have to give them a good smack from time to time. Otherwise they walk all over you, those little *shetan* . . .'

Fouad could easily have contradicted Bouzid by reminding him that he had not had any children, and that things were always easier in theory than in practice. Fouad, angry with his uncle's anger, went as far as forming the words in his mouth but, at the last moment, repelled by their venomous taste, preferred to stare at the bottom of his empty glass and conclude emptily, 'Ah, yeah . . .'

'Well,' Bouzid continued, 'I think it's best Rab and Dounia stay out of things, you know. For a little while, so as not to cause a scandal. It's not that Granny or Rachida are angry with them, but . . .'

He shut up. All thought seemed to have abandoned him.

'Otherwise, everyone's left,' he went on mechanically before making a list: 'The ancients, Raouf, even Kamelia.'

'Even Kamelia?'

'Yeah,' confirmed Bouzid. 'There's only us.'

Us, the family of Saint-Etienne, understood Fouad.

Fouad had become a Parisian in the last few years, and it had taken just one weekend for him to return to the sticky weight of this 'us'.

'Only us,' he repeated so as not to lose his temper.

4.

After Fouad had left his uncle, it took him an hour of walking through the city in the sweltering heat to calm down. He took off his jacket as he passed the Design Centre and its metal monument overlooking the former factory. His steps soon led him to the North Hospital, where his mother no longer worked. She now worked at a retirement home in the south of the city.

He wondered if Zoulikha and Ferhat received regular visits and was preparing to check this for himself when he was seized by the splendour of the diaphanous light covering the line of hills behind the entire hospital complex. It was a light that did not exist in Paris, not even in Lyon, if truth be told: a light that seemed to belong solely to the South and which the wooded hills of Forez, not yet Mediterranean in their flora and vegetation, constituted a sort of foretaste.

Letting his gaze wander across the carpets of sunlit greenery behind the city, Fouad eventually thought for one moment that he had seen the same landscape when he travelled with Jasmine through northern Italy: the sensual clouds of light green foliage on the hillsides, the haughty poplar trees lining the crests, not burning as brightly as they would when summer returned.

Fouad walked back along the tramline. Without meaning to, and while trying to avoid focusing on Nazir – a mass of confused and heavy thoughts, as crushing as the thought of death – he found himself wandering along the hill of Saint-Christophe, where the private school stood that he, his brothers and most of his cousins had attended. The only exception had been Luna, who was studying sport at Tézenas-du-Montcel, and Krim, who had dropped out of the Eugène Sue Technical School.

The summit of this pine-covered hill had, for some years, been capped by the large mosque of Saint-Christophe. Fouad took the steps up to it. Two men in light-coloured jeans and leather jackets followed him at a distance. One of them murmured into his sleeve microphone, 'Well, look at that, he just happens to be going to the Saint-Christophe mosque . . .'

The wind, which had grown stronger in the past few hours, sent a slanting rain of variously coloured pollen – yellow, brown, red – that landed on the corners of the pavements, gathering in small, solid, yet volatile mounds.

The mosque was a pale pink concrete building, decorated with oriental ornaments and domes. But the most remarkable feature of this temple was its missing minaret. The infamous minaret whose construction had been debated, begun, called off, refused, and of which now there remained just a pile of stones drowsing in the dust. With or without a minaret, this building would have been the highest point in Saint-Etienne, as Fouad could see on turning towards the six other hills and the tiled roofs of a city that tried its best to exist, to proclaim its presence under an already setting sun that shone on billions of other roofs across the surface of the globe.

He sat on a wall in front of the deserted entrance and took out the sheet of paper he had brought with him to write a letter to Jasmine. They – this 'they' of which he knew nothing but in which he had chosen to believe so as to explain his beloved's silence – were surely watching his phone and his emails, but no one watched mailboxes any more. Besides, no one wrote letters any more.

The men observing Fouad from a distance could only see him from behind. Hidden behind the trunks of the pine trees that climbed towards the mosque, they explained to the captain in charge of the team, 'He's sitting down in front of the mosque.'

'What's he up to?'

'Looks like he's praying, Chief.'

Fouad soon left the hill of Saint-Christophe and posted his letter. He paid extra so it would arrive faster. The employee gave him a sorrowful smile, which Fouad had difficulty returning, all the more so as he could not understand the reason for it.

He could no longer feel his legs, and yet he walked for another hour, furiously, to escape the thought that Nazir had spent the last months walking in the same city, staying in the same house, enjoying the same light. Fouad's stroll led him to the Geoffroy-Guichard Stadium, and then along the football and rugby pitches of Etivallière. A highway encircled the sports complex, and its reassuring buzz interfered with the warm-up exercises of the teenagers who had come there without teammates, some of them without even a ball, but with the conviction that they would meet at least ten like-minded people and so be able to play a game.

The synthetic grass was brightened by the six o'clock sun. Fouad thought of Jasmine: he would have liked to have told her about these long expanses, the balls flying in the oblique sunlight, the bursts of laughter, the perfect passes, 'just like in practice', launched from the outside of the foot by amateurs who weren't even wearing football boots.

Suddenly, the chattiest kid in the group recognized him, one of those Sunday players who never play defence and get their only pleasure from scoring. The kid had the look of an artful dodger: streetwise, slightly snub-nosed, with mischievously retracted nostrils.

A crowd gathered around Fouad.

'*Wesh*, cousin! The man of the match! On the Koran and Mecca, respect . . .'

Fouad was wearing his old Camper trainers and a pair of

jeans he rolled up to the knees to turn into shorts. He played until the ball of the sun had disappeared behind the highway, leaving in its wake a kind of pink vapour. He stayed mostly in defence, but made some good passes, and even, thanks to the smooth talker who had begun to play left wing, treated them to a heroic break where he dribbled past four opposing players and scored by wrong-footing the goalkeeper.

5.

When he returned home by bus, totally exhausted, he saw that he had missed calls only from Yael and a few other friends. At the foot of the slope, he remembered Jasmine's voice, and a peculiar question she had asked him at the start of their relationship, last autumn:

'Do you prefer a very beautiful girl with an average voice or an average girl with a very beautiful voice?'

Fouad had understood that she considered herself average that day, and that there were objective reasons for that: her hooked nose, essentially, but also her canines, which were ever so slightly too long.

Back at his mother's, he went into the bedroom, where he hoped he would not have to awaken Luna. He knocked once on the half-open door: Luna was standing on her hands, her body lined up perfectly against the wall. Upside down, her cute teenage face seemed tense, sorrowful, and as hard as her abdominal muscles, the six-pack clearly revealed.

'Hey there, little monkey . . . *tutto bene?*'

Luna said yes with difficulty, before launching into a series of push-ups in this superhuman position. At the end of the fifth, she dropped down, her legs as straight as scissors.

'You know I was supposed to have a competition next month?' said the young girl, her mouth twisted in a sign of disappointment.

'Why do you say "supposed to have"?' asked Fouad, sitting on the edge of the bed. 'Aren't you going?'

'Well, no! How could I, with all this?'

Fouad stood up and took his little cousin's shoulders.

'Listen to me closely, my love: Krim's situation is not going to change if you go to the competition or not. On the other hand, if you don't go, it'll be as if . . . What I mean is that we mustn't change our habits. You have to treat these events with contempt, honey. You understand? You have to treat them with contempt, be stronger than them.'

Luna liked the expression but did not understand its exact meaning.

'And it's the most important competition of the season. If things go well . . .'

'Where is it?'

'At Bercy. I might – in fact I'm sure I'll be selected for France's junior team, if things go well. Can you believe it?' she asked, her sparkling eyes lighting up her whole face. 'The French team, the Olympic Games, the real top level! It'd be such a dream come true.'

'I'll come and see you,' declared Fouad. 'I promise.'

Luna looked up at her elder cousin. He had never been so unlike the actor from *Man of the Match*. Yet the fatigue, the two-day growth and the knitted brow made him almost as handsome as he was on TV.

Luna put her arm around him and did not hide the immense pride she felt at being part of the close entourage, the inner circle of her celebrity cousin. She wanted to write to her friends at the gym that there would be a VIP at the competition next month. But not one of them had called her since Sunday, not even Chelsea, and Luna had not yet dared go on Facebook to see what they thought about the attack – for fear that her 808 'friends' had mysteriously melted into air in the space of a few hours.

On the ground floor, Rabia was not sitting still. She insisted on cleaning everything from top to bottom before Dounia returned. When Luna sprayed water in the bathroom she had just polished, she got angry, saying, 'There you go: "I don't give a shit" in all its splendour!'

'But it's only water!' said Luna indignantly, stopping herself from adding the words 'you crazy bitch' that burned her lips.

Fouad wanted to speak to Rabia while she did the windows. He just took her hand and whispered a kind word in her ear. Her hair was now stiff but it was no thinner. If Fouad understood why she wanted to change her appearance, he was not admitting it.

He went to the bathroom to freshen up and saw the hair straightener on the lid of the linen basket. For the first time in his life, Fouad felt hatred for an object, the way you might hate the corner of the table where you hit your elbow or the edge of the wardrobe against which you stubbed your toe.

Of course, it was not the hair straightener that made Fouad or Rabia suffer, really. It was worse than that: the straightener had done something wrong by appearing to have done something good, by being designed to efface one of the most obvious stigmas of Africanness. For that, Fouad hated the object.

A phone call from his cousin Kamelia tore him from these

musings. Desperately tense, Fouad picked up immediately and waited for her to speak.

She began with the bad news that she had had to leave: she was returning to work tomorrow morning, the investigators had taken down everyone's numbers and addresses, but had authorized them to get on with their daily lives . . .

'But Fouad,' she said hurriedly, 'I'm coming back on Friday. I swear I don't want the aunties to think they're being abandoned.'

'I'm not the one you have to tell,' said Fouad impatiently. 'Call them.'

'I'm going to. I was going to do it anyway. I just wanted to tell you. I'm . . .'

On your side. That was what she wanted to say. But to do so would be to confess that a civil war had become inevitable among the Nerrouches, and certain words were like self-fulfilling prophecies once you uttered them: to speak of a break between Rabia and Dounia and the rest of the family was to make it happen.

Faced with Kamelia's panic, Fouad could not remain steadfast for long. He thanked her for the phone call and told her he found it very courageous of her to return to Saint-Etienne at the end of the week – exactly what she needed to hear, exactly what he found so repulsive to have to tell her.

6.

Slim had arranged to meet his big brother at the Taverne de Maître Kanter outside the railway station. He wanted to speak to him about something, and Fouad was surprised to see Kenza waiting with him at one of the three metal tables on the terrace. Fouad greeted Kenza warmly. His new sister-in-law was wearing a flower-patterned summer dress, topped by a black long-sleeved cardigan. With her protruding chin and girlish physique, Fouad had never found her attractive. But that evening – no doubt because of the heat and the fact that he had not seen Jasmine for almost three days – he found himself suppressing looks that she could have interpreted, if she were slightly paranoid, as ambiguous.

Slim was shifting in his chair, crossing and uncrossing his legs. Fouad asked him why he was so agitated. Slim put his hand on Kenza's and loudly took a deep breath.

'Fouad, we have to speak to you about something.'

Kenza was looking at the ashtray, painted by the slanting rays of sunset.

'I've been thinking about this for quite a while, and so: I've decided to stop my studies. Not to sit around and do nothing. On the contrary. Kenza and I, we've decided it would be a good idea to get a small apartment in Lyon. But to pay the rent, I've got to have a job, you know. I mean . . . We can pay the deposit with the money from the wedding, but we have to think of what comes after.'

'Slim,' said Fouad, passing a hand over his hairy neck.

He did not want to make Slim uncomfortable in front of Kenza – but Slim had obviously asked Kenza to be there so Fouad could not make him uncomfortable.

'We've thought about it, Fouad. We've even made a plan, a budget – see?'

He took a piece of paper from his jeans pocket.

'Wait, Slim, listen. This is not the right moment to think about this. And if . . . Let me say, I think it's a good idea that you're getting an apartment, but why would you give up your studies?'

'But Fouad, sociology will get me nowhere! Everybody says that. The faculty just produces unemployed people. There's no point in it. I'm not going to wait five years to become a teacher or I don't know what. And then the labour market . . .'

'Yes, but Slim, think a bit more about this: if you give up your studies, what are you going to make of your life, your life in the broadest sense? Even if you manage to find some casual work—'

'He's already found a job in a pizzeria,' interrupted Kenza in a porcelain voice. 'And I'm going to get a part-time job near the university.'

'Fine,' retorted Fouad. 'You'll have to do that as well, Slim. You stay at the university and you take a job on the side.'

Slim felt that even if his resolve was not crumbling, the debate was nonetheless undeniably escaping him. He bit his lip and raised a hand to his chin, as if to give himself the confidence of an adult, or at least of someone who has thought hard about his argument.

'But I'm sick of sociology, Fouad. It doesn't interest me. He was right, Chaouch: you have to do what you enjoy in life.'

'Ah well, then, now we're onto the real subject, the one we should have started with.'

'Fuck, but this is incredible,' said his little brother. 'Anyone would think you were Nazir, I swear. Why don't you support me instead of humiliating me?'

Fouad was aghast.

'You're crazy, Slim. How am I humiliating you? I'm just saying you're cheating: if you want to stop university because your exams went badly' – Slim suddenly uncrossed his legs, hearing the truth that his big brother had just guessed – '. . . but don't pretend that it's so you can take on responsibilities that . . .'

of those Roma who had been haunting the city centre for a few months, but Fouad had the impression of having seen him before. The Rom stood up, while giving Fouad a frightened and sorrowful stare.

Fouad realized the man was going to approach him, but he felt no fear: the Rom had the build of a sparrow and his shoulder looked as if it was dislocated.

He babbled something in his direction. Fouad bent down to ask him to repeat. In a voice midway between male and female, the Rom repeated, 'You Slim's brother. I know. I seen you is Slim's brother. He owes thousand euros me. If no give thousand euros me tomorrow afternoon no normal. Say this Slim.'

Fouad wanted to ask him for more details but the Rom was already moving away.

He did not dare follow him and stopped at an ATM where he discovered the exact sum that had been taken out with his card a little earlier in the day, Monday 7 May at 1.45 p.m., if he was to believe the statement: one thousand euros. He now remembered giving Slim his card so he could do some shopping, and Slim had given it back to him with a guilty look. But as he almost always looked that way, Fouad had not given it a second thought.

He finally decided, after a quarter of an hour's reflection – a quarter of an hour to stifle his anger, in truth – to tear up the statement and to speak about it with Slim only if his brother broached the subject first.

8.

The towels hanging on the bathroom door formed a sort of soft and protective padding: Rabia, who had taken refuge on the bidet, did not need to cover her ears to avoid hearing the sounds in the house. Nevertheless, she was massaging her temples, as if to erase the poisonous thoughts writhing around in her mind. Fouad's knock on the door soon made her fear a new disaster. She did not reply, awaiting the next round.

Fouad pressed his ear to the door and knocked three times, less and less loudly.

'Auntie, is everything all right?'

The gentler his tone, the more it penetrated Rabia's attention like an icy drizzle.

'Yes, yes, don't worry, my dear.'

She sensed that he had not left the corridor.

'You don't want to come out, Auntie?'

'We weren't prepared,' Rabia said in a slightly fuller voice. 'We were never prepared for this.'

Fouad hoped that she was not going to start crying. He delicately placed his hand on the closed door.

'No one's prepared for this, Auntie.'

The door suddenly opened upon Rabia's high and beautiful cheekbones. She had not been crying. Her eyes were stable, resolute, almost piercing.

'I'm going out for a walk,' she said, leading her nephew down the corridor.

'You're not going far?' asked Fouad anxiously. 'The lawyer says we have to avoid journalists, you know . . .'

'I must go to the cemetery,' Rabia explained.

'At Côte Chaude? No, no, Auntie, it's at the other end of town, it's really too far.'

'I need . . .'

As she did not dare speak about her husband's grave, Fouad got there before her.

'I understand, of course. But . . .'

'I can't, Fouad. I'm suffocating here . . . I'm just going out for a little walk,' she said decisively. 'I promise: I'll stay in the area.'

And so it was that the plainclothes policemen of the ATSD charged with trailing Rabia received a phone call from the team that was watching Fouad. Along the street that climbed towards the cemetery, two cars followed Fouad, who followed his aunt. At the head of this stretched-out procession was Rabia, whose dishevelled hair, less lively since it had been straightened, undulated gently in a wind that enveloped her in fleeting gusts.

At the top of the hill, an oblong park surrounded the walls of the cemetery. Not one of her dead was waiting for her there. Rabia shook, crossed her arms and proceeded through the dramatic half-darkness of that handful of minutes when evening had fallen but the streetlamps hadn't yet been lit.

At the foot of the square, on the pavement opposite, Fouad closely watched the hesitation of his aunt, who had stopped in front of the open gate of the cemetery, on the ochre gravel path that was lined with trees, concrete benches and unlit lamps.

A red dust rose towards the foliage of the plane trees, taking with it Rabia's shadow, the shadow that had led her to the top of the hill, but left her with her doubts and memories, her shame and despair.

She entered just as the bulbs of the streetlamps began to flicker in their metal casings. Gravestone followed gravestone: on the marble, Rabia noticed occasionally the senseless dates of the dead who had lived just ten years. There had been a time, just after the death of her husband, when anything served to put out the fire, notably the comparison with worse fates. Now that no longer worked, and this cemetery was irrefutable proof: you died alone, as alone as you had lived. The little mausoleums topped with 'Something Family' could do nothing about it, no more than the monumental cenotaphs and vaults adorned with floral decorations and lovingly crafted windows.

Lost among these foreign graves, Rabia would have liked to take in her arms those she called her dead. Her father, her husband. Krim, who had been torn from her, had now joined that list. It was intolerable. Rabia thought of a time when he could again be with her; but that future did not exist, and when she tried to imagine scenes of joy and reunion, they bolted immediately, like rabbits made of smoke.

At the end of the cemetery, linked to the rest by an untended path of paving stones, the Muslim section displayed the round tops of its gravestones. Rabia remembered a visit from Nazir, two years earlier – that is to say, three years after Zidan's death. He had led her to the cemetery of Côte Chaude and, while Rabia silently remembered the most beautiful episodes of her husband's life, Nazir had raged against the poverty and narrowness of the Muslim section. Rabia had explained to her nephew that sobriety was required for Muslim graves. But Nazir would hear nothing of this; he who was usually so self-controlled, and seemed never to be overcome by his feelings, had that day pointed a trembling finger at the marble sculptures of the Christian graves, and uttered a terrible sentence that Rabia remembered only now, in this other cemetery that looked like the end of the world:

'Even when they're dead, they make us feel unwanted . . .'

Rabia jumped and wheeled around: a shadow was walking up and down the path leading to the Muslim section.

Her legs became heavy. She suddenly felt in her hand

again the glass of grenadine she had dropped when Mouloud Benbaraka broke into her home.

The relief she felt on discovering that this shadow was only Fouad almost made her smile. Her nephew kissed her and led her far away from the ghosts.

'We loved elephants,' she suddenly said in a dreamy voice. 'Zidan and I ... we wanted to go to Africa one day, to see an elephant graveyard ...'

Fouad did not know what to say.

'We thought we'd grow old together,' Rabia went on, before adding, without looking at her nephew, and in a tone that was not even interrogative, 'You will stay, won't you? You won't abandon us as well, will you...?'

8

GENERATION CHAOUCH

1.

Stubble surrounded the tube-filled mouth of the president-elect. Some of the bandages had been removed and something surprising and terrible was happening: on recovering a human form, his face, because of these cheeks scattered with short hairs, was beginning to resemble that of someone else. Jasmine had never, since her early childhood, seen him let his beard grow longer than a day.

A nurse came in. Jasmine looked at her for a long time. Then, pointing at her father's motionless body, she asked, 'Can we speak to him?'

'You *must* speak to him!'

'But does he understand?'

An air of clinical compassion appeared in the nurse's eyes.

'Hm, well. We can't know for sure, Mademoiselle.'

The nurse left as Madame Chaouch entered the room.

'They've retrieved your phone, by the way. You'd left it at home, honey.'

Jasmine took it and rushed to see the list of missed calls. There was not a single one from Fouad.

'What have you done?' Jasmine asked.

'What has who done?'

'Why are there no calls from Fouad?'

'My love,' ventured Esther Chaouch, 'it's hard, but you've got to get it into your head that Fouad is perhaps, and I'm saying *perhaps* . . .' – she breathed in and closed her eyes – '. . . connected to everything that's happening to us . . .'

Jasmine felt her jaw crack as she stopped herself from hurling insults at her mother.

'You should go home, Jasmine.'

Esther was trying to stay calm but the emotion of her previous conversation with Vogel and Habib showed on her face. Jasmine had imagined that the backroom manoeuvrings were turning against her father. No one told her anything, but it was probable that Françoise Brisseau, who had come second in the Socialist presidential primaries, was in the process of becoming the new leader of the Socialist Party.

In the struggle between the supporters of Chaouch and those who had decided that he would not wake up, Esther had gone to the front lines. And Jasmine was not reassured by the idea that her mother would throw herself body and soul into this fight. She was a university professor, not a politician: she risked being gobbled up by those piranhas who considered her to be a false First Lady while still offering the hypocritical respect due an almost-widow.

Jasmine crossed the corridor, which hummed with hushed telephone conversations. In the cobblestoned courtyard, she was astonished to see Valérie Simonetti emerge from a grey car. She was wearing a drab trouser suit. It was the first time Jasmine had seen her like that: without her earpiece, and without those glances to right and left. She seemed at a loose end.

So many contradictory emotions mixed in the 'First Daughter's' head that she remained motionless on the steps.

'Mademoiselle Chaouch—' began Valérie Simonetti.

'Valérie,' Jasmine said, stopping her with a wave of the hand. 'Are you coming to see my father? He's upstairs. I heard you've been suspended, and that . . . we can do nothing about it. But . . . I want to tell you that I don't find any of this normal.'

'Mademoiselle, I—'

But, yet again, Jasmine stopped her and gave a smile that was worth more than any words of forgiveness. However, one last thing happened on the suddenly crowded steps of the building at Val-de-Grâce. Though Valérie Simonetti was standing on the second-lowest step, she was still a foot taller than Jasmine standing on the highest one. Jasmine saw a shadow pass over the cerulean eyes of the bodyguard, who saw someone appear in the background, in the doorway.

Jasmine swung around: there was no one suspicious, no one whose presence would have justified such a wary look. Only Aurélien Couteaux stood behind her – the youngest of her father's security officers, who had been spared investigation by Internal Affairs and who had been assigned to help guard Jasmine, whose every habit he knew and with whom she had always said she had no problem.

2.

There had been, during the campaign, a big scene involving Chaouch and his daughter, who could not stand being subjected to even the most discreet protection. She'd had to resign herself to it but she made no secret of her hatred for these elite cops who followed her everywhere she went: to the café, to the Opera, jogging along the Canal Saint-Martin, riding a rented bicycle to Fouad's apartment on the place d'Aligre in the 12th arrondissement. The giants in dark suits had spoiled some of her sweetest moments with Fouad. Couteaux, however, thanks to his youth, his relaxed style, and a certain shyness and humanity in his eyes, could pass for a slightly clingy friend.

He was sitting next to her on the back seat while the car drove up rue Saint-Jacques. Jasmine took a long look at his sharp-nosed face outlined against the mauve and violet sky of dusk.

'What about you?' she asked him abruptly. 'Do you think he'll wake up?'

Couteaux took out his earpiece and turned to Jasmine, though he didn't actually look her in the eyes. Jasmine suddenly had the intuition that what she took for shyness was a simple technique taught in training: never look in the eyes of the person you are paid to protect with your own body, in case a bullet is fired in his or her direction.

Couteaux replied in an anonymous voice, 'Yes, yes, of course, Mademoiselle.'

And, as if conscious of how inadequate his words were, he added softly, after having glanced into the left wing mirror, 'You know, a lot of people are praying for him.'

Jasmine too wanted to pray for him. But she did not believe in God. She also wanted to call Fouad. But she couldn't do that either, persuaded as she was, after having noted her mother's unease when she handed back the mobile phone, that she had been put under surveillance and that the policemen in headphones were just waiting for the moment when she would give in: scroll down to the letter F in her address book and recount intimate things to her lover, innocent things that their suspicious brains would seek to use against him . . .

The car took an unusual route: a crowd had gathered at the bottom of the Canal Saint-Martin, where Jasmine's apartment was located. Since the tragedy, she had insisted on returning home instead of accepting her mother's invitation, repeated ten times a day, to come and stay in their second home in the Yvelines. 'You have to maintain,' Jasmine systematically replied, 'the illusion that life goes on.'

When she was finally back home, she slumped onto the sofa and turned on the TV. The news was starting on Channel 2. She switched between channels and chanced upon a new episode of *Man of the Match*. She was unable to turn her eyes from the screen, knowing that no more than a minute could pass without her beloved appearing. The wait was longer than expected, and Jasmine began to wonder if it was even conceivable that his character had been written out because of the attack, when at last he appeared with his open face, his eyes that creased almost to slits when he smiled, his vigorous neck, and his full and gentle voice.

Jasmine turned up the sound and took out her iPhone.

'But why is *he* not calling me?'

She scrolled down as far as 'Fouad'. Remembering the day when they had met, on the terrace of a café near Pigalle. Fouad in his red-checked lumberjack shirt, basking in the sun while glancing over discreetly at her. Jasmine was arguing with Christophe Vogel, the son of her father's right-hand man, whom she had been seeing for two months and who accused her of being too unadventurous. That day, she was wearing dark slim-fit jeans, ankle boots and a long-sleeved grey top, which hugged her nicely curved chest. Christophe, sitting on a stool at their high table, tried desperately to whisper – and ended up making more noise than if he had spoken normally.

The way Fouad had described this scene to her was not at all kind towards Jasmine: he had told her she spent all her time wriggling, hands on hips. From time to time, her face lit up, but even then, even in those smiles, her freshness came across as a slightly bourgeois sophistication.

'Bourgeois?' asked Jasmine indignantly.

They had already been going out for two months at that moment.

'Let's say a bit polite. Forced, you know.'

Fouad did not want to hurt her, but instead of going back on what he had said, he remained faithful to the profound sincerity of his nature, and expressed his impression more fully.

'That's how it seemed to me: like a fake casualness. The way you moved, it was like you were acting more casual than you felt. Like all those posh girls, you didn't look natural, that's all. And then afterwards . . . I saw.'

But in fact, he had 'seen' well beforehand, right from the first contact. As soon as Christophe had left in a fury and Jasmine had come over to Fouad's table, a smile in the corner of her lips, asking him simply, leaning her head sideways, 'Rony?'

She really was waiting for 'Rony' in Pigalle, a journalist who worked for a music magazine and whom she had never seen before. Fouad had understood this, and, since he was in a mischievous mood that day, he had replied with a look of being falsely surprised but truly charmed, showing himself as cheerful and warm as if they had always known each other.

'Yes, that's me.'

'Rony, from *In Tune* magazine? I'm Jasmine Chaouch . . . for the interview?'

'Yes, yes, I've been expecting you.'

And Jasmine had believed this for at least twenty minutes, letting herself be asked questions on Baroque music by an imposter with whom she was to end up spending the next two hours and the following six months.

Jasmine suddenly interrupted her flow of memories. Behind one of the plane trees hiding the canal from view, she thought she caught sight of a candle's flame. A murmur now rose from the street. She opened the window and heard admiring exclamations. Looking through a different window, she noticed that it was not one candle but a flotilla of candles, dozens, hundreds of candles that floated down the canal, held afloat on red lifebuoys.

The vision of these flames in the soft evening air brought tears to her eyes.

There was almost no wind, not the slightest gust to trouble the foliage of the trees, and the candles, thousands of them in fact, covered the entire surface of the canal, for dozens of metres, surrounded by a procession of onlookers on each bank, who Jasmine finally saw were also carrying candles and cigarette lighters, some of whom – no doubt those who had organized this demonstration – wore white t-shirts bearing her father's face.

3.

The images went all around the world. They were seen on CNN, CCTV and Al-Jazeera, as well as on the Russian, British and Brazilian channels. They were presented as an unexpected counterpoint to the urban violence: the candle flames versus the flames of Molotov cocktails. For an entire evening, it seemed that France had truly become the media centre of the world: its president-elect in a coma, its people marching to keep him from sinking into the beyond.

In Saint-Etienne, Fouad saw a young woman on LCI, in a t-shirt bearing the face of Chaouch and the words 'GENERATION CHAOUCH', who was being interviewed on the meaning and origins of this demonstration. She explained, with big doe eyes, that it had nothing to do with the Socialist Party, even if some people who had taken part in the campaign – including her – were present. The idea of the procession had spread spontaneously on social media. A few dozen people had gathered at the start, but word of mouth had worked very quickly. Still more people were expected: all Parisians had been called on to show their support for Chaouch and his family. 'Come along, everyone!' she concluded with an ardent but ever-so-slightly contrived look.

Fouad put down the remote and ran upstairs. He threw the doors wide open and encouraged everyone to join him in the living room.

When they came downstairs, Slim and Luna were dumb-founded by the images on TV. Dounia and Rabia, who had been listening to old songs in the other bedroom, followed and were equally affected. Fouad put his arm around Rabia's shoulder and smiled sadly as he watched the screen. He hoped the vision of these thousands of candles would give his aunt some solace, but this was not the case. After having taken the remote and flipped through the international channels, she suddenly felt desolate and began to sob.

'It'll be okay,' Fouad reassured her, pressing her head against his chest. 'Things are going to work out, you'll see.'

Rabia nodded and let ten seconds pass before protesting, 'But how will it be okay? What on earth are you talking about? Seriously, tell me: what do you mean when you say it's going to work out? Tell me!'

Dounia gestured to Slim and Luna to return upstairs. Fouad tried to comfort Rabia but her whole appearance seemed to have changed since her hair had been straightened: she was no longer going to be pushed around.

'Why don't I have the right to call my son?' she screamed. Silence fell like a curtain around her. 'How is this possible? What right do they have to stop me calling my son?'

'Szafran thinks you'll surely be able to call him in a couple of days. After they've finished questioning him . . .'

Rabia stood there gaping with outrage. Her face was ravaged by tears.

'Two days, and after that what are they going to tell me? Ten days? Two months? No, I don't care, I want to phone him right now. Fouad, *raichek* Fouad, get me the number of the inspector, the *rhla*, the one who questioned us.'

'There's no point, Auntie, there's no point in—'

'Fouad, you know what she said to me?'

'Who? Who are you talking about, Auntie?'

'Annie! The woman whose children I look after. When I came back from the cemetery, I called to ask her . . . to ask her how she was, how the kids were. She told me: there's no point in bothering about it, because they're no longer going to need me. You know what she said? You know what that bitch said? That she and Jean-Michel, they've brought the kids' grandmother to the house, and as she's got nothing to do, *zarma*, she insists on looking after the kids herself! Can you believe it? I heard the kids crying in the background, saying "Rabia, Rabia". I can't even . . . I can't even see them one last time . . .'

Dounia came back into the room and also put a hand on Rabia's shoulder. But it was too much for Rabia, all this concern, like some vain reminder that light had once existed in her life. Instead of exploding into sobs, she dropped to the floor, slowly, dramatically, crying silent tears that came in regular bursts, from a seemingly never-ending source.

'Cry, cry, my love.'

Dounia was caressing Rabia's head, holding back her own tears and encouraging her sister's. She knew how to handle the situation. But Fouad did not and, for the first time, he cracked and began to cry: faced with the immensity of his favourite aunt's distress but also, perhaps, out of hope, the crazy hope awoken in him by the image of that flotilla dappled with flames and illusions.

4.

From the window of his cousin's studio flat in Ivry, Fat Momo had a panoramic view of the capital, its majestic tower blocks and its roofs glittering with gold and silver. Despite the stress that prevented him from going out and eating several baskets of chips with Djinn, Fat Momo felt privileged to be able to look through his binoculars at the Sacré-Coeur and the Montparnasse Tower.

Granted, the monuments were far away, but at least they were there. And, for the 'small' boy from Saint-Etienne, who had never travelled further than the Gerland Stadium (and then only to beat up some Lyon football fans), the complaints of inhabitants of the Paris suburbs seemed like baseless whining: how could you complain, with a view like this? At no moment did the thought occur to him that the capital gleaming with glamour and so magnificently close was, in reality, further away from where he now stood on the wrong side of the Paris ring road than from the tranquil and boring banks of his native river Loire.

Of course, Djinn was there to remind him of this.

'What's the point, *zarma*, of seeing the Eiffel Tower from the window if, when you want to see it for real, the cops stop you ten times in a row?'

Since the day after Fat Momo's arrival, Djinn had found himself getting angry merely at the sight of his fat provincial cousin standing in front of this bay window.

'*Wesh*, Momo, come inside. I've gotta talk to you about something.'

As a good 'Parisian', Djinn always had something on the go. Some mysterious shopping to do, an urgent favour. He said 'Greek sandwich' instead of 'kebab' and talked of 'doing a mouff' to suggest going to hang out on the rue Mouffetard. Fat Momo was very impressed by him. Djinn also had his little business in addition to dealing weed: jeans he bought at factory prices from a wholesaler 'colleague', and which he resold on Facebook. At just eighteen, he could already pay for his own flat, as well as a scooter and the latest iPhone. There was always some Coke in the fridge, but nothing else: in the evening, he brought back a Greek sandwich or McDonald's. Every evening. He was living the high life, was cousin Djinn. You just had to see his Lacoste polo shirts and his bottles of Hugo Boss aftershave. And then there was his personal consumption: they weren't meagre bars of bad hash, but beautiful and voluminous bags of Amnesia – Krim's favourite kind of weed.

Krim became the subject of their conversation when Fat Momo joined him in the kitchen, away from the suspicious looks of Paris and the high-powered beacon on the Eiffel Tower.

'You want to see what your mate's done? Turn on the TV . . .'

Fat Momo looked for the remote, Djinn got impatient and pressed the button at the side of the flatscreen television.

All the channels had been interrupted and were now showing, from different angles, the Canal Saint-Martin covered in candles. The image was both spectacular and comforting. After a few minutes, Fat Momo understood that it was an homage to Chaouch, a march to encourage him back to consciousness. Standing there, mouth agape, he would have liked to communicate to his cousin the very peculiar feeling that had suddenly taken hold of him, a strange and slightly hysterical joy at this mixture of beauty and goodness – but Djinn was smiling sardonically and shaking his head in condemnation.

His phone vibrated, and his face darkened.

'I've got to go. I'll come back tomorrow. Don't do anything silly, okay?'

Fat Momo changed the channel and listened, without understanding it all, to a debate between experts on *The France that Voted for Chaouch*. Women and young people had voted massively for him, as had – 'the biggest surprise of the poll', said one of the guests – a large section of the working class, who had abandoned the extremes, unpersuaded by the right's violent attacks on the Socialist Party candidate's elitism.

Geographically, Chaouch had conquered the West and the North of the country, the eastern half of Paris and, of course, the restive suburbs, about which the two specialists on electoral mapping could not manage to agree: one claimed that the registration of immigrant children from the infamous 'third generation' had constituted a massive and decisive movement in the election result, while the other argued to the contrary. Fat Momo would have liked to believe the first expert, but he looked very severe and resembled his old maths teacher. The other one was round, bearded and sympathetic: he considered that the phenomenon of the suburban vote was interesting but marginal. Fat Momo concluded that he had been right not to vote, that it would not have changed Chaouch's victory, or, at least, that he had not prevented it.

'Phew,' he sighed.

At that moment, he had completely forgotten that it was his best friend who had fired on Chaouch. The last time Krim had spoken to him – in the bushes around the gym – it was to ask if he was going to vote. He had replied, stupidly, 'Vote for what?' Words that now made him feel ashamed while the show's presenter, in a voiceover on the candles of the Canal Saint-Martin, sang the praises of the nation's youth who had resolutely chosen their candidate, and who deserved, today more than any other day, the nickname 'Generation Chaouch'.

5.

In his office, Montesquiou was looking at his own smooth face smiling out from a dozen framed vignettes: next to President Noyer, Bill Gates, Tony Blair, the famous fictional cop Jack Bauer (actually Kiefer Sutherland) and obscure European Ministers of the Interior whose names even the experts couldn't keep straight. This display of famous encounters was not unusual. What was unusual was another photo, stuck to the back of his safe door, which his visitors were therefore not supposed to see, but which was glimpsed briefly by the IT engineer who came to the young chief of staff's office that evening.

'What's this photo?' the technician could not help asking.

The picture showed Chaouch at the platform, covered in sweat, ecstatic, as he made that famous speech between the two rounds of the Socialist primary. In the first round, he had come in second, to general surprise, and many people believed that his speech to French youth – so strange, impassioned and unusual to hear from the mouth of a politician – had been the throw of the dice that truly launched his unstoppable rise. Montesquiou had been in front of his TV set that evening: three days before the second round that would crown this virtually unknown member of the European Parliament as candidate for the main opposition party, Vermorel's right-hand man had understood that, for his camp, the Angel of Death had taken on the unexpected features of an Arab with an actor's physique and a warm voice, a man who gave his all to the galvanized crowd.

Montesquiou never wanted to forget the image of the man who might cause him to leave this office, this ministry and his privileges. That photo of Chaouch was his own *memento mori*: remember that your padded armchair is an ejector seat. Although he said nothing of this to the engineer from the CDII who had come discreetly to bring him a dozen annotated pages, analyed with red felt pen and at the top of which were stamped the words 'Top Secret'.

'That's all the messages from the last four months?' asked Montesquiou with a hint of annoyance.

'All of them,' replied the computer technician in a hushed voice, 'including those he deleted.'

'I'm impressed.'

It took him only half an hour to digest the comments in the margins. He finished reading them in the car that drove him to the ATSD.

When he went through the headquarters of Levallois-Perret, no one paid him any attention, and certain underlings, embarrassed to recognize him at the wrong moment, greeted him awkwardly.

Captain Tellier nodded deferentially but with a perplexed frown. That Krim's interrogation could interest the Ministry of the Interior he understood, but one visit per day from the minister's deputy chief of staff? That was too much. With a deceitful look, Montesquiou asked, 'Are you managing to make him talk, Captain?'

Tellier replied that he was 'chewing' a bit, in other words, the interrogation was not eliciting much information.

'But I have to say he doesn't seem to know very much . . .'

'Captain, I would like to speak with him alone for a few moments.'

Tellier did not hide his discontent, but he could hardly refuse. Montesquiou had the power, in one phone call, to have him moved to the security department in Rillieux-la-Pape.

'Would you prefer me to be present or . . .'

'No, I would prefer you to give me a cigarette,' Montesquiou replied brusquely without even looking at the captain.

Tellier had stopped smoking two months earlier. He asked for one from a colleague and handed it to their powerful boss.

When Montesquiou entered, his first gesture was to turn off the webcam and lean his walking stick against the desk where the computer sat.

'Do you smoke?'

Krim did not reply. He had scarcely the strength to frown and show all these cops how much he hated them. But ever since he started smoking, he had never gone twenty-four hours without a cigarette; he remembered having smoked one before seeing the red-haired guy. And he even remembered stubbing it out when there were at least four drags on it left. When he thought about those four casually sacrificed drags, it choked him even more than his physical craving.

'All right, you don't want to smoke, you don't want to reply, so I'll do the talking. Put it this way, whether you speak to the cops or not, you are going to be sent to prison. I think you have worked that out yourself. But after some time, tomorrow or the day after tomorrow, the captain is going to make you a sort of offer: if you spill the beans, perhaps he'll be able to speak to the judge, to find some mitigating circumstances for you. All that stuff you've been constantly repeating since yesterday: I have been manipulated, etc., etc.'

Krim was horrified by this guy's voice. It was the voice of someone for whom nothing had any real importance. It reminded him of Nazir.

'And when he offers you that, you can be sure he is lying. He is just a police captain. He can always speak to the judge, but that will change nothing.'

'So then, what?' interrupted Krim, more to stop the feeling of being invaded by this unhealthy voice than because he really had anything to say. 'It's best I keep my mouth shut, isn't it?'

'You have understood perfectly.'

Krim did not understand anything.

'Now I am going to speak to you about myself. You still don't want to smoke?'

Krim moved his chin very weakly. Montesquiou offered him the cigarette.

'And how do I light it?'

'I will give you the lighter once you have listened to everything I have to say.'

6.

'Well then. My name is Pierre-Jean de Montesquiou and I am the chief of staff of Madame Vermorel, the Minister of the Interior. All those cops who have questioned you? All their bosses? I order those guys around. They hate me: I am twenty-nine years of age, I went to an elite school to become a top civil servant and for them I am the plague, the devil: a pretentious politician who has never held a gun in his life and who can ruin their career in three minutes. Because I see the minister every day, you understand, I whisper words in her ear, and she listens to me very carefully, Vermorel does. Everything I say. So these guys, and I'm talking about the top cops, you know, they hate me, but there are some who hate me even more: those are the judges. The judges, and I'm not going to lie to you, are more difficult to hurt: they have their own office – the Ministry of Justice – and they hate taking orders. But in the gravest situations like this one, they don't have a choice. What you did by shooting Chaouch was to provoke a crisis bigger than anything you could ever imagine.'

'But I—'

'No, no, listen to me, I know that you were forced to do it by Nazir. I know exactly what happened. And I am going to tell you a secret: I know Nazir very well. I have been watching him for some time. I was tapping his phones. I've read your text conversations with him, for example . . .'

Krim was stunned into silence, so stunned that his fingers ended up dropping the cigarette.

He was about to lean down to pick it up when Montesquiou's voice started off again and prevented him doing so by the sheer strength of its volume.

'So, now, it is very simple: there is one small thing that bothers me. It is nothing, you will see, just a short message. A text written in Italian where he arranges to meet in "G" on Thursday 10 May. Does that ring a bell? A text in Italian, that shouldn't be hard to remember, it's not like you've received hundreds of them . . .'

'A text in Italian? Uh no, I dunno . . .'

'Listen, I have something those guys who scream at you do not. I know who Nazir is. And I understand completely that you have let yourself be influenced by him, and I am telling you what I think.' He placed a long, fine hand on his own chest. 'It would hurt me greatly if you alone paid for what he has done. What is going to happen now is that he will get out of this and you will be singled out as the only culprit. The truth is that they do not care, the people who are going to put you in the slammer. What they need is a sexy culprit, a good story to serve up to the press. A young thug from the suburbs, a third-generation immigrant, a total dropout, all that kind of shit. What's more, he's a little bit crazy, he listens to classical music while smoking joints. He wants people to know who he is, so he shoots the next president. Well, believe me, Krim, there are not two people in this country who can stop that from happening. There is only one person and that person is standing in front of you right now.'

Montesquiou took the lighter from his pocket and made an immobile flame appear beneath Krim's chin. Krim picked up the cigarette with his free hand and breathed in the first puff, which was so pleasant that his head began to spin.

'So what do I have to do?'

'This text in Italian: why does he arrange to meet in "G"? There was another one in Italian, just before. "*Como stai, babbo?*" And after that one, "G". Try to remember.'

'Ah, no, those were texts he sent me by mistake. He told me to delete them, but there were some I forgot to delete . . .'

Montesquiou saw that Krim was trying to remember but that the stress was preventing him from concentrating.

'All right,' he finally decided, 'think again about Nazir, think again about those texts, and I am sure that in a moment you will remember something. I don't know, a place in a foreign country he spoke about all the time, some strange people he had to meet, a city . . . And when you remember something, say nothing to the little cops, who can do nothing for you. Keep it in a corner of your brain and wait for me to come back. Okay?'

For the first time, Krim felt he was not being looked at by Montesquiou like a specimen of some inferior life-form.

He seized his courage in both hands and asked, 'Is Chaouch dead or not? They say he is but I don't believe them . . . those bastards, they just want to make me *khalai* . . .'

Montesquiou observed him with amusement.

'And what does that mean: "*khalai*"?'

'That means scared,' replied Krim, returning the elite civil servant's gaze.

The strangely dormant shape of his eyes contrasted with their icy blue; nor were they pulled upward in a nasty or ironic manner. It even seemed that just one detail would have sufficed to make that cruel gaze morph into its exact opposite: gentle and melancholy.

But this detail was invisible, or at least impossible to identify. And Montesquiou leaned on his walking stick and left without informing Krim of the state of health of his illustrious victim.

7.

Fleur, the young woman now driving Nazir, had almost the same eyes as the minister's deputy chief of staff. And in her, too, the melancholy and gentleness inherent in her features had been dispelled by life's adventures. Except that, for one thing, it was not political cynicism that lit up Fleur's eyes, but rather a sort of perpetual panic; and, for another, their equally arctic blue had been hidden for some months by a pair of green contact lenses that Nazir had given her as a present and which he considered it a point of loyalty that she replace, every week, with a fresh pair.

To begin with, Fleur hadn't understood this obsession of the one she called the love of her life. Nazir had explained himself but in a confusing way: he said he never saw her look more beautiful than when she was asleep, and green eyes produced better than blue ones the illusion of that sleepiness.

One evening, in Zurich, he had confessed to her that his girlfriends had all been more or less the same girl: ersatz Fleurs – young, sleepwalking creatures, with open mouths, sulky, pouting lips, a fine white neck wrapped in scarves and neckerchiefs in tones of pale pink to accentuate the aquatic green of those eyes that remained in the land of dreams.

At nearly twenty-one, Fleur now corresponded only very imperfectly to this fantasy of which Nazir claimed she was the ultimate paragon. Exile in this isolated village in the Swiss Alps had made her robust. Her neck and her shoulders had lost their romantic curves, her palms had become square, her forearms had hardened and her sulky lips had become badly chapped.

Besides, she had changed the colour of her hair twenty times since puberty: from mahogany to pink with violet streaks, alternated with browns that were each more disastrous than the last. It was only on exiling herself in Switzerland six months earlier that she had resigned herself to rediscovering her ash blonde origins. But so as not to look like the well-brought-up girl she had been until the age of fifteen, every aspect of whom she abhorred – from the way she held her head to the way she sat down in a chair – she meticulously neglected her hair. Tied up with an ugly fuchsia bow, it fell in a vulgar ponytail on the headrest of the driver's seat. Not to mention the fact that, as Nazir blurted out in an uncontrollable fit of irascibility, it *smelled*.

'For fuck's sake,' commented Fleur, 'we haven't seen each other for two months and this is the way you treat me?'

'Well, what did you expect? That I was going to join you in the hideout and we were going to make passionate love amidst candles and roses?'

He spent his time turning around to check that no one was following them on this mountain road. But the night was veiled by thick fog: when the 4×4 veered round a hairpin bend, Nazir would never have been able to make out the gleam of enemy headlights.

Fleur wiped the corner of her eyelids and opened her mouth so as not to cry or throw up.

Nazir returned to his close examination of a road map. The faint blue light of his BlackBerry forced him to place the folded sheet just under his nose. Fleur looked upward and turned on the small bulb by the rear-view mirror. Nazir immediately turned it off. To control the rage that was taking hold of him, he closed his eyes and forced his lips into a broad, fixed smile. He'd noticed that Fleur had put on her best clothes for their reunion: she had chosen the most beautiful flower-patterned dress and her faded blue-grey Converse sneakers. Nazir banished the mental image of his young girlfriend receiving his text and rushing to reply, dropping whatever she had been doing.

'Fleur, I'm sorry,' he said, putting a hand on her chafed knee. 'It's the stress of . . . Waldstein, the guy who drove me here. I'm sure he was sending them our coordinates, maybe just with the GPS. I couldn't take any more risks. Listen, I know it's cost you, all these months preparing the hideout, and then . . . the loneliness . . . the impossibility of us seeing each other . . .'

'It was hell.'

'I know. I know what you've been through. But the hardest thing—'

'The hardest thing is that I couldn't see you! I couldn't call you!'

'They were watching me, Fleur. I didn't have any choice. They were listening to all my phones at the end. Even the one I used to speak to my . . . mother.'

'Yes, but it was . . . There were times when I couldn't take it any more. Afterwards, I wanted it, and I think it did me some good, life on the farm. To no longer see all those ugly faces—'

Nazir interrupted her with a wave of the hand. They had now reached the top of the mountain pass.

'Park behind that bush. I want to check no one's following us.'

'Nazir, you're going crazy. We've been driving through the middle of nowhere for three hours! And anyway, for fuck's sake . . . are you sure we can't go back to Sogno?'

It was the place where Fleur had spent the last few months. There was an abandoned farm a few kilometres from the village, amid wooded hills and undulating meadows full of flowers. Fleur had built up a larder of vital necessities. She drew her water from a well, read poetry by candlelight, and lived without electricity, in the wild, far from the treacherous lights of urban civilization.

'We'll sleep here tonight,' declared Nazir. 'And tomorrow . . . we'll see.'

Fleur turned off the engine and saw Nazir bizarrely checking the texture of his black jacket.

'What are you doing?'

'I sewed some papers into the lining. Some important papers.'

Fleur listened to the hooting of owls.

The 4×4 was stopped just a few metres from the road, and was completely visible. Fleur tilted back her head and took off her fuchsia scrunchie. Her hair did stink, but she hadn't noticed this before Nazir pointed it out.

She opened her mouth again and remembered all those evenings of reading and solitude, the candles burning out in their holders as night thickened around her.

She began to cry like a madwoman.

'I've missed you so much,' she said, looking up at Nazir through eyes flooded with tears.

Nazir helped her to slip onto the back seat so she could stretch out and calm down a little. Her calves, bristling with short blonde hairs, were covered by mud and small scratches. On her naked forearms, Nazir saw that she had goosebumps. He took off his jacket for the first time since the day before and placed it over the body of his accomplice, which now shivered with fatigue.

'Go on, sleep a little,' he said in an almost gentle voice, 'everything's going to be okay.'

And when she was asleep, he passed over her still anxious face the screen of his brand new BlackBerry, and murmured in the same tone of voice as two minutes earlier, 'My little savage . . .'

8.

The candlelight procession was fizzling out as Commissioner Maheut supervised the Operations Centre of the Police Department, situated in the building's basement. A special badge was required to gain access after passing through several security checks. The officers working there were all in uniform and stood to attention when the commissioner passed.

The 'room' was an immense command post, equipped with dozens of screens linked to the hundreds of video-surveillance cameras in the capital. Maheut had led the Directorate of Public Order and Traffic for a year now. He had never seen this bunker so full and active as since Sunday's attack, but this evening every record had been smashed. All the departments were on the warpath: riot police, local cops, interior intelligence and all the other forces.

One team watched the cameras on the Canal Saint-Martin. The commissioner walked over to another bank of screens and asked the operators to zoom out on the Champs-Elysées. A band of fifteen individuals were making discreet signs to each other so as to avoid being noticed by the cops on the ground. Maheut was soon convinced they were up to something. He alerted the nearest company, sent two teams of reinforcements and observed, on the night screens, the forceful intervention that followed. At the scene, the major moved away to speak into his walkie-talkie.

'Commissioner, we've found golf clubs on them, but also some handguns.'

'Loaded?'

'With real bullets, Commissioner,' declared the major anxiously.

One minute later, the commissioner ordered, 'Alert the American Embassy that things are moving towards them.'

The Canal Saint-Martin team spotted some movement at the exit from the Jaurès metro station, where the candlelight procession was ending.

'Commissioner, come here quick!'

Maheut bounded over to where the captain was manipulating images.

A few cameras captured those who had taken too long to cover their faces with black scarves. The images were instantly transmitted to a processing centre, which checked them against the police database for the Ile-de-France region.

'How many sections of riot police do we have to control the demonstration? Send all of them!'

Dieuleveult, the chief of police, had forbidden all demonstrations, but this one, initiated at the last moment on the 'social networks', as journalists would say, had escaped the prying eyes of interior intelligence.

At Maheut's command post, onlookers had been seen massing on the banks of the canal, but the few units on the scene had been unable to disperse them. So as not to create an incident, Commissioner Maheut had decided to let the march take place for four hours, and he had sent some sections of riot police to place Jaurès, at the end of the procession, to prevent the arrival of hooligans from the suburbs.

They were apprehended without difficulty, except for one, who jumped into the canal to escape the police. Maheut observed the riot police in heavy boots as they descended the steps and invaded the two quays to pick up the runaway. But this one continued to swim. Maheut had to make a decision: he ordered his men on the scene to join the culprit in the water to prevent him from drowning. It was impossible to know if he had taken drugs, for example. It was out of the question that this peaceful march should end in a death.

The riot police were reluctant but obeyed. A few minutes later, the demonstration had dispersed and the chief of police congratulated his young commissioner, by telephone, on his intelligent management of the situation.

There was, however, one image, amid the room's applause, that haunted Maheut for the few hours that followed: the young man who had almost drowned had his head in his hands on a screen that no one was watching any more. He was handcuffed, far enough away from the edge of the canal so as not to be tempted to jump back in, flanked by a few policemen, and he was crying, crying like a kid, trembling in the pitiless yellow of the quay's neon lights.

TUESDAY

9

CONSTITUTIONAL SORCERY

1.

The editorial entitled 'EMERGENCY POWERS' sent into the stratosphere the number of page views on Avernus.fr, the news site that had shown itself to be – by far – the most hostile to Chaouch during the campaign. The three paragraphs, written in the form of a letter to President Noyer, dealt not only with invoking the emergency powers, unprecedented in the history of the Fifth Republic – at least since General de Gaulle in 1958 – but also with the electoral campaign and a France that had experienced a *genuine phenomenon of collective hallucination*, having let itself be *charmed by a neoliberal snake with a Socialist Party membership*, and finally, with the toll of two nights of riots, here termed *pillaging*, which had started, let us remind ourselves, in Grogny – (*one may wonder what the urban policy would be of a president who has turned his own town into a powder keg*) – and which gave to the rest of the world the shameful image of a country on the brink of eruption. The editorial concluded:

It was a barbarian named Clovis who founded France. Enough of the cunning and cynical calculations. Let's say it loud and clear: we will not let a handful of savages destroy her. Monsieur the President of the Republic, do not shirk your responsibilities. Be, in this storm, a bold and strong captain: take emergency powers.

The man who had written these lines, the man who had been accused of 'incredible indecency' on all the shows to which he had been invited, the man who had singlehandedly defended himself against everyone and who had, in fact, been the first to break the media consensus around the idea that things had to be calmed down at any price, this grandiose adversary of peace waited quite peacefully, on this Tuesday 8 May (cloudy over the whole northern half of the country, with heatwave temperatures caused by the warm front that arrived last Thursday from North Africa), in a famous bar in Saint-Germain-des-Prés, where he had been invited by his former university classmate, Henri, now Judge Wagner, who was obviously as casual as ever about punctuality.

Judge Wagner arrived ten minutes late, tie-less, his head still heavy from a night spent reading the phone taps on Nazir Nerrouche.

He held out his hand towards the most irresponsible editorialist in France. Puteoli did not get up to shake it, making do with an excessively warm 'How are you?'

'Ah well, that editorial,' ventured Wagner, sitting down in front of him. 'The least that can be said is that you know how to make people talk about you . . .'

Puteoli smiled through his rodent teeth.

'It's a pleasure to know you are a faithful reader.'

Wagner tapped his fingers on the table and tried to catch the waiter's attention, so as to suppress his desire to reveal to Puteoli all the disgust his sly ways inspired in him.

The discussion, which had scarcely begun, fell dead, the two men sizing each other up without looking at each other, neither of them wanting to break the ice. Wagner, who needed this exchange to go smoothly, put his fist in his pocket and asked for news of Puteoli's family.

They spoke thus for a few minutes and soon silence fell again on the table. Puteoli raised an eyebrow and asked coldly, 'What do you want from me, Henri?'

'You're right: screw courtesy. Listen. I want to know how you got a sneak preview of that video of the arrests. I'm asking you this as . . . a friend.'

Puteoli shook his head.

'Well, I'm not going to reveal my sources and you know that very well. I hope it's not for this that you insisted we see each other. I've got a very busy schedule these days.'

'At least tell me how your journalist, this Marieke Vander-whatsit, how could she get access to the organizational chart of the CDII . . . And what's the sequel to the article? The "massive failures", what's that about? How does she know all that? She had access to the preliminary investigation files?'

The eyes of the head of Avernus.fr were, as usual, mobile and wary, but a slight veil of jubilation had just appeared in them, creating irrepressible movements at the corners of his lips.

Wagner, who was too tired to humiliate himself any more, grew sullen.

'Believe me,' he blurted out, staring at the edge of his metal chair, 'I have no desire to *force* you to tell me how you know all that. It's against all my principles.'

Puteoli declared triumphantly, 'Your principles! Ah, those subtle minds . . . those sensitive souls . . .'

Now the two men were looking at each other. Puteoli went on, placing his hands on the empty table, 'Henri, we're not going to lie to each other. The whole country is waiting for the decision of the Constitutional Council to rule on whether Chaouch is fit to serve, a terrorist network that no one saw coming has succeeded in shooting a presidential candidate, our country is turning into the Wild West, and you're here threatening me over some trivial thing? What are you going to come out with: violation of the secrecy of an investigation for the video of the arrests? Well, the secrecy of an investigation doesn't exist, so let's stop bullshitting . . .'

Wagner wanted to take out the Code of Penal Procedure and smash it over Puteoli's head.

Puteoli affected a victorious gravity, as if to justify, beyond his editorial, the turn his life had taken in the last few months – a turn that had made it thrilling, and whose thrill had become a drug: the TV shows, the impassioned homilies, the death threats, the support of voices stronger than his own, from greater and deeper minds who nevertheless had to bow before his pugnacity and media savvy.

'This is war, Henri. You would do well to realize that.'

'Go to hell.'

'This is war,' he repeated before quoting Shakespeare: '"In cities, mutinies; in countries, discord; in palaces, treason"' – his face lit up with duplicity – '"and the bond cracked 'twixt daughter and father." He said daughters or sons? I've forgotten . . .'

Overwhelmed by his inner tumult, Wagner did not understand the insinuation.

'All right, well, you leave me no choice. You remember Jean-Christophe? Jean-Christophe Habert? He's become Director General for Inland Revenue, the bastard. He was the best, you'll say, the best one among us. We spent a few days on holiday together last summer. I invited him down South with his new wife. A very pretty woman. We got along very well . . .'

This thinly veiled threat of an audit should have instilled panic in Puteoli's eyes, but, for the first time, those shifty orbs did not move. The duplicity did not leave them. He got up calmly from the table and readjusted his bow tie. With the unshakeable self-assurance of a man who had the protection of God Himself, he declared to his old classmate with a smile, 'Ah yes, they're beautiful, your principles . . . The great left-wing judge who threatens to break my kneecaps like some mafia boss . . . Go on and do what you have to do, Henri. I'm not going to tell you a thing.'

2.

As Mansourd had expected, the bank in Zurich refused to hand over the surveillance tapes. The commander hoped that Wagner was right, and that the diplomatic route would bear fruit. Of course, while the French and Swiss Justice Ministries tried to come to an agreement, Nazir was still on the run; but the checks at the airport had been doubled and, thanks to Interpol, there were Wanted posters pinned up in every Swiss police station, particularly those on the borders with Germany, Austria and Italy. The local television channels generously relayed every last detail on Public Enemy Number One. Unless he buried himself in a cave or got hold of a potion that made him invisible, it was not unreasonable to believe that the fugitive stood no chance.

Back at the ATSD headquarters, and after having studied the dozens of calls from people claiming to have spotted him in a nearby bar, the commander asked about the electronic surveillance and phone taps on the Nerrouche family. The lieutenant in charge replied with a shake of the head. He was accompanied by an Arab interpreter who did not understand Kabyle.

'And Fouad? Has he spoken with Chaouch's daughter?'

'No, he's tried to call her several times, but Chaouch's security is on it.'

'And not a word on Nazir?' the commander said angrily, obviously lacking sleep. 'No one?'

But it was true: two nights after the attack, as the hidden angels watching Dounia's house could attest, not once had Nazir's name been uttered within its walls. Nonetheless, he occupied everyone's mind, gradually spreading there like a black and extremely toxic smoke.

But they had not yet found a way to listen to people's minds.

3.

The first to wake up, Dounia seemed to succumb to this black smoke by washing the dishes to stay busy while the coffee brewed. She let the water run for a minute and her mind wandered. She turned the tap handle for hot water, but it stayed lukewarm for a minute, while she was trying to remember Nazir, her first born, as an infant, as a child, as an innocent. No, it was something that her maternal heart could not comprehend, something that made her recoil as soon as she imagined it: the fact that, now not only undeniable but a matter of public infamy, she had given birth to a monster.

'Ouch!' she cried.

The water was burning hot. It had been burning hot for a while, long enough to burn the skin on top of her hand.

There was still no noise upstairs: she smoked a cigarette at the window overlooking the sleepy car park beyond the lawn. She was not entitled to paid leave in the private retirement home where she was a nursing assistant, so on Thursday morning, she had to return to her job, take care of the sixteen old people on the floor she was responsible for, look after their bedsores, their IV drips, perhaps even lay out a corpse as she did last week, that old woman suffering from colon cancer whom she had left for two hours in her locked bedroom, looking after the other patients while a continuous flow of green shit flowed from her dead mouth.

When only one puff of her cigarette remained, Dounia lit another with the end of the first. Halfway through this guilty second cigarette, she heard Fouad's alarm go off in the adjoining room and rushed to finish smoking it. Fouad was thus awakened more by his mother's umpteenth coughing fit than by the ringing of his mobile.

Irritated by just three hours' sleep, as well as by his impression of having bad breath, he asked his mother as he poured some coffee, 'What the hell were you doing at the hospital on Sunday afternoon?'

'Oh, you're not going to start that again,' said Dounia, leaving the room with her head bowed.

'Mama, answer me: is something going on? Are you ill? Tell me, for God's sake!'

Dounia almost replied that it was not cigarettes that made her ill, but she preferred the truth, the banal and reassuring truth.

'I went to see Zoulikha! The poor girl, we weren't going to leave her all alone . . .'

She went upstairs to wake Rabia.

It was half past three in the morning when Rabia, Dounia and Fouad left Saint-Etienne in Dounia's Twingo. Rabia, who did not have access to her wardrobe, had borrowed a suit from her sister. You had to be well dressed to meet a judge. But Dounia did not have a variety of smart outfits to choose from: they therefore wore the same black skirt, a short-sleeved shirt of different colours (pale pink and cream) but of identical make, and a similarly tailored blazer. Some instructions had been left for Slim and Luna concerning the telephone and going out (don't use it, don't do it); a phone call to the college had explained Luna's absence for the next few days: the principal 'understood'. For the rest, the fridge was full and there was no reason to be worried.

Fouad preferred to drive, even if it meant passing the wheel to his mother halfway. They had five to six hours' driving in front of them. Fouad had paid for the first tank of petrol and had to put up with Rabia's embarrassed thanks.

Three days before, Fouad had been sitting next to Krim in the back seat. Krim had tapped him affectionately on the knee and asked for the meaning of the words to the song by Ait Menguellet, 'We, the Children of Algeria'.

Now, Krim was in police custody and Fouad was driving his mother and his aunt across France to see a counterterrorism judge.

So there, Fouad said to himself, you have the meaning of the words to 'We, the Children of Algeria'.

Beside him, Rabia was dozing. Her face, with its sharp cheekbones, was gilded by the sun rising over the fields of Cantal, but her knitted brow left no doubt about the nature of her dreams. Krim caught in the vice-like grip of the judicial system. Her hair caught in the irons of shame. Uncle Ferhat's neck caught in the hands of a madman, who had placed him in a headlock while he shaved his scalp, before drawing on it unspeakable obscenities . . .

In the back seat, Dounia also seemed to have her eyelids closed but she was not sleeping: she was looking at her hands placed on her knees, and striving to control the coughing fits that attacked her from within.

When Rabia woke up, she asked if they'd mind if she put on the radio. Fouad could not help seeing this as a good sign, even if the only static-free station in this remote corner of the country was France Info, which was reporting on a second night of rioting more violent than the first. A gymnasium had been burned down, some firemen targeted, a suburban town hall vandalized and tagged with the now famous word 'Murderer'.

An expert in criminology, who was apparently an early riser and known to be close to the Ministry of the Interior, claimed there had been three thousand arrests that night alone. He added that these arrests had led to two thousand people being held in custody and ended his telephone interview by expressing the hope that the Constitutional Council was going to re-assess its 'silence'. The evening before, the Elders of the Constitutional Council had officially validated the election of Idder Chaouch and indicated that they had been asked by the prime minister to give a ruling on the president-elect's *fitness to hold office*.

But they had revealed nothing of their intentions, and the criminologist seemed to lay at their door some of the responsibility for riots spreading to the suburbs of towns that had not even seen any trouble during the unrest in 2005.

Sensing that there was a good chance the next story would involve Krim, Rabia asked Fouad to switch off the radio. He did not hesitate, even if behind the silence that followed, they could hear the whistling of tear gas grenades in flight, the roar of charging riot cops, the boom of explosions and the crackling of thousands of cars on fire. And all because of him, the young cousin, the little nephew, the adored son.

4.

Upon waking, Fleur passed a hand over her dried tears, certain that they had flowed spontaneously while she slept. She stretched her stiff body on the seat and sensed she was alone in the car.

'Nazir?'

She opened the door and walked barefoot in the icy dawn. At the edge of the thicket where she had parked in the middle of the night, she saw Nazir from behind, absorbed in contemplation of the mountains. His right hand was stuffed between the middle buttons of his closed jacket. With his left hand, he tapped on his BlackBerry.

'What are you doing?'

Nazir must have heard her get out of the car: he did not jump. He did not even bother turning around to utter his enigmatic reply, which he spoke as if he had been preparing it all night.

'I'm gathering my troops.'

Was he speaking metaphorically about his strength? Fleur realized that this was not the case when she saw, on the wide screen of his phone, a Facebook page with accumulated 'likes' at the top of it.

'Have you nothing better to fucking do than go on Facebook? We're hunted by all the police in Europe, and you, you continue with your fake profiles . . . Anyway, how can you get wifi in the middle of nowhere?'

'Hence the need to have a phone on a cellular network. That said, it doesn't pick up very well. Hey, let me finish, will you?'

After a few years of creating fake Facebook profiles, he now had seven of them, which was more impressive than it seemed. Under his false identities, he had achieved staggering numbers of friends – even if, to appreciate the size and the scope of the phenomenon, he had to pass for a female: there was nothing easier, when requesting girlfriends, than to pretend to be one – and, the world being what it is, a rather young and pretty one.

In the long and secret history of voyeurism, Nazir took the dawn of Facebook to be an event as revolutionary as the birth of Jesus or the invention of electricity. Every day, the hard-working Facebook voyeur colonized new continents of nymphets. The family albums of a good tenth of mankind were no longer inaccessible at the back of dusty cupboards, but infinitely clickable, zoomable and cut-and-pastable.

Of course, some girls blocked their profiles, but few refused a detailed friend request if it included the assurance of one or several mutual friends. And Nazir, who liked nothing more than teams of young girls, possessed, in his evil, virtual collection, hundreds in every part of the globe. No detail escaped him. Knowing when they were depressed or enthusiastic, their tastes and when they were angry. Learning, often live, that a female gymnast from Utah had just got engaged, or that a cheerleader from the Pas-de-Calais, by becoming friends with half a dozen Polish girls after an international competition, had no doubt unknowingly opened doors for him, through the capillary action of *mutual friends*, to a terra cognita that perhaps would lead him to spend part of the night chatting – one on one and in that awful standardized English that everyone, absolutely everyone, spoke – with a young and innocent blonde girl from Lvov or Katowice…

This virtual harem of some five and a half thousand virgins did not, however, merely fulfil an erotic mission for Nazir. On at least two of his false profiles, he, or rather 'she', was only friends with inhabitants of Grogny, aged from thirteen to nineteen, all of them alienated males from the Rameau-Givré housing estate, who would never have dreamed of refusing a friend request from such a teasing little slut. 'The girls' regularly posted sequences of addictive photographs of various parts of their bodies, taken at arm's length on their smartphones. Nazir thus knew from the inside what the counterterrorism services would only discover afterwards, masking their impotence in long technical reports that the Ministry of the Interior manipulated according to the emergencies of the moment. And he waited for the right moment to begin to post, instead of nipples that drew thousands of 'likes' and almost as many comments, those slightly more substantial messages that he wrote and carefully translated into text-speak.

Nazir's eyes had closed at the thought of the most beautiful specimens in his collection. He had to reopen them on hearing Fleur repeat that she was dying of hunger. Nazir put away his BlackBerry and pointed out, eastward, the triangle painted in the space between two summits that seemed to overlap: the still-resolutely night-blue sky was on the verge of turning purple.

'That valley, over there, is the Valley of Schlaffendorf. We have to go along the lake, which should take another hour, if we drive fast.'

Nazir was not mistaken. After an hour driving by the side of the lake, which was just starting to reflect the sky above it, their 4×4 passed through the first few silent houses of a small village. The Grisons district was one of the least populated places in Switzerland: in Schlaffendorf, there was less than one inhabitant per square kilometre. There were no lights on in the houses, without exception. The cars, if there were any, slept in hidden parking spaces. Snow refused to melt on the shoulders of the road. On some roofs, weather vanes in the shape of cockerels or rabbits waited motionlessly for the wind to tear them from boredom and rust. Just then, a grey dog began to bark, as if to remind the visitors that they were not driving through a dreamscape.

The main road was poor quality, and Fleur noticed, as she accelerated to lose the dog, that, after having driven the 4×4 all last night, she was suffering along with its wheels, its rims and its shock absorbers as if they were extensions of her own body. On imagining the bodywork covered in dust by the journey, she felt the need to wash her face.

Instead of speeding towards the end of the valley, Nazir asked Fleur to turn off towards what looked like a dead end. He assured her, however, that it was the road they had to take. After a few kilometres through thick forest, the road became a scarcely passable dirt track. Fleur and Nazir drove by a meadow that did not exist on any map, a steep meadow behind which the sun was rising.

As the track climbed, Nazir saw a horse galloping across the slice of hill they seemed to be aiming for. The horse was black and ridden by a young girl, whose long and abundant blonde hair seemed to the astonished Nazir to melt like the first cloud set ablaze by the dawn. The horsewoman made her mount rear up, then vanished over the hill as day finally broke, illuminating the sky until Nazir had to squint so hard his eyes closed completely.

Nazir, who thought he had been hallucinating, tried to open his mouth to ask Fleur if she had seen what he had seen. But Fleur was just gaping ahead, imitating with her lips the reassuring jolts of her 4×4.

'Stop!' screamed Nazir. 'Didn't you see that?'

Fleur braked and Nazir got out.

She parked the car next to a meadow spangled with white and blue flowers, which, in the infant light of dawn, looked like a flying carpet at rest.

Nazir rushed across it, seemingly in search of someone. He ran right to the edge of some undergrowth and came back almost immediately, staggering, out of breath.

'I thought I saw . . .'

'What?'

Fleur wanted to place a hand on Nazir's chin. He seemed to be in a state of shock. Nazir pushed her away and gave her a horrified look, as if her head had been replaced by Medusa's.

It took him a few seconds, eyes closed, to rediscover some semblance of a sense of reality.

'Let's go,' he said, getting back into the car. 'To Schlaffendorf.'

5.

Esther Chaouch insisted that she and her daughter have breakfast together, but, as Jasmine was reluctant about returning to 'her place', mother and daughter met up in the restaurant of a hotel in the 5th arrondissement, a few hundred metres from Val-de-Grâce, where a makeshift private room had been created for them with some screens that had been erected around their table. Jasmine kept her eyes closed to ignore the whispers and furtive looks that had surrounded her when she came into the hotel, preceded and followed by her bodyguards. Beneath the screen decorated with unbearable fleurs-de-lys, she could see the loafers of Couteaux, who was going to spend the morning keeping his eye on the other customers.

'Jasmine,' her mother began, unfolding her white napkin, 'there are two or three things we have to talk about. But, first of all, how are you?'

Surprised, and almost shocked by her mother's tone of voice, Jasmine sighed like a teenager.

'I don't know, Mama. I'm incapable of knowing if I'm okay or not. Story of my life.'

'No, listen. I thought you might want to know how the investigation's getting on—'

'Well, you're mistaken,' Jasmine cut in.

'Jasmine—'

'Seriously, I can't take this any more. I don't give a damn about the investigation! What I want is for Papa to wake up, wake up and drop politics, and for us not to have anything more to do with all those . . .'

Her voice went silent of its own accord.

'Jasmine, I know it's hard, but this is not the time to show signs of weakness. On the contrary, we have to show the country that we're strong. That we've kept hope.'

The 'country': Jasmine didn't give a damn about the country. What hurt her, what offended her at that moment was the fakeness of her mother's voice. She could not hate her for this fakeness: Jasmine knew all too well that beneath her commanding demeanour, behind her resolute gestures, that upright posture, her mother was in pieces.

The young woman took advantage of a moment when her mother consulted her phone to observe her knitted brow, her jet-black hair, which she still dyed herself.

'Mama, what's going to happen if he doesn't wake up before the Constitutional Council decides to annul the election?'

'Well, that's simple,' replied Esther Chaouch, clearing her voice to adopt her professorial tone. 'According to the Constitution, on 17 May, i.e. next Thursday, the President of the Senate, Cornut, will become interim president. All electoral operations must be repeated, in twenty to thirty-five days' time, which takes us up to—'

'So Noyer's going to be re-elected? After all that's happened?'

'No, of course not, nothing's certain. Why do you say that?'

'Well, there's no one on the left if you take away Papa. No one who can beat him. And with all these riots, people are going to vote for security, stability . . .'

Esther hesitated before replying.

'Listen, Vogel will be prime minister. He'll be taking care of the everyday governing. In the scenario we're talking about here, I think he would have . . . a lot of support, and an undeniable mandate for carrying forward your father's programme, the policies that they—'

'Vogel? Are you serious? Vogel? You see him as president?'

'Honey, nothing's that simple. And then, we may never have to get to that. Come on, this is absurd, it doesn't have to come to that, it's . . . obvious . . .'

244

Silence fell. Jasmine bit her thumbnail. Her mother looked at the anxious face of her only daughter.

'And Brisseau,' Jasmine suddenly asked. 'She lost the primary to Papa but everybody likes her. I heard her on the radio just now. I get the feeling she wants to take advantage of his coma, don't you think?'

'That's politics, honey.'

'Mama,' said Jasmine, changing the subject and lowering her voice, 'there's something I want to confess to you. This is going to seem stupid, but . . . I have difficulty talking about it to anyone, and . . . I can't sleep. I feel like I've betrayed . . .'

'What's wrong, Jasmine?'

'I didn't vote for him. I didn't vote for Papa.'

Esther did not react. She just laid the cutlery on the side of her plate and looked into space. Jasmine threw her head back.

'I didn't vote for Noyer either, you know. I just . . . left my ballot blank. I think that, in my heart of hearts, I didn't want Papa to be elected. I felt that . . . it was going to change our lives forever. Even though I'm sure he would have made a good president.'

'Jasmine!' her mother admonished her. 'Your father is in a coma, he's not dead! I refuse to let you speak like this. As for this story of a blank vote, just promise me you won't tell anyone, okay?'

Jasmine was no longer hungry. She claimed she was tired and replied feebly to the few questions from her mother about the concerts she had cancelled. Just before letting her daughter leave, Esther took her hand and said something that, when spoken aloud, appeared to Jasmine to have been her sole concern from the outset.

'I have to say something. Promise me you won't get angry, but... Fouad ... How can I say ...'

Jasmine flushed with anger. She tore her hand from her mother's.

'Goodbye, Mama.'

'Jasmine, I must warn you: do what you like but... Fouad is in a hearing today with the judge investigating the attack on Papa ...'

This information did not make the young woman turn around but perceptibly slowed her pace.

Couteaux stood in front of her and asked her to wait for a moment, to give the car time to come up to the hotel entrance.

'Really, Aurélien?' Jasmine complained. 'Really? We can't walk ten metres?'

Couteaux looked at her in a strange, almost personal way, which troubled Jasmine so much that she looked down at the floor and agreed to wait in the hotel's air-conditioned lobby. It was then that she received a text from her ex, Christophe Vogel, who said he was thinking of her, that he was always there for her, that he did not dare call her but was just waiting for a 'sign'.

6.

The elegant sixty year old who introduced himself in the waiting room looked exactly like the man Fouad had seen and admired on TV. A slim and energetic figure in a tailored suit, Szafran's forehead was high and open, scarcely wrinkled, as if to testify to a still youthful intelligence. His dark hair was accentuated rather than softened by the white strands that were beginning to invade his crew-cut. There was one detail that bothered Fouad, though: the star lawyer was frantically chewing gum.

'I'm sorry, Monsieur Nerrouche, but I was held up in coooourt... Mesdames, Monsieur, follow me into my office, please.'

From the abrupt way in which Maître Szafran apologized, Fouad thought he heard a reproach. He attributed this discomfort to the lawyer's remarkable bass voice, so deep it almost made the blue walls of his office shake.

'I had Judge Wagner on the phone this morning. You are going to be heard as assisted witnesses, separately, and that should not last very long.'

'Assisted witnesses?' asked Rabia. 'Does that mean you'll be there?'

'Yes, I will be there, but that is not what "assisted witness" means. Assisted witness means you are not implicated in the case, but that you will not be heard as simple witnesses.'

Szafran continued chewing gum, his jaws moving violently from side to side.

Fouad did not often feel small in front of older men, but this lawyer's piercing eyes, the hardness of his attitude and, above all, his reputation reminded Fouad that he was only twenty-six.

Fouad's unpleasant first impression turned into unconditional admiration when Szafran swivelled on his padded chair and announced that he could already boast of a first – modest – success: thanks to his good relations with one of the investigators from Levallois-Perret, Rabia could phone her son before the end of his interrogation, and just before he was brought before the courts.

'When?' asked Rabia, almost leaving her chair.

'Well, the prosecutor has extended his custody by forty-eight hours, so I'll say Thursday evening, probably.'

'Not before Thursday evening? But . . .' Rabia closed her eyes to stop herself from crying. 'But he's my son. They don't have the right . . .'

'Madame,' the lawyer continued gently, 'the heaviest charges in the Penal Code weigh on your son. It is useless hiding from the facts: even if we manage to make it look like he was just obeying orders as part of a wider conspiracy, it is nonetheless he who fired the gun, who shot at a candidate for the supreeeeme office.'

'So his only chance,' interjected Fouad, 'is to pass the blame onto . . . my brother?'

'I am afraid so, yes.'

'Maître, I wanted to ask you what we can do to stop Krim from being defended by this Maître Aribi. I heard him yesterday. He was speaking on behalf of Krim, but also the whole family. And without being familiar with defence strategies and all their subtleties, I'm pretty sure that it's a bad idea to speak like that on TV . . .'

'Well, I was coming to that. Not only is it a bad idea, but it is punishable by sanctions. If he has spoken in your name when you have not appointed him, he is wrongfully taking on a client. I spoke with him yesterday, on the phone, and I asked him to let me take charge of Krim's defence and . . . I'm not going to lie to you, the tone soon became heated. I threatened him with taking the affair to the Paris Bar.'

'Anyway, who's going to pay?' cried Fouad. 'Not Krim, us! After all, we do have the right . . .'

'Absolutely. Listen, I am going to tell you: it will not go as far as the president of the Bar. Maître Aribi has not yet visited Krim. Custody in a terrorism case allows the police to delay the presence of a lawyer for up to seventy-two hours. It is scandalous, but that's the way things are. What we are going to do is that when you speak to Krim on the telephone, tell him to change lawyers and appoint me. Now then. We have to prepare for the hearing this afternoon.'

'You told me yesterday,' asked Fouad, 'that you knew the investigating judge who's looking after . . . us?'

'Wagner? Yes, yes,' replied Szafran, slightly evasively. 'From what I have understood, interior intelligence was still investigating your brother and this movement, the SRAF. And given Wagner's closeness to the new Paris prosecutor, Lamiel, he was appointed to investigate the attack on Chaouch even before the end of your cousin's custody. Which must annoy quite a few people. Anyway. Apart from that . . . He is a strange, unpredictable man, but I do not think he is as crazy as Rotrou. You know, they're all crazy in counterterrorism. Too much power, and also too close to power . . . But Wagner is not a hardliner, if I dare say so. He is cultured, married to a great pianist. He's still a judge, but the fact that he was appointed instead of one of the big shots on Islamic terrorism proves one thing, in any case: they have known from the beginning that it has nothing to do with Al-Qaeda in the Islamic Maghreb or I don't know what Islamist movement . . . Besides, in his press conference, Prosecutor Lamiel did not mention the slightest religious line of inquiry.'

Fouad nodded. Szafran loosened the Windsor knot in his tie, seized a notepad and slipped his jacket onto the back of his chair.

'So, now, let's get down to serious business. I am going to ask you to repeat to me everything that you said in custody. And, above all, tell me about Nazir. At length. Would you like a coffee? A glass of miiiineral water?'

7.

An hour after learning through Poussin that the Saint-Etienne police had found no one at the home of 'Fat Momo', Wagner received a second phone call from his young colleague. He had just left the Palace to go to lunch, and his security officers asked him to get into the car while he took the call. Wagner could not suppress a gesture of irritation and held the phone against his chest while he ranted at one of his guards.

'Look, we're right outside the Palace, between the ministry and police headquarters, with the highest density of police and armed officers in the entire capital, and you really believe I'm at risk by taking two minutes of fresh air?'

Ever since his wife had scolded him about not remembering her concert that evening, the judge had been in an execrable mood. His bodyguards didn't hold his bad temper against him, however, and drove him to the restaurant on the Left Bank where he was to meet Prosecutor Lamiel.

'Poussin, I hope it's good news,' Wagner sighed, once in the back seat of his mobile prison.

'N-n-not sure,' replied Poussin. 'In any case, it's interesting. I s-s-searched Fat Momo's place myself, and on the desktop computer we looked at the recent emails, notably in the spam box for F-F-Facebook notifications. And there, in the F-F-Facebook message box, the kid talks about how he must go and hide at his c-c-cousin's in Ivry-sur-Seine.'

'Good, very good. Find the cousin's address and contact the Ivry police so they can go and arrest him.'

'No, no, your Honour, that's not it.'

Wagner looked to the heavens. With his stammerer's sixth sense, Poussin understood. He got his breath back and added,

'On l-l-looking through the F-F-Facebook messages, we d-d-discovered a whole thread of conversations that look like the p-p-preparation for t-t-targeted operations during the riots.'

Wagner had kept his mouth open and his brow knitted since the start of the phone call. If he heard 'Facebook' one more time he was going to lose patience. He had to uncover a plot to assassinate the President of the Republic and Poussin was talking to him about Facebook, for heaven's sake!

'Listen, I'll let you see about all that with Mansourd.'

He hung up and got out of the car. Thierry Aqua Velva fell in behind him, and went out in front just to check that the place was safe.

'Come on, you've got to be kidding me, Thierry!'

'Your Honour?'

The constancy and courtesy of these men was unflappable. Wagner let him enter the restaurant and check, from the ground floor to upstairs, that there was not hidden in the abundant draperies, the chandelier or – why not? – under the thick wall-to-wall carpet an assassin with a dagger between his teeth. Lamiel, too, had just arrived; standing at the bar, he was reading the salmon-coloured pages of *Le Figaro* while fidgeting with the stick around which the prestigious newspaper was wrapped.

'Oh dear, my friend. You look awful.'

'A bit of trouble sleeping,' replied Wagner, avoiding the bulging eyes of his colleague.

Lamiel insisted on going upstairs where they would, he claimed, have some peace and quiet. Wagner agreed because, contrary to what he had feared – a fear that had a lot to do with his current irritability – the prosecutor had not asked someone high up to accompany him to put pressure on a mere judge. Upstairs, there were a dozen round tables and, at theirs, just two place settings. So this was no 'trap', but Lamiel, with his smarmy gestures and the Ricola cough drop he passed noisily from one molar to another, seemed to be hiding something all the same.

'Have you heard about the Constitutional Council? I've been told by a reliable source that they will soon be speaking with the chief medical officer at Val-de-Grâce.'

'I didn't know that,' replied Wagner, raising his eyebrows in the manner of a man for whom gossip, even those whispers heard in the hushed corridors of the ministry, held no interest.

'At this level, it's no longer a decision that they are being asked to make. It's sorcery! And when you look at the make-up of the council, it's quite . . . spellbinding, don't you think? Debré and Giscard would do anything to block Noyer, and the other eight were all directly or indirectly nominated by him! I'd love to be a fly on the wall in the room where those beloved Elders are going to deliberate . . .'

Wagner at last looked up and stared at Lamiel's protruding eyes. He almost told him that his transformation into a fly was already in the works. He preferred to talk to him about the transcripts of the phone taps he had requested from the CDII.

'On rereading Nazir Nerrouche's mobile phone records, I discovered, with my court clerk, that at one moment he mentioned a third phone. That can't have gone unnoticed, but I truly wonder why the CDII did not automatically include the taps on this third phone in the file . . .'

'Perhaps they quite stupidly didn't listen to it.'

'No. Mansourd spoke with his counterpart at the CDII,

Boulimier, who himself was leading the investigation. He confirmed that there were indeed three phones being tapped.'

Lamiel said nothing.

'We'll see this evening. I've asked for them to be delivered urgently.'

Lamiel approved. He did not dare look Wagner in the eyes.

'Well, Henri, we know each other too well for me not to cut to the chase. Since you started investigating this case, I've made a lot of enemies, starting with the chief of police, who will never forgive me for getting Mansourd's ATSD involved, which I did because I know you like working with him. Fair enough. Enemies are part of life. Who cares. I'll even tell you this: your choices are your choices, and the fact that you prefer to tap the Nerrouches' phones rather than take them to court, I respect that. The problem is that there are people, here and there, who gossip, who think you're not tough enough. Our friends in the press, of course, but also other friends . . .'

'Jean-Yves, you said at first that you wanted to cut to the chase. Please do!'

'Listen, I've seen the transcript of the questioning of Nazir's mother, Dounia Nerrouche. She says in black and white that she sent money to her son in an account in Zurich. If that's not enough to have her go to court for criminal association in relation with a terrorist enterprise, we might as well abolish that charge . . .'

Wagner was not reacting. He was playing with his silver knife, moving its blade towards the empty glass, but stopped just before contact, just before the desire became too strong and provoked that clinking which would not have been noticed in a casual place but which, in the dim light of this respectable red-carpeted restaurant, would have the effect of an energetic burp at a meeting of the Rotary Club.

'Henri, if you don't charge anyone in the family, people are going to think that we're getting nowhere. And they'll be right! For the moment, we know nothing about the Nerrouche network! Abdelkrim, the half-wit body-builder, and Benbaraka, who says he did a favour without knowing what it was about. With a bit of luck, the criminal records office will soon give us the name of the infamous goateed redhead who supposedly helped Abdelkrim on the day of the attack, but that's all. None of the sleeper cells followed by the CDII have the slightest link to the attack. The Nerrouche network is neither Islamist nor separatist nor anarcho-autonomist, nothing at all! I'm telling you, as far as we know, even if this is not much: it's a family. You cannot sincerely believe that they've got nothing to do with the projects of Nazir Nerrouche! He was living with his mother, he gave work and money to his cousins, his uncles, he was the hero of the community. They knew, Henri. They knew.'

'Well, as for me, I don't know,' retorted Wagner. 'I don't know yet, and so long as I don't know, I don't incriminate people. I'm not going to charge an entire family and ask them to prove to me that I'm wrong. You remember the burden of proof? I learned that at college, I know it's a bit old-fashioned but it basically said that it's not for the accused to prove his innocence, but for the accuser to prove his gui . . .'

He fell silent. Two shadows were approaching their table. Two shadows in three-thousand-euro suits, and Wagner did not take long to recognize the elder of the two: it was no less a figure than the First President of the Court of Appeal, the highest magistrate in France. Lamiel had stood up, almost as if standing to attention. Bafflement and anger nailed Wagner to his seat.

'Your Honour,' said Lamiel, clearing his throat to introduce the other man, 'you know Marc Fleutiaux, from the Ministry of Justice.'

Fleutiaux pushed his small spectacles up his long, condescending nose.

'Your Honour,' he said in a voice used to imposing silence, 'I wish to tell you that Monsieur the Minister, as well as his whole staff, are very closely following the investigation you are leading. A faultless performance, don't you think, Monsieur President? A faultless performance – so far.'

The First President nodded. With his light skin and white hair separated by an impeccable parting, he gave off an air of bourgeois dignity that nothing and nobody could ruffle. As Wagner was not reacting, not even with a nod, Fleutiaux sent Lamiel a dark look. He added, raising his chin, 'Of course, there's the video of these arrests. Terrible thing, that video. Terrible. The most terrible thing is that it forces us to make the most of the operation, if I dare say so. Don't you think, Monsieur President?'

The First President replied in the affirmative. Fleutiaux frowned and both men returned to their round table, situated at the other end of the room, in front of the bay window.

Lamiel did not say a thing. When a waiter in fine livery brought the dishes, Wagner threw his napkin on the table.

'So what's the next step? A challenge to my impartiality, to have me taken off the case? Well then, go through Maître Aribi to make the petition. If you're into underhanded tricks, you might as well go the whole hog!'

'Don't be naive, Henri. We're not dealing with a case where some kids have thrown fireworks at a police station. We're talking about a plot to assassinate the President of the Republic. It's an attack on the very foundations of the state . . . It's hardly surprising if there are pressures . . .'

'Yes, but what's not normal is the speed, the diligence and above all the servility with which you are relaying this. Oh, and you know what else? It's ruined my appetite, your little ruse.'

He abruptly stood and left the table.

8.

The office of the head of Human Resources of the Saint-Etienne Transport Service was situated on the first floor of the audacious complex of glass, lawns and steel that housed the headquarters. Bouzid had not had time to put on a tie, nor, given the urgency of the summons, had he managed to find a clean shirt. He had tidied up his driver's uniform (dark green suit, with a shirt chosen by the driver; in the case of Bouzid, a stranger to questions of style, dandelion yellow) and spent half an hour in the magazine-free waiting room looking out at the parking places reserved for management, scratching the armpits of his jacket, hoping to erase the unfortunately indelible rings left by two weeks of sweating as he piloted the bus on the sadly notorious Line 9.

The head of Human Resources was a brunette with blonde streaks, not ugly enough to spend her time taking revenge on others, but not pretty enough to show real self-confidence. She was struggling to open a sophisticated Tupperware tub when Bouzid was finally invited to sit down in front of her.

'Do you mind?' she asked, grabbing her plastic fork.

Bouzid looked at the unfriendly face and replied with a vaguely polite nod of the head. The woman was fifteen years younger than he, had a few dark hairs on her forearms, and the contemptuous voice of people who have degrees.

However, she was not at ease, and it was not impossible that she had waited for Bouzid's arrival to gulp down her salad, in order to show her superiority at the fateful moment. Bouzid knew in fact that it was bad news, but when he saw her fiddle with her files without daring to look up at him, he realized that the news was not bad, but rather the worst he could imagine. Theoretically, rumours of redundancy did not concern the drivers, and the status of the Transport Service employees was coveted by many inhabitants of Saint-Etienne in casual work. Despite everything, the woman began by recounting the difficulties the company had gone through since the start of the economic crisis.

Bouzid looked at the giant poster swallowing up one of the office walls: it was a proverbially heavenly sunset, an enormous ball slumped on the ocean horizon, so blazing and luminous that the beach's palm and coconut trees were visible only as black silhouettes.

'… You will therefore understand that we cannot offer you another post in the immediate future. My advice is therefore—'

'Why me?' Bouzid cut in with an unusually calm voice.

'Monsieur Nerrouche, I have just explained this to you. We have drawn up a list of criteria—'

'Monsieur Nerrouche, yeah,' he repeated, almost smiling.

The head of Human Resources pushed away her Tupperware and put on an indignant air.

'What are you insinuating?'

'Yeah, that's it, *zarma* you don't know what I'm insinuating . . .'

Bouzid got up.

'I will say,' added the woman, solely in order not to lose face, 'it did not help that you have already had two official warnings.'

Bouzid gave her the finger.

'And we were made aware of a third incident only yesterday.'

For her to try to persuade herself that there was sense in firing him rather than someone else made Bouzid's infamous vein bulge. He turned around and pressed his trembling hands on the desk.

'Listen to me closely, you fucking bitch: you've decided to sack me because I'm called Bouzid Nerrouche, and you've been watching the TV for the last two days. If you keep giving me this bullshit...'

He was going to say: I'll smash your face in. But the phone vibrating in the back pocket of his trousers brought him back to reality. It was probably Granny trying to get through to him. He announced that he would finish his day's work. The woman wanted to reply that it was not necessary, but with one gesture Bouzid made her understand that there was no point in insisting.

Too angry to pick up his phone straight away, Bouzid went, as he did every day, to the drivers' changing room. He put on another shirt, tied his tie bearing the company insignia, and treated himself to a cigarette while he waited to start his shift. The driver he was to take over from arrived slightly late and seemed surprised to see him. Bouzid shook his hand and sat down on the soft seat, closing the cab door on which were laid out the ticket machine and rolls of coins.

It was most probably the last time he would hear that harmonious clicking noise that indicated he had taken possession of the driver's seat. He had known good and bad days at the wheel of this bus. Occasionally, the blocked traffic forced him to wait for long minutes in an unexpected traffic jam. Sometimes, it was an idiotic driver who cut him off and then got out of his car to provoke him by tapping on the side window. One day, he too had got out to show that he would not be pushed around.

The hardest hours, however, were those in the evening, during times of unrest. When the suburbs were in flames across the whole country, the Montreynaud neighbourhood where he worked was the front line of riots in Saint-Etienne. With time, he liked to believe that he had learned to be treated with respect. The thugs knew that they could not smoke at the back of the Number 9 when Bouzid was driving.

The dashboard radio crackled and signalled to him to return to headquarters immediately. Bouzid just turned on the other radio and found the RMC channel. The indefatigable Brigitte Lahaie was giving relationship advice to the early afternoon listeners. A regular passenger greeted the driver and took her favourite seat just behind him. Bouzid drove off at the moment when he saw two men in polo shirts running towards his bus.

He drove as far as the first stop without feeling particularly worried. His phone was ringing constantly. Granny urgently wanted to speak to him, hanging up just before the last ring and calling back immediately.

'Why doesn't he reply, that damned *arioul?*' she said, sitting down on a bench in the small square where the Eurolines buses arrived and departed.

A blonde girl gave her a compassionate look, the kind you give to an old lady who is out of breath. Her cute face was hidden by an enormous backpack topped by a rolled-up camping mat. Granny glared at the young woman, who had never been the

259

victim of anything, not war, not men, not the French and especially not old age.

She knew Bouzid's work schedule, because she interrogated him at the start of each week to find out when she could phone him, if needed. And Granny always had lots of needs. She lived a carefully compartmentalized life of intrigues, one of those lives that demand the constant availability of a private chauffeur. The city's sheiks respected her, and she made a lot of money reading fortunes at their homes. Bouzid took care of the shopping, for which his mother summoned him day and night, as if he owed her something more precious than birth.

The Eurolines coach she was waiting for arrived from Madrid. According to the itinerary posted on the bus shelter, it had passed through Zaragoza, Barcelona, Saint-Jean-de-Luz, Périgueux and Clermont-Ferrand. It finally appeared at the edge of the square where there were bus shelters and temporary parking spots. Granny called Bouzid again. She knew he was working the night shift this Tuesday. Bouzid slept lightly and was tacitly obligated to leave his phone on all day long, even when taking a nap. If he did not wake up, thought Granny, how was she going to transport to a safe place, where he could not be seen, the man she had come to meet?

Uncle Moussa saw his elderly mother from his seat in the middle of the coach. He took a cigarette from his jacket inside pocket and grabbed the small piece of hand luggage that he'd kept with him rather than storing it under the bus.

Bouzid eventually turned off his phone. After the fourth mandatory stop on the line, the bus had to take the motorway for a few hundred metres before re-entering Montreynaud. Bouzid saw in the rear-view mirror that there was just an old man left sleeping in the bus, an old Moroccan who had told him the previous week that he had had a cataract operation. At the moment when he was about to swerve into the right lane for the turn-off, Bouzid had a sudden, crazy impulse: he continued along the motorway.

He did not know if he had enough fuel to reach Lyon. He did not know if he would be intercepted by highway police before he even got past the little town of Saint-Chamond. What he knew was that to miss the turn-off, to depart from this strictly defined and monitored road map, to drive freely amid the usual motorists on the A45, who must have wondered why the Number 9 was following them on the open road . . . all of this gave him a feeling of liberty that he did not remember having experienced since he began to lose his hair.

9.

A rental car was supposed to wait for Djinn between the place de la Bastille and the Gare de Lyon, or more precisely, at the corner of avenue Daumesnil and avenue Ledru-Rollin. Fat Momo's cousin arrived well in advance and waited in a laundrette whose dirty window overlooked the intersection. A pink brick viaduct went along avenue Daumesnil: the Green Axis, the famous promenade linking Bastille to Vincennes, was suspended ten metres in the air and planted with flowerbeds and lime, maple and cherry trees. Between glances at his phone, Djinn stared at the box hedges and bamboo that hid the female joggers from view, sometimes trying to follow, over a few unobstructed metres, a woman's blonde hair or a pair of bouncing breasts. But from down there he saw almost nothing, or just chests depressingly flattened by sports bras.

Finally, the car appeared and parked beside the cycle path. Djinn came rushing out of the laundrette and was making for the passenger seat when the driver gestured for him to get behind the wheel.

'But why?' asked Djinn.

The driver did not reply and went around the car, hiding his face. Since the attack, he had been wearing sunglasses and was thinking of dying his red hair. But he had not dared to go into a supermarket, never mind to a barber's. He had shaved off his goatee but, on top of utterly failing to make him unrecognizable, this new beardless chin made him feel oddly exposed, as vulnerable as a porcupine deprived of its needles.

'Where are we going?' asked Djinn.

Yet again, the red-haired man did not reply.

'Romain,' Djinn insisted, 'where are we going?'

Romain was shaking his head while staring at the rear-view mirror. He took off his sunglasses: his eyes were bloodshot and he looked possessed.

'To where we agreed to meet,' he explained, signalling to Djinn to drive. 'Up there, on the walkway: that's where we have to hide the bags. You come and fetch them here and you take them up there.'

'What do you mean by "here"? I thought they were in the car.'

The red-haired man asked to be dropped off at the bottom of a street close to the Gare de Lyon.

'Rue d'Austerlitz,' he explained to Djinn. 'Number 17. I'll wait for you there with the bags.'

'But why not just give them to me right now?' asked Djinn, who no longer understood anything that was going on.

'If you get stopped on the way, we're fucked,' Romain replied.

'One last thing,' ventured Djinn. 'What about my cousin, Fat Momo?'

'What about him?'

'I would like him not to be . . . you know. I'd like him to be left out of this. I've done everything, haven't I? Now I'm just asking for him not to be mixed up in . . . You see what I mean?'

'You're the one who needs to see, pal. Either you do what's planned, or you return to your little life of peace and quiet. Up to you. I've got nothing else to say to you.'

Romain swallowed painfully and looked at himself in the mirror. Feverish, sickly and pale, without his goatee, he looked like what he truly was: an overgrown, insecure adolescent.

Djinn drove fast to Ivry. He found Fat Momo slumped in front of the TV.

'*Wesh*, Fat Momo, come here for two minutes.' He dragged him into the kitchen. 'Look, you've got to do something, as a favour *zarma*, okay?'

Fat Momo looked down at the warped lino of the kitchen floor: he had seen a cockroach there the previous evening, a sight that had kept him from sleeping all night.

'Honestly, it's nothing much, just looking after some mutt this evening. It's a dog belonging to a friend. I have to do something, you see. Okay? No problem?'

'No problem,' replied Fat Momo.

It was no problem at all, in fact: he was thrilled. Not only was he going to have a bit of company while Djinn wandered off, but it would be canine company. But when the dog appeared in the doorway with its master an hour later, Fat Momo was brought down to earth. It was not an Alsatian with Sultan's tender eyes. It was a muscular, short-haired pit bull, prevented from barking and devouring the children of the neighbourhood by the most impressive muzzle Fat Momo had ever seen. Around this huge dog's chest a harness restricted its movements, and its master advised Fat Momo against removing one or other of these obstacles.

Fat Momo asked what the dog's name was. His master didn't reply. Djinn noticed his cousin's astonishment and replied that it was just a dog, who cared about a dog's name. Because the dog rode in big cars, because he was small but cantankerous and gifted and, above all, because he was formidably intelligent.

Fat Momo looked at the dog's little tobacco-brown eyes: they were so dead that they could have been replaced with the buttons of a teddy bear.

'If I were you, I wouldn't look him in the eyes.'

The master was from Mali and had the same build as his dog.

'He's an attack dog,' he explained with a ferocious smile. 'Crossed with I don't know what. One day, I made him fight two bulldogs. I swear to you he ate them whole. If I get nabbed, it'll be straight to the slammer.'

Fat Momo passed a hand under the monster's muzzle. Djinn turned on a computer in the room next door and logged onto Facebook. In the mirror above the broken couch, Fat Momo saw his cousin and the dog owner look at the profile of a scantily dressed girl. To amuse himself, Fat Momo tried to prove he could read backwards by noting her first and last name. The girl was classically cute, and yet the two friends did not grin lewdly; on the contrary, they were frowning and the words they exchanged, along with lots of glances in his direction, were hushed, as if in a library.

When they left, Fat Momo felt pity and unmuzzled the monster. After a few violent licks and a brief series of barks, the dog calmed down and accepted the bowl of water that had been prepared for him by his master for the evening.

Through the window, Fat Momo saw that a dozen cars had gathered in the courtyard at the foot of the red-brick buildings. Djinn was giving instructions, with some little slaps to impose his authority. After this sinister briefing, the men got into their cars in pairs. Some of these cars had tinted windows, but not one of them had their windows opened wide to blast their playlist for the rest of the neighbourhood. Djinn's car was the first to drive off. The others followed like shadows.

10

THE WANDERING SHADOWS

1.

Unable to get through to her father, Aurélie let herself be swept up by her classmates, who went to lie out on the banks of the Seine every day at noon as the school year wound down, to get some sun and pretend to study. Among them was Nico, one of the four boys who had stayed last Sunday after the big party they threw at her parents' place.

Nico, who dreamed of getting into Paris Institute of Political Studies, had begun to wear suit jackets and blue-striped shirts and to speak like Noyer. He used the first names of people he harangued in a debate, and spoke of his 'political family'. However, it was a portrait of Chirac he had in his bedroom, a fact that had been revealed on Facebook along with the creation of a satirical group ('If you have a poster of Chirac in your bedroom like Nicolas Bachelier'), that pushed the young man to come out as a Chiracian and thus distinguish himself from Tristan, the most zealous Noyerist in school. Some claimed that it was precisely to show he was different from the charismatic bully of the senior class that he had allowed the leak on Facebook.

Aurélie suspected this was true, but honestly, she didn't really give a damn.

When she saw Nico approach her, she walked quickly over to the far edge of the quay and looked up at the sky.

'Has Tristan sent you? What do you want?'

'Well, I see you're not in a good mood. I've come to tell you that neither Thibaud nor I have said anything about you-know-what. And yes, if it makes you happy, it's Tristan who told me to tell you that when I saw you.'

Aurélie's look softened, and she licked her lips in relief. Nico took advantage. He shrugged his shoulders nervously and frowned.

'Just one thing, though, and it's me now who's asking. What was that letter you were writing just now in philosophy class?'

'Fuck off,' said Aurélie indignantly. 'Since when do I owe you explanations, arsehole?'

Nico made a show of taking this in his stride. He must have read or imagined from reading the memoirs of the former president he idolized that this is what politics was: learning to take things in your stride.

Aurélie put a hand in her cardigan pocket: the letter wasn't there. She had, in fact, left it in her bag, the large handbag where she put her papers and swim gear for when she had lunchtime practices. Back among the small group, where a joint had just been rolled, she checked that the letter folded in three was still there. It was, but a shady look she detected in Nico's eyes from the other side of the circle of friends persuaded her to keep it as close to her as possible.

Her jeans pockets were too small to put it there, so she finally opted for the one in her cardigan, from which, in fact, it scarcely stuck out.

The joint was handed to her and she took at least six drags. The din of the cars vanished, along with her bad mood. She began to laugh prematurely at the jokes made by the resident comic, and she was the first to get up and give the finger to the idiotic tourists waving to them from the deck of a passing riverboat. When she took off her cardigan to reveal just her t-shirt and do some sunbathing, one of her female rivals pretended to be shocked and asked her to flex her biceps. Generally, people noticed two things about Aurélie: her eyes of different colours and her muscular shoulders and arms. Slightly stoned, Aurélie, who was, in any case, very proud of her muscles, obeyed with a defiant smile.

And then she began to listen to Nico, who had a thousand fascinating theories about the current political situation.

'... But you'd have to be stupid not to see what's happening! Noyer's going to stay president whatever happens. Next Thursday, he's resigning, resigning officially – not unofficially. In fact, he's been manipulating Cornut, the President of the Senate, from the very start. Cornut's a dummy. He'll do exactly what Noyer whispers in his ear, and do anything to expedite the Constitutional Council's decision in the event that Chaouch wakes up ...'

'And how do you know all this?' someone asked, laughing.

Nico, who was too carried away to detect the ironic tone of the question, replied, taking off his jacket like a seasoned politician, 'It's obvious! Look, the problem is the riots. If there weren't any, the Constitutional Council would wait until after the inauguration, after the official end of Noyer's mandate. In order to give Chaouch a chance. But that's too dangerous. In my view, they are going to declare him definitively unfit for office at the end of the week, because, in this country, it's unthinkable not to have a head of state. Ever since we cut off the heads of kings and replaced them with presidents, we've always had a head, a strong head in charge. And a strong head is the complete opposite of a head that's asleep!'

Aurélie burst out laughing. Nico's beardless, aggressively pointed chin and his scrawny voice that swept over centuries and concepts – he was so ridiculous, this poor Nico, and yet it was almost cute.

'I'll leave you guys to Chirac Junior. I've got to go.'

A few voices protested: there were no classes that afternoon. Aurélie explained that she had to go to one of her mother's concerts at seven and needed a shower to rinse off all the stupid things Nico had said.

2.

'Your name is Fouad Nerrouche. You were born in Saint-Etienne, in the department of the Loire, and you are twenty-six years of age.'

Fouad nodded. The judge did not look up from his files. His fountain pen remained suspended above a sheet of paper. His vigorous white hair seemed to wait for something else, some extra information or perhaps just oral confirmation.

'Yes, your Honour,' ventured Fouad.

And this sufficed: the judge started writing again.

'Why is your last name Nerrouche, when Nerrouche is your mother's maiden name?'

'My father was also called Nerrouche. He was a cousin of my mother, or rather a distant cousin, a member of the Nerrouche tribe, quote unquote. That happened often in Kabylia... At least, I think it did.'

'You mean that you do not really know Kabylia personally? You were born in France. Have you ever gone over there?'

'No.'

'And your brother Nazir?'

Fouad glanced to his robed lawyer. The latter gestured for him to reply immediately.

'I don't think so, your Honour. I must tell you from the start that I have not had any relationship with my elder brother for three years, since our father's death.'

'Yes, that's convenient, isn't it? Why?'

'A disagreement about... I don't know how to explain.'

Fouad remembered the way the meeting with Szafran had concluded. There were not ten thousand possible strategies: he had to clearly distance himself from Nazir, remembering that he had not hesitated to drag them all down in his fall.

Fouad turned towards the court clerk sitting behind a desk perpendicular to that of the judge.

'I believe I hate him at least as much as he hates me. It's a psychological disagreement, if you like. Everything is opposites with us, your Honour.'

'Everything? When did it take place, this... break?'

'Three years ago,' repeated Fouad half-heartedly. 'At my father's funeral. We disagreed about... the way of burying him.'

The judge was looking at him without batting an eyelid, waiting for him to continue.

'Nazir wanted a very religious ceremony, but my father had

not cared about that, he had even said he wanted the opposite . . . We argued, and . . . well, there you are.'

'Would you say that Nazir attaches great importance to Islam?'

'I don't know. I believe he attaches importance to nothing and to nobody. I believe he is simply evil. Nihilist is the word.'

Wagner put down his pen and revealed beneath his white hair a pair of thick black eyebrows. His sculptural, serious face gave Fouad an impression of strength and suppressed anger. Yet he changed the subject casually.

'I saw you in that series, *Man of the Match*. My daughter adores you. She says you look like a young Alain Bashung.'

Fouad and his lawyer were speechless.

'Monsieur Nerrouche, you must understand something: while you were bewitching viewers, a whole team from interior intelligence was watching the movements of your elder brother. I already know what you are going to tell me now. I am telling you this detail so you don't try to rewrite history or play-act when you answer this question: what *exactly* did you know about your brother's plans?'

Fouad snapped back. The question had been prepared with Szafran.

'I only knew two things: that he financially helped a part of my family, but without asking anything in return, and notably my mother by sending her, to my great despair, some money from time to time. And the second thing was that he campaigned actively for the construction of that infamous minaret on the central mosque in Saint-Etienne. He was actively involved, but I did not and still do not know exactly how. I also understood that he was in contact with my cousin Abdelkrim, but I understood that too late, your Honour.'

He had a lump in his throat. He almost asked for a glass of water but preferred to continue.

'On the wedding day of my little brother Slimane, last Saturday, I found it a bit odd that Krim received an envelope from Nazir. I talked to Krim in person and asked him what was in the envelope. He refused to tell me.'

'Well, I'm going to, Monsieur Nerrouche,' murmured Wagner after he had scribbled a note. 'In this envelope, there was an express train ticket for him to go to Paris and assassinate Idder Chaouch. Who in your family knew of the existence of this envelope?'

In a panic, Fouad looked to his lawyer. The latter spoke: 'Your Honour, my client knows nothing about that.'

'Well, let him say it himself!'

'I don't know, your Honour.'

Wagner saw he was lying. All the bad temper he had accumulated since the start of this day concentrated in the fingers of his right hand, the thumb and the index that pinched the top of his nose as if to clean the corners of his tired eyes.

'Monsieur Nerrouche, you are being heard as an assisted witness, which means that at any moment I can decide to charge you. Do you understand what that means, being charged?'

Fouad raised his eyebrows to indicate yes, he understood.

'Well, we'll return to that. I would now like to ask you about your relationship with Jasmine Chaouch. How long have you known her? How did you meet her?'

Fouad did not have the time to reply: an ultra-powerful siren made the floor of the office vibrate.

Wagner turned to Alice. She shrugged her shoulders and put her hand on her belly. Accompanied by two police officers, the military commander of the Palace opened the office door.

'Your Honour! It's a bomb alert. We have to evacuate the Palace.'

'A bomb alert here? But that's impossible!'

'I assure you.'

The military commander's voice was not that of a man carrying out a simulation. Wagner let Fouad and Szafran leave and accompanied Alice onto the landing. He took great care to lock his office and came across Rotrou at the entrance to the Saint-Eloi gallery. Covered by the siren's din, the two judges did not speak to each other. But in the Ogre's eyes there was a flood of recriminations, as if this alert were a consequence of Wagner's 'humanist' methods.

While crossing the waiting room, Fouad felt the tingling of a strange and entirely unfamiliar fear: that of an explosion. The roofs would collapse, and the blown-out walls would project enormous bricks at their tiny and already charred bodies. But it was the explosion itself that terrified him: it was the thought of an unimaginable sound, louder than thunder and more violent than death itself.

'It's just a false alarm, my dear,' said Dounia, on seeing that her son was having difficulty breathing.

When they were out of danger, behind the security cordon, the judge, surrounded by his bodyguards, seemed to confirm Dounia's prediction.

'It's probably a false alarm, but the checks are going to take hours. We must arrange another meeting. In the coming days. Tomorrow perhaps?'

Szafran protested, 'Your Honour, my clients live 480 kilo-metres from Paris. They are hunted and literally harassed by the press. Their every trip is terribly costly, in terms of money as well as energy.'

Alice had left behind the office diary. Wagner saw her hand was on her belly and her face was doleful and worried.

'The day after tomorrow,' conceded the judge. 'Let's put it off to the day after tomorrow, at the same time.'

He took a few steps back to ask Alice if she was all right. She put on her usual smile.

'Very well. A bit tired, but trust me, I would tell you if it was becoming too difficult.'

And as if to prove that she very much intended to work until the last hours of her pregnancy, she added, 'It's true he looks like Alain Bashung.'

'Yes, but it's very probable that he won't have the same career,' commented the judge, turning on his phone to listen to his most recent messages. 'Ah, there you go, speak of the devil . . . my daughter just called me.'

He rang Aurélie back, who answered after the third ring.

'Hello, my terrible daughter. What did you want to tell me?'

Aurélie hesitated at the end of the line. She wanted to confess everything: the afternoon with Krim and the letter for him she had just written and which she needed her father to pass on. She did not have a choice: Krim must receive that letter; she had to tell him the truth about that Sunday. But even if her father seemed better disposed towards her than the day before ('my terrible daughter'), she was too afraid of his reaction.

'It's . . . I don't really know how to say this . . .'

'How to say what?' asked the judge in an inquisitorial voice. 'I'm listening.'

'Papa, I can't speak about it on the phone. When are you coming home?'

'Aurélie, what's happening? Are you bloody well going to explain to me or not? Aurélie? *Aurélie?*'

She had hung up.

3.

It took the bomb disposal teams three hours to confirm that it had, in fact, been a false alarm. But at around four o'clock in the afternoon two other phone calls warned that bombs were going to explode at the Havre-Caumartin metro station and at the François Mitterrand National Library. The mass evacuations were filmed by a horde of cameras, but, once again, no explosives were found. Prosecutor Lamiel, who was already managing the hallucinatory calls from 'witnesses' claiming they had seen Nazir in all four corners of the globe, launched a preliminary investigation and entrusted it to the counterterrorism section of the judicial police. He refused to talk to a journalist from Agence France-Presse and called Wagner to find out how the hearings with the family had gone. Wagner explained to him that he had had to postpone them, and was strongly opposed to the prosecutor's hypothesis that it was a manoeuvre by the Nerrouches to avoid being questioned in due form.

To stem the psychosis that risked spreading among Parisians, the prime minister gave a press conference, encouraging people to go on living as they did before the assassination attempt. No serious threat had been recorded since this attack, and the false alarms that Tuesday afternoon were attributed to practical jokers whom the police would do everything to apprehend and punish in exemplary fashion.

After the departure of Szafran, who had again spoken very reassuringly ('we're lucky to have such a good judge'), the 'close family' went into a café. Fouad had chosen an unassuming place: his mistrust of journalists was turning into a phobia.

The toothless waiter at their table made a strange impression on him: he spoke like a former drug addict numbed by medication for his nerves, and on observing his extremely meticulous gestures and a politeness that seemed to hover on the brink of anger, Fouad was somehow convinced they were dealing with an ex-convict. When he brought their coffees, he moved Fouad's papers a bit further up the table, so the hot cup was right in front of the customer's chest, but accompanied this intrusive movement with a frankly reproachful 'if you don't mind'.

Fouad proposed to Dounia and Rabia that they spend the night in Paris at his apartment in the 12th arrondissement. He would sleep at a friend's place, and, anyway, he had things to do in Paris before returning to Saint-Etienne.

But Rabia could not bear being in the same city as her son without seeing him, and did not want to leave Luna alone any longer.

'I'll drive,' decided Dounia. 'If we leave now, we'll arrive around eleven or twelve tonight.'

Fouad was reluctant for his mother to spend six hours behind the wheel after the day they had just had. But Dounia insisted. And when he accompanied them back to the car and closed the door, her son could not help feeling an enormous sense of relief. For the first time since Saturday, he was alone: he did not have to appear strong, and the only immediate decision he had to make was which way he should take to get home.

Forgetting his resolution to remain incognito, he crossed the place du Châtelet and went along rue de Rivoli before it became rue Saint-Antoine. On this main road, which he knew by heart, he was surprised by the unusual number of police vehicles parked on the emergency lanes and accompanied by soldiers who now patrolled the pavements. If he had taken the metro, he would have been even more surprised: the memory of the bloody bombings of 1995 by Islamist terrorists, revived by the attack on Chaouch, had convinced the authorities to place a security detail in each carriage. Instead of staying at the back of the train carriages, the soldiers patrolled the aisles, checking the seats, and asking all dark-skinned passengers to show the contents of their bags.

An overexcited old man asked Fouad for the time and kept talking to him for five endless minutes during which Fouad learned that: 'If there are so many soldiers, it's because the Security Alert System has been raised to red. Ah yes! You know what? As long as we don't have a president, we're vulnerable. And it's going to last, I'm telling you. Chaouch isn't going to wake up . . .'

This loquacious passer-by suddenly stopped talking when it occurred to him that Fouad might be North African.

'Well, I'm telling you, I voted for him, you know, and I'd prefer he woke up, but, you know, we should be realistic. A ruptured aneurysm in the brain? Well, frankly . . . My brother-in-law had that, near Menton, you know Menton? Nice place, isn't it? But I'm telling you, he stayed in a coma for two months and afterwards he collapsed just like that. Oh yes! Well, I'm telling you all this just to say: when's Noyer going to go? In ten days? Next Friday, I think. Well, what's going to happen after that? The President of the Senate will replace him, but who's the President of the Senate? That drip Cornut! I mean, frankly, Cornut? Winner of the political humour prize for the last three years! Three consecutive years! And you think they're going to wait for us to have someone proper in charge before they attack us, Al-Qaeda and their friends?'

Once he had shaken off this unwelcome attention, Fouad removed his jacket and continued on his way under a sustained series of female looks, accompanied by smiles on at least three occasions. After Saint-Paul, he stopped and was seized by a violent sense of déjà-vu. He sought a familiar notch in the pleasantly curved architecture climbing towards the July Column – a garret, a corbel, a wrought-iron balcony, just something to break the uniformity of the ribbon of narrow buildings after the church of Saint-Paul.

But the entire landscape refused to respond.

A petite brunette with blue eyes suddenly stood in front of him, where the street crossed rue de Turenne. She had a pixie cut, and wore a black sleeveless t-shirt with a subtly low neckline.

'Are you trying to make me believe you don't recognize me?'

Fouad rubbed his eyes. He remembered sleeping with her two years earlier. He remembered it was a stormy night and that she had freckles between her breasts. But he could not remember her name.

'Fuck, it's been years, Fouad,' the young woman declared, lighting a cigarette. 'You never called me, you bastard!'

Fouad slapped his forehead.

'Amazing…!'

He would never retrieve her name, but at least she seemed unaware of his involvement in the nation's psychodrama.

'Well, I've seen things are going well for you. *Man of the Match*. I love it! You still filming, or is the season finished?'

Fouad remembered that she worked in cinema: production, finance, marketing, something like that.

'Yeah,' he said, slightly ill at ease. 'We start again in two, three weeks.'

'Are you going to Cannes this year?'

Fouad put his hands behind his neck and nodded as if he was doing a set of crunches standing up.

'Cannes? Not sure. I don't feel too much like sunbathing at the moment, with all that's going on . . .'

'It's not sunbathing,' insisted the young woman. 'It's partying! You're hilarious. And anyway, everyone's expecting you down there.'

Ah, so she knows, Fouad thought. But looking straight into her eyes, he wasn't so sure.

In fact, the young woman didn't know. What she did know was that she was exaggerating: not everyone was expecting Fouad, due to his popular success in *Man of the Match* and the supporting role he'd had in the summer's upcoming hit comedy, which was already starting to attract the overt contempt of a large number of critics. But he was in contact, or more accurately, his agent Yael was in contact with a respected director who, two years previously, had won the Oscar for best foreign film, and who had an excellent reputation in French cinema.

As the conversation languished, Fouad revealed a professional secret to his former conquest, as if to earn forgiveness for not remembering her name.

'You shouldn't talk about it, obviously, but I'm maybe going to act in a sort of biopic of Emir Abdelkader. Filming's supposed to start in the autumn. It's very ambitious: a five-hour film in three parts. It'll recount the life of Abdelkader, his youth, his captivity . . .'

'Holy shit, that's fantastic!' exclaimed the young woman, opening her eyes wide with amazement.

'Yeah, although I do wonder if . . .'

'If what?'

Fouad sighed. He was really not on top form. The confessional mode suddenly seemed to be the least evil, the only possible way forward.

'You know, I just wonder if I have what it takes to play Abdelkader! I mean, frankly, what do I do? I make people laugh on a cheap sitcom. I go and play a nice Arab in the comedy blockbuster of the summer . . . There are times when I wonder . . .'

'Don't wonder,' the girl reacted solemnly. 'Don't wonder . . . But hang on, we're not going to stay here in the street, looking like idiots, are we? You want to get a drink?'

Fouad glanced at the freckled flesh of her firm, white young bosom. The flashing lights of a procession of unmarked cars woke him up. He thought of Krim, Ferhat, Jasmine, and his mother coughing.

He said no, claiming he was already late for a drink with someone else.

4.

Yael had put on a flared skirt and high heels when Fouad arrived at her place. He asked her if she was going out, and she replied on taking his hand that *they* were going out. The sound of her heels on the staircase awakened Fouad and reminded him why he loved Paris so much, especially at this time of year. In the sunlit street, Yael's red curly hair had never seemed so exuberant.

They passed by a supermarket, bought a six-pack and a screwtop bottle of Muscat, and settled on one of those fashionable lawns in the Parc des Buttes-Chaumont. Fouad recounted his afternoon, and the bomb threat. Yael had a hyperactive way of listening to people. Her open mouth devoured the words, digesting them with 'oh yeah?', and 'oh my God!'

'So that's it . . .'

He stretched out on his back and looked at the clouds fraying in the blue sky above.

Yael opened a second can of beer and spilled some foam on her multicoloured blouse. Wiping herself unceremoniously, she realized that she was not yet ready to get to the point.

'I wanted to ask you, about Jasmine . . . I've thought a lot about this. You don't think it's a bit dangerous to . . . I dunno . . .'

'What are you talking about?' Fouad asked.

'Well, you know, it's a bit risky there, in Chaouch's entourage. They're maybe going to take civil action. Well, I just think you should start to see them as . . . as enemies, legal enemies. I suppose Szafran explained it better than me . . .'

'Szafran hasn't talked about that. And I'd like you to do the same.'

Fouad felt he had been a bit too harsh. He tapped his agent's shoulder and changed subject.

'Well, anyway, when do I start filming again? I don't know how I'll do it. I can't leave Saint-Etienne now. My aunt, my mother . . .'

Yael kept silent. Fouad lifted himself onto an elbow to grab his phone, which was vibrating. It was Slim. He chose not to reply.

'Yael, are you okay?'

Yael had never heard this tone in Fouad's voice. She opened her second can of beer and took a deep breath.

'Well, Fouad, I tried to tell you this on the phone, but ...
these are not things you say on the phone. God ... I think I've
got some bad news for you, Fouad ...'

5.

At that very moment, Jasmine felt the bathwater in which she
had been meditating for half an hour beginning to cool. But
she was too weary to turn on the hot water tap and wallowed,
immobile, in the tepid liquid, fascinated by her own laziness.

Two knocks on the bathroom door made her jump.

'Mademoiselle Chaouch? Is everything all right?'

It was the voice of Couteaux. Out of defiance, Jasmine did
not reply. But when Couteaux knocked again and repeated his
question, she had no choice but to splash noisily in the soapy
pool.

Couteaux's shadow was moving in the tiny strip of light at the
foot of the door. This made Jasmine feel an annoyance bordering
on hatred. She turned on all the taps and let the water pour
out. When Couteaux tried to open the lock, Jasmine screamed,
'Leave me alone! Leave me alone, for fuck's sake!'

To calm down, she closed her eyes, and breathed slowly. The
words at the end of Rameau's *Les Indes galantes* came back to
her. She had missed the previous day's rehearsal, as well as her
singing lessons. It was the rondeau from 'The Savages' that she
sang in a low voice at the surface of the water, as if breathing into
the sails of an imaginary vessel:

> Peaceful forests, peaceful forests,
> Never here does vain desire trouble our hearts.
> If they are sensitive, if they are sensitive,
> Oh Fortune! It is not at the price of your favours ...

She dreamed of those peaceful forests. She would have liked to have one of those hearts that no vain desire troubled. The thought that Fouad had attended a judicial hearing haunted her now.

The six months they had spent together, their weekends in London and Venice, the evenings under the covers watching DVDs, those spent with friends where they shared a mischievous glance before slipping away – perhaps all of that had been a hoax, and Fouad himself, Fouad the actor, had played her to get close to her father. The songs they had loved and to which Jasmine already attached so many memories; a whole period of her life imbued with those melodies: the Fouad period. The music of her love – which dignified her love just as her love dignified the music, in a lovely circle – suddenly went out of tune because of this tiny but persistent suspicion that was growing because it could not be simply waved away.

And the percussion sections, the cello's entrance, the major chords that, after a few months, had contained all the joy of her love, were now just artifices meant to dupe her, reverberating in her soul only the bitter certainty of her own ridiculousness.

'No, no,' she murmured. 'I can't believe he lied. I can't believe he's taken me for an idiot . . .'

Mad with rage, Jasmine got up and unlocked the door. She came out of the bathroom completely naked. She passed in front of the gawping Couteaux and walked resolutely over to the low table where she remembered leaving her phone. But the phone was not there. Nor on the couch either.

'My phone, where is it?' she asked the bodyguard, who was trying not to look at her. 'Where is it? So I don't even have the right to phone Fouad? Well, let's see what happens if I don't have the right to call Fouad! I want to speak to him. I *have* to speak to him! This is absurd! He loves me!'

And thus, still in the nude, she began to search the apartment for her phone, quickly turning it into a battlefield.

6.

A battlefield is what Fouad's mind looked like after hearing Yael's bad news.

'But they've got no right! We can do something about this, no?'

'You'll have to see with Szafran—'

'A paparazzi shot on the cover of *Closer*! Is that possible, with me and Jasmine like that? Can't we ban its publication? And what do we look like in it?'

'But I just told you, Fouad. I haven't seen it. It was an old friend who works there and who told me they'd decided to publish it.'

'But publish what, exactly?' said Fouad angrily.

'Fouad, everybody knows. It's awful, I know, but . . . Everybody knows in these circles that you're Krim's cousin. And so long as you haven't been cleared—'

Fouad stopped her mid-sentence. As if to make it resonate.

'Cleared? Cleared, my arse! I'm not even charged. Not me, not my mother, not . . . It's Krim who . . .'

It was Krim, therefore it was Fouad. The subtleties of the justice system obviously had no effect on the media's propensity to presume culpability.

'And what about *Emir Express*?'

This was the forthcoming summer comedy in which he played a young Algerian immigrant who discovers an oilfield in his village in Loir-et-Cher.

'What are they going to do?' he asked with a dry laugh. 'Are they going to cancel the release?'

Yael had not noticed that she was drunk before Fouad became angry. She bit her lip, felt ridiculous and opened the Muscat. She took a big swig from the bottle.

'No, the film's going to be released. And I'm telling you as it is, Fouad: I'm going to fight, I'm going to do all I can . . . And it's horrible to think about this but, knowing these people, the distributors are maybe going to think this could be a good thing: whatever happens to you, it's a godsend for publicity . . . I mean, it's awful, but . . . Listen, let's not think of that yet. Just try . . . try to keep a low profile while we wait for—'

'While we wait for what? For me to publicly distance myself from my cousin? While I change my name and birth certificate?'

Yael wanted to reply, but Fouad had stood up and started walking.

'Where are you going, Fouad?'

'To take a piss,' he replied coldly.

Yael looked at the bottle, of which she had drunk a third on her own. 'He needs me,' she thought.

Just then, she heard the ringing of a phone that was not hers. Fouad had left his phone on the grass, next to his linen jacket. Yael took it: Jasmine was calling. She turned around to be sure that Fouad could not see her and stopped the call after the second ring. A few minutes later, a beep rang out, indicating a new voicemail. Yael hit 'Listen' to hear Jasmine's message:

'My love, I don't have the right to call you but I can't take it any more, I miss you too much, they're telling me things about you, I know they're talking crap but I need to hear you say it, come on, please pick up the phone,

I just want to talk for two minutes . . . I don't know what you think, if you think I'm angry with you or . . . Just call me back, please.'

The voicemail service asked if she wanted to press 2 to save the message or 3 to delete it. Yael turned around again and saw Fouad at the top of the slope, leaning against a tree trunk, lost in thought. Not one of the pretty boys who buzzed around her could hold a candle to him.

She bit her lip and pressed 3.

7.

In the Montpensier wing of the Palais Royal, the ten members of the Constitutional Council were interviewing Professor Saint-Samat, chief medical officer at Val-de-Grâce, in order to thoroughly inform themselves of the president-elect's state of health.

The interview lasted two hours. The honourable ladies and gentlemen of the Constitutional Council finally dismissed the doctor and the neurosurgeons who had carried out the delicate operation on the presidential brain. And while the most eminent professors of constitutional law were urgently invited to appear on TV panels, while in police stations all over the country officers prepared to confront a third night of violence, former President Valéry Giscard d'Estaing walked towards the window lined with beige curtains overlooking the main courtyard.

President Chirac had had to relinquish his seat on the council in summer 2011, after being found guilty of corruption. Ever since, voices were constantly denouncing the rule that allowed former heads of state to automatically have a seat on the council. Valéry Giscard d'Estaing had no intention of giving up his seat, but the way in which he distanced himself that evening, with hushed steps, was not unsurprising to his peers, especially when they noticed that his lips were moving in empty space and that he seemed to be talking to someone. They wondered to whom he could be speaking, that backlit silhouette who looked like a ghostly incarnation of the republican monarchy itself, a presidential monarchy that the president-elect, on whose fate they had to give a ruling, had promised to bring down.

One great jurist whispered his perplexity into a colleague's ear. The latter facetiously replied by humming a melody by Couperin, accompanied by a wave of his palm, which was far better suited to the full sound of a cello than the tinkle of a harpsichord's unsingable tremolos.

'Do you recognize that?' he asked, once out of breath.

Faced with the stunned look of his younger colleague, he explained, 'It is the most beautiful piece for harpsichord by Couperin, the famous twenty-fifth *Ordre*... And to indicate the tempo, just one word...' – he took a dramatic breath – '"Languidly". It's called *The Wandering Shadows*...'

Within this seventeenth-century palace, accustomed to the old-fashioned calm that accompanied the examination of burning questions of constitutionality and other esoteric legal quibbling, the Elders decided not to impose a languid tempo on their much-awaited deliberation. It would be said that they had conceded to the emergency sirens and bomb threats. But beyond the classical courtyard of the Palais Royal, as had been mentioned on RTL radio by a Minister of the Interior restored to her high horse, the country was in turmoil and the shadows were no longer wandering. Resolutely out of step with the prime minister, Vermorel had argued that there were even strong reasons to think that these shadows were gathering, organizing and arming themselves, with a goal that could only be described appropriately with one word and which the minister had uttered by aggressively separating each syllable:

'The de-sta-bi-li-za-tion of the state.'

It was impossible to suspect the President of the Council, Jean-Louis Debré, of collusion with Noyer, any more than with Valéry Giscard d'Estaing.

As for the socialists, they had increased their behind-the-scenes manoeuvrings and off-the-record remarks to the media to delay as much as possible the declaration of unfitness for office, which would amount to invalidating an election that, after all, they had won handsomely.

This was a majority of socialists, but not all socialists: the fine political newshounds of the main daily newspapers had revealed that the supporters of Françoise Brisseau were quietly sowing the idea that a declaration of unfitness was inevitable, because even if Chaouch woke up in a few days' time, you could bet he would not be able to hold office. The neurosurgeons, phoned by the TV and radio news shows between operations to offer their expertise, turned out to be more objective: the bullet had not touched the brain, they reminded the interviewers, the operation had consisted of repairing the ruptured aneurysm and everything depended, once he woke up, on the physical and mental condition of the patient. This was also what Professor Saint-Samat and the specialists who had operated on Chaouch had said.

And yet, after two nights of rioting and a nervous tension brought to a head by unseasonably high temperatures, the Elders could not make do with 'that depends', and they had no choice but to announce *the definitive unfitness for office of Idder Chaouch*, the man elected president with 52.9 per cent of the vote.

Jean-Louis Debré himself wrote the communiqué sent to the press, after it was read and approved by the ten other members. The eight o'clock news programmes were reaching an end and the red sun had long since dipped below the Arche de la Défense, when they set up the lectern from where the decision of the guardian angels of the Constitution would be solemnly announced to the French people.

8.

'How do you manage to be so strong?'

These were Rabia's first words since they set off. Dounia had taken a wrong turn, had not found the highway and was now driving on the wrong side of the river. The Twingo was driving around and around through the traffic jams at the Porte de Charenton. Amid the car horns and the city lights, it was like being held prisoner of a traffic game whose rules were indefinable.

'Maybe I'm strong,' Dounia joked, dropping her forehead on the steering wheel, 'but my sense of direction is rather weak!'

However, Rabia was not in the mood. She insisted, 'Look, you're making jokes, you can take anything! Doune, it's too hard for me. I can't manage . . . *Wallah*, Rachida's right: I didn't know how to bring up Krim. Yet . . . Zidan and I did everything. We gave them so much love! What happened?'

Dounia turned to her little sister with a face filled with kindness.

'Don't say you're not strong. When Zidan died, *ater namah rebi*, you started to live again right away, my dear. You did everything for Krim and Luna. But you can't control everything in life.'

'What life? What life?'

'*I* didn't know,' Dounia insisted. 'I didn't know how to live after Aissa died. Without you, I would have killed myself! You continued to laugh, to love. Look at me, look at me, Rabia, look at my hair. And look at you!'

It was true – it always had been: a vitality, an invincible youth had lived in Rabia's eyes. But not any more. She gritted her teeth. She no longer even registered Dounia's words of comfort.

'Where did they say Krim was?' she asked, staring at the invisible enemy beyond the windshield. 'Which prison?'

'What?'

'Fleury,' she replied to her own question. 'Fleury-Mérogis! Dounia, drive me to Fleury.'

'What are you talking about, Rabia?'

'If you don't drive me, I'm taking a taxi, *wallah*, on Granny's life I'm taking a taxi!'

'Rab, even if I wanted to go to Fleury, I don't know where it is. Anyway, I don't want to go there! It's complete madness!'

Dounia looked at her sister out of the corner of her eye. Her chin was trembling: her contradictory thoughts seemed to be contained there, quivering at the edge of her lower lip before they died from not being spoken.

She suddenly jumped out of the car. A coupé was entering the right lane. It honked furiously but stopped just in time. Dounia pulled on the handbrake and ran after her sister.

'Rabia, stop!' she screamed.

A look behind told her that the traffic was moving more freely, and that their Twingo was blocking a line of enraged drivers.

'Rabia, what are you doing?'

'I'm going to Fleury,' she declared, her eyes rimmed with cold tears that slipped down her cheekbones and fell into the void.

'Rabia, stop,' her sister repeated, grabbing her sleeve.

The horns redoubled in intensity. The driver of the car blocked just behind was shouting at them. He was a big, red-faced fellow, in blue overalls.

'What the hell are you going to do in Fleury? What's the point of it, Rab? *What's the point?*'

'I'm going to wait for him,' Rabia shouted. 'He's my son! Dounia, he's my son, you understand? Flesh of my flesh! I carried him in my womb, Dounia! I carried him in my womb. I protected him all his life and now . . .' She leaned on the guardrail of the two-lane highway; she had a cramp. 'And now everyone hates him! My little Krim, my blood, Dounia! My blood!'

The traffic was roaring. Some lorries were passing, whipping up gusts of polluted air that mingled with exhaust fumes and the heart-rending sounds of horns that remained long after the heavy lorries that gratuitously set them off had passed.

'Everyone hates him,' Rabia repeated, 'everyone hates him.'

'Not us!' ventured Dounia. 'Come on, we're going home. Think of Luna, the poor girl . . . You can't give up now. Think of her, think of me . . . Come on . . .'

Rabia's resolve was about to crack, but the red-faced driver came up and began screaming at her. He was much taller than they were and probably weighed as much as the two of them put together, but Rabia stood her ground and began returning insults. The words 'sand nigger' soon got thrown around. Dounia started coughing blood at the side of the road.

Three men then turned up out of nowhere, two of them in jeans and tight jackets.

'Is there a problem, Monsieur?' one of them asked the driver. 'Who are you?'

'Highway police,' the other lied, turning him around for a body search. He looked at Dounia and asked about her coughing.

'Are you all right, Madame?'

'Yes, yes, I'm all right,' she said, raising her eyes and mouth to the sky. 'Come on, Rabia, we're going home now.'

Rabia bowed her head, intrigued by these highway policemen whose arrival was too convenient not to mean something.

Indeed, when Dounia and Rabia finally found their way to the road to Lyon, the three men of the ATSD informed Commander Mansourd that they had been forced to abandon their cover. Mansourd understood. Besides, he was preoccupied by this story of the horsewoman who had claimed Krim's mobile by showing a police badge.

In the corridors of the ATSD, he came across Tellier, who was also supervising the interrogation of Mouloud Benbaraka.

'I'm going to speak to him for two minutes,' the commander decided. 'Turn off the camera. What's he like?'

'Not easy,' Tellier replied. 'He's been up to his neck in shit for so long, he thinks it's a joke.'

Mansourd would certainly have preferred to discover a man with his back to the wall rather than the blinged-out and self-assured gang boss he saw on entering the cell next to Krim's. At ease in his designer clothes, Benbaraka caressed his wrist with the flourish of a man used to swapping, from time to time, the bracelet of a Rolex for a handcuff.

But the inconvenience was not a passing one this time: this was more or less what Mansourd explained to him. Benbaraka licked his lips, raising his eyes to the ceiling. When Mansourd made it known to him that he was sure to be charged for criminal association in relation to a terrorist enterprise, the godfather of

Saint-Etienne whistled and, his thoughts seemingly elsewhere, declared, 'Charge me as much as you like, pal. What do you want me to tell you?'

'How you helped Nazir Nerrouche to prepare an attack on the president-elect, for example.'

'But nobody will believe that kind of crap. I'm a businessman, and sometimes in business you come across fanatics. That's life . . . A professional risk.' He chuckled. 'I had no idea he wanted to kill Chaouch!'

'And yet he did ask you to illegally confine his aunt and to drug her, and you did exactly what he told you to, like an errand boy. Nazir speaks and everyone lies down . . .'

Benbaraka's voice changed.

'Oh fuck, this supercop's amazing! You're going to make me confess. So who was the boss? It was Nazir, right? Wow, this is amazing, I'm telling you . . . What can I do against such a good psychologist? I don't have a chance,' he added sarcastically.

The commander got up suddenly, put his hands round Benbaraka's neck and started to squeeze, until the latter was obliged to stand up as well. The handcuff attached to the table was tugging on his wrist, and he lacked some of his earlier pride.

'Where's Nazir hiding? Where's he going? Tell me or I'll strangle you!'

Benbaraka had difficulty breathing. Mansourd had begun to squeeze his neck more tightly. When he let him fall back on his chair, the gang boss coughed and raised his bloodshot eyes towards the commander, who repeated his question. In response, Benbaraka extended the middle fingers from which his gaudy rings had been removed.

11

THE UNCLE FROM ALGERIA

1.

Her father was a Muslim, her mother a Jew, neither of them really practised their religion, and yet, it was in the wormwood odour of a small church on the Right Bank of the Seine that Jasmine Chaouch went to seek refuge at the end of that stifling day when she had changed her mind a thousand times about everything.

Fouad had not called back, while everyone else continued to bombard her with messages. Habib wanted her to appear with her mother for a feature in *Paris Match* – 'I know, I'd promised, but this is urgent: everything your father represented and represents is at stake.' Her mother wanted her to agree to speak to Habib again after having hung up on him the first time. Christophe Vogel, probably on the orders of his father, wanted to have lunch with her, go for a coffee, anything. The people at the Aix music festival were beginning to harass her about whether she still planned to perform in *Les Indes galantes* in July. Some journalists had got hold of her number. There was evidently something in the air, and the two human beings to whom she most wanted to speak had disappeared behind a wall of silence – one wasn't returning her calls, and the other was in a coma.

Jasmine sat down on a pew in the back row, assuming it was where the non-believers sat. Three officers from the Security Group for the Presidency of the Republic (SGPR) were waiting outside, while three others, including Couteaux, were walking up and down the aisles, occasionally looking up at the stained-glass windows, not to admire their shapes and colours, but to anticipate the arrival of some suicide bomber.

Their charge was slumped on the pew, her shoulders hunched and her head like a deflated balloon. There were two old ladies in the front row, motionless on the creaking pews. They had the same white hair tied up in a bun, the same mouse-like stature and, as Jasmine noticed as they walked up the central aisle after crossing themselves, the same serene and delicate smile, the same evangelical tranquillity. Jasmine responded with a nod of the head and plunged back into her hell.

For the first time since the old ladies' departure, she noticed the altar and the monumental cross on which Jesus stuck out his knees at an exaggerated distance from the post. The idea of adoring a suffering and dying god had always been repugnant to her, but for the first time she did not think of it in this way: she did not think with ideas, she perhaps was not thinking at all, in truth, but she undeniably felt something, something more than an attraction, like a gravitational pull.

She got up and slowly made her way through the enchanting scent of old stone and candle wax. At the end of the aisle, she looked up at Christ, whose stone face seemed to come to life.

Ideas of universal love filled her from every direction: Jasmine reduced them to Fouad. Fouad who used to check, when she sang a 'la', that her tongue was properly flat and her mouth correctly round. Fouad who used to go downstairs and buy croissants after they had spent the night together. Fouad who did not care about the girls throwing themselves at him. Fouad who did not know what vanity was, who was perhaps devoid of ego.

Jasmine felt a warmth spread through her. She then had a series of visions: great stones turned to gold by the sun, churches surrounded by oaks and plane trees, monuments that embodied republican majesty like a perfume embodies the ineffable grandeur of one's own past. She thought that she had been a very privileged little girl. With her father, she had spent entire afternoons hopping from bus to bus. He explained Paris to her through its most important places, great men by their street names, from the Three Musketeers to the kings of France.

These memories were another prayer, which lasted perhaps half an hour. But this half-hour seemed like an entire life.

Jasmine lifted her head again and reopened her eyes. A dozen people were scattered across the pews. Couteaux signalled to her that it was time to go home. She accompanied him calmly. And when she left the hospitable shade of the church for the heavy air, the heat and the car horns, she turned to her bodyguard and asked, 'Aurélien, would you take a bullet for me?'

Couteaux raised his eyebrows.

'Uh . . . I don't understand, Mademoiselle.'

'If I was shot at, would you put yourself between the bullet and me?'

'Well, yes, that's my job. Mademoiselle, your mother's calling you, and I think you should reply. Things are happening . . .'

'I'm going to call her in the car, Aurélien. Thanks.'

Couteaux watched her slip into the armoured car. He sat down next to her and told the driver the route he had chosen for getting to the canal. But Jasmine lifted her chin.

'Couldn't we go join my mother at Solferino?'

'Of course, Mademoiselle,' the driver replied after having consulted Couteaux with a glance into the rear-view mirror.

'*Thank you*,' said Jasmine, emphasizing the words as if this was the first time she had said them with real conviction.

The car set off. Couteaux looked at his charge out of the corner of his eye. Her temples were covered with small beads of sweat, and her untidy hair half-covered her eyes. A terrifyingly soft smile floated on her face.

2.

The headquarters of the Socialist Party once again looked like what Chaouch had called 'the hive' after he installed his campaign HQ there, so as to solidify the marriage of convenience with the party that had chosen him. The walls were covered with posters of roses, of Chaouch, some that had become famous, like the one of the candidate posed against a background of church spires and windmills, with the slogan Habib had come up with in the bath: *The future is now*. And everywhere could be seen people on the telephone, exchanging photocopies, bandying about figures and opinion polls as if their lives depended on them.

Jasmine was led into Vogel's office, where the campaign manager was surrounded by his closest aides. The campaign had been managed by the martial duo of Vogel (policy) and Habib (communications). Also present at this evening hour, slumped around the flatscreen television, were the four spokespeople of the 'thematic areas' thought up by Vogel. Esther was chatting in a low voice with one of her husband's speechwriters when she saw her daughter standing by the wall. She cut short her conversation, then came over and put her hands on Jasmine's shoulders, like she used to do when Jasmine was a child, when she had to carry a schoolbag that was too big for her.

'Well, that's it, it's all over. The Constitutional Council has declared him unfit for office.'

'Okay.'

'Did you hear me? Jasmine, are you all right?'

'I'm fine, Mama. I know you must be disappointed, but there are more important things, I think.'

Esther had difficulty recognizing her daughter's voice through her motionless smile. Habib screamed into the telephone and demanded everyone leave the room. Jasmine was beginning to turn on her heels when her mother said to her, 'Not us, honey.'

Habib put his stump into his trouser pocket, sent away an assistant with a wave of his remaining hand, and walked over to the daughter of the now ex-president.

'I'm sorry, Jasmine. We're a bit on edge at the moment. Listen, the good news is that I'm not going to bother you with photos for *Paris Match*.'

His bitterness was perceptible. Esther shook her head to reprimand him. But Habib was inconsolable.

'Fuck,' he swore in his usual straight-talking manner, 'what a bunch of cunts, though, seriously ... They spent the whole campaign searching for scandals, and they found nothing. We were ahead all along, in the middle of an economic crisis. We were faultless, for fuck's sake, fucking faultless! And yet, despite everything, those bastards are going to win ... They lost and they're going to win! Well,' he said, pulling himself together, 'the main thing, of course, is Idder. Let's hope . . .'

Jasmine put him at ease.

'Yes, yes, let's hope.'

'You know, what your father did is extraordinary. It's unparalleled in this country's recent history. I . . . it's not over, of course, but even if . . .'

'I understand, Serge. It'll be all right.'

Habib was terribly embarrassed at having nothing more to say. Jasmine bowed her head and pretended to have a question to ask him.

'And what if he wakes up next week? What'll happen?'

'Exactly, that's the whole problem! You can't appeal a decision by the Constitutional Council. The new election takes place in one month. It's an accelerated process and it's already begun, you understand. There's nothing more we can do.'

'Or what about a *coup d'état?*' joked Esther, before her face darkened. 'No, but we've got lawyers considering the possibility of challenging some members of the council, going to the European Court of Human Rights, etc. After all, the majority of the members were nominated, directly or indirectly, by Noyer and his administration. You need a quorum of seven members to make a ruling, and if those who appear not to be impartial are challenged, then you've got . . . Well, there you are. It's . . . Well, this system of institutionalized political gratitude is absurd, *absurd*, and people are eventually going to notice it. What we need is a Constitutional Court like in Germany. We cannot ask the . . .'

But tears seized her, as if the technical nature of her speech revealed, rather than masked, the very scale of her disillusionment.

Jean-Sébastien Vogel, who was speaking on the phone in front of the TV, turned his head and stared at Jasmine.

'Yes, yes, she's here. Shall I tell her to wait for you?'

Jasmine wanted to shake her head, but it was too late. Vogel had already hung up.

There was a whole procession of leading party figures in the ten minutes that followed. They all eventually spotted Esther and Jasmine sitting on a velvet couch at the back of the room: they then felt obliged to cut across the room to present what felt too much like condolences. Every one of them, of course, repeated the same thing.

'But it's not over: we're going to fight.'

Except that their dejected voices conveyed the opposite.

'Well, I've also got to tell you,' Esther said to her daughter without looking at her, in a low voice despite all the noise, 'the Internal Affairs inquiry into Valérie Simonetti is continuing. She's probably going to be cleared but she's accused of serious failings in the security arrangements. Would you agree to reply to the investigators' questions? It's the Inspectorate-General, the police of the police, nothing to do with ... Would you?'

'Yes, of course, Mama.'

'Given that you like her, that you trust her ...'

'That's perfectly fine, Mama.'

'You know what we did on Sunday?' Esther suddenly said. 'We danced. Idder closed the door and had everyone wait outside. For a quarter of an hour, it was just the two of us. He sang me some Jean Sablon and we danced.'

Jasmine took her mother's hand.

'Mama, he's going to come out of this. I know it. I feel it. I hope you still believe it, right?'

'But yes, of course, honey. How can you . . .'

'No, but seriously, Mama. I hope you really believe it. Not like when you say: I believe it's going to snow. I hope that you *believe* it.'

Esther furrowed her brow, troubled by what her daughter had just said. She kissed her forehead and resolutely sat up straight.

'Of course I believe it, honey. I truly believe it. But what do you want us to do? Rediscover the wisdom of the Ancients? There are things we can control and things we can't control . . .'

Jasmine wanted to tell her what had happened to her in the church, but the crowd of blue and black suits split to enable a departure, or an arrival, offering the young woman a view of the television. Jean-Louis Debré's lips were moving behind a lectern, with the face of Chaouch on the left of the screen. The face of her father, whom Jasmine was now just beginning to understand would never be President of the Republic. What she had feared, wished for, and feared and wished for again before no longer wanting it at all after the attack. And now that reality was cutting through the Gordian knot of her indecisiveness, she realized not only that she had no idea what she wanted, but, above all, that she did not care. She did not care at all.

What the Elders had done by untying the rope that had linked the president-elect to his people was to give a father back to his daughter. And nothing else mattered now, as far as Jasmine was concerned.

3.

Montesquiou's Vel Satis stopped outside the gate of the minister's private residence, an elegant property in the 8th arrondissement, near the Champs-Elysées and within the glow of the Eiffel

Tower. The two police officers at the entrance stood to attention and let the car advance into the courtyard. There was a swing and some tables and chairs in polished copper. In the middle of the lawn, a majestic chestnut tree cast its shadow over a grove of blooming plane trees. The snaking gravel path led to the house itself, an imposing three-storey building covered in pleasingly lush ivy that gave the main facade the tranquil look of a bearded man.

There was certainly no risk of finding a bearded man inside: the minister's husband, a former chief adviser to the National Audit Office, had shaved himself bald when he became a sculptor. He occupied an outbuilding converted into a workshop and spent his days making strange porcelain crosses. Montesquiou's understanding was that they slept in separate buildings, but, in fact, they even lived in separate buildings, and only saw each other for family lunches that Vermorel insisted on organizing on the first Sunday of every month, after Mass.

Montesquiou had been to one of these at the beginning of the year, a sign of the absolute trust his boss placed in him. He had attended the spectacle of the minister's six sons-in-law, young men from good families, lined up neatly to present their respects to the tsarina. They were bankers, business lawyers, an auctioneer. One of them taught political science at the Sorbonne; respectably conservative, he had, however, dared to bring up at table the question of public policy reform. His wife, Marie-Caroline, had given him a withering look while Vermorel simply asked the cook to bring them her famous strawberry cake. Things had gone no further, but Marie-Caroline had been asked to keep a tighter rein on her 'intellectual' husband.

The youngest daughter in the family was considerably

younger than the others. She was nine and suffered from Down's Syndrome. Anne-Elisabeth was the favourite of the minister, who regularly went into raptures about her inner beauty. These children, she would say, staring into your eyes, are living proof that grace is possible. In the moment, you were not to frown or show the slightest hint of suspicion. And this was the real reason why Montesquiou hated being invited to the minister's private residence: he could control his facial expressions with anyone except her. Vermorel knew what his wolf-like smile was hiding: if he heard that an ugly pre-adolescent was a paragon of the opposite, she had no difficulty guessing what he truly thought.

Little Anne-Elisabeth came to greet him at the car. She was trying to find her balance on a scooter with fluorescent yellow handlebars.

Montesquiou avoided the little girl's eyes. Her mother was still wearing her trouser suit. She looked closely at her young liegeman, while inviting him to sit down on the terrace in the last rays of sunlight.

'I forgot to ask. Your sister? Florence, isn't it? Do you have any news?'

'Madame?' replied Montesquiou, caught off-guard.

She took off one of her high-heeled shoes and put her foot on a chair. Montesquiou stopped himself from looking at the minister's toes playing in the air through her pale stockings, as if on a virtual keyboard.

'The last I heard, she had run away, and your mother had taken on a private detective . . .'

'Yes, Madame,' said Montesquiou stiffly. 'But they eventually gave up. Florence has been an adult for a long time. She's twenty-one now.'

And as the almost warm casualness of the exchange seemed to allow it, he added, 'My father had stopped her allowance. She was warned about what was going to happen. He's written her out of his will, Madame.'

Vermorel looked at him with no perceptible reaction. She had wary little eyes like two almonds within the haughty bags of her eyelids. After slipping her shoe back on, she declared, 'You are an elite soul, Pierre-Jean. And like all elite souls born in these barbaric times, you believe in nothing. But bear in mind that, when all is said and done, when everything has been submerged by the calamity of life, there remains only one substantial loyalty, a sole island of meaning and value: family.'

The minister's red mobile phone vibrated on the table. It started ringing after two seconds, like an old alarm clock. It was encrypted, reserved for communication with the president.

'Go with my little Anne-Elisabeth to the foot of the chestnut tree, will you? She's lost her doll around there, I think.'

Montesquiou got up and left the minister to speak with Noyer. The child seized the young man's hand and trotted over the lawn in pursuit of a fat white pigeon, taking arbitrary turns and murmuring nonsensical words. The pigeon flew off and disappeared behind the thick foliage of the chestnut tree. Faced with the little girl's disappointment, Montesquiou had the impression that she too would have liked to stretch out a pair of fabulous wings to escape the weight of her poorly shaped flesh, melting like a butterfly into the yellow-grey sky.

But the airspace had been closed since Sunday evening, and Vermorel was gesticulating from the terrace for him to rejoin her.

Montesquiou picked up the doll and handed it back to the

little girl, who burst into tears on seeing the violence with which he twisted its plastic wrist.

When he was relieved from his babysitting mission, Montesquiou felt so hot he almost loosened his tie. He could practically visualize the acid molecules of sweat attacking the fabric of his jacket at the level of his armpits. He and Vermorel waited at the door for the car that had just entered the property to disgorge the evening's latest visitors.

It was Boulimier, the boss of the CDII, who had – just this once – personally supervised the investigation of Nazir Nerrouche. His head spinning from the heatwave, Montesquiou could not work out if Boulimier's smile was one of satisfaction or just a grimace. Regardless, his bearing contrasted with the look of a beaten child he had shown two days before to the chiefs of police, when the minister had given him that memorable dressing-down.

After offering his 'respects', he handed the minister a file with a padded cover. His smile, which was indeed one of contentment, slid as far as Montesquiou, and he declared in a strangely fake tone, as if to dupe any hidden microphones, 'I told you they weren't honest, these Nerrouches . . .'

Before passing the document to Montesquiou, the minister confirmed, 'Ah yes. I suspect our dear Judge Wagner is not going to like this . . .'

4.

For now, our dear Judge Wagner had returned to his chambers in the Saint-Eloi gallery and was preparing to send Alice home, who was yawning as she reread the dozens of pages of phone taps on Nazir. The temptation to put this tedious task off until the following day was great, but Wagner felt that something was going to leap out at them if they continued late into the evening. The air-conditioning had stopped working a little earlier in the afternoon. Alice had done all she could to procure a fan, but the ancillary staff were in a hurry to go home and the office now felt more and more like a furnace.

Alice was beginning to see double. She got up to stretch her legs, then realized that the judge, engrossed in his reading, had not even noticed her move. He was scratching his white head with the hand that was not taking notes. The other tightly gripped his multicoloured pen. His lips were tight, his brow furrowed. He suddenly looked up and said in a soft, almost fragile voice, 'Alice, can you check with the reception desk whether a courier has brought the records of the third phone?'

It was the fourth time in an hour that he had asked her to do this.

The office phone rang. Wagner picked it up while his court clerk went on the pointless errand he had given her.

'Mansourd here. Your Honour, there's a new development. I'm on my way to the Palace. We may be able to locate Nazir within the next hour.'

'Okay, but why are you coming here?'

Wagner was on tenterhooks.

'I'll explain. I'll be there in five minutes.'

Alice came back empty-handed. The judge told her about Mansourd's call and suggested she go home. It was purely a formality: Alice knew very well that he was going to need her.

He received a call on his personal phone. Paola wanted to know if he was coming to her concert 'as promised'. Wagner almost lost his patience. He could not tell her why he would not be able to come. If she knew, she would not hold it against him. But for her, it was simply 'work'. Whether it was staying up all night to read transcripts of interrogations, or personally searching a suspect's home, or issuing an international commission request to have a terrorist arrested on the other side of the world, it was uniformly 'work' in Paola's mind. And that evening, even though he tried to explain to her, as a last resort, that he was in the same state as she was in when about to go on stage, she replied with a weary sigh and hung up without sending her love.

Wagner did not have the time to feel sorry for the state of his marriage: Mansourd was at the door.

'Well, your Honour,' Mansourd said excitedly, 'you can thank your colleague Poussin. He has put us on the scent of Facebook profiles, starting with that of Mohammed Belaidi, Fat Momo. A team of experts has meticulously examined the messages left in the last few days, and that has led them to secret forums where rival gangs from the suburbs arrange to meet in Paris for fights. But what really amazed us was a supposed girl, who has a Facebook profile with lots of contacts, including, as of a few hours ago, the infamous Fat Momo, and this girl seems to be giving instructions, and seems to want to make peace between the gangs. What set the investigators thinking was the fact that her texting language is not perfect, i.e. her spelling is too correct. They have done a search and discovered that the messages were sent from a cellular smartphone located in Switzerland. A village called Schlaffendorf.'

'It's him.'

'Probably. We have two secret service agents in Bern, and we're in contact with them. Given the difficulty getting swift collaboration from the Swiss, maybe the simplest thing would be to set up an unofficial mission, your Honour.'

Wagner wiped his brow.

'A surveillance mission, you mean. Well, for that you'll need to lodge the request with a bit more precision.'

'It's a question of minutes, your Honour. I propose that as soon as we have an exact location, we put together a mixed team: DGSE, RAID, plus me and my group.'

'No, no,' baulked Wagner. 'Think of procedure, for God's sake. Mansourd—'

'Your Honour, we can arrest him now or we can let him vanish into thin air. Given the precautions he has taken up to this point, the fact that he's left his BlackBerry on proves that he's got his back to the wall. It's not going to last. If we lose the signal, it could take weeks, months, even years to find his trail again. That depends on you, your Honour.'

'Well, yes to the surveillance mission. But no intervention. There can be no question of a team of cowboys catching him. What would it look like, a clandestine mission in Switzerland? Can you tell me? And why not use nukes, while we're at it?'

Mansourd was chomping at the bit. Wagner continued, 'And what about these gangs plotting on Facebook? The chief of police is doing what must be done, I assume . . .'

'The Public Order and Traffic Directorate is on a war footing. Paris is completely cordoned off.'

'Good. Well, good work, Commander. I'll buy Poussin a new jacket with elbow patches to reward his perspicacity . . .'

At that moment Alice received a fax that intrigued her. She gestured the judge over, but Wagner first accompanied Mansourd to the door. When he had closed the door behind him, he put his hands around his neck and heard himself pray that things would work out. Even the organized disorder of the chambers now appeared to him less depressing. There was only one poster on the wall, depicting a street in his native Longwy, with the smoking chimneys of its factory and black brick walls. On seeing this factory at a time when it was not yet derelict, it seemed to him that his investigation was going perfectly, without having to take an unjust decision, without having accepted the slightest favour from on high. Up until now, the pressures from the courts had in no way modified the spinning of the turbines. The road was still long, but not endless.

'Your Honour?'

Alice had called him three times. She looked worried.

She handed him the fax. The CDII was refusing to hand over the records of the third phone. They had been classified.

Wagner gaped in astonishment.

'Top Secret,' murmured Alice to break the silence.

'But . . . I don't understand . . . why . . .'

The judge stopped talking. He slumped in his chair and reread the fax several times. Hypotheses jostled in his overworked mind. Top Secret: it could mean everything and anything. What was certain was that neither Wagner nor any other judge would ever know more about it, or at least not for several years. And suddenly it was as if the lights were going out, as if the machines were grinding to a halt, as if all those with whom Wagner had believed he worked on the same assembly line had only been a team of holograms, and the judge, brutally confronted with the ultimate limits of his investigative powers, found himself alone again, irredeemably alone in the impenetrable darkness of a cold factory.

'Okay,' Wagner said, pulling himself together. 'Alice, call the CDII immediately. If it's a war they want, then that's what they'll get.'

5.

Rabia had slept all the way through the second half of the journey from Paris to Saint-Etienne, even when Dounia had stopped at the service station. It was night when the two sisters arrived on the familiar A45 that circled their hometown. Rabia, curiously, seemed to be in a less dark mood than at the beginning of the evening, as if her fit of hysterics in the middle of the traffic jam had somehow relaxed her. Her features were still hard but her face less closed: she put on Radio Nostalgie, and even sang along to the track by Demis Roussos, 'When I Love You':

'*When I love you, I feel like I'm a king, a knight, the only man on ea-ea-ea-rth . . .*'

'*Wallah*, you should have been a singer,' Dounia complimented her in a low voice, as if not to risk awakening her rage.

When they parked by her house on the hill, Dounia saw her niece waiting for them in the doorway. Luna asked right away why Fouad was not with them.

'Ah, you like Fouad, don't you . . . I'm sorry, honey. He had to stay a little longer.'

Luna's lips opened with disappointment. Dounia, slightly surprised, added, 'But he's coming back tomorrow or the day after tomorrow at the latest, don't worry. Did things go all right with Slim?'

Rabia gave her daughter three big kisses on the cheek. The last one lasted a long time, and it was on finally detaching her lips from her daughter's neck that she noticed that her phone was ringing.

She stepped away to take the call while Slim and Kenza came downstairs. The children had prepared a real feast and Dounia was almost in tears when she saw the table set in the warm light of the hallway.

'Look at this, Rab!'

But Rabia's eyes were sparkling. Dounia could not imagine any good news in the current configuration of events.

'Guess who's just arrived in Saint-Etienne?'

'No? Really, is he here? Moussa? But how did he get the visa?' Luna put her arms around her mother.

'Uncle Moussa? He's come from Algeria?'

'You know, sweetie,' Rabia replied, 'when I see what you're like with Fouad, well, your aunt and I, it's the same with Moussa. When we were girls we loved him, I swear we loved him. You can't imagine.'

'Because he was blonde and handsome, is that it? I mean, when I saw him two or three years ago, he was still good-looking, but . . .'

'But a bit old, is that what you mean?' Dounia said, bursting out laughing and pinching the young girl's cheek. 'You're pitiless, you young people. There's nothing we can do. Once you get past forty, you're ready for the scrap heap. I swear . . .'

The conversation about Uncle Moussa continued around the table while Slim served the meal.

'Uncle Moussa, you can't imagine, sweetie. He was our god, on Granny's life I swear he was our god. He was blonde, with green eyes, he was tall, strong. I swear, when he entered the room, everyone fell silent! Isn't that true, Dounia?'

'No, no, she's right, it's true,' Dounia confirmed, raising her eyebrows to try to convince Luna who was sitting on the edge of the sink devouring an apple while she laughed.

'And then he was always well dressed,' continued Rabia, overwhelmed with retrospective pride. 'All the girls in Saint-Etienne were in love with him. They said he looked like an

American actor. Isn't that right, Dounia, he looked like an American actor? All the same, if truth be told, he was a bit hard with his sisters. No, but I'm telling you, with Bekhi or Ouarda, it wasn't easy. They used to say that he would hit them if he suspected them of smoking a cigarette or going out with boys. No, he had a backward mentality, but that's what boys were like back then.'

'Not all of them,' corrected Dounia. 'It may sound funny now, but Bouzid was not at all like that back then. Besides, Bouz just went out with French girls. When did he become backward like he is now?'

A melancholy smile wavered on Rabia's face. She did not want to speak about Bouzid but rather of the one who had so totally eclipsed him – and made him suffer so much – in their youth. The older brother. The hero of the family.

'Your older aunts can say what they want, but Moussa always adored me. I was his little pet. Tell her, Dounia.'

'Ah, you couldn't lay a finger on Rabia! "Whoever touches my little Rabinouche is going to have to answer to me," he used to say. Honestly, it's the truth!'

'It's such a pity he left for Algeria so young.'

'But why *did* he leave for Algeria?' Luna asked.

'Well, we never really knew much about it. He fell in love with a girl over there, and that's that.'

Rabia had something to add, something she could not tell her daughter but which amused her greatly while filling her with a slightly unhealthy pride: it was that Uncle Moussa, a ladies' man of the dark ages, before condoms and contraception, had left countless little Moussas throughout the region, from Saint-Etienne to Lyon, along the whole Gier valley. Kabyle girls, Arab girls, French girls, and Italian girls – his favourites. Rabia could see him again on Granny's balcony in the seventies, smoking Craven As, his muscular torso in a tight-fitting shirt with a fancy collar – a shirt she thought she remembered as pink but that could well have been yellow – open, in any case, to reveal an undeniably blonde and curly fleece, where the passionate adolescent she had once been had liked nothing more than to rest her cheek.

6.

'No? Really? Shit . . .'

Dounia's disappointed voice called Rabia back to the present. She was speaking on the phone.

'What's happening, Dounia?'

'Well, I've just called Bouzid. He says that Moussa's at Granny's, and that he's just gone to sleep. So we won't see him until tomorrow . . .'

So that the good mood generated by the prospect of seeing Moussa did not disappear in one go, Dounia proposed to Rabia and the children that they go to the cinema. But Rabia did not want to and Luna wanted to go and get ice cream.

Slim and Kenza were tired. And so, forgetting for a moment the hell they were living through, Rabia, Luna and Dounia went to eat ice cream on the terrace of a café, while continuing to talk about Moussa, to explain Moussa to Luna, who imagined Fouad while hearing all these stories, but a blonde, tetchy and apparently rather nasty Fouad. Luna did not have any very precise memories of Moussa. He was an uncle like the others, whom she had seen only three times in her life, on the unfortunate occasions that made him come over from Algeria: among them, the death of the grandfather whose body he had repatriated to the village of his birth and her own father's funeral, when Luna had had things on her mind other than observing this character that Aunt Dounia and her mother were now describing.

Rabia, who always fiercely defended her favourite brother, was forced to recognize more and more that Granny's favouritism towards him had created 'traumas' in the family, involving Bouzid, whom Moussa regularly humiliated, and especially Granddad.

'You're grown up, sweetie. You can hear everything now. So, much as I adored and still adore Moussa, I have to confess that he was unjust, and that he eclipsed Granddad's authority, God rest his soul. Sometimes I have the impression that he replaced him. You see, he was the one who shouted at the sisters when we did something silly, and above all, Granny did everything for him, and, truth be told, she spoke disrespectfully to Granddad. That's what couples were like back then, sweetie. They got married but they didn't love each other. It wasn't even a problem, not loving your husband. On the other hand, when it came to the children, *that* was love. And with Moussa, it's true, Granny treated Moussa differently. She served him first, and, look, memory is a funny thing, the details that come back to you . . . When I think about it now, I have the impression that Moussa was always at the head of the table and Granddad at the side. The poor guy. *Wallah*, he said nothing, he just worked, chewed his tobacco . . . Like Ferhat, *miskine*, gentle, shy. And on the other hand, Moussa . . .'

Rabia stopped talking, shaking her head. However much she suffered at the thought of the ungrateful son and the shy father, Moussa was so good-looking, so blonde, so sure of himself! He was the pride of the family. He was the one who got into clubs while his brown and curly-haired colleagues were left outside to fight with the racist bouncers. The one who made them forget their poverty, the crushing weight of prohibitions and injustice, the hostility of the French.

'Ah yeah . . . '

As there was nothing left to say about Moussa, Rabia suggested she call Fouad. He was out for a walk, 'chilling out'. Dounia sent her love and watched her sister lost in thought.

'All the same, it's a pity Moussa's sleeping. Hey, shall we have another one?' asked Rabia with a mischievous look, as if the pastel ice creams were liquor strong enough to tear her from the nightmare of reality.

7.

In fact, Uncle Moussa was not asleep. Standing next to Granny's shrivelled but invincible figure, he leaned over his Uncle Ferhat's hospital bed. His big hands gripped the railings. He had a fine blonde moustache but his forehead was wrinkled, wrinkles that were all the more visible as his forehead had been enlarged by a baldness that had come late but was now relentless. His green eyes also seemed to have darkened because of the furrows digging into his eyelids.

For ten minutes, he had been grilling old Uncle Ferhat. The latter, wearing a ridiculous frayed bonnet, did not know what to say about his assailant. He stuck out his chest and raised his shoulders in an attempt to imitate the monster. He soon remembered that he had had a shaven head and skin as white as aspirin.

Granny sensed that, not until he provided this description – the gestures, the doomed attempt at puffing out his chest – had she truly felt hatred for poor Ferhat's unknown assailant.

315

A nursing assistant opened the heavy door and came in to check on the patient.

'So, Monsieur Nerrouche,' she said loudly as if to a child, 'how are you today? You've got a visitor, haven't you?'

While she checked the drip in the old man's pale forearm, Moussa turned towards the window, hands behind his back. Granny asked when they were going to remove the obscenities from his scalp.

'The operation is planned for Friday morning, Madame.'

Moussa laughed nervously. The nursing assistant noticed this and almost reacted, but the tall man with his back turned did not look very accommodating. She left. Moussa continued his interrogation in Kabyle.

'*Did you recognize him?* Khale? *Think! Have you ever seen him before?*'

'*No, no, my son, no.*'

Realizing he would get no more information, Moussa wanted to leave, but he first let his eyes stray over the old man's emaciated torso: the collar of the light blue shirt they had given him was too wide for his thin and wrinkled neck, but it was his old man's collarbones that struck Moussa most forcefully. The distended skin there had a corpse-like whiteness. The bones were so fragile and delicate that you would have thought they no longer had the strength to jut out, to resist the shrunken flesh covering his torso.

Moussa kissed his forehead, muttering some superstitious words in Arabic, swearing to himself that if his father had lived long enough to grow old, he would have looked after him in the same way. Ferhat's profile disappeared into sleep at the same moment that Moussa noticed he resembled a bird. There were two sorts of old people: those who ended up looking like rodents (like Granny), and those who ended up looking like birds. Moussa liked to believe that the latter faced the prospect of death more lightly than the former.

What was not in doubt was that he had never been as little at peace with himself as when he left that hospital room filled with darkness and Uncle Ferhat's feeble breathing. He swore in Kabyle that he was going to find his uncle's assailant and break him in two. But, for the immediate future, he made Granny understand that he could not stay in this public place a minute longer.

'Eh, eh, bailek ammehn,' his mother admitted, pushing him towards the exit.

8.

Montesquiou loosened his tie in the back of the official car and looked at the black cover of the confidential file the minister had given him. This little trip to Levallois-Perret was not his first errand of the day but it was the most important. He went through the drastic security checks before entering the ultra-safe headquarters of the CDII and was led into the offices of the ATSD, where Mansourd was waiting for him on the stage of the meeting room, surrounded by the chiefs of the three investigative teams hunting Nazir. There was also Captain Tellier, who looked at Mansourd like a man ready to die for his boss.

Montesquiou slipped into the room and asked the commander to continue with his briefing.

Nazir had been located by means of his phone, in a small village in the Grisons region of Switzerland. The powerful satellites of the secret services left no doubt. Although it was clandestine – or because it was clandestine – the mission would be followed live from the Interministerial Crisis Centre by the Minister of the Interior, who had authorized it over the judge's prerogative, as well as by the Minister of Defence, to whom some of the men on this mission reported. The helmet of the chief of special forces would be equipped with a camera. The difficulty of the mission would be apprehending the suspect without attracting the attention of the local authorities. There would therefore not be any extensive surveillance operation, just fifteen men in an Air Force helicopter undetectable by radar, and whose mission was no more and no less than to kidnap Public Enemy Number One and bring him back to France.

At the end of the meeting, Montesquiou asked to speak with the commander alone. All the other men left.

Vermorel's chief of staff handed the padded file to Mansourd and watched his reactions. Mansourd detested this arrogant young product of elite schools and did nothing to hide it.

'We received this from the Algerian secret services.'

'This' was a file that showed that Moussa Nerrouche belonged to the AIG, or Armed Islamic Group, which had been responsible, among other things, for the series of attacks on French soil in the mid-nineties.

'And that's not all,' Montesquiou added. 'Aissa Nerrouche, Nazir's father, as well as Zidan Bounaim, the father of Abdelkrim, both of whom are now dead, made regular visits to Algeria during the worst of it.'

By 'worst of it', Montesquiou meant the dirty war that had covered Algeria in blood during that decade.

'There are files on them at the end, less detailed than those on Moussa, but still . . . That should interest your friend, Judge Wagner . . .'

Mansourd did not take his eyes off the documents, which he scanned with lightning speed.

'Of course, I suppose all that can wait,' said the young man. 'Besides, if you'll allow me, you haven't told us these last two days how your investigation is getting on . . . What do you think, Commander? I mean, what is your personal view?'

'My personal view?'

'The people for whom you work would like to know some more about what you think . . .'

'I do not work for people, Monsieur. The Republican Police serve the French people. They taught you that at your fancy college, surely? The ATSD is a branch of the Republican Police. It is not a political department.'

'You're about to cross the line, Commander.'

'Let me step to the side, then,' Mansourd retorted, closing the file. 'My personal view? It's simple: I don't yet know if Nazir Nerrouche ordered the assassination of Chaouch or if he has himself been . . . how shall I say . . . *employed* by bigger fish. But we won't know that for weeks, perhaps months.'

'Sooner would be better,' concluded Montesquiou, slightly thrown. 'Good luck with the mission this evening. *Commander.*'

The sarcastic inflection did not please the addressee. Montesquiou banged his walking stick on the floor and left without turning around.

Mansourd called Captain Tellier and passed him the file.

'What do you think?' Mansourd asked his captain.

'It looks like the Algerian secret services all right. But that doesn't really surprise me. Without going as far as saying terrorism is hereditary, there's rarely smoke without fire.'

Perplexed, Mansourd was fiddling with the medallion on his necklace.

'I've got the impression this bothers you, boss,' said Tellier.

'Yes, I've interrogated them, Krim's mother and Nazir's mother. I don't know, but it doesn't stand up. Either they knew nothing about what their husbands were up to, or . . .'

'Or what?'

Mansourd's medallion came loose from being fiddled with so much and fell onto the floor. Tellier picked it up and saw in it the face of a woman in black and white, a beautiful fifty-something with a tragic face.

'Who is it?'

'My mother,' Mansourd replied. 'It's funny, but she's the spitting image of Nazir's mother. If you saw her . . . Well, that would mean nothing to you. I'm being stupid.'

The captain did not know what to say.

'Boss, are you telling me you have a soft spot for the mother of this lunatic because she looks like—'

'Thank you, Captain,' Mansourd cut in.

Tellier bit his lip. His harelip seemed to dilate, like the lung of a tuna.

'Commander, there's one last thing. It's about Vermorel's chief of staff.'

Mansourd turned his head, suddenly interested.

'Well, he came to Levallois on the first day, which is normal of course, but he came back the following day, and he asked to speak with Abdelkrim alone . . . As we were going nowhere and, anyway, the kid had told us everything he knew, that's to say . . .'

'You let him?' Mansourd snapped.

'What else could I have done?'

Mansourd drew a considerable volume of air into his powerful nostrils.

'All this is beginning to get on my nerves,' he growled before breathing out. 'And the redhead?'

'That, on the other hand, is going well,' Tellier hurried to explain. 'I'm looking after it. His fingerprints are those of one Romain Gaillac, converted to Islam, known to interior intelligence because he frequented a Salafist mosque . . .'

'Good, you look after that. And listen, there's no question of letting that vulture Montesquiou get his dirty claws on our investigation, okay?'

Tellier made a gesture of impotence that he transformed at the last second into one of approval, then left the room.

Mansourd reopened the file from the Algerian secret services. 'Strictly Confidential' had been stamped in red on each page. A classified photo showed Moussa leaning against the hood of a jeep, near a stony wadi. His thin blonde beard had something desert-like about it, too. He was wearing green combat fatigues and raised his chin in a sign of defiance to the lens. Under his left armpit appeared the wooden grip of a pistol stuffed in its holster.

12

WAITING FOR THE STORM

1.

Kenza had wanted to take advantage of the absence of Luna, Dounia and Rabia to spend a private moment with her new husband. But after half an hour of fumbling and forced intimacy, Slim turned the light back on and sat down at the foot of the bed where the warm rumpled sheets bore witness, like smoking ruins, to the battle in which he had just been defeated yet again.

Breathless, he shot a worried glance at Kenza's profile. Her pretty round forehead was glistening. It took just a twitch of the eyebrow, a girlish wink, one of those clever movements women knew, for him to think he desired her and, with her lascivious and panting consent, set off once more for boarding. But when he parted her knees and found himself up against the inner curve of her thighs, which trembled with mystery and warmth that smelled of guilt, his good intentions dissolved. No ardour and no urge, which made him want to die. But he did not die:

he went back up to that face he could love unconditionally and covered it with tender, chaste and clumsy kisses.

Except that, this evening, it was all too much for Kenza. She passed her left arm over Slim's naked torso and turned on the bedside lamp.

'Slim, we've got to talk.'

Slim froze on his side of the bed. Anticipating Kenza's next sentence, he turned off the lamp and heard those few words that sounded like the first rumbles of the end of the world:

'Slim, I saw you earlier, behind the Design Centre.'

Darkness was a bad idea at that moment. Slim felt the shadows invade him and he began to tremble. Saliva accumulated on his palate but he couldn't swallow. If his mouth produced another drop, he was going to have to spit it out, then probably vomit.

'I saw you earlier with that guy, that tranny.'

'What . . . what did . . . what did you see?'

'I saw that he was trying to touch you. I saw you were pushing him away, but . . .'

She began to cry. Slim tried to embrace her with his long white hands, but she abruptly and violently left the bed.

'But no, you're making a mistake. He's a guy I . . . owe money to!'

In the total silence that ensued, Slim heard the sound of a vibration that he thought he had heard a little earlier while he was trying to concentrate on Kenza's breasts. He lifted the sheets and found, at the back of the bed, Luna's mobile.

'Shit . . .'

He had let the interjection pass in the hope it would attract Kenza's attention to something else, in the hope that she was going to ask him what was happening.

But Kenza, sitting in front of the sleeping computer, covered her head and ears with her hands. Slim took the phone and turned it off. He got up, approached Kenza and touched the base of her neck.

'But I love you, Kenza,' he murmured. 'Trust me, we'll get there.'

Kenza's only response was to crouch on the chair and pretend to fall asleep in that impossible position, which said more than words ever could.

2.

Fouad walked past a concert hall. 'Paola Ferris plays Mozart.' It was the intermission. The pavement was teeming and he soon found himself lost in the crowd. He received a text from Yael, who wanted to know how he was 'coping'. That expression was starting to get on his nerves, and was definitely one of the reasons why Fouad now claimed to be too busy to have lunch with her tomorrow.

Once he had sent the message, he suddenly felt extremely ill at ease: this white and bourgeois population, the false laughter that rang out in every direction and the people who looked at each other out of the corners of their eyes. Like the fear that draws you as close as possible to its source, Fouad's disgust immobilized him amid these people he kept telling himself he wanted to flee like the plague.

But what enraged him the most was to catch sight, in the tinted window of a luxury car that was stopping to pick up some old fart, of his own reflection, which did not look at all out of place in this prestigious gathering of starched collars: jacket and trousers, light-coloured shirt, dark loafers – his uniform for daily life in

Paris, neither too smart nor too casual. It enabled him to be as at ease in a scruffy bar in Belleville as at a classical music concert in the company of creatures he despised. Creatures he despised but who he could not help wanting to please, as proven by the polite and discreet smiles he shot at the ladies and gentlemen with whom he made eye contact. They wanted to know they were dealing with an integrated nigger, a specimen of that new race of Arabs who could be journalists and lawyers, who certainly took it badly when asked where they came from over an innocent flute of champagne, but who at least did not burn cars, did not cut the throats of sheep and did not want to replace the good old French nation with an Islamic State. France might sometimes be the Church's favourite daughter, sometimes a devourer of priests, but it was certainly not ready, and wouldn't be any time soon, to accept gender-specific timetables at swimming pools and exclusively halal menus in the fast-food joints of the Republic.

Horrified at the idea that all these pointless musings were Nazir's, and not his own, Fouad pinched the top of his nose and shook his head vigorously.

On the way home to place d'Aligre, Fouad felt certain on three different occasions that he was being followed.

He got off at Bréguet-Sabin instead of Bastille. The station did not have a connection, so he could see from the end of the half-empty train if the two men in dark jackets he had spotted would jump out when the bell went. And there certainly was a person who waited till the last minute to jump out of the carriage, but it was a young woman. Consequently, he thought he must have been imagining things. But, crossing this lively intersection of the 11th arrondissement, he found himself pursued by a car that drove so slowly it was being passed by bicyclists.

In order to shake off the car on his way to avenue Ledru-Rollin, Fouad was forced to take rue de Lappe, a depressing pedestrianized street with a row of bars and girls in high heels tripping on the cobblestones. When he arrived at place d'Aligre, he decided he wanted to have a drink on the patio of his favourite café. He went upstairs to get changed.

When he came back down, he had swapped his good Arab's shirt, loafers and jacket for a deliberately untidy outfit: old tracksuit bottoms, his worn-in Reeboks, a printed t-shirt and, most importantly, a dark green hoodie. Sitting on the veranda with his hood blocking his face, he ordered a beer from the proprietor, who did not seem to notice his sudden change of attire: in fact, judging by the cold way in which he served him, Fouad realized the man had simply not recognized him.

The place d'Aligre offered an astonishingly representative tableau of the Parisian social classes, distributed between the bars at its three edges: the bar for rich hipsters, the bar for poor hipsters where Fouad (as an imposter) had his usual table, and finally, the bar for more or less swarthy proles who worked at the famous market. This bar opened at five in the morning; the customers there drank espressos from plastic cups and then went back to setting up their stalls. Fouad felt guilty about shunning the clientele of the market's official bar for his dear artists' café: diaphanous girls with pen caps between their lips, highlighting lines in scripts where they had a small role; trendy dads in sandals; the neighbourhood's community organizers – people who all worked in the cultural sector, who had all, without exception, voted for Chaouch, and who were sipping three-euro pints of lager in the soft evening air.

Fouad observed with horror this harmonious landscape of

which he was a representative member, this haven of social peace that was reinforced rather than destroyed by the loud conversations about politics and the anger expressed against those still in power. And it was not the hypocrisy or the comfortable life of his fellow aperitif-drinkers that aroused in Fouad such a sense of rejection: it was the peace itself that disgusted him, this peace that he could almost feel – smiles between strangers, the benevolent wind lifting the collars of jackets, the prospect of returning home after a second mojito to a well-lit apartment protected by two separate door codes changed every three months.

He was thus in the process of turning into Nazir when he saw a young woman appear in front of his table. It was the girl with fair hair who had got off at Bréguet-Sabin at the very last moment.

'I'm sorry to bother you,' she said in her high-pitched teenage voice, 'but I recognized you and . . .'

Fouad could not hold back an ill-tempered gesture: would she have spoken to him if she had not recognized him? Would she have spoken to a hooded Arab if he had not been the star of a successful TV series? How was she going to react when she learned that his career was probably fucked?

'No, it's not that, it's . . . I recognized you at my mother's concert, at the intermission. I immediately started following you. I'm sorry . . . You're Krim's cousin, right?'

Fouad blinked. A new light had just appeared in his eyes.

'I'm Aurélie, I got to know Krim last summer down South. We spent part of our holiday together, and . . .'

Fouad got up and walked a little way with her along the pavement.

'Last Sunday, Krim came to my place before he ... Well, I was wondering if you could give him a letter from me.'

'But ... well, of course, if I can, but ...'

Aurélie rummaged in her bag for a good twenty seconds. Then she moved on to her grey cardigan, the grey cardigan whose pocket she had slipped it in earlier that afternoon. The letter was not there either.

'Fuck!'

It was all too obvious to her now: Tristan had arranged for it to be stolen, on the banks of the Seine. She had been right not to trust Nico. No: she had still been wrong! She should have been twice as wary.

'Listen, it's not a problem,' Fouad reassured her. 'We can meet tomorrow. Anyway, when you're dealing with all these lawyers, it's complicated to—'

'But no! No! You don't understand! It's ... my father ... If that letter ...'

Fouad pleaded with her to calm down. She spluttered incomprehensible explanations, asked him to forgive her, contorting her anxious face, and suddenly sprinted off before the astonished eyes of the people on the patio.

3.

'We should have been in Italy hours ago.'

The 4×4 was hidden at the edge of a wood crowning the hill at the foot of which extended the two hamlets that made up the village of Schlaffendorf. Fleur had eaten away the nails of her two index fingers. Her plaintive tone exasperated Nazir, who showed his nervousness by just slightly sticking out the tip of his tongue.

Fleur tried again.

'So you lied to me? No one's expecting us in Italy! We're going to stay here in this fucking car for days and days until they catch us?'

Nazir had already replied to her legitimate questions at the start of the day. His young accomplice's lack of patience was not a surprise, but it annoyed him all the same.

'Fleur, there's something you don't understand, and I'm going to repeat it calmly: when all the police forces in Europe are looking for me, a border like the one between Switzerland and Italy cannot be crossed any old way. You have to prepare it carefully beforehand, and that's what I'm doing.'

'No,' said Fleur indignantly. 'All you're doing is looking at the screen of your phone, hoping that someone will call you! It's night-time and I'm cold! Is this going to be our life from now on: hiding in a car all day then coming out at night like vampires? Are we going to get out, at least? Fuck, this is ridiculous. You've prepared nothing. I'd have been better... Anyway, why isn't Waldstein here? He was supposed to help us, right? I don't understand what's going on! Tell me! What the fuck am I doing here?'

With just one look, Nazir reduced her to silence. His large black eyes changed shape with the hours: anger enlarged them, while forced patience seemed to have made them sphinxlike – what did not change was the terrifying invisibility of the white at the corner of his irises.

'When I found you,' he declared to the young woman, 'you had just run away from home like a capricious child, and you were giving lessons in martial arts and Andalusian poetry in a squatter's commune. At that time, all it would have taken was for your papa to beckon with his finger and you'd have gone back to the family fold. Florence—'

'Don't call me that,' Fleur interrupted, widening her eyes bloodshot with nervous exhaustion. 'I've changed my first name, I've changed my surname. Do you know many people who have that much . . . courage?'

Nazir looked at Fleur's wan face, her girlish fragility that suddenly filled him with powerful and contradictory feelings. Contradictory but rooted in the same evil: pity.

'No, that's true. You've been very brave. That's why I don't understand why you're losing your nerve now. I need you, Fleur. We need you – both of us. When we're in Italy, I won't be able to go out. You'll be my eyes, my hands, you'll be . . . my body.'

This hint of enthusiasm in her lover's voice drew Fleur to him. She seized him by the neck and wanted to kiss him. Nazir resisted. She had lost her green contact lenses and continued to smell bad.

'Anyway,' said Fleur in a resigned voice, returning to her driver's seat, 'we're like Bonnie and Clyde, don't you think?'

Nazir raised his eyebrows mockingly. Cut to the quick, Fleur changed the subject.

'It's weird. Why do you never think about your family? You sacrificed them, I know. Are you going to make me believe that doesn't keep you up at night?'

Nazir did not reply.

'All you can do is say "fuck off". With your little manipulations on the internet, your attempts to send all those towns up in flames . . .'

'The flames are in people's heads,' Nazir instantly reacted. 'I'm not lighting any fire. The fire's already there. Has been for generations.'

'You're not answering my question.'

'People are burning in silence. TV cameras can't film what's inside people's heads. I'm just making the fire emerge, so it can be seen. And, in France, you only see clearly what's happening in Paris. I am a stage director of the truth, and if you think I'm just shit-stirring, then you're free to . . .'

'But why drag your family into it?'

'You know nothing about my family, so shut up.'

'Oh no, Nazir,' she said, losing her nerve, 'let's not argue. Not now.'

Nazir took a deep breath and, while staring at the cigarette lighter, told her, 'I'm going to confess something, because you've got it completely wrong. Try and imagine me, obligated to convince people, to play a role, to plot and scheme, to be ten different people in a single day, until I don't know what my true feelings are. The fake mobiles, the true secrets. And all of that for months, while the whole country had a crush on that imposter, that clown Chaouch . . . Well, in the evening, every second or third evening, I called my mother. I recounted to her what I did during the day, inventing as I went along: How are you? Explain to me what you're doing . . . I invented honourable projects, flattering meetings. I just wanted to hear her voice. But with every lie she swallowed, I felt I was further away from her. And yet I continued. Her voice, I wanted to hear her voice, that's all. And then I wanted her to worry about me, because as long as she was worried about me, I didn't have to worry about her.'

He stopped, and his voice seemed to soften, his armour cracking.

'She's the only person in the world that I love. I've never loved anyone but my mother.'

Fleur stared at him, horrified, and yet full of feelings: of love for him and of respect for this filial passion.

'And I wanted her to be proud of me. So I told her I had created a public relations company as well as the private security agency in Saint-Etienne. I told her I was settling down in the countryside. The exquisite pleasure of those imaginary lies was irresistible. During the day I lied to society, and at night I lied to my mother. And it was worse than lying to myself. We were being listened to, but she knew nothing of this, of course. Each time she expressed approval, each one of those remarks that meant that she believed my bullshit, that she had no doubt about the truth in what I was saying, was like a fibre detaching itself from the sacred cord that tied me to her. And when I hung up, I changed the SIM card, I stood at the window, I checked my messages, my emails, the calls I'd missed, and I cried.'

'You cried . . .'

'I cried. And I knew that the day when I no longer cried after those phone calls, I'd be ready.'

Just then Nazir heard the powerful sound of a horn broadcast through a loudspeaker.

'The trumpets!' he exclaimed. 'They've arrived!'

'Who's arrived? Were we expecting someone?'

'Fleur, get out of the car and tell me what you see.'

Fleur obeyed. She left the car and walked out of the woods. In the distance, on the only road through the lifeless village, she saw a convoy of a dozen vehicles.

It was a travelling circus. The loudspeaker crackled with information in a language that Fleur did not know: neither German, nor French, nor Italian, nor even Romansh.

'What's with the circus?' she asked, returning to the leather smell of the car.

'Our passport to Italy,' Nazir replied, tapping on his BlackBerry.

4.

Fat Momo heard his mobile ring for the third consecutive time. He had not answered because he was busy preparing some pasta and, when the water began to simmer, he noticed a cockroach on the cupboard and decided to exterminate it as an example to the others.

But when the landline began ringing continuously, he became worried and abandoned the hunt and his saucepan. At the other end of the line, Djinn screamed at him.

'There's a car waiting for you downstairs, a white taxi. You take the gym bag I put on my bed, grab the dog and you come downstairs. Get in the taxi with the dog and you're driven away, okay?'

'But I haven't eaten yet . . .'

'Come out right now! There are cops about to smash down the door!'

'Cops? But . . . why the cops?'

Fat Momo did not wait for Djinn to start shouting again. He ran into Djinn's bedroom, weighed the bag in his hand and realized it was full of weapons. Covered in sweat, he brought the bag into the entrance hall and suddenly remembered that the pan was on the gas flame. He turned off the gas and the kitchen light, and put the muzzle back on Sarko, who was starting to become agitated by his new master's stressed-out state.

Before leaving, he had a bad feeling about what was going to happen and decided to rummage in his own bag to take Krim's

9mm gun. Instead of putting it in the sports bag, he concealed it, as in Saint-Etienne, in his tracksuit jacket. And so it was, out of breath and dressed far too warmly for the sweltering temperature outside, that he raced downstairs. A white taxi was indeed waiting for him in the courtyard. The sun had set, but the heat remained. The sky had clouded over, there was not a breath of air and the birds were flying low. Fat Momo, who had never taken a taxi before, went to sit next to the driver.

'Excuse me, does the dog bother you?'

'Get in the back, you damned *arioul*! And get the mutt off my seats!'

Fat Momo obeyed. His jowls were trembling and his hands seemed to weigh a ton. When the car drove off, he put them in his pockets and stared at the big dog. Its eyes were lit up with sparks that glowed red in the car's darkness.

A quarter of an hour later, men from the Search and Intervention Brigade smashed down Djinn's door with a battering ram. The brigade major took off his earpiece and called the first number on his phone.

'Negative, Chief. But the saucepan's still warm. I think they've just left.'

5.

Commander Valérie Simonetti had asked Judge Wagner to meet with her privately. Wagner suggested one of the bars on the boulevard near the Palace, but Chaouch's ex-chief of security preferred an anonymous pub on the other bank of the Seine. Wagner alerted his two bodyguards that they were going for a short walk. They arrived at the door of the Saint-Eloi gallery and insisted on making the hundred-metre trip by car.

The traffic lights in the place Saint-Michel seemed to be conspiring against the judge's car.

'We could have gone there and back on foot by now,' he complained to Thierry.

Aqua Velva did not bat an eyelid.

From the pub chosen by Simonetti, you could see an oblique profile of Notre-Dame that the judge wasn't used to seeing. No more than he was used to the police vans that blocked access to the bookstalls all along the Seine.

Wagner stopped at the door. Behind him, the cathedral seemed to float in the electric evening. The Ile de la Cité shivered, like a ship on the verge of sinking, dragging with it the Conciergerie, the police headquarters and the Palais de Justice into the depths of the Seine, along with the Saint-Eloi gallery, Wagner's chambers, files, state secrets and all his cares.

'Your Honour, I'm sorry to meet you like this.'

The judge was immediately struck by Valérie Simonetti's athletic build and nervous demeanour. A powerful vein bulged in her bare forearm. She had ordered a lemon-flavored Perrier and wanted to get straight to the point.

'This is unlike me, but I have to tell you that after the attack I was suspended and subjected to a full inquiry by the Inspectorate-General. They want me to take the blame and . . .' – her posture stiffened and her jaws dilated at the thought of all the service she had given and the sacrifice to which she had consented – '. . . And I won't shirk my responsibilities. I accept them. But I have my doubts, your Honour. Doubts about Major Couteaux, Aurélien Couteaux. He was sent in during the campaign by the Security Service of the Ministry of the Interior, directly into the SGPR and Deputy Chaouch's bodyguard. I would not like you to think that I am motivated by personal feelings – these things happen, not often, but they happen. I had Major Couteaux under my command when Monsieur Chaouch asked me to lead his security team. And, it's difficult to explain, but I always had a bad feeling about it . . .'

'You had a bad feeling?'

'Your Honour, last Sunday, Major Couteaux expressly requested to take up a post in the first ring of protection. As I felt he was stressed, I refused. All the members of the first ring are now suspended, so I'm not alone. But Couteaux has been cleared after just one interrogation, and is now directing the bodyguard of Chaouch's daughter.'

'What are you trying to say, Madame?'

'I have only suspicions, but the situation is urgent, which is why I have taken the risk of speaking to you about them. I believe you should investigate the SGPR. The special placement, the major's behaviour, the fact that he came out of it unscathed, all of it seems very fishy to me, your Honour.'

Wagner was taking mental notes. When he left the commander and returned to the heat of his armoured car, he took out his notebook and transcribed the conversation. He called Alice to ask her to draft a summons for the former boss of the SGPR.

'You'll have to put it in the special file, Alice.'

In the special file: that meant the courts and Lamiel would not be informed. This lead must be kept confidential for the time being.

On arriving in the Palace's underground car park, Wagner bounded out of his car and ran up the stairs, galvanized by the complexity of the investigation that, one hour before, had seemed hopeless. His security officers even had difficulty keeping up with him as he raced to the third floor, something that Wagner joked to them about.

But at the door to the Saint-Eloi gallery, his laughter died in his throat: in front of him, Prosecutor Lamiel had the look of a man who has come to announce that your daughter has died in a car accident.

'Jean-Yves, what's happening?'

'Henri . . .'

'You know we're going to catch him this evening?'

'Henri . . .'

Prosecutor Lamiel sat on the bench opposite the gallery's secure door. A half-open window looked onto another wing of the Palace. Lamiel took a deep breath and declared, 'I've just come from Jeantot's office.'

'The President of the Tribunal? Why?'

'He received an anonymous letter this afternoon.'

'Go on.'

'An anonymous letter left on his secretary's desk, with another letter attached.'

Lamiel seemed to be testing his friend, gauging the sincerity of his surprise. He stuck out his tongue and licked his lips.

'The anonymous letter is denouncing you, Henri, and demands that you be taken off the case investigating the attack on Chaouch. Or that you withdraw from the case . . . Well, for God's sake, don't look at me like that. You're not going to make me believe you've no idea why?'

'For Christ's sake, what's going on, Jean-Yves?'

'It's your daughter. She wrote a letter to the kid, to Abdelkrim. That's the letter attached. In the main letter, it says that she and three of her friends, including Puteoli's son, spent the afternoon with him, at your place, Henri, at your place, just before he carried out the attack in Grogny. According to this letter, because of your family ties with the girlfriend of the accused, it is inconceivable that you could investigate in an objective fashion, etc., etc. . . .'

He got his breath back and hastily removed his glasses.

'Fucking hell, what is all this shit, Henri? Can't you tell me? You do realize I can't do anything for you here? My advice, now, is that you decline to act in the case, and as for the rest . . . Rotrou is inevitably going to be appointed to take on the case. There's nothing else to be done. He'll retire after that, it'll be his swansong. This is not going to be pretty . . .'

Wagner loosened his tie and murmured, 'Puteoli . . .' and almost immediately, while moving his head from right to left, '*In palaces, treason* . . .'

Without even glancing at Lamiel, the judge descended the stairs Aurélie had clattered down the day before, when she seemed on the point of confessing something. Holding his tie, he did not reply to his bodyguards who wanted to know where he was heading.

They discovered this at the same time as he: Wagner took the main staircase, crossed the courtyard and wandered aimlessly along the boulevard du Palais, right up to the riverbank, swaying like a man lost on the deck of a ship in distress.

6.

Fouad lived in a curved building overlooking the place d'Aligre. Through the shuttered window of the Asian supermarket that shared the ground floor with a Franprix store, Fouad's eyes met those of a white man with short hair who was idly fiddling with a bottle of soy sauce. As he slowly climbed the stairs leading to his apartment, head down, Fouad thought he was going mad. Could he be followed as far as here? Was that why his custody had been so short – because they intended to follow him, track him in the hope of . . .? In the hope of what? Proving that he had something to do with his brother's madness?

A young woman he had never seen in the building before was waiting on his landing, tapping a set of keys against the door opposite his. She had a motorcycle helmet and a leather jacket. Seeing Fouad, she turned around, adjusted her jacket and cleared her throat.

'Excuse me.'

Fouad saw her approach and understood that something was up. She was as tall as he was and exuded a peculiar, almost menacing energy. She was strangely beautiful, with her wide face and square jaw. Her heels clattered on the floor as the light went out. When Fouad pressed the switch to turn it back on, she was right up against his face.

'Don't be afraid,' she whispered loudly. 'My name's Marieke. I'm a journalist and I've come to warn you. Can I come in?'

Fouad swallowed painfully. Although she spoke in a whisper, this journalist's voice seemed too indiscreet, and when he opened his mouth to reply, it was a thin and precarious dribble of sound that came out.

'I don't speak to journalists, leave me alone—'

'No, no, you don't understand,' Marieke insisted. 'I don't want to interview you. I want to warn you, to tell you to watch out. There are things that are beyond you, that are beyond all of us. I've been working on the counterterrorism investigation into your brother. Listen, I'm sorry to meet you like this . . .'

'Goodbye, Madame.'

Fouad wanted to open his door but Marieke put a big hand on the lock, without taking her eyes off him. The term 'fearless' had never seemed as appropriate to Fouad as it did in describing the boldness of this journalist.

'It's your family, Fouad. They're going to try and scapegoat you. You can't trust anyone. Listen to me. Have you at least noticed that you're being followed?'

'I don't give a damn,' replied Fouad, who did not want to lose face. 'I'm not guilty of anything.'

Without realizing, he had agreed to talk with her. It would have been surprising if he hadn't: Marieke was very engaging, her voice was pleasantly husky, and there was something striking about her sculpted physique, something that forced you to look at her and listen.

'You believe you're not guilty of anything, but believe me, they'll find something to bring you down. And I'm not just talking about you. I'm talking about . . . Can we talk more freely?'

'No!' said Fouad, coming to his senses.

A smile opened on Marieke's face, unveiling teeth that were strong and charming, perhaps because of their crookedness.

'I'll be in touch,' she concluded in an improbably playful way. 'Once you've understood what's happening, I think you'll be a bit more cooperative . . . Well, at least I hope so . . .'

'Because you're not working for anyone?' ventured Fouad.

'Exactly!' exclaimed Marieke, who had in fact just offered her article's sequel to the competition, unsuccessfully for the time being. 'I work for the truth, Fouad, the *truth*.'

On this, she disappeared down the stairs, leaving Fouad with the inexplicable impression of having been simultaneously kidnapped, seduced, rejected and stripped naked. He checked the contents of his pockets as he opened the door to his apartment. In his sweatshirt pocket, he found a business card: MARIEKE VANDERVROOM, REPORTER, with her email address and phone number. On the back, she had written in English, pressing a ballpoint pen into the cardstock: 'Call me!'

His apartment didn't look real when he raised his eyes from the words on the back of the card. Faintly lit by the naked bulb dangling in the entrance hall, his large living room smelled of cold cigarette ash and neglect. He wanted to do a bit of tidying up but preferred to have a drink first. In his cupboard, a bottle of Platte Valley whiskey was all that remained. The small stoneware pitcher looked like an ancient amphora and was three-quarters full.

Fouad turned on the light, and found the untidiness of the apartment reflected all too faithfully in the balcony's French windows. He turned the light off again and poured himself a first glass of Platte Valley. The liquor was pale yellow, and sparkled when he moved the glass. Fouad downed it in one and immediately poured himself a second.

After the fourth one, he noticed that the faces of his family had stopped passing through his mind. He poured a fifth and larger glass and sniffed at it for a long time, detecting the vanilla aroma and the sweetness of the corn, envying the solid tranquillity of those distillers in Missouri who almost certainly had never had anything to do with counterterrorism law enforcement.

7.

Commissioner Thomas Maheut, in a short-sleeved white shirt embroidered with his grade and the insignia of the Police Department, was coming out of the Operations Centre, surrounded by men to whom he was giving instructions. His natural authority meant he never had to raise his voice. He then began speaking on the phone, sounding fairly relaxed, with Valérie Simonetti. He was telling her about the clashes at the place de la République, around Père-Lachaise, and even in rue de la Fontaine-au-Roi.

'We've never seen this before,' he explained. 'They've become organized! A paramilitary organization. The eastern neighbourhoods are all mobilized. There are hoax emergency calls in the north to create diversions. I've just sent reinforcements to the town hall in the 11th arrondissement. They're burning cars from Voltaire to Charonne. It's completely crazy. They've even burned the chairs on the patio of Le Vidocq!'

'Oh my God, Le Vidocq . . .'

Maheut frowned.

'It's most dangerous at Bastille. We've got information that these savages were planning to unroll a banner at the Opera, a huge banner with "Noyer Murderer" written on it. Can you fucking believe it? "Noyer Murderer"!'

'You've arrested them?'

'No, not yet. I've never seen anything like this before, I'm telling you. Such a massive deployment of police forces in the capital. GIPN, GIGN, BRI . . . Dieuleveult has seen it all in XXL, as usual, but I'm beginning to wonder if we won't have to get some guys from the RAID . . . Well, I've got to go. But, wait, are you outside? What the hell are you doing?'

The bells of Notre-Dame were ringing out, and Maheut thought he also heard them in Valérie's telephone. He stared up at the sky: the wind was beginning to move the blanket of cloud that had been weighing on the city since the start of this accursed day.

'Where are you?' he suddenly asked.

'In the area,' Valérie replied in a dreamy voice. 'I had a little something to sort out . . . with my conscience . . .'

'Well, we'll talk about it soon.'

The commissioner hung up. A voice in his earpiece alerted him that the chief of police wanted to see him urgently. Maheut took the stairs leading to the chief's office suite, all padded doors and thick carpets. He identified himself in front of the smoked-glass security door, and then a series of attendants led him through a labyrinth of silent corridors to the large double doors of the chief's office. The two-colour light turned to green and Commissioner Maheut entered, nodding to the other commissioners.

They spoke in hushed tones in this Vatican-like room. The office's giant screen, which generally broadcast news or the current session of the Paris Council, was this time divided in four: three screens for video conferencing, one of which was connected to the Operations Centre, and the fourth which, unusually, consisted of a real-time weather report. And this was all Dieuleveult talked about, sometimes walking over to the window to see the movements of the sky above the towers of Notre-Dame. He beckoned Maheut.

'What's your opinion, Commissioner? Will it rain or not?'

A storm had been forecast for the early evening. Two hours later, the sky was heavy and low. The wind had picked up but there was still not a drop of rain. It was strongly hoped that a storm would dampen the rebellious passion of the gangs of thugs planning to sack the capital.

Maheut made his report on all of the latest manoeuvres. The chief of police's orders had been categorical: he wanted no policeman in Ile-de-France to sleep at home that evening. Apparently these orders had been followed. Maheut thought of those men who had been on duty since Sunday evening. He then learned, directly from Dieuleveult's chief of staff, that they had ordered a blimp to reinforce the helicopters observing crowd movements on the main roads. The blimp was seventy-five metres long. Equipped with satellite cameras, it would fly over Paris beginning less than thirty minutes from now and broadcast its videos to the underground control centre commanded by Maheut. The chief of staff was finishing his briefing when a massive bolt of lightning split the sky over the Ile de la Cité, followed a few seconds later by the noise that everyone had been hoping for: the rumble of thunder. It sounded like God Himself was storming down the steps of heaven, furious.

A soft voice declared it was time. Dieuleveult nodded, hands behind his back, staring out the intimidating bay window of his fortress. Then he sent Maheut away with a meaningful look that communicated a great deal about the immense responsibilities now weighing on him, as well as with an injunction, two words that seemed to rise directly from his guts:

'Crush them!'

8.

While the blimp flew towards the French capital, Nazir was negotiating, in a mixture of Italian, French and German, with the owner of the travelling circus he had waited for all day. He was a bald man with a jutting jaw and a Mussolini-like profile. He unashamedly stared at Fleur while Nazir tried to persuade him.

After about ten minutes, he turned on his heels. Nazir gestured to Fleur for her to stay close as he followed him. The last vehicle in the convoy was an enormous lorry from which emanated a stench so nauseating that Fleur stopped in her tracks.

'What the hell is that stink?'

'Wait for me here,' Nazir replied.

Fleur watched him climb into the lorry's passenger seat. He stayed there a few minutes. When he got out, he led Fleur without a word to their 4×4 and asked her to check that no one was watching them. He stuffed a few wads of banknotes into a plastic bag and came and sat down next to Fleur.

'Are we going to leave?' she asked anxiously, not understanding anything that was going on. 'Is it okay? Can we escape?'

Nazir turned his shoulders towards her and framed her anxious face with his long hands, a gesture so warm and manly that it took Fleur's breath away.

'Fleur, you've got to be brave, now,' he said in a gentle voice. 'We're going to cross the border. It's going to be very difficult. You've got to be braver than you've ever been . . .'

He got his breath back. His facial muscles twitched as if some reptile hidden for years beneath his skin had just woken up.

'You trust me, right?'

Fleur squinted so as not to cry. Her chin moved its pretty dimple up and down: yes, she trusted him.

At the same moment, Djinn was reaching rue d'Austerlitz: a narrow street with very narrow pavements, a row of about fifteen hotels, many of which did not even have one star, and at least two of which were used mainly by prostitutes. They risked being seen if they parked in the middle of the street; a scooter could not have passed them because of the rubbish bins piled on the pavements. Djinn drove around the block and, on a parallel street, spotted an open parking space not reserved for the disabled. He turned off the engine and the headlights.

On the fourth floor of 17 rue d'Austerlitz, Djinn discovered a tiny studio occupied by Romain, who was pacing around, shaking his head, as well as by a young, veiled woman studiously staring at a laptop. There was just a single bed in the little room, a kitchenette, and no place to piss: no doubt the toilet was out in the hallway. A row of cube-shaped cupboards on the walls made the room look like the cabin of an ocean liner. Or was that because Djinn's head was spinning? How could he know if it was him or the world that was unsteady?

'It's amazing what's happening, just amazing, it's unheard of, they're going to lose their minds, I'm telling you, they're going to lose their minds . . .'

Romain was overexcited. He was waving his hands clumsily from right to left. He had never looked so pale and impassioned.

'Are the bags in the cupboards?' asked Djinn, who wanted to show that he was focused.

Romain could not hear him: strange, feminine cries were coming from outside, probably from the hotel opposite.

'We're here,' he continued grandiloquently. 'In the eye of the storm. People are rising up everywhere. Do you understand what's happening?'

Djinn could now hear the woman's cries distinctly, punctuated by panting and moans of pleasure. Romain heard them too, and began to blush when he realized what was going on.

The young woman in the veil said nothing, remaining glued to the laptop screen, which she moved needlessly.

'Who's the girl?' Djinn asked in a low voice.

'She's with us,' Romain replied, taking Djinn's elbow.

'But what does she do?'

'She works in a library but she's with us,' Romain repeated. 'She might not look it, but she's a Sicarii too.'

'A Sicarii?'

Djinn felt annoyed: both because of the effect the cries from the brothel were having on Romain's complexion, but also because of the shameless way in which he mimicked Nazir in his moments of fervour, his moments that swept away your scruples – only here Romain persuaded no one with his schizophrenic babbling, not even his own reflection.

'The dagger-men,' he replied disdainfully, while the panting accelerated and Djinn discovered in the bags hidden under the bed the weapons he was going to distribute to his colleagues. 'The Sicarii were the dagger-men, Jewish dissidents who wanted to kick the Romans out of Judea.'

'So what?'

'What do you mean "So what?"?' he repeated with a cold, flinty laugh, like air spat through the nostrils. 'Well, Nazir's recreated them, that's what! It's you, me, us. But now instead of daggers we've got nine millimetre guns. We're everywhere, they're everywhere, in the shadows, defeated hearts he revived, broken lives he armed! Here we are! In the heart of the capital. Look around you: now that it's done, it's starting!'

'Yeah,' murmured Djinn, observing the engraved grip of one of the pistols he had taken from the bag.

But Romain did not dare agree: the cries of pleasure were increasing in volume, in a terrifying crescendo of groans and creaking bedsprings, until the final scream, that last explosion of an orgasm that humiliated and paralysed him, because he did not know how to ignore it.

'Come on,' he finally said in the humid, unhealthy atmosphere that followed that piercing cry, 'there's no time to lose. He told me to tell you that he trusts you. He trusts you, Djinn. Don't let him down, okay?'

13

THE STORM

1.

All of Paris was sirens, cars and burning rubbish bins, charges by riot police and arrests that were either arbitrary or the result of breaking a curfew that the Police Department hadn't announced properly or early enough for people to be aware of it. While the barracks of Paris and the adjoining suburbs were emptying at the same time as the streets, hooded shadows in small groups of eight to ten were meeting at arranged places and burning everything in their path.

Tristan Puteoli, returning home from Nico's place in Oberkampf, where he had tired himself out playing video games, was driving his scooter along boulevard Beaumarchais in the direction of Bastille when he was passed by a dozen riot vans, sirens blaring. Moving onto the bike path, he was hit by a cyclist and lost control of his scooter. The fall left him with only grazes, but his scooter had careened into a parking meter and was in a very bad state.

The cyclist abandoned his bicycle and ran off. Tristan

screamed after him and noticed at the end of the boulevard, at the foot of the July Column, a huge cloud of tear gas. He was wondering what he was going to do with his scooter when, from an adjoining street, he saw five hooded thugs emerge, their mouths protected by black scarves. The riot police were far off on the place de la Bastille, and Tristan could see no one who might help if he were attacked.

He took off his helmet and started crossing the street to reach rue des Francs-Bourgeois and the place des Vosges. He had his hands in his pockets, with the normal look of a high-school student returning home after a few drinks. But he also had blonde hair. And, in the perfectly lit night in this posh neighbourhood, his blondeness suddenly seemed to him horribly conspicuous. The five guys set off after him at a distance.

He walked faster and faster, but did not dare run for fear he might provoke an altercation. He discreetly called the police, but no one replied. The switchboards were all busy. Tristan thought to himself that the nightmare was just beginning.

Aurélie called. He had not had any news from her since the nasty thing he had done, and this was the moment she chose to call and lambast him. Tristan, who was out of breath from his speed walking, took the call after the first ring, only too happy to have something to give him some composure if the thugs fell upon him. He couldn't say anything to them or 'provoke' them with a look if he were in the middle of an important phone call.

But, at the end of the line, Aurélie began with silence.

'Aurélie, this is not the right moment for insults. For fuck's sake, there are some guys following me, some scum from the suburbs, and I can't get hold of the police. Aurélie, can you hear me?'

'You realize what you've done, you fucking arsehole?'

'Aurélie, I'm telling you it's not the m—'

'My father's been forced to drop the case. You know what that means? His career is finished. It's completely fucked now. Fucked. You understand?'

The five guys had started to run and hide behind the arcades on the pavement opposite. They were kicking the security gates and all the wing mirrors in their path.

Tristan gambled everything.

'But what are you talking about? Drop the case? What have I done?'

'What have you done? What have you done?' Aurélie screamed. 'You stole the letter I'd written to Krim and you threw in an anonymous note to say we spent the afternoon with him before he carried out the attack. That's what you did, you fucking arsehole.'

'But it wasn't me, Aurélie. It was my father! I swear it was my father.'

'There's a limit to being an arsehole. This isn't some sexcapade. What you did wasn't showing everyone a video of some girl sucking you off at a party . . .'

One of the thugs was shouting at him. Tristan did not dare say a word back. He stopped in front of the closed gates to the place des Vosges.

'Wait,' he said, pretending to concentrate on listening to her. 'Wait.'

'Hey, pretty blonde boy?' the thug from the suburbs was shouting. 'Hey, whitey! Come on, hand over the phone. Come on, is that an iPhone? Can I borrow it?'

The rest of his colleagues were yelling at one of their own, who had finally managed to light his Molotov cocktail but couldn't decide where to throw it. Sirens could be heard in the distance, on boulevard Beaumarchais.

Tristan lifted his head and looked across at the high, incredibly high but dark, despairingly dark windows that formed a series of Cyclops' eyes set in the elegant pink brick walls of the buildings surrounding the square.

One of the thugs he hadn't seen kicked his legs out from under him. He fell to the ground and saw his iPhone roll into the gutter. He wanted to get back up and defend himself with his helmet but the suburban scum had run off. Not because of the police vehicles and fire engines, which only arrived a minute later, but because of why they were there: the Molotov cocktail that one of the thugs on the other pavement had thrown into a window of the building that almost completely encircled the square. The flames could obviously never spread through the whole of this brick structure, and yet that was what Tristan thought of as he took his pulse to chase away the fear: the place des Vosges completely surrounded by flames.

He retrieved his phone from the gutter and looked up as the cops came to ask what had happened: two helicopters were hovering over the Marais, as well as a gigantic shadow that resembled a space ship. With ultra-powerful searchlights, these monsters swept the zinc roofs, the tiled domes and the narrow streets of the Marais corseted in stone. Their loudspeakers made a terrifying sound as they gave garbled instructions to the people of Paris, who hid behind their television sets.

2.

Dounia, Rabia and Luna had finished their ice creams and walked through the centre of Saint-Etienne, ignoring the advice of Fouad and Maître Szafran. They were at the foot of the steps leading up to their street, paralysed by hysterical giggles. The bar section of the café where they'd been had a karaoke machine, which was being used by a table of bank clerks at happy hour. One of them had concluded the evening with a flourish: he was a stocky little fellow with a massive head, and his workmates had made him sing a song by Patricia Kaas, 'He Tells Me I'm Beautiful' – which he performed with the most unexpected voice you could imagine coming out of that body: smooth, lyrical and, above all, unbelievably high-pitched.

'We can make fun of him, but he sang really well, don't you think?'

Dounia could not reply: she had her hands on her knees, and the veins of her neck looked like they might explode if she did not stop laughing. Rabia began to sing, imitating the voice and the vibratos of that clerk.

'*He tells me I'm beauuuutiful . . .*'

'Stop! Stop! I'm going to piss myself . . . Stop, I'm telling you, I'm going to piss myself . . .'

Luna observed her Elders with a slightly puzzled smile.

Rabia raised her eyes and the umbrella she was carrying to look at the dozens of steps they would have to scale once the laughter had subsided.

Her smile suddenly twisted into a horrified grimace. Dounia, surprised at the absence of her sister's laughter, took her by the sleeve.

'Rab?' she asked in a still cheerful voice. 'What's wrong?'

She looked at what Rabia was looking at and brought a hand to her open mouth. At the top of the steps, a dozen hooded young thugs were pushing a burning container to the edge of the stairway.

'What the fuck are they doing? Luna, sweetie, come here!'

'They're going to push it down!'

It was true: the unbalanced container tumbled down the steps of the first section of the staircase and ended up in a bush next to an old-fashioned lamppost, which buckled under the weight but did not break. What happened next was worse: the bush caught fire, and the fire spread to the straw screen protecting the veranda of one of the chic residences looking onto the staircase.

Dounia called the fire department but sirens were already wailing at the end of the street.

Two police cars passed at full speed, in front of Dounia, Rabia and Luna, who did not dare move. Two other cars, unmarked this time, disgorged a dozen men in civilian clothes who ordered the three passers-by to return home immediately before they rushed up the steps.

Another car, from the local police, arrived as reinforcement and parked on the wrong side of the street. Its driver lowered his window and told Rabia, 'You shouldn't be outside, Madame. It's very dangerous.'

'But we live up there, Monsieur. We live just beyond the top, in the street by the cemetery!'

The policeman spoke for a few moments with his colleague then said, 'Get in the back. We'll take you home.'

'But what's going on?' asked Rabia, closing the door. 'Now there's even riots in the city centre?'

'What does it look like?' replied the policeman.

When the car dropped them off at their address, they saw a police helicopter flying to and fro across the rainy sky above the hill of Montreynaud.

'Look,' Rabia stammered, 'it's coming towards the city centre! *Wallah*, you'd think we're at war . . .'

Yelling could be heard at the end of the street. Dounia forced her sister and niece inside without delay and followed the advice of the policeman who had been their chauffeur: they deadbolted the front door and closed the ground-floor shutters.

3.

Fat Momo found Djinn at the foot of a staircase where some tramps were sleeping. Djinn took the bag and the pit bull's leash and climbed the steps, giving a few kicks to the slumbering drunks. The stairs led to an elevated garden hanging a few metres above the avenue. To escape the cops' surveillance, Djinn communicated with his commando groups by means of prehistoric beepers, old Motorolas bought on eBay. When the two men were well hidden in a clump of bamboo, Djinn checked the bag's contents and began to do breathing exercises as he loaded the pistols.

Fat Momo asked him what the hell he was doing there. Djinn wanted to whisper to him to shut his big mouth, but he had one of those croaky voices that could never crack the secret of whispering.

'You watch the dog and don't move. When I give the signal, some guys are going to arrive from all sides of the square, and you, you stay here and protect the guns with the dog. That's all. And if you say anything else, you'll get my fist in your face.'

Fat Momo wanted to leave, alert the police, return to his Alsatian and the games of *Call of Duty* in Krim's cellar. Instead of which he took in his palm the 9mm they had used for training, convinced that, with this piece of metal in hand, he would be safe if things turned ugly.

4.

Krim would be able to name each of the notes. First the harmonica with piano accompaniment, and then the voice going on about a screen door slamming. Fouad got up unsteadily as the radio played Bruce Springsteen's 'Thunder Road', realizing, although he had not listened to it for years, that it had always been his favourite song.

> The screen door slams
> Mary's dress sways . . .

But instead of identifying the song's Mary with his Jasmine (besides, why would he, since she had been born in a posh neighbourhood?), Fouad began to think about Nazir. He was too drunk to know whether he was thinking about Nazir because it was his brother who had first introduced him to this song, or for some other, more obscure reason. As teenagers, they used to exchange CDs, without comment or a simple 'listen to this'. And now, ten, fifteen years later, like some silly little girl who believes that the current pop hit truly speaks to her and only her, Fouad was in tears as he listened to The Boss singing that he and his brother had also had to take Thunder Road, to escape the shithole where they had been born . . .

The song only lasted a few minutes, but in those few minutes his whole adolescence came back to him. Not in precise moments but in fragments of landscape, and always in winter colours.

Saint-Etienne, New Jersey: one long road lined with factory chimneys, piles of dead leaves in the high-school yard, footbridges crossing unused railway lines, wasteland. And in front of each of these wastelands there was Nazir to look at it with him and make him understand what Bruce Springsteen was yelling at the end:

> It's a town full of losers
> And I'm pulling out of here to win!

The saxophone channelled the song's rage, the piano was played by a virtuoso, but before the dramatic final decrescendo, the song suddenly stopped.

When the suave voice of the idiotic presenter announced the next song, Fouad ran over to the radio and clumsily tore the wires out of it. It fell on the carpet.

He wanted to call Saint-Etienne to be sure that everyone was safe, to be sure that his town full of losers still existed. But he was not yet drunk enough to believe that he was sober. After downing a bottle of water, he turned on the TV. The twenty-four-hour news channels spoke only of Paris, and broadcast copious images of the blimp floating over the capital. He turned off the TV and went onto the balcony. From the top floor, Fouad had a stunning view of the zigzags lighting up the sky for a fraction of a second before it returned to its dark brooding of clouds and electricity. The thunderclaps were following more and more quickly, but even though Fouad checked every few minutes in the halo of the streetlamps, he could still see no drop of rain on the square below.

He suddenly heard his phone vibrate on the coffee table. Before he even saw the name of the sender, he knew it was her, telling him:

> I have just received your letter.
> I have never been so moved in my
> entire life. I want to see you tonight.

With the bourbon's help, Fouad decided to stop asking himself millions of questions and to show a bit of spontaneity — the reason everyone loved him. He scrolled through his address book as far as the letter J and, with a lump in his throat but his heart feeling certain, he pressed the green button.

'Jasmine?'

On the other end of the line, Jasmine was silent, as tears welled in her eyes.

5.

The dozen police vans stationed in front of the Bastille Opera included an anti-riot van equipped with water cannon, as well as a real armoured vehicle from the Search and Intervention Brigade, decked out like a tank and containing the mobile command post. It was from in front of this triceratops and its gleaming black hide that a police sergeant observed the surrounding area. He was tapping his fist on his chest, which bore the famous red badge of his force, waiting desperately for the order from the police commissioner to be sent into action.

The command post radio spat out information on violent clashes at place de la République or on the Champs-Elysées, and he had been ordered to protect a supposed target confirmed by interior intelligence but where no one, except for a small band of thugs, had appeared for two hours now.

The sergeant took his walkie-talkie and asked to speak to

Commissioner Maheut. The commissioner ordered him to stay where he was.

'But there's nothing going on here!'

'Sergeant,' the commissioner cut in, 'no redeployment before I say so. Over.'

Finding this immobility unbearable, the sergeant took three men and walked around the Opera to inspect the entrance to its underground car park. He thought he noticed some movement up above and raised his eyes. A helicopter was flying above their position, headed towards the Seine. Nearly a hundred metres behind the last van, the tree-lined elevated walkway began. It was closed at night but the sergeant had a premonition and thought he saw the trees move.

'It's just the wind, Chief.'

The thin voice of Fredo, a corporal recently assigned to the riot police unit, annoyed him. Fredo had difficulty breathing in his gear. His small face disappeared into the helmet, making him look like he was on a reality TV show called *One Day with the Riot Police*, and who was only now realizing just how unfit he was for the violence of this job.

'Chief?'

Fredo reluctantly followed his boss. The two men climbed the steps leading to the elevated walkway while the last corporal on their team watched the intersection of rue de Lyon and avenue Daumesnil. All three of them were in full riot gear: heavy boots, bulletproof vests, fireproof trousers and jacket, and a helmet with a fine foam lining at the neck to soften blows and prevent whiplash. They were equipped with batons and Tasers. But it was their Flash-Balls that they held at the ready when they discovered that the tall metal door to the walkway had been smashed in. Beyond the broken padlocks, a long corridor opened up before them, a long corridor surrounded by luxuriant and dense vegetation that reduced the light from the streetlamps on the avenue below to thin yellow rays illuminating nothing but the little gaps in the leaves through which they came.

6.

Racing eastbound on the highway at 185 kph, Mansourd noticed that his hands had started to shake. He needed to clear his mind, so he mechanically glanced down at the last calls on his secure mobile phone and saw that he had made a mistake when he saved the name of Judge Rotrou: he had replaced an 'o' with an 'a,' which could be easily explained because that was the nickname he gave him in his heart of hearts . . . 'Ratrou' had indeed been appointed to take over the Chaouch case with Judge Poussin. Mansourd had never liked the Ogre of Saint-Eloi, but he had to admit he was more flexible, more at ease than Wagner was with the principle of clandestine missions.

In the basement of the Ministry of the Interior, Montesquiou constantly fiddled with the knob of his walking stick. Vermorel was reading through reports in this futuristic room where, two days previously, she had inflicted a Napoleonic humiliation on the chiefs of police who had allowed a presidential candidate to be shot.

The giant screen silently broadcast several twenty-four-hour news channels. Technicians were busy in the shadows, and occasionally a memo or document was brought to the minister's attention to provide her with the latest update on the number of burned cars. When the number reached 1,100 in central Paris, the minister lost her temper. Montesquiou felt he had to say something. He looked at the corner of the screen where they had just been watching the video feed from the commando operation.

'The main thing is that there haven't been any deaths yet. Two nights of rioting as violent as this without a single fatality is good news for the president.'

Another message reminded the minister that the president wished to be kept constantly informed of the operation's progress.

'Any news on the kid?' the minister asked in a low voice, continuing to read.

Montesquiou checked automatically that the letter had not disappeared from his jacket's inside pocket. It was the original of Aurélie's letter to Krim: two naive and perfumed pages that Puteoli had passed onto him out of a desire for revenge.

'I think I have ways of making him talk,' replied the young chief of staff.

7.

'I doubted you, Fouad. They told me you were working with your brother, that you were interrogated by a judge. I doubted you.'

'That's normal, my love. Anyone would have had doubts. Anyone.'

Fouad had difficulty holding the phone to his ear and stringing together whole sentences. He danced from one foot to another, without realizing.

'Not you. You would never have doubts about me. I've had a revelation, Fouad. I don't know where to start. I was at church, and I understood ... I understood everything ... Love! That's all that counts, Fouad. Love! Oh my love, I've really missed you. I've missed you ... so much ...'

'Jasmine, what can we do? Where are you? Can I come and see you?'

'It's impossible,' Jasmine replied, sniffing. 'Oh my God, the streets are blocked, there are cops everywhere, and there are no taxis.'

She closed her eyes to keep back another flood of tears and declared, 'I'll come to you. Get ready.'

But she had to clash with Couteaux for ten minutes. It was out of the question for her to leave the apartment that evening. Even if he agreed, the team of riot police sent to protect her street would never authorize the departure of a convoy.

Jasmine called Vogel, Habib and finally her mother, who eventually agreed. Why? Jasmine had no idea and that worried her: the ease with which her mother had given in, the strange, disappointed tone in her voice . . . Had she *given up*?

Two cars were called in as reinforcements, and it took half an hour to prepare the convoy that set off at full speed along the Canal Saint-Martin headed towards place d'Aligre.

8.

Sitting on the bed, Aurélie covered her ears so as not to hear the violent argument between her parents, who were at the other end of the apartment, in the piano room. When the shouting ceased, she tried to recall what she had written in that letter so she could rewrite it. But the harder she tried to remember the exact phrases, the harder it was to write anything down.

She crumpled up several sheets of paper before deciding to write another letter from scratch. A letter that began in Bandol last summer, where it was all about the sea, pink laurel trees, stone pines, and the pergola of Virginia creeper covering the patios where they sat every afternoon, the leaves already turning brown at the edges. Suddenly inspired, Aurélie remembered having often seen Krim silent. It was as if he had been trying to erase time by unconsciously murmuring inaudible tunes, and, more curiously, by poking with his straw at the dense speckles of light that the sun projected onto the towel through the thick foliage. While she, wrapped in her turquoise sarong, talked about everything and nothing – mostly nothing – with the bare-chested boys on the beach who followed her around like a halo of mosquitos.

She screwed up the sheet of paper, took another one, and scrunched that up too before even writing a single word on it.

At the other end of the apartment, the arguing had started up again. Upset, Aurélie stuck her tongue out at them through the walls. Her mother had sat down at the piano and was playing fortissimo to drown out her father's explanations and lamentations.

'Fuck,' she sighed, going out onto her bedroom balcony. 'Fuck, fuck, fuck . . .'

She tried to call Nico. He hadn't replied to any of her messages since she realized the letter had been stolen. This time, an electronic voice announced that the number she had dialled was not in service.

9.

Fouad had changed back into his all-purpose suit and his finest white shirt. He saw two black vehicles arrive at the corner of the square. Some men with earpieces got out and checked the entrances to the square and the area around the boarded-up shops. They then went into Fouad's building and knocked at his door. Fouad was used to this little circus: he let them come in and check the apartment. Fifteen minutes after the advance party, Jasmine's car arrived at the foot of the building. The VIP, as the security officers called her, was escorted to the top floor. Three police cars cordoned off the square, and Jasmine's two protection vehicles kept their engines running in case they had to exfiltrate her at once. Such arrangements weren't typical for a member of the family of a person at risk, but the attack on Chaouch had made heads roll at the SGPR, and no precaution now seemed over the top.

Major Couteaux knocked at Fouad's door, which had remained ajar. In tears, Jasmine looked at Fouad while her bodyguard inspected the apartment. Fouad stared at her as if he hadn't seen her for years. He didn't notice the dark look the major sent him. Couteaux had smelled the alcohol still on his breath, despite the three endless minutes Fouad had spent brushing his teeth.

Couteaux left the door open and waited outside. Jasmine leapt on Fouad, forcing him to carry her a few centimetres off the floor.

'I want you to come with me. I want us to go and see my father together.'

Something had changed, in the space of three days, in his lover's face. Fouad said nothing, obviously, but he had the impression that she had gone a bit crazy.

'Jasmine, they'll never let me in, you know that . . .'

Already, he no longer dared look her straight in the eye, thinking of Nazir, of the thunder road he could never have taken if his big brother had not given him the idea.

An inexplicable anger lifted the young woman onto her tiptoes, and made her breathing increasingly frantic.

'Well, we'll see about that,' she said, grabbing her lover's wrist.

10.

At police headquarters, Commissioner Maheut was called over urgently to view the images from Bastille. Some apparently diversionary attacks had just been launched simultaneously on the main roads leading to the plaza. Two Molotov cocktails had set the base of the July Column on fire.

'Send reinforcements!' he screamed to the captain sitting behind the command post.

'Commissioner, the last available units are guarding the Ile de la Cité. Aren't there enough men there to defend themselves?'

While the vans along the Opera esplanade deployed to confront the rioters' hail of stones and homemade explosives, the commissioner tried to get through to the sergeant. The latter had unplugged his earpiece.

'Find me the cameras along avenue Daumesnil!'

The cameras did not extend as far as the elevated walkway, except one that overlooked the open-air section of the promenade, at the spot where it crossed over avenue Ledru-Rollin. The captain turned this camera and zoomed onto the sergeant accompanied by a corporal. Completely alone, they advanced along this bridge, carrying their Flash-Balls.

The young commissioner's mouth went dry at the sight of this striking image, and he opened his mouth in the hopes of finding, in the air, a little moisture.

11.

Jasmine and Fouad drove towards Val-de-Grâce. When the car stopped in front of the gates, the bodyguards asked to speak with Couteaux. From the rear window, Jasmine saw some heads and eyes say no, reinforced by oblique movements of the palm that signified more than no, that actually meant: under no circumstances.

Jasmine got out of the car. Couteaux abandoned the conversation with his colleagues to order her to return to her seat.

'You let him come in or I'll make a scene!'

'Mademoiselle Ch—'

'Shut up! Shut up!'

She began screaming her head off. Couteaux took charge of the situation and tried to calm her.

'All right, we'll let him in, all right—'

'Now!'

'Yes, but we'll have to search him, Mademoiselle.'

'Well then, search me as well!'

In the back seat, a petrified Fouad could only make out every other word of the exchange. He was asked to get out and was led over to an entrance behind which two men passed their hands over him and asked him to take off his shoes. Fouad lost his balance trying to take them off without leaning down. He fell and was not caught by either of the guards.

A few moments later, he was led across a courtyard into the intensive care unit. Other men in uniform guarded the entrances, and there was even a small detachment of soldiers armed as if for war. On the ground floor, he saw Esther Chaouch at the foot of the steps trying to calm her daughter. Fouad had met her several times but the effect she had on him was always the same: more than a celebrity (he eventually got used to celebrities), she was the wife of the man he admired most in the world. Part of Chaouch's aura had attached itself to her, and Fouad's mouth was always dry when he tried to greet her correctly.

Esther Chaouch gave him a half-smile. Not completely glacial, but certainly lacking in humanity.

The bodyguards, standing at a distance, missed nothing of the exchange that followed between mother and daughter. They also kept an eye on Fouad. Fouad wanted to intervene to explain that he did not mean to cause any trouble, but Jasmine would have felt ridiculous and even more alone, and, at that moment, his own discomfort seemed nothing next to the passion his girlfriend felt.

Outside the hospital, the team charged with the non-stop surveillance of Fouad were speaking to the new man in charge of protecting the Chaouch family. Esther Chaouch eventually agreed to have Fouad taken upstairs, on the condition that he did not go into the patient's room. Jasmine stamped her feet on the courtyard cobbles.

'That's my father!' she cried.

'Calm down, Jasmine. Control yourself a bit, for God's sake. This is a hospital. You're . . . making a scene . . .'

Fouad had never felt so uncomfortable. He was regarded as a problem to be solved by negotiating the confluence of security imperatives and the caprices of a little princess. Jasmine accepted the compromise proposed by Couteaux under Esther's control: Fouad would stay in the waiting room, while Jasmine went to spend a moment with her father.

Couteaux's gentleness, and his apparent good feeling towards Fouad, the moment he turned to face him, got the better of Jasmine's anger.

Esther accompanied them to wait in a comfortable but closely guarded room. Jasmine covered Fouad with kisses, as a provocation, and left him in front of the coffee table, on a stool where he was soon subjected to the contempt and indifference of the woman who, a few hours earlier, had been the First Lady.

12.

No matter how many times Fredo repeated the commissioner's instructions being screamed into his earpiece, the sergeant continued to advance, convinced he had seen some movement in the thicket. He suddenly turned around to order his corporal to unplug his earpiece. He seemed to want to give him a lesson in courage. To give him a taste of action the hard way.

Fredo could not unplug his earpiece because of the visor on his helmet. So he took the helmet off, happy to get some fresh air.

At that very moment, a shadow surged from behind the bushes and crossed the bridge at full speed. A pit bull. It ploughed into him with such power that the sergeant was thrown against the guardrail of the bridge and instantly fired a Flash-Ball into thin air. Off-balance, the shot knocked him over the guardrail and he only stopped himself from falling ten metres by grabbing with one hand to a greasy drainpipe. He heard screams but couldn't see what was happening. Consequently, he did not know that the pit bull had leapt at the throat of the corporal, who had not been able to grab the emergency knife from one of his trouser pockets.

Commissioner Maheut called for reinforcements and loosened his tie. He could no longer breathe; it felt as if it were his own throat that the monster's jaws were crushing. He suddenly saw a trembling figure appear at the end of the bridge.

Fat Momo was brandishing his 9mm gun. Commissioner Maheut could not know this, but he was aiming it in the direction of the dog, to save the corporal.

'Stop! Let go! Let go!'

However much he screamed, the dog wouldn't let go. The sight was unbearable. Fat Momo fired twice into the dog's powerful chest.

At that moment, the sergeant, who had managed to haul himself back onto the bridge, thought that Fat Momo had fired on his young colleague. In a fit of rage – rage that had built up these last three days, these last thirty years – he seized Fat Momo by the collar and, of course not hearing Maheut's shouts from the command centre, pushed him over the guardrail. From the bridge, Fat Momo was now just a silhouette, lying broken on the street like a puppet.

A thunderclap sounded as the sergeant gave first aid to his young colleague, trying to stop the bleeding with a makeshift tourniquet. The rain finally began to fall, reaching peak downpour in the space of a minute. A few gusts of hailstones hammered down on Fat Momo's inanimate body as well as that of the last dog he had loved, one he had loved even if it was trained to kill. Thus was the last thought of Mohammed Belaidi, aged eighteen and a half, native of Saint-Etienne, department of the Loire, before he slipped into oblivion: unlike men, it wasn't the pit bull's fault if he was trained to attack because – as he had seen in the tobacco-brown eyes of that mutt – dogs were all good creatures, lost in an inexplicably ferocious world.

13.

At precisely 3.47 a.m., in the darkest hour of this stormy night, while Jasmine Chaouch contemplated her famous father's motionless hand, a man named Frédéric Mulot, a corporal in the fifth section of the third company of riot police called as reinforcements to the Bastille neighbourhood, died of his wounds in the emergency room of Saint-Antoine Hospital, where he had been taken with his sergeant, who remained in a state of shock.

At the same moment, Jasmine heard a new noise in the electrocephalogram sitting to the left of the bed. She opened her eyes without letting go of her father's hand and anxiously looked at the deserted corridor through the half-open door. A minute later, two nurses came in and asked her to move aside. Jasmine got up with a limp: her legs had fallen asleep. Someone helped her sit down again and she soon saw the floor's nursing staff arrive. The medical chief had been woken urgently. Professor Saint-Samat's heels made a lot of noise on the floor: he had had to grab the first pair of shoes he could find. He asked the family to wait outside.

Jasmine stopped a nurse who was rushing into her father's room.

'What's happening?'

She did not get a reply. She threw herself into Fouad's arms.

'Jasmine, honey, are you okay?'

Esther – who had stopped smoking when she started university thirty years before – had just asked Major Couteaux for a cigarette, which he got from one of his men. The open window overlooked the chapel and, turning around after stubbing out the cigarette, Esther saw her daughter kneeling, head down, her hands joined above her chair. Fouad looked lost, watching her sudden piety and unable to understand it.

Esther did not dare interrupt her but felt acutely anxious when her daughter's prayer was punctuated by the sign of the cross. The waiting room had gone silent so as not to bother

Jasmine. The bodyguards had stiffened and lowered their heads in a mark of respect.

What Jasmine heard, however, was not the solemn silence of the waiting room, but the song of the first birds, the dawn chorus, the richness and variety of God's creation. And it was soon His infinite goodness that appeared against the pregnant silence it had aroused in her: from the once hostile exterior came the metallic patter of Professor Saint-Samat's heels, the footsteps in the corridor that she had noticed first but which she did not count, deliberately, seized by the intuition that to count was to sin. And when he appeared in the waiting room, everyone rushed over to him, but not Jasmine. She remained motionless and only lifted her head to return the kisses and tears of joy her mother rained down on her.

14.

All over Paris, telephones began ringing, including that of Serge Habib, Chaouch's director of communications. But he did not hear it. Around midnight, he had decided to catch up on some sleep. He had closed his curtains for the first time since the campaign, found some earplugs in one of the cupboards and set his alarm for 6.15 a.m. To the continuous ring of his mobile phone was soon added that of his landline, but it was another fifteen minutes before Habib was torn from sleep, when someone began to hammer at his front door.

He looked at his mobile and the dozens of missed calls and floated into the hallway, knocking against the round table at its centre.

'Who the fuck is it?'

'The doorman!'

Dressed in pyjamas, Habib opened the door and saw that it really was the doorman, also in pyjamas and in a filthy mood.

'Listen, it's not part of my job, you know, dealing with all this crap! So next time, I don't care if it's the campaign director, the prime minister or the Queen of England, I'm unplugging my phone!'

Habib understood. He got dressed in a flash and phoned Vogel, who was already waiting for him at Val-de-Grâce. Ten minutes later, the director of communications, who had not had time to wash, entered the hospital and climbed the stairs. The waiting room contained three times as many people as it had seen in the last two days. All Chaouch's closest advisers greeted him with the same half-smile. Faces were exhausted, expressions cautious, skin tightened by the sudden wake-up call and the hasty wash.

Habib used his stump to make his way through the crowd and was led to the bedroom by a bodyguard. In front of the door waited Esther, Vogel, Jasmine and – surprisingly – Fouad Nerrouche.

He greeted the first three and began talking about a press conference. Vogel was in a short-sleeved pyjama top underneath his jacket. He took Habib to one side and told him in a low voice, 'Something's happened, and it has to stay between you and me.'

'And Jasmine's boyfriend. What the—'

'Doesn't matter. He's heard nothing. Well, Idder said things when he woke up. I mean, he spoke.'

'Fuck, that's fantastic! He's already talking! What did he say?'

'Well, you see,' Vogel replied, 'we don't really know ... He spoke in Chinese. He hasn't opened his eyes yet but he spoke in Chinese, for fuck's sake!'

Habib was about to react when a nurse came rushing out of the room. She didn't close the door completely behind her. Through the forest of doctors around the bed, Chaouch's two closest advisers saw the boss's hand move, detaching one finger after another.

'In Chinese? But why Chinese?'

Habib was at a loss.

'This changes everything,' he added in Vogel's ear as he looked around.

'What, Chinese?'

'No, the declaration of unfitness... The Constitutional Council made that decision last night. I mean, fuck, just a few hours ago. You're not telling me that...'

'That what? That they can't change their minds overnight? Well, precisely: they can't! Their fucking decision is set in stone... Listen, we'll talk about it later. For the moment, we've got to think about the communication plan. Get your team together. It's useless going back to HQ. We're going to borrow a room and work here till sunrise. Okay?'

15.

Jasmine would not stop kissing her mother. Fouad felt he did not belong here, in this corridor, with the nearest and dearest.

He quietly walked away to the open window in the waiting room. Leaning against the armoured car, Aurélien Couteaux was talking on the phone. He fidgeted and looked nervous, tense, *human*.

Jasmine came over to Fouad, put her arms around him and, giving him a look full of suffering, love and hysteria, said, 'It's all thanks to you, Fouad. It's all thanks to us, because we found each other again, you understand? It's because we're in love!'

Fouad caressed her black hair, but said nothing.

Jasmine moved her arms in the direction of her bodyguard and gestured for him to come upstairs. Couteaux lifted his palm to say: just a second, I'm coming.

'I can't talk any more. It's an emergency,' he said into the phone.

'For fuck's sake!' shouted the voice at the end of the line. 'Don't hang up! You hear me! Do *not* hang up!'

'Given the latest news, it's not you I'm taking orders from. So change your tone, stop calling this number, and leave me alone.'

He hung up and rejoined the commotion upstairs.

16.

'Couteaux!' screamed Nazir. 'Couteaux!'

He punched the telephone box several times and dropped his head against the window dripping with dew.

Fleur's eyes were bloodshot from the sleepless night they had just spent. Their lorry had gone around an endless lake and stopped to allow Nazir to make his umpteenth phone call. Fleur took advantage of this to breathe some fresh air. Inside the lorry, they were hidden among black pigs, and a mobile pigsty stank just as badly as any other kind.

Nazir rejoined her and signalled to their new driver to wait a minute.

The telephone box overlooked a chalet topped by a motionless weathervane. For two hundred metres, the lakeside was untouched by mankind. Although not completely: there were the roadside guardrails made from logs of calibrated wood. On the other side of this lake, half an hour away, the circus tent had been raised for the next day's show.

Fleur observed the mist that floated on the dark surface of the water, tinged with imperceptible shades of blue and red, while the sky, which could at last be made out from the mountains, was violet, turning to a sumptuous orange-red where the sun was beginning to rise.

Nazir watched the sky as the shapes below it grew more precise, the contours emerging from sleep. The mist now moved only on the lake, receding from the bank where at that moment Nazir saw two lights appear. It was not a motorcycle headlamp the mist had blurred a few seconds before, but two very distinct lights, racing along the lakeside.

He thought it was *them* but the cars passed the circus lorry that was to take him and Fleur over the border – if, that is, they survived the smell, this smell which reduced Fleur to tears. She turned to Nazir and asked, 'We're going to stay together, right? We'll never leave each other? Not after all this . . .'

Nazir saw a shadow pass through the sky, a metal crow that flew low and whose actuality he could not comprehend: the thing suddenly took the form of an army helicopter flying towards the other end of the lake.

17.

The images were shaky despite the stabilizer on the camera attached to the commando chief's helmet. The Minister of the Interior kept clenching her jaw, sniffing bizarrely and fidgeting in her chair. The barrel of the commando chief's assault rifle pointed at the horizon like in a first-person shooter video game.

The commando team penetrated the trailers one by one, meticulously ransacking the circus and screaming at those they woke up to tell them the whereabouts of the man whose photo they brandished.

Not one of them spoke French. 'But all of them can recognize a face!' thought Mansourd angrily. He was convinced they were deliberately refusing to help.

The agent who had stayed behind in the helicopter indicated to Mansourd that they were still receiving the BlackBerry's signal.

In Paris, the minister uncrossed her legs and shifted onto her other buttock. Montesquiou was apoplectic.

Mansourd followed the chief and three other men towards the most distant trailer. They gave no warning before they smashed the door down. Inside, the commando chief's camera and gun barrel swept over a cooking area, a couch and finally another door that led to a small bedroom. Vermorel and Montesquiou expected to see Nazir there, his hands up, surprised, perhaps in a moment of athletic intimacy with a young contortionist.

Instead of which they were astonished to discover a chimpanzee, all smiles, dressed in a little blue, white and red suit, who cheerfully jumped up and down on the bunk bed.

The commando chief lowered his weapon and searched the ape. In the pocket of its tailored jacket, he found Nazir's BlackBerry.

Maddened with rage, Vermorel cancelled the operation and ordered them to return to France immediately, before they were spotted by the Swiss authorities. Mansourd suggested that Nazir was perhaps within a few kilometres, that maybe they should—

'Shut your mouth!' the minister screamed. 'You're coming home!'

Montesquiou became tense at the sight of this creature

taunting them. Vermorel waited for the screen to go blank before she exploded with rage and began looking for a scapegoat.

An urgent phone call gave Montesquiou the pretext for escaping the minister's wrath. He slipped into the anteroom and checked that no one could hear him after realizing who it was.

'What's with all those horse noises? Where are you?'

'I'm at home,' replied a female voice at the end of the line.

'The ATSD are looking for you because of the mobile phone,' the young man replied gravely. 'Those cretins call you the "horsewoman"? Are you there?'

'I'm back on Waldstein's trail.'

Montesquiou said nothing for a moment, then, 'It's too late now. Nazir escaped the commando team. We don't have the time to deal with Waldstein. You agree, right?'

'He's preparing to take a break in the country. South America. Do you confirm I should let him go?'

'Yes, I confirm,' sighed Montesquiou, who was increasingly irritated by the linguistic habits of these experts in secrecy to whom, in the end, he was obliged to give orders.

18.

Rabia had heard a neurologist explain in a TV programme once that our sleep is divided into ninety-minute cycles: since that day, she mentally noted the time at which she fell asleep and checked, in the early hours, that she had slept x times ninety minutes. It was foolproof: she always slept seven and a half hours or six hours, never eight hours or six and a half. Her naivety had often been mocked, but Rabia still believed it. Until that Wednesday morning, when she spontaneously got up exactly four hours after she had closed her eyes. She checked the clock and tried to remember how long it had taken her to fall asleep, to deduct from the four hours. But it seemed impossible: she could have sworn she found sleep as soon as her head hit the pillow.

Surprised and a little dazed, she got up, listened to Dounia's difficult breathing, nodded her head with a sigh and left the bedroom on tiptoe. She was no longer sleepy and did not understand what was happening to her.

She went downstairs and drank a big glass of water in the kitchen. Some strips of daylight were appearing between the gaps in the shutters.

Images of Mouloud Benbaraka seized her like a shiver up the spine. She'd had this waking nightmare several times since Sunday: she was alone in the living room of the flat on rue de l'Eternité. She was watching TV, and suddenly she felt a presence, a hostile presence. She was looking out of the windows between the open curtains, but it was the door someone was trying to break down – and she woke up at the very moment when the intruder succeeded. As if Fear, reaching its maximum intensity, mechanically ejected her from this universe that it had custom-built.

In the world of dreams perhaps, Rabia thought, but not elsewhere: she turned her head quickly, sure that she had heard the front door move. She switched on the radio and heard the news: Chaouch had woken up. She did not believe it, until she heard that a press conference by the chief medical officer at Val-de-Grâce was planned for 7.30 a.m. and would 'obviously' be broadcast live. Rabia opened her eyes wider than she had in the last ten days. She wanted to shout, to alert the household, turn on the lights, open the shutters, let daylight into the kitchen. Suddenly she was no longer afraid. She would never be afraid again!

But her enthusiasm was broken by a series of violent knocks on the front door.

She switched off the kitchen light and felt her legs turn to jelly. Terror attacked her limbs first, it seemed, even before it set her heart racing. She crept stealthily back into the living room, hoping to reach the phone and alert the police, but she heard the harsh voice of the man who was trying to destroy the door.

'Police! Open up!'

She turned on the living room light, then the one in the hallway, and began to turn the key in the lock.

'Police! Open up! Open up!'

'Who . . . is it?'

'Police! Hurry up or we'll smash the door down!'

Why were they shouting so loudly? Why had they come so early? Before she could open the door herself it was torn from her hands to let a dozen men in plain clothes, carrying weapons, armbands and bulletproof vests, rush into the corridor.

'Rabia Bounaim-Nerrouche? Judge Rotrou of the counterterrorism division of the Department of Justice is taking you into custody.'

'But I've already—' Rabia started to protest.

'Come on, no point discussing.'

She was pushed against the wall and handcuffed unceremoniously.

'But I haven't done anything!' she said, weeping. 'When are you going to leave us alone? *We haven't done anything!*'

'Yes, yes, that's right, no one's done anything. Until they have. Is your sister upstairs?'

She didn't recognize this captain from the ATSD from when they had interrogated her on the night of the attack. He was a small, fat man with a square face, cat-like eyes and thick eyebrows slanting upwards – the very face of nastiness.

Between sobs that suffocated her chest, Rabia found the time to say, 'I have a lawyer. Maître Szafran ...'

But the captain did not react. He readjusted his armband, tightened Rabia's handcuffs and led her outside.

'You're hurting me! At least let me get dressed!'

She was wearing a pink nightgown and slippers. Seeing that the captain was still not reacting, she began to shout, 'But I haven't done anything! I haven't done anything!'

'Oh yes you have,' the captain finally replied. 'We have new evidence that directly incriminates you and your sister. And, besides, why would Judge Rotrou arrest you if you hadn't done anything?'

19.

At home in his pyjamas, Judge Wagner crossed the hallway to go to the bathroom. He saw the light was on in Aurélie's bedroom. He knocked twice, softly. Aurélie shifted on her bed. He went in. His daughter's hair was a mess, her eyes sorrowful. Dozens of scribbled and crumpled pages were spread across her pink quilt. She gathered them frantically and rested her face between her fists.

'Why are you not asleep at this hour?'

'Papa ...'

The judge looked down at her. It was this thoughtless young face, this teenage mouth, these pretty eyes of different colours that had ended his career.

He gave his daughter a pained smile, thinking that children were monstrous because you could not hold it against them, because it made no difference when they caused you pain.

'Come on, get some sleep,' he said, turning off the light.

After going to the toilet, he got dressed and found Thierry, who was dozing in the living room.

'We don't have much time left together,' he murmured on waking him. 'I'd like to go for a ride if you don't mind.'

Ten minutes later, the car was on the highway. The judge touched his driver-bodyguard's shoulder as they approached Levallois-Perret.

'Monsieur?'

'Wait, Thierry, slow down. But don't stop.'

Some cranes stood above the watchtowers of the CDII headquarters and Judge Wagner could not help noticing how they stood out against the raw and faded sky. The rain had just stopped and some spots of blue were exposed between the dark and still dominant clouds. The judge remembered the saints at the Vatican and the clouds they had set in motion. It was the same thing with the cranes and the watchtowers of this highly protected site, which looked like androids brought to life by the shifting sky.

Someone was trying to call him on his personal phone: it was Poussin. He answered and heard the uncertain voice of the man he once considered a protégé. Poussin informed him that Rotrou had taken the inseparable Nerrouche sisters back into custody, just before the legal amount of time for an arrest had passed, a limit that any file marked 'Counterterrorism' admittedly authorized him to ignore.

Wagner shook his head in a sign of disappointment and powerlessness. As his young colleague was about to hang up, he cleared his throat and added in a tone that, for the first time, was not strictly professional.

'Guillaume, we've got to fight. Rotrou wants to screw us with all the others. You understand what I'm saying?'

'Y-y-yes, Monsieur.'

'It was a bad idea, Saint-Etienne,' Wagner added. 'It's in Paris you have to investigate. The plot brings together . . . Listen, this goes well beyond the Nerrouche family . . . Everything is in the records of that third phone. If that's been classified, it's because it contains crucial information . . .'

'It's also p-p-prooof that they're p-p-panicking,' Poussin observed.

'Of course. But in their position they have the means to panic calmly . . . I'll also give you my notes on a testimony that could be recorded in the proceedings as a testimony by a person unknown. It's by a commander of the SGPR, Valérie Simonetti. You have to . . .'

Wagner stopped, remembering that he had resigned, and that it was no longer his business.

'Good luck, Guillaume.'

'Th-th-thank you, your Honour,' stammered young Poussin. 'You c-c-can t-t-trust me . . .'

Wagner raised his eyebrows and hung up. He looked at his bodyguard.

'I'm sorry, Thierry. Let's turn around.'

He dialled Valérie Simonetti's number as Aqua Velva drove him to the Palais de Justice. He explained to Chaouch's former head of security that he had withdrawn from the case and that from now on she would be dealing with his colleague, Judge Poussin.

His chambers in the Saint-Eloi gallery looked like the aftermath of a party: files scattered around the coffee-maker, his desk strewn with hurriedly scribbled notes and spattered with brown stains. He sat down behind his court clerk's desk and, without switching on anything other than the desk lamp, contemplated the vast room from an angle that was not usually his – Alice's.

A few knocks on the door jolted him. Rotrou's enormous face appeared, horribly lit up by a smile of unhealthy joy.

'You're an early bird for someone who's unemployed . . .'

As Wagner did not reply and seemed to ignore his presence, the Ogre added, 'You'll have to give me your notes on the case. So you might as well do that now.'

'You're mistaken, Rotrou,' Wagner said without moving his eyes, his hands placed on the armrests of Alice's chair. 'That poor family has nothing to do with the plot. It's here you have to investigate . . .'

His mouth gaping, Rotrou panted without being out of breath – he panted out of pure excess of respiratory energy. He was in shirtsleeves, his braces hanging down. His hairless forearms looked excessively large and devoid of all muscle tone, like two fat thighs.

From the doorway, his bear-like paw pointed at the desk with a weak gesture, which was intended to include, by extension, the entire chambers and the whole judicial system.

'This isn't a place for humanists, Wagner. You want to look good. You want them to write articles that say: the good Judge Wagner, the kind Judge Wagner, Henri Wagner, man of integrity, independent Henri . . .'

Wagner gave him the finger.

The Ogre let out a huge snort that gathered an entire flotilla of mucus at the back of his throat. But instead of spitting, as you might have thought he was preparing to do, he declared, 'Man is neither angel nor beast, and unhappily whoever wants to act the angel, acts the beast.'

20.

Captain Tellier had just finished his breakfast. He had spent the night trying to put together the puzzle of Krim's Sunday itinerary, rereading the transcripts of the interrogation of the whole family, of Mouloud Benbaraka, constantly returning to gnaw on the bone that was the statement by the manager of the Pont-Neuf riverboat company, who described 'the horsewoman' as 'a tall blonde', who 'looked strict', wore 'perfectly credible' police insignia and had 'something hard and a bit crazy' in her eyes.

No department that might have wanted to retrieve Krim's mobile had declared they knew of an officer answering this description. She was probably, then, one of Nazir's accomplices. Which added a twist to the plot, another one, another one too many, thought Tellier as he felt fatigue weigh not only on his eyelids but also on his back muscles.

He suddenly heard the noise of a familiar gait: a three-legged gait.

Montesquiou materialized in the doorway. Tellier rose with difficulty.

'Hello, Captain. I'd like to see Abdelkrim Nerrouche.'

Tellier gulped down his last mouthful of croissant and declared, ill at ease, 'I'm sorry, Monsieur, but that won't be possible. The kid's asleep, and you're not... I could get in trouble...'

'Well, you'll certainly get in trouble if you don't let me in.'

Tellier sighed.

384

'You'll have to see Commander Mansourd. I can't take responsibility for . . .'

Montesquiou raised his voice. 'You work for me, Captain. You don't have responsibilities. I decide and you obey. Is that clear?'

Tellier touched his harelip with the tip of his tongue. He led the minister's chief of staff into Krim's cell.

21.

Krim was sleeping like a baby. A blow against his bed from the walking stick made him jump.

'Come on, come on, get up. We've got things to discuss.'

Montesquiou leaned against the door and took out the second page of Aurélie's letter.

'I have two bits of good news for you, Abdelkrim.'

Krim was rubbing his eyes like a little boy.

'Firstly, Chaouch was in a coma, and he has just woken up.'

But the second piece of good news managed to make Krim forget the magnitude of what he had just heard.

'And your girlfriend asked me to give you a letter.'

Krim was completely awake. He went over to seize the page but Montesquiou withdrew it at the last moment.

'You remember our little conversation last time? If you want the letter, you have to give me something in exchange . . .'

'But . . .'

'Frankly, it would be a pity if I had to leave with this letter . . . It would be such a pity. Come on, make a little effort . . .'

Krim had thought of something before falling asleep four hours earlier. He had nothing to lose and everything to gain. He said, 'Well, the text Nazir sent me by mistake . . . He seemed angry that I'd received it. He told me I had to delete it straight away . . . It seemed to be incredibly important and . . .'

Montesquiou passed a hand through his blonde hair. He knew all this. Krim's slow grasp of the situation was making him so mad that his walking stick was trembling, shivering like a naked leg in the cold.

'He was talking about a city where he had to go. I don't know if it's related . . .'

'What city? We're talking about "G", right?'

If Krim's face was about to become distorted now, if he had forgotten it was all about retrieving the name behind that accursed initial, Montesquiou sensed he was going to lose patience.

'Well, I'm not a hundred per cent sure, but it was something like Geneva in Italy.'

Montesquiou straightened up, victorious.

'G. Genoa, of course . . .'

'What?'

'Did you talk about it with your friends?' asked Montesquiou, his head pointing to the cell door.

'Uh, no. I'd been told—'

Montesquiou slammed down his walking stick and dropped the page on the floor.

'That's good. Continue to tell them nothing and perhaps I'll give you other little presents . . .' He remembered his original promise. 'While waiting, of course, for the big present, but that's for later, as I'm sure you understand . . .'

He left without adding anything, keeping the first page of the letter in his pocket.

And so Krim discovered, in the stifling and windowless

cell where he had spent the last three nights, while morning broke outside and Chaouch's eyes opened with difficulty upon the moving figures in the intensive care unit at Val-de-Grâce, a letter from Aurélie that contained only nine words:

I'm thinking of you, all the time.

Aurélie, xxx

Nine words that he read and reread a hundred times over the following hours, until he knew by heart each circle of the 'a', each bulge of the 'o', each arch on the 'e', each cross on the 't', and so on as far as the careless scrawl that formed the 'xxx' from his beautiful Aurélie.

The comma punctuating the first sentence brought tears to his eyes, but there was something else, for the first hour at least, something stronger than the contents of the letter: her lavender perfume. This lavender perfume that Krim did not know the name of and would never know how to describe was proof that the earth continued to turn in his absence. It was all the love of the world distilled into a handful of atoms. It was a tiny drop of hope, precarious, fleeting and paltry, and yet it had the power to light up the entire ocean with the same astonishing rapidity of daylight conquering the sky after night's reign, which had seemed, only a few moments earlier, fated to last for centuries and centuries.

To be continued . . .